NOV 2 7 2015

WICKED
RELEASE

Books by Katana Collins

THE WICKED EXPOSURE SERIES

Wicked Shots (novella)
Wicked Exposure
Wicked Release

THE SOUL STRIPPER SERIES

Soul Stripper
Soul Survivor
Soul Surrender

Published by Kensington Publishing Corporation

WICKED
RELEASE

KATANA
COLLINS

KENSINGTON BOOKS
www.kensingtonbooks.com

KENSINGTON BOOKS are published by

Kensington Publishing Corp.
119 West 40th Street
New York, NY 10018

All Kensington titles, imprints, and distributed lines are available at special quantity discounts for bulk purchases for sales promotion, premiums, fund-raising, educational, or institutional use.

Special book excerpts or customized printings can also be created to fit specific needs. For details, write or phone the office of the Kensington Special Sales Manager: Attn. Special Sales Department. Kensington Publishing Corp., 119 West 40th Street, New York, NY 10018. Phone: 1-800-221-2647.

Kensington and the K logo Reg. U.S. Pat. & TM Off.

eISBN-13: 978-1-61773-640-7
eISBN-10: 1-61773-640-6
First Kensington Electronic Edition: November 2015

ISBN-13: 978-1-61773-639-1
ISBN-10: 1-61773-639-2
First Kensington Trade Paperback Printing: November 2015

10 9 8 7 6 5 4 3 2 1

Printed in the United States of America

For Krista. 2,801 miles is no match for us, my friend.

Acknowledgments

There are always so many people to thank throughout this process of creating a book—and the list just keeps getting longer each time!

Many thanks are owed to the large team of people who helped get this series off the ground: Martin Biro, Vida Engstrand, Paula Reedy, Jackie Dinas, and everyone at Kensington who works so hard to put these books out! Also sending loads of gratitude to my agent, Louise Fury, and her group of rock stars—Jenny Bent, Kristin Smith, Kaitlyn Jeffries, Kasey Poserina, and everyone who is a part of Team Fury.

I don't know where I'd be in life or career without my friends and fellow writers, Krista Amigone, Derek Bishop, Alyssa Cole, Sofia Tate, and Hope Tarr. You all keep me sane, you keep me laughing, and you keep me far away from that ledge!

As always, so much gratitude to my friends and family—Mom, Dad, Bridget, Bo, Adam, Adelynn, Harrison, Maddie, Liza, and my husband, Sean, for their love and support through the years. I'm sure it's not always understandable as to why I choose to hang out with the characters in my head versus real people!

PROLOGUE

The brake was tight beneath my foot as I pulled my black sedan behind the Lincoln. My partner in the other car was a smart man. But intelligence doesn't always translate fluidly into the real world. And *I* was smart, too. Something everyone needed to be occasionally reminded of. Rolling my window down, I knocked twice against my car door, to which he responded with the proper one knock back before sliding out of the space and driving off.

I coasted into his spot, putting the window back up so that no passerby could see my face from behind the tinted windows. Moments later, I received his text: *The house has been quiet all weekend. She opened the door only for food deliveries.*

But that didn't account for the damn tunnel that extended from the beach right into her basement. Which she now knew about. That tunnel was the single, most important reason we needed Cassandra to join our operation in the first place. Our main means of transport to move the drugs without anyone seeing and for everyone to have an alibi—the masquerades. And now it was gone. Soon that tunnel would be crawling with uniforms like ants on a cookie. Well, I suppose that just meant I needed to find them another cookie to distract with.

A tremble rolled through my body at the memory of a few nights ago; the way Jess froze when she saw me running, escaping after I attacked her detective boyfriend. How the handle of my gun pressed into my gloved hand, my fingers tickling that trigger. Thank God I had the mask on—played along as always at those parties. I hadn't counted on her finding the tunnel so quickly. Which only proved that she was sticking her nose where it didn't belong.

Oh, how I wanted to kill Sam that night. But adding a cop murder on top of everything? It would have resulted in a manhunt and the last thing we needed was more attention brought to us. Maybe now with Zooey as our fall, everyone would back the fuck off—particularly Jessica.

I shook my head, inwardly chastising her. Tugging my camera from its bag on my passenger seat, I zoomed in on the windows of the house. The curtains were drawn. Squinting, I focused on the guest room just as a breeze from a passing person caught the corner of the curtain.

Leaning back in my driver's seat, I relaxed. If Jessica was anything like her sister, it could be a while before she was ready.

But even as I settled in and reclined my seat, preparing for a long morning, the bright pink door of the house swung open and she exited, keys in hand and dragging a rolling suitcase behind her. My spine straightened, hairs all standing on end. Was she leaving town? If she knew what was good for her, that's exactly what she should be doing.

With a tentative look over each shoulder, she loped down the steps and into her car. *Just where are you off to, Jessica?* There was a new sort of hesitancy in her demeanor. A . . . fear. My smile widened and I felt a raw chuckle rasp at the back of my throat as excitement danced in my veins. Yes, she was definitely afraid.

She pulled out of the driveway and I shifted into gear, following behind at a respectable distance, keeping at least two cars between us. In my business you get damn good at following without being spotted. Two rights. A left. Another right.

A chill rocked my entire body, turning my blood to ice, as we took the last right turn. *Fuck me.* I knew where we were going.

I parked my car into a spot in the farthest corner of the parking lot, out of view of the security camera.

The cold metal of my gun scraped against my ankle. Cracking my neck to each side, I took a deep breath, putting the car in park just in time to see Jessica stop at a coffee cart and purchase two cups of coffee, still dragging the suitcase behind her.

Jessica had only parked a few cars away. Flipping my jacket collar up, I also tugged my hat lower onto my eyes, shielding my face. Grabbing the five-by-seven glossy images from my passenger seat, I flipped through them one last time. Running a gloved finger down Cassandra's face in the image, I sighed. It really was such a waste. She was one of our best distributors. Coy, unassuming; no one ever suspected her. But she had to go and ruin it for everyone.

As I flipped through the photos, goose bumps lifted on my arms. I scanned the curve of her hips as she stretched to zip her dress. My groin tightened as I remembered her last scream before my bullet penetrated her heart.

Unzipping, I ripped off one glove and gripped my dick, squeezing hard as I stared at her face. I flipped to the next image—the moment she looked out the window and saw someone there on the sidewalk. Her eyes were wide, mouth turned down. Forehead wrinkled. *Terror.* I groaned and came hard as I bit the inside of my cheek, coppery blood filling my mouth.

Pain. Sex. Fear.

Blood.

I dropped my head back against the seat and closed my eyes for a second before wiping my hand and putting my glove back in place.

Get out of that house, Jessica. Get out and let us do our job, find what we need. And if these images didn't scare her? Well, I could find ways to make the message clearer.

I glanced through the rest of the pictures, making sure all the photos were accounted for. There were three of Cassandra getting dressed and three of Jessica dressing before Friday's party. I slid them evenly into an envelope before I opened my door. I knew the location of every security camera inside and out of this building and up until the eighth row of parking you couldn't be spotted in the far corners. Keeping my hat over my eyes just in case, I made my way across the lot. As I passed the front of Jessica's car I dropped the envelope onto the hood and then walked around to the back of the building.

1

Jess waited patiently in the reception area of Elliot Warner's office. The white marble was smooth beneath her as she scuffed her toe back and forth against the floor. Only two weeks ago, her sister would have been coming into this office to work. She would have arrived on that same elevator—maybe even *with* Elliot, her boyfriend—and she would have gotten off on the tenth floor while he rode all the way up here to his office. The penthouse.

Jess shook her head, gripping the flimsy paper cup tighter in her hand. *His office,* she thought, inwardly rolling her eyes. The whole damn building belonged to him, even if he used only the penthouse for his personal operations. The rest of the floors were rented out to various businesses, including the pharmaceutical company where her sister works. *Worked.* Past tense. Because her sister was dead. Cass was *dead.* It still didn't feel real. Like she expected at any moment, her sister would come barging in off the elevator, pull Jess's shirt closed over the little bit of cleavage showing, and demand that she get home to do that growing load of laundry piling up at her bedroom door.

Jess's hand trembled, causing a bit of coffee to fall and splatter against the white marble floor.

"Shit."

She set the cup down on the receptionist's desk beside the second cup of coffee that she had bought for Elliot. Pinching the bridge of her nose between her burning eyes, she took a deep breath. She needed to pull it together. Though she'd only briefly met Elliot Warner once before during a shared elevator ride, she knew him all too well from the e-mail account she'd found on her sister's iPad. The iPad she found buried beneath the floorboards of her sister's house, along with stacks of money, a fake passport, and a skeleton key that unlocked a secret tunnel in the basement.

Is this what her life was now? Secret tunnels and stacks of cash, mystery men and murder?

Jess sat back down, pulling the iPad out of her purse and flipping it open. She didn't know why the hell it was so calming to read her sister's old e-mails. Maybe it was because she could almost hear the words as though Cass were actually saying them. Maybe she was clinging to any memory her sister had left.

She scrolled through the e-mail history, choosing a random entry. She'd read almost all of them already, but it didn't matter.

> My dearest Cassandra,
>
> I have an intensely special evening planned for us. One that will be forever documented—but for yours and my eyes only. I believe that you've earned it. You've been working hard and I love that you aim to please me, even if you don't love being my submissive. There's so much for you to figure out about yourself, and I have to admit . . . I enjoy figuring you out as well. You're so different than my other trainees. I know you want to be here. I believe you enjoy your time with me as much I do—and well, to be frank, if the way you

came against my tongue last night is any indication, I'd say you're more than sexually fulfilled by
our dalliances. And yet, you resist. Constantly.
And not in the way that suggests defiance or playful opposition; your resistance runs deeper. It is
instinct in the same way an unbroken horse resists
its training. You resist submission because it goes
against your very nature. And I must stop to consider what this means for you, for your training—
and for us. Because while some dominants may
enjoy the challenge of breaking the wild mare, I
much prefer to see her run free.

    Always yours,

    Master

Master. Her sister actually addressed this man as Master in
their relationship. Jess grabbed her coffee back from the receptionist's desk, craning her neck to see down the hallway. What
the hell was taking so long? Settling back onto the bench, she
clicked Cass's response open.

    My Dear Master,

    Isn't it possible the wild mare wants to run be-
side the stallion and not be forced to trot behind
him? I fit in this lifestyle. I know I seem to fight it,
but at the end of the day, you are the person I wish
to talk to. I feel more like myself when I'm bound,
gagged, and spanked around you than I do amidst
the dozens of friends and colleagues I've had for
years.

    Don't give up on me yet.

    Cassandra

Jess dug inside her purse for the tissues she kept in there.
Tears danced at the edges of her eyes. Had he given up on her?

Given up on her so much that he felt the need to shoot her and leave her to die in the ocean? Jess wasn't sure; she had spent the last week reading the dark details of their relationship and the man in the e-mails clearly loved her sister. And even if Jess and Elliot "Master" Warner had nothing else in common, the fact that they both loved Cass was enough. It had to be. She had no one else to turn to now that Sam wanted her to give up and get out of town—to leave Portland and forget the fact that her sister's death was so much more than the "robbery gone bad" Portland Police labeled it as. Besides herself, Sam, and Captain Straimer, no one else was in on the underground drug dealings her sister had gotten involved in. Not even Sam's partner, Matt.

Everyone who used to bring Jess comfort now only brought pain. Her parents had passed away years ago. Cass was dead. Her sister's former friend/handyman, Dane, had lied to Jess the very second he met her. And then there was Sam.

Sam was the boy Jess had grown up with. Her first kiss, her first cigarette, her first everything—and she couldn't even trust *him* anymore. And if she was being honest with herself, she never could. He'd been lying to her since they were fifteen. Ever since the night her parents died and he covered up the fact that his mother had been at the wheel of the car that struck them.

Jess winced as the memory of Sam in his hospital bed, vulnerable and bloody, rushed into her thoughts. Yes, she was mad at him. No, she didn't trust him anymore. But that didn't mean she wanted him in pain or suffering. Someone had attacked him, hurt him, as a way to get to her. And now, she had nowhere else to turn. No one else to believe in . . . except for Elliot. Wetness stained her cheeks and she wiped it away, looking at her reflection in the mirrored elevator doors. She had to pull it together. If there was ever a man who wouldn't respond to tears, it would be Elliot. She was sure of that much.

Jess slipped the iPad back into her purse as she gently wiped below her eyes and pinched her cheeks to get some of her color back. "Don't be desperate," she said to her reflection. "And don't show weakness."

"Mr. Warner's ready now," the receptionist said from behind her.

Jess grabbed her things and followed the receptionist with her smooth, bouncing ponytail down a long hall. After a moment, Jess entered through heavy double doors into an oversize office that screamed of an inferiority complex. She scanned the long floor-to-ceiling windows that looked out over historical Portland's wharfs and docks.

"Ms. Walters." Elliot Warner's voice was quiet, with the low trill of a wolf's warning growl. Her attention drew to where he sat behind his desk and she felt her chest hitch with a sharp inhalation. His lips quirked and damn if he didn't sense her nervous energy. Of course he did. A wolf always knew which prey was the easiest capture. His eyes never once left hers. "I've been expecting you." He gripped a set of car keys in his hand before setting them down onto the desk next to him.

"It's Jess. Not Ms. Walters." Nerves bounced around in her empty stomach. "Going somewhere?" Jess asked, nodding to his keys.

"Just getting back, actually." He cleared his throat. "You discovered me last week, in the elevators. And yet it took you days to actually confront me." He grabbed the cup of coffee Jess had brought for him from the coffee cart outside, which, according to his e-mail exchanges with her sister, was the best in all of Portland.

"Was there a question in there somewhere?" Jess took a sip from her cup. Though it had been a while since she arrived and bought the coffees, it was still hot, and she savored the smooth, creamy liquid as it slid down her throat.

"Let me rephrase," he said. "Why did it take you so long to confront me when you've clearly known who I was for several days now?"

"Well, I was busy and had business to attend to this weekend. This felt like it could wait. I usually have good instincts about these things," Jess answered.

Elliot took a long swig of his own coffee, but unlike when Sam drank coffee, Elliot's sip was refined. Smooth. Whereas Sam would slug it back in a quick gulp no matter how piping hot the liquid inside was. Tightness closed in around Jess's throat and she turned her attention outside of Elliot's window. She could not think of Sam right now. He didn't deserve her. And while she wasn't so foolish to believe that once they broke up she had some sort of magical immunity to their chemistry, it didn't change the facts. You only get one second chance, and Sam blew his. Matt could take care of him now that he had been released from the hospital on Monday.

"I wouldn't say that," Elliot responded.

"Huh?"

"About your instincts?" he continued, pressing his palms to the lacquered desk and pushing to his feet. The exquisite three-piece navy pinstripe suit fit his body perfectly, as though it was sewn for his exact specifications. And hell, maybe it was. This guy was freaking loaded. "In fact . . . I'd say other than coming to see me today, your 'instincts' have damn well nearly killed you and your boyfriend."

Jess's cheeks heated. "He's not my boyfriend."

"Your . . . dom, perhaps?" There was a teasing tone to his voice that Jess hated.

Sam's voice from last week echoed in her memory. *"I'm going to tear that dress from your body, press your breasts against that wall, and show you what you've been missing all these years by paddling that tight ass of yours."*

Lifting her chin in a false show of confidence, Jess shook her head. "No. He's my nothing. My colleague, perhaps, and that's all."

"Well, that's an interesting development."

A sense of unease slid through Jess's body, landing at her fingers as they trembled around the coffee cup, despite the heat that burned through. "How do you know so much about me?"

"I make it my business to know." He swaggered around to the front of his desk, then tugged at the knees of his million-dollar pants. "So, Sam's out of the picture . . . pardon the photography pun."

"Yes. He's out." With a deep breath, Jess gave herself the mental pep talk she needed. She could do this. She had to do this. Not only for Cass now, but also for her own life and for Sam's. Even if they wouldn't be together, she didn't want him dead. "You know more than you let on. It's painfully obvious. I think you probably know more than the entire Portland Police force ever could. And I need your help." Jess resisted the urge to look at her feet. "*Cass* needs your help."

"I don't see how a dead woman would need my help." But even as he said the harsh words, pain sliced through his cold features.

Jess slammed her coffee down on the corner of his desk. A bit of the steaming liquid sloshed out the top and splattered onto her knuckles. She gritted her teeth and refused to show any acknowledgment of the pain. But despite her efforts, Elliot's eyes flicked down, noting the moment as a smile turned his lips.

"Don't be an ass," Jess said. "Don't pretend as though my sister meant nothing to you. She may have been your sub, but she loved you. And I think you loved her."

"That's a lot of thinking you've been doing." Elliot's eyes locked into hers and they stood there, momentarily frozen in time. He walked over to a small bar area on the opposite side of the room. "Can I offer you a little Irish in your coffee?" He wiggled a bottle of whiskey, the caramel-colored liquid sloshing around inside the bottle.

Jess shook her head as he poured himself two fingers worth

of whiskey. "Yes," Elliot said after a long sip. "I loved Cassandra. And if you're not careful, you're going to end up with the same fate as her."

"Except that her colleague, Zooey, is being pinned for both Cass's and Dr. Brown's murder. And I don't think she killed them. At least not Cass—as for Dr. Brown . . . well, I don't know."

Wrinkles framed his eyes as they narrowed for just a fraction of a second. "Zooey? That mousy girl that Cass worked with?" He shook his head. "Wow. They're really straining to close this, aren't they?"

"Yes, they are. And it certainly doesn't help Zooey's case that she confessed to Dr. Brown's accidental manslaughter and then disappeared. But even still, I think she's being set up." Jess brushed a hand against Elliot's arm to emphasize the point, and immediately regretted doing so. He looked down at where her finger had dared to touch his suit as though he may need to burn the thing now. She pulled her hand back to her side. "Come on. We both know she didn't do this."

Elliot sighed, dragging his hand down over weary features, his entire body seeming to relax with the breath. "I don't know anything. Which is exactly how you should answer should anyone ask you, Jessica."

"*Jess*," she corrected once more. The last man to call her by her full name was Sam. In the bedroom. She'd rather not have that memory hanging over her.

One side of Elliot's mouth lifted into an arrogant half smile. "I prefer Jessica."

"And yet, that's not really your call."

His grin twitched higher. "And yet, I don't care."

A breeze gusted through his open window and Jess shivered, resisting the urge to hug her arms to her chest. Just who did he think he was? And what the hell was it about men who were assholes being so damn magnetic? Jess hated herself for liking that quality in Sam, and she hated Cass for having liked it in this guy. Because at the end of the day, all it did was make them shitheads. Sexy shitheads, but still . . .

"Are you going to help me or not?"

"Of course. But only if we do this my way, *Jessica*."

Jess gave an inward curse. He knew exactly which buttons to push and relished her agitation.

She opened her mouth to answer, when her cell phone rang from within her pocket. The sudden noise made her jump. It was a small action, but damn if Elliot didn't notice it. Jess gnashed her teeth together, grabbing her phone from her pocket and checking the number. *Sam.*

Emotion burned through her chest at the sight of his name.

Jamming her finger onto the silence button, she slipped the phone into her back pocket, unanswered. Sam was no longer a player in this game. But this man in front of her? Her sister's ex-lover and the man who ran the masquerade parties? He was her only hope. He was Cass's *only* hope.

"Deal."

2

"Son of a bitch," Sam grumbled, tossing his phone on the bed beside him. Placing a damp palm against his forehead, he closed his eyes, willing away his pounding headache.

"Still not answering, huh?" Matt, his longtime friend and partner on the force, nudged open Sam's bedroom door, resting a bowl of soup and a glass of water on the nightstand.

"That better be vodka," Sam said, eyeing the glass.

"I don't expect to earn my 'naughty nurse' title for nothin'," Matt laughed. "C'mon, man. You gotta eat something. The doc told me I'd have to drag your ass back in if you're not drinking enough fluids."

"Jesus Christ," Sam grumbled. "You've gone soft since you became a dad."

"Shut up and eat your soup, asshole."

Sam leaned over the steaming bowl and took a sip of the salty broth. It felt good going down. But damn if he'd admit it to Matt that he was right.

"It's good, isn't it?" Matt grinned knowingly.

"Fuck . . . this isn't any sort of canned shit."

Matt shook his head. "No way. Nothing but the best for my partner. Kelly made it. It's some family recipe or something. But it's damn good."

Holy hell. Sam lifted the bowl, resting it in his lap. After two days of hospital food, this was like a Thanksgiving feast.

"She left a full container of it in your fridge, as well as two casseroles. With your stomach? You should be good until breakfast, fatty." Matt gave him a gentle slap on the back and Sam grunted in response.

After another moment of silent eating, Sam dared another glance at his buddy. "How is she?"

Matt tucked his hands into his pockets, a disingenuous smile crossing his face. "Kelly's good. Busy with the baby and we're both fucking exhausted—"

"That's not who I'm asking about and you know it," Sam interrupted.

Matt's smile faded. "Yeah, I know. We have uniforms driving by and checking in on Jess a few times a day. She seems fine."

"No one shady hanging around?"

"Dude, we caught the guy—or girl, in this case. Zooey's unconscious but handcuffed to her hospital bed. Jessie's safe. You're safe."

And yet, that uneasy feeling in the pit of Sam's stomach wouldn't go away. Zooey wasn't their perp. There was no way she was the brains behind the newest drug being distributed in Portland. Not that Sam expected Matt to have any knowledge of that. To his friend, this probably did look like a clear cut-and-dried case. What they initially thought to be a robbery gone bad with Cass—and what Sam and Captain Straimer were relying on everyone to believe to better solve her case and find the mole in the department—now looked like a crime of passion. A love triangle between a scorned woman; her boyfriend, Dr. Richard Brown; and Cass, the woman he was flirting with on the side.

"You really think a girl attacked me in that basement?" asked Sam.

"I've seen stranger things," Matt said.

"When she wakes up, she'll be able to—"

"*If* she wakes up," Matt interrupted. "She's in rough shape."

Fuck. Then all will have gone to Cass's murderer's plan. Zooey will be the fall person for Cass's and Dr. Brown's deaths and they can carry right on distributing drugs. "You've got a uniform watching Zooey's door, too, right?"

Matt rolled his eyes. "Of course. What do you think this is? Amateur hour?"

Well, at least that's something. A small relief, but Sam would take his wins when he got them. "Have you at least talked to Jessie?"

Matt shook his head, running his fingers down the length of his trimmed goatee. It would have looked ridiculous had Sam not known the guy well enough to know that was his habit when he didn't want to admit something. "Matt—what?"

"She won't answer my calls, either," he said, dropping his hands. "Not since we found Zooey."

Maybe she'd finally taken his advice? Realized just what was good for her and gotten the hell out of this investigation. Now that her sister's murderer thought that they had wrapped the case up in a neat little bow with Zooey's arrest, maybe, just maybe, they'd let Jess go back to her life. Go back to Brooklyn. And even though it hurt like a sock to the jaw, it was the only way Jess could survive this. The person who attacked him at the masquerade Friday night had made that perfectly clear.

Get her out of Portland.... The attacker's hot breath and raspy voice rang in Sam's ears as if it had happened seconds ago. He had tried. He had broken up with her and confessed to the one thing he was certain would make her forget all about him and move on—the fact that his mother had been the drunk driver who killed her parents in a car wreck when they were fifteen. Sure, he was just a boy when he came home that night to find his intoxicated mother sweaty and panicking. She had begged him to be her alibi.

"And . . ." Matt broke through Sam's thoughts, hesitating before continuing.

Sam froze with that one little word. His already sore and stiff muscles bunched beneath his pajama pants and undershirt. "And?"

"According to Officer Donnelly, she left this morning. And she was seen loading luggage into her trunk."

"Why didn't they follow her? Find out where she was going?"

"He wasn't actually on watch for her. He happened to be in the area and just did a quick drive-by. But . . ."

"But *what?*"

"I mean, her leaving with a packed suitcase. It can really only mean one thing, right? She was leaving."

Jess was leaving town. The mixture of relief and pure, empty sadness was overwhelming. She needed to get out of Portland for her own good. No matter how hollow his life would be without her. He did it once . . . he could do it again.

"It's okay, Matt. I knew her stay wouldn't be permanent."

"Yeah, but this is sooner than you thought, isn't it? Weren't you two just getting back together—"

Sam gave his best casual smile. "Jess and I are like a carton of milk. We always had an expiration date. She's just tossing us out now, *before* we spoil, instead of after."

"Whatever you say, man. I think it's pretty fucked up, though. She didn't even say good-bye. I thought for sure you two would work it out."

"We don't all end up with our high school sweethearts, Mattie."

Though it was silent, his partner held his glare, a tense energy passing between them. Matt only came to about Sam's shoulders when they were both standing tall. He was stocky, but short. And like a bulldog, he could deliver as loud a bark as any of the big dogs on the force. And he knew Sam better than he sometimes knew himself.

"Well, I need to get going. Captain Straimer is assigning me a temp partner," Matt snarled, his lip curling. "Apparently Officer Laura Rodriguez is training to be detective and so she's gonna shadow me while you're out of commission."

"Jesus," Sam grunted. "Good luck with that. Keep it in your pants, man. Kelly will eat you alive if you—"

"Yeah, yeah, I know." Matt laughed, opening the bedroom door. "But she won't know if I look or not. Just no touching." He held both hands up at his shoulders, palms out, as he backed out the door. "I'll check on you later. Call if you need anything."

The sound of Matt's heavy footsteps clomped down the stairs and with a slam of the front door, Sam was alone in his apartment again. For the first time in years, he felt lonely. The boring white walls, crappy particleboard furniture, and simple navy décor was suddenly massively depressing.

Without thinking, he grabbed his phone and called Jess again. Just one more time to say good-bye . . . and yet, as the phone rang against his ear, he knew it was a stupid idea. She hated him—or at least she *should* hate him. Her voice mail clicked on and he ended the call without leaving a message. And really, what was there to say? All those years; all that time he had lied to her about his mom. A lump lodged in his throat and he took another slurp of soup to help it go down. All those years of hiding the truth and covering for a woman who, nine times out of ten, would have chosen a bottle of gin over her own son. But what was he supposed to do? Turn his mother in to the authorities? Go into the foster system and be parentless? Unlike Jess, he didn't have an older sibling to step up and become his legal guardian.

He shook his head, tossing the almost-empty bowl of soup back onto the nightstand. *Fuck.* Turning his mother in was exactly what he should have done. He had been a total and utter coward. A young coward, yeah, but even as he got older, even now that he was a grown man and knew his mistake, he never took steps to right that wrong. Not to mention that he was also the world's biggest hypocrite, serving as Portland, Maine's lead detective.

And now he had lost Jessie for good because of it.

Which was precisely what should have happened, because she deserved better than him. Her very life depended on finding someone better than him.

3

"So, Jessica . . . why don't you tell me what you *think* you know?" Elliot's eyes glistened, ripe with authority in a smug way that Jess just freakin' hated. It elicited anger and a frustration deeper than she cared to examine.

"Let's see," she said, and dropped the handle of the suitcase she'd found in the back of Cass's guest closet, kicking it out of her way. "I know that my sister was involved in drugs. Not doing them herself, but distributing. It was pretty obvious when I started putting the pieces of her life together. I know that the two of you started as some sort of master-apprentice, dominant-submissive relationship before you fell in love. I know that the masquerade parties are some sort of front to get the drugs transported out of my house through the hidden tunnels in the basement and that you were the man who began these parties." She paused for emphasis, and stopped pacing, standing in front of him. His breath was shallow and he smelled like a mix between coffee and whiskey. Grabbing his cup, she took a drink of his spiked coffee and then thrust it back into his hands. "And I know that I fucking go by *Jess*. Not Jessica."

"That's a lot you *think* you know."

Jess jerked her head toward the luggage, not breaking eye contact. "Why don't you have a look?"

He gave her a curious glance before bending and lifting the suitcase, dropping it on a side table. He carefully unzipped it with a tenderness that reminded Jess of unzipping the back of a silk dress.

Elliot inhaled sharply as he flipped the suitcase open. Inside were stacks of cash from Cassandra's floorboards and her fake passport.

"*That's* how I know," Jess sneered. "Now, can you stop treating me like a child?"

"Did you touch these?"

"What?"

"Did. You. Touch. These?"

"Yes, I—"

"Did you wear gloves?"

Jess gulped and suddenly she felt like she was back to being a chastised little girl. Just as she thought she was gaining some traction with this man. "No. But, I mean, I found them. I haven't *done* anythi—"

"Shit," Elliot grunted, running both of his hands through his inky hair.

"What the hell are you freaking out about? None of this is even *mine*."

Elliot's eyebrows jumped as he shot her a fiery look. "You think that matters?" His voice was gruff and he rushed to the window, scanning the parking lot below before pulling the blinds closed. "You think that innocence ever matters in times like these? You believe your friend Zooey to be innocent, right?"

Jess nodded slowly, her throat burning.

"And did the cops care that the evidence didn't quite line up?"

Jess didn't answer. She didn't need to. They both knew the truth.

"You need a place to hide this money," said Elliot.

"Cass had it all in the house—"

"Not a literal hiding place. A place to invest. Tie the money up in a way that won't raise any flags when and if they search your financials. It's what Cass should have done initially. I should have helped her."

Jess backed away from him and the cash. Her stomach turned like she had a loaded gun pointed directly at her chest. "You can't actually think I plan to keep this money? I'm turning it over to the police."

Elliot grunted his opinion of that. "Don't be ridiculous. You're a photographer, right?"

"But this money isn't *mine*—"

"It was Cass's," he snarled, and Jess jumped as he swiveled away from the window, nearly knocking her over. He barely noticed and continued walking, backing her against the wall.

"Yeah, but—"

"And Cass left everything to you, yes?"

"*Yes*, but—"

"Then this money *is* yours. There is no but. Cass put her life on the line. I doubt it was for the cash, but even so. She worked for this money. She risked everything for it. And now it is *yours*." He spoke with such authority. Head high, eyes straight ahead, shoulders stiff. He truly was magnificent to watch and Jess couldn't help but stare at him in awe. She'd always tried to hold that sort of command in conversations—hell, in life. And compared to this man? She was worse than a rookie. She was the runt on the little league team.

But that didn't mean she was ready to back down just yet. Jess snapped her mouth shut, her jaw twitching, and stood a bit taller. "It's illegal. And I don't want it."

"Then you're fucking stupid," he said, forgetting his coffee and pouring himself a highball of straight whiskey, neat, instead. "I could hire you to photograph images of my buildings that are on the market and slowly put the money into your account as a paycheck. You'll have to pay taxes on it, but considering you were going to turn it over to the police department, I'm going to guess you're okay with that."

There was a knock at the door as another man, also in an immaculate three-piece suit, poked his head into the office.

"Excuse me a moment," Elliot said, and followed the man outside the office keeping the door propped open with his foot. There were murmurings, but Jess wasn't listening.

Her cheeks burned hot as she stared at his marble floors.

Elliot finished with his colleague, coming back in and shutting the door behind him. Jess opened her mouth to speak but Elliot cut her off.

"Just think about my offer. Don't answer now." He swirled his tumbler in his palm, and whiskey sloshed along the side of the glass. "So. What else did you find?"

"What else?"

"Well, you found the money. Her passport. Obviously, you found me." If Jess hadn't been so utterly convinced this guy had no sense of humor, she would have thought she heard a twinge of amusement in his voice at that. "So, yes. What else?"

Jess racked her brain . . . other than the skeleton key and the tunnel, there was nothing else.

Elliot's rigid shoulders tightened around his ears. "You didn't find her stash?"

"Stash of what?"

He cursed before tossing his head back and swallowing the rest of the copper whiskey in one motion. "Jesus, Jessica. Her stash. The drugs she's been sneaking in and out of the house— hell, probably even the country."

"There are drugs still in that house?"

Elliot pressed his lips together, not answering. Not that he needed to.

Jess fell back into the club chair that was behind her, landing on the soft leather. It groaned in protest beneath her weight.

"What—what do I do?" she asked herself more than Elliot. She knew exactly what she needed to do. She needed to call Sam. Get the DEA in her house immediately and sweep it.

A hand on her knee caused her to jump and she looked to find Elliot on his knees in front of her. His velvety, dark blue eyes seared into her. How the hell did he move so quietly? Or was she just that zoned out?

"You came to me for help, Jessica. Let me help."

She nodded. "Can you c-call the police for me? I don't think I can do it." Even as she reached for her cell, her hand trembled. Pulling it from her pocket, she handed it to Elliot. The screen felt smooth beneath her quivering touch.

He gently took her phone, but instead of calling anyone, he tucked it into his back pocket. "The police in this town are dirty, Jessica. There's a mole down there. Maybe more than one. Calling them will only get you killed. *Especially* if you show knowledge of the drugs. You need to trust me."

"Trust you?" her voice cracked with a bitter laugh. "You mean like Cass did?"

Sadness washed over his face, the waves of sorrow pulling his expression deeper under water. "And I'll never forgive myself for not trying harder. . . ." His voice faded away, eyes drifting somewhere over Jess's shoulder. "She trusted me as much as she could," he finished, bouncing back into his usual hardened demeanor.

"Why would she do this? Why did she allow herself to get caught up in this? And who—"

His jaw tensed. "I don't know."

Right. Yeah, fucking right. "Bull. You know something. Okay, fine. Don't tell me. But then don't sit there and wonder why I can't trust you when you won't tell me everything."

"Look," Elliot growled "The less you know, the safer you are. Why do you want to find out, anyway? Because if it's for some vigilante reason, then you can count me out. I already feel responsible enough for Cassandra's murder—I'm not going to take part in yours, too."

All the moisture in her mouth evaporated. *Well, if he can keep secrets, then so can I.* With what little she knew about this man, she doubted he'd ever agree to join her on a quest to find her sister's killer and avenge her death. Nibbling her bottom lip, she took a slow breath, channeling her theater classes from high school. "My life is in danger. I want to find whatever it is these assholes want from me, get it to them, and then get the hell out while I can."

A smile flickered briefly at Elliot's lips. "That's what I needed to hear," he said. He pulled her phone from his back pocket and handed it back to her. "I don't know where Cassandra's stash is, but I think I know who does."

"Okay . . ."

His eyes flashed. "And you're going to call him."

Rolling the phone over in her hands, Jess circled her thumb over the smooth plastic. "Who would know that?"

Elliot worked his jaw hard, grinding his teeth. A cloud darkened his eyes before he spoke. "Dane."

4

Dane, Jess thought, wanting to protest, but knowing it was useless. Just another person she could add to her list of liars. With numb fingers, Jess dialed Dane's number, her hand shaking the whole time. What exactly was she supposed to say to the man who pretended to have no knowledge of her sister's death when Jess told him about it? He was supposed to have been Cass's friend. Someone she could rely on, but he hadn't even come to her funeral. He answered almost immediately on the first ring.

"Jess," he said quickly into the phone. "Jess, I am so glad you called. I was hoping you would after I left my note—"

"Dane," she said, and as she opened her mouth to say more, Elliot snatched the phone out of her hand.

"Ah, Daniel. Hello, my friend." Elliot's voice boomed with arrogance.

"My name is Dane," Jess heard on the other end of the receiver. Elliot tossed her a wink to which she responded by folding her arms. At least she wasn't the only one he played name games with.

"Jessica and I need your assistance. Today. As soon as possible, actually."

Jess could feel Elliot's attention following her as she wandered around the room. There was a large, built-in bookshelf along one wall. She dragged a finger along the book spines: *Robinson Crusoe, A Tale of Two Cities, The Catcher in the Rye.* On some of the books, the edges were worn so thin they were frayed.

Her shoes clicked against the marble floor as she continued her march around the room. She dared a glance at Elliot. He had angled features sharpened like the sheer edge of a deadly cliff and a lock of bluish-black hair fell over his brow, adding a boyishness that was contradictory to his beauty, softening his severity. And while he wasn't her type, she could absolutely see how Cass had fallen so hard over the edge for him.

"Uh-huh," he said into the phone, and yet, somehow it felt as though he were talking directly to her. "We can explain more when you get to Cassan—" Her sister's name caught in his throat and after taking only a second to compose himself, he continued. "I mean, Jessica's house. Though, I'm sure you could figure it out if you think really hard. You're a smart guy."

Yeah, not quite a compliment. And she was pretty damn sure Dane knew it.

"One hour?" Elliot checked his very expensive-looking watch. "That will do."

Jess wandered behind Elliot's desk, running her hand along every surface she could find. Damn, she wished she had her camera in here. Photographing this place would give such insight into this man. She could see things through the viewfinder that she simply couldn't see with her own eyes. It was what she loved so much about photography. Her camera was like a second set of eyes; eyes that could capture motion, freeze a moment in time, evoke mood and emotion with a quick click. And, more than anything, she wanted to dissect this man. Know what the hell he had been like with her sister. In a way, he knew a side of Cassandra that Jess never would—she couldn't even imagine her sister in an office like this, let alone dating a man who owned the whole damn building.

Tears pricked the back of her eyes, but instead of succumbing to the emotion, Jess brought her teeth down hard onto her tongue, dulling the emotional pain with a physical one.

When Elliot hung up, Jess plopped back down into his leather desk chair. His lips tightened and she felt an odd sense of joy at getting under his skin. Everything was so perfect; so orderly. She relished throwing his tidy life around in a heaping mess.

"So . . . *El*," Jess said, "Why didn't *you* just call Dane? Why have me do it if you were going to take the phone from me anyway?"

As quickly as the scowl surfaced, it was replaced with a small smile. "Because Dane never would have answered my call," he said. "Nor would I blame him for that."

Well, that was an honest answer. And for once, Jess had no idea what to say in response. "Why?" she asked.

Elliot gave her a thoughtful once-over before lifting her purse off the club chair where she had left it and zipping up her suitcase. "I think we've both had enough questions for one day. How about some answers?" He walked over to her, her purse dangling by the strap from his fingertips.

"I would love some answers," she said.

"Would you mind if we kept this luggage here? It's probably one of the safest places to keep an amount of cash this large." He walked briskly behind his desk, not waiting for her answer before opening a bottom cabinet. After sliding out a series of filing shelves with a few clicks he opened a hidden safe.

Whoa. That was some serious shit. Jess's feelings must have been pretty damn apparent because when Elliot caught her glance, he answered her unspoken question. "I keep cash on many of my properties. And if Cass had gotten a safe as I suggested, you may not be in such a predicament."

"She had a safe. In the basement."

"That wasn't *her* safe," he said, pushing to his feet after securing the cash inside. Using a tissue, he lifted Cass's fake passport and held it up in front of Jess's face. "Would you like to hold on to this? Or should I?"

Jess stilled beneath his stare and even though it was a simple question, it felt like a test. A test of whether or not she trusted him. She grabbed the passport and tucked it into her purse.

Elliot sighed. "Well, then, shall we?" he said with a gesture toward the door.

They exited the building together, walking in silence the whole way. As they slipped off the elevator, Elliot brushed the small of her back. A minor gesture, yes. A gentlemanly motion, but not one she was entirely comfortable with. How could Cass trust someone so . . . so . . . demanding? Someone with such a clinical desire to be in constant control? But her sister *had* trusted him. That's what she had to remember. And Cass wasn't one to trust easily—he must have earned it. Then again, as judging from Cass's life choices, maybe her sister wasn't exactly the best judge of character.

Elliot held the door open for Jess, nodding at the man behind the front desk before once again placing that icy touch on her lower back. A chill skated down from the base of her neck to the back of her heels. This man completely unnerved her to the core. And why? Because he had money? Because he had walls up? Who didn't?

She shook the idea from her head, bringing her thoughts back to Dane and how he would be at her house within the hour. Sure, Jess had assumed Dane knew *some*thing about Cass's situation, but for him to know exactly where her sister was keeping God-knew-how-much money in drugs?

As she dragged her thoughts back to the present, Jess realized that they had stopped walking. Elliot had been leading the way in the parking lot, right to her car.

"How the hell did you know which car was mine?" Jess demanded.

"Shh," he said, snapping his palm out behind him to quiet her. She damn near slapped his hand out of her face except for the tight look that passed over his features. The same awareness that she had seen up in his office had returned as he now scanned the parking lot. "Did anyone know you were here?"

"Huh? No . . ."

"Did anyone follow you?"

This time goose bumps lifted along her arms as a chill careened a path down her whole body. "I-I don't think so." Moving around to the other side of Elliot, she froze, seeing what he was talking about. An envelope sat tucked into her windshield wipers. Which normally wouldn't be all that alarming, but the envelope had a lobster claw seal. The same seal on the letter she had received from the people using the masquerade to distribute their drugs. And it was the same stationery she had found in Dr. Brown's office after he was murdered.

"You don't think so?"

"I wasn't really watching, I guess."

Elliot smoothed a palm down his clean-shaven jaw. A sprinkling of black stubble was pushing its way through his soft-looking skin. Even though it was similar to the stubble that Sam sported, on Elliot it just looked . . . different.

"You should know how to spot a tail, Jessica. I can teach you."

Jess didn't know what it was about Elliot, but something told her not to fight him; not on this. She backed away from the envelope, as though walking away from it would delete its existence entirely. "No. No, this is ridiculous. That note's not for me. They messed up—whoever delivered it mixed up my car for someone else's—"

"Jessica," Elliot warned, closing in on her. It only made

breathing harder. He was the problem here. He was making it impossible to get air. "Jess!" His hands were gripping her shoulders, clenched tightly; not so hard that it hurt, but enough to apply pressure and bring her back to the reality of the situation. "You could run," he said, and her eyes widened with his statement. The late September air was crisp and cool and made her eyes dry as she blinked. "Run, Jessica. Take your sister's cash. Get the fuck away from Portland and don't come back. They only attack when threatened and if you're not here, then you're not a threat."

Emotion clogged her throat; it fogged her mind, her thoughts, her chest—just about everything. When did life get so damn difficult? Why couldn't she just have a normal person's problems? She'd already lost her parents at a young age— why this, too? It was maddening and suddenly that sadness that was hazing her thoughts cleared away and was replaced with pure, crystallized anger. Hatred for the people who took the only family she had left from her. She *could* run. She *could* start a whole new life. But then, there would never be any justice for her sister. Zooey would be blamed, the drugs would continue being distributed, and everything she'd worked so hard for would disappear along with whatever small dose of integrity she had left.

Elliot's grip suddenly felt less binding and more secure. Solid. Strong. In control. He was exactly the kind of person she needed on her side for this. His bright eyes narrowed, almost as though he were reading her thoughts. "What's your end goal here, Jessica?" he said.

"What do you mean?"

"You can't take them down. You will not win. Do you understand me? And I'm sure as fuck not going to participate in some sort of suicide mission."

Jess shrugged his hands off her. "I have no idea what you're talking about. I don't want to run . . . I don't want to leave my life and everything Cass worked so hard to get in this town. But

I don't want them coming after me anymore. And I think you know how to get them off my back. I think you know what they want." Because more than anything, she wanted to find that motherfucker who had pulled the trigger on her sister and lock him away for life.

They locked into another stare down for what felt like an eternity. Did he believe her? Hell, she almost believed herself.

"It could be anything. Drugs . . . money . . ." He backed away from her, snatching the envelope from her windshield. "Maybe this will tell us."

Jess moved with as much confidence as she could. She took the envelope and carefully pried the seal open. Six black-and-white glossy images slid into her palm. There were three photos of Cass getting ready for one of her parties. Behind those were three images of Jess, half naked, dressing for the party that had taken place the past Friday. It was a warning. A warning that they were watching.

She should have felt fear. She should have been frozen where she stood, shaking with terror. She should have gone straight home and started packing and gotten the first ticket out of this godforsaken town. But all those images did was add gasoline to her rage-fueled fire.

Elliot took the pictures from her hand, gently holding the edges, careful not to smudge them. His face twisted as he stared at a photograph of Cass, her dress unzipped, twisting to look behind her out the window at the camera.

"This was the night she died," he said, his voice hoarser than after a concert. He was quiet for another moment before tearing his gaze away from the image and looking at Jess. No . . . not looking at her. Those eyes were cold. Hardened. He looked *through* her.

"You want to know what they *really* want?" He dropped the pictures back into her hands. "They want a bullet in your head."

5

The pounding in Sam's head had dulled to barely an ache. Not bad for it being only a few days post-concussion. *It also isn't great by any means,* Sam thought as he slipped his arms into a button-down blue shirt. He wanted to look more than capable if someone came by from the force to check on him. The sooner they signed him back into active duty, the better.

The TV was on in the background, the local news offering a white noise background as he spooned Kelly's casserole into a bowl and popped it in the microwave. Once it was done, he settled onto his black leather sofa, propping his feet up on the glass coffee table and cupping the steaming bowl under his chin as he ate.

As he finished his meal, he stole a glance at the clock. Seriously? Only ten minutes had passed? He groaned and let his head fall back against the back edge of the couch. Time moved fucking slowly when you were stuck at home like a man on house arrest.

His cell rang and Sam tossed his bowl to the side, muting the TV. An unknown Portland number blinked on the screen of his phone. Swiping to the right, he answered.

"This is Sam McCloskey."

"Mr. McCloskey, this is Dr. Adams from Mercy Hospital. How are you feeling?"

Sam sighed. *The doctor, of course.* Other than Matt or the captain, who the hell would be calling him? His mother and stepfather had long since passed away. And Jess . . . *Well, it wasn't as though she's going to be calling me,* he thought, driving her delicate face from his mind. "I'm feeling great, Doc," Sam lied. "Could run a marathon tonight if you let me."

Dr. Adams gave a quiet chuckle from the other end of the line. "Somehow I doubt that, but I'm glad to hear you're feeling better." There was a pause as something sat static in the air between them.

"Dr. Adams? Is there something else you need?"

The older man sighed. "I tried calling your partner, a Detective Matt Johnson, but he didn't answer and I didn't want to wait—your suspect, Zooey Devonshire, woke up about thirty minutes ago. I thought one of you should know. Detective Johnson had mentioned he wanted to speak to her the second she came out of her coma."

Sam's pulse flicked, pounding against his wrist. *Where the hell is Matt?* It wasn't like him to not answer a call . . . particularly not in the midst of such a high-profile murder case. "I thought she wasn't doing well? I thought the chances of her waking up were slim to none—"

"The human body is a mystery. With the extent of her injuries, it was most definitely a surprise to see her bounce back within a few days. I don't think she'll be up and escaping anytime soon, but . . ." His voice faded away.

"But what?"

"She's extremely disoriented. Can't remember a thing and, understandably, had a massive anxiety attack with what little energy she had when she saw herself restrained to her bed."

Shit. He thought that restraining her had seemed a little extreme when Matt said that. Then again, she had supposedly run from Jess when she was found . . . and the first thing he ever learned as a detective was that only the guilty run. If his head wasn't hurting before, it was now.

"I'll be—I'll send someone down there right away to talk with her. Thanks for the call, Dr. Adams."

"Of course. I'll see you Friday for your follow-up." With that, the doctor hung up. Sam grabbed his badge, cell, and wallet, stuffing the various items in his back pocket as Matt's face on the television caught his attention. The local news was showing various cops scattered along the wharf, below the docks. The area that led directly to the tunnel into Jess's basement. Sam gulped. *Fuck.* If Jess wasn't out of Portland yet, she better be soon.

Jess pulled into her driveway with Elliot following her closely the whole way. As she walked up the front steps, Jess noticed that her sister's ceramic frogs were turned with their backs facing out. "Dane's here," she said.

She turned to look at Elliot as he scanned the house's perimeter. "I know. I saw his truck parked down the street." Elliot raised a brow in her direction as she unlocked the door. "How did you know?"

Jess glanced quickly at the frogs; her and Dane's signal for when he would use a house key Cass gave him long ago. It was the result of Jess thinking he was an intruder and nearly blinding them both with pepper spray. "I saw the truck, too," she lied.

She looked away as she said it and shouldered the door open. Why did she feel the need to keep the frog thing a secret? It was such a minor detail to keep to herself and yet she couldn't shake the feeling that she needed to maintain control over this man, even in the littlest ways possible. Even if no one else in the world knew that she still held some secrets, *she* would know.

And she would hold on to those secrets as her own personal reminder that she was in control of her fate. Not Sam. Not Elliot. Not Dane. Jess Walters.

"Hey, Dane," she said as she walked in, finding him propped against the doorframe that separated the foyer from the dining room. He had a mug clenched in his fist and was sipping something that had steam billowing from it.

He was six foot something of pure, hardened muscle. Sandy brown hair. Light, kind eyes and the no-bullshit attitude that accompanied a heart of gold. His mouth turned up in a slight smile as he saw Jess.

"Hi. I hope you don't mind . . . I made some coffee," he said before glancing behind her to Elliot. The soft look he awarded her froze into a scowl. "I'm here for her. Not you."

Elliot's sigh was barely audible. Jess was pretty certain he hadn't meant for her to hear it. "I know that."

Dane took a sip of his coffee. "So long as we're clear."

"Crystal."

They had a stare down as Jess glanced between the two powerful, but extremely different, men. She couldn't stand the silence for another second. "What happened between you two?"

Dane's jaw twitched, the tight scowl softening as he met Jess's eyes. "He's a thief. He stole from me."

Jess's jaw dropped as she stared at Elliot. "You're rich. And you stole from him?"

Elliot rolled his eyes, shuffling out of his suit jacket. "Calm down. He's being dramatic. He means that I stole Cass from him." Tossing his jacket onto a nearby hook, he rolled his shirtsleeves up to his elbows. "And don't let those ripped jeans fool you. He's not hurting financially, either."

Jess opened her mouth to retort, only no words would form. Instead she clenched it shut and moved beyond Dane into the kitchen. He towered over her and as her shoulder brushed his bicep, he laid a gentle hand on her elbow.

"Can we talk?" he asked.

The taste of something acidic burned in the back of Jess's throat and she swallowed it down. He wanted to talk about the night of the party. About how he stole a prescription pad from her. About how he didn't care that stealing something like that could potentially put Jess in even more danger than she already was. At least when Sam lied, it was under a delusional pretense of trying to protect her. Dane on the other hand didn't seem to have the slightest concern for her well-being, no matter how many times he had apologized in his note to her.

And in the end, what were all of Dane's lies for? For a prescription drug problem he had? An addiction that apparently Cass's involvement had clearly not helped. Jess never thought her sister would be an enabler. Cassandra Walters was a lot of things, but she cared about her friends. She'd dive off a cliff for the people she loved. That's almost exactly what her sister had done in the last moments of her life. And Jess needed to find out why. So that her sister didn't die in vain. "We do need to talk. But not right this second."

"So," Dane said, drawing Jess's attention right back to him. "Why am I here? What can I do for you?"

Elliot took a step forward. "We need—"

"Did it look like I was asking you?"

Elliot looked at Jess with lifted brows.

The testosterone in the room was palpable. *My sister would have been able to handle these guys,* Jess thought. And for the millionth time, she wished Cass were here to jump into the frame. "Look—I don't quite know why you would know this, but apparently Cass may have . . . um, hidden some things. In this house. And for whatever reason, Elliot thinks you may know something about it."

"Does he?" Dane asked.

There was more silence as Dane's crystal-blue gaze swept the length of her body. She liked Dane. She had liked him almost from the first moment they met. And yet, there was something alarming about the guy. He was quiet and scrutinizing in a way that wasn't creepy. And he was always kind. Yet, he was a liar. She was beginning to think that the word *liar* was synonymous with "man."

"Look," she said. "If you're not going to help us, then just leave. Now, do you know where she may have hidden these things, or not?"

Dane paused while he sipped his coffee. "Follow me," he said, pushing off the wall and heading up the stairs.

His heavy work boots clomped up the stairs one by one, a stark contrast to Elliot's leather dress shoes, which had a lighter clack to them; more graceful, calculated. They reached the second floor, but Dane just kept going, climbing higher.

"When Cass bought this house, it needed a lot of work. Nothing foundational, but cosmetic changes and polishing." He got to the top floor—a refurbished attic that had an office and spare bedroom. Swinging the door open, he barged through. "When I was gutting up here to put in insulation, we found a weird room that had been plastered over. Based on the odd lighting choices, I thought the previous owners maybe had a darkroom or something. Cass was completely enchanted by the idea of a hidden room."

Nerves jumped in Jess's belly. A hidden room in the attic of a one-hundred-year-old house? Of course Cass had loved it.

Dane stopped in front of a wall, running his hand along the smooth plaster. Halfway up was a '70s-style wood panel design and then it switched to the normal cream-colored plaster. He smiled as he stroked the section of panel, as if remembering an old, lost friend. "She loved those ridiculous murder mysteries. So I created this for her as a joke." He tugged a nearby wall sconce shifting it down to reveal a keypad. "Unfortunately, I don't know her code to get in. It's different from her other ones."

Meaning that he had tried it before, Jess thought. That little voice in the back of her head that was telling her not to trust this man became louder.

"May I?" Elliot asked, stepping forward. Dane didn't answer, but took a step back. Elliot punched in some numbers and within seconds, a section of the panel popped open, revealing a small half-sized entrance.

"I told you she trusted me," Elliot said. Then, pulling his phone out, he showed Jess a series of four numbers on the screen. "Memorize it. Don't tell anyone." He jerked his chin toward Dane. "I mean that—no one. Not even him."

Zero four two zero.

Dane shouldered around Elliot, and turned on the sconce, illuminating the back room as well. "Go ahead," he said, and jerked his head in the direction of the secret doorway.

Jess stole a look back at Elliot, who stood tall, chin high, but his mouth was tightened into a firm line. Ducking under the half-open wall, Jess entered her sister's secret room. It was painted white, with lots of little lamps to light the room. An old, ornately carved desk sat against the wall with a cozy-looking chair tucked in beside it. But most notable were the shelves lining the walls from floor to ceiling. Not a single space was empty. Every inch of the shelves was occupied by bags of pills.

Jess felt sick, her head spinning and the walls closing around her. There were so many drugs. Shelves and shelves of prescription pills surrounded them. "Oh God, Cass. What were you thinking?"

6

They weren't the typical street drugs Jess thought of when she heard about dealers. There was no cocaine or white powders of any kind. No marijuana, no heroin. The entire room consisted of prescription medication. The exact sort of drugs Cass would have an easy time getting ahold of thanks to her job at a pharmaceutical company.

"Biophuterol," Jess read from one of the labels. "I've never heard of it before—" She reached to pick up one of the bags when a firm grip pinched her wrist.

"Don't touch anything," Elliot snarled. "Not without gloves on." He pointed to a box of latex gloves sitting on the edge of Cass's desk. "I'm guessing your sister was meticulous about that. One of the reasons she was never caught."

"It's a new drug," Dane said. "Biophuterol. Not FDA approved. It's replacing the demand for Oxy on the streets."

More cobwebs filled Jess's brain than she could handle. It was as though a spider were living in her head, constantly spinning a web to fog her thoughts. How in the hell could this be her sister's doing? How could she be so involved? This was beyond just a little bad judgment. Cass was officially neck deep in drug dealing. Or so it seemed. "M-maybe someone else was using this room?" Jess offered as an explanation. But even she didn't believe it.

Elliot strolled over to the back shelves as easily as if he were on a walk in the park on a summer day. Tucking his hands into his pockets, he smiled just a bit. "Who else do you know who would color-code the pills based on when they arrived and when they're supposed to go out?" he said, nodding his head toward the different bins.

"That's what these dates are?" Jess asked.

"I would assume so. Each bin has two dates on it. I would assume the earlier date is when the drugs arrived to her and the second date is when the drugs have to go out to the dealers."

"Prescription drugs are like anything else—they expire," Dane explained, looking around the room, his eyes lit. "And as they expire, their effectiveness . . . or their high would lessen."

Jess spun to face him. "You seem to know an awful lot, don't you?"

"About what?"

"*This*. The drugs!"

"I knew she had gotten involved with the wrong people. But it was for the right reasons," he said.

"What does that mean?" Elliot asked.

Jess had been thinking the same thing, only Elliot had beaten her to the question.

Dane didn't answer, keeping his eyes focused on Jess. "I didn't know about all this. I just thought she had to pick up a handful of pills from Canada each month and bring them across the borders for the dealers." He shook his head, rubbing a hand down his face. "But all this? This is just nuts."

"No," Elliot said, gesturing to the walls of pills. "You wanted to know who keeps threatening you and why? Well, *this* is what they want."

"Now what?" Jess asked. "You say the cops are dirty, so I can't call Sam. I can't just leave all this here."

"We need to find a way to leverage it to save your life. If these drugs are what they want, then this is what they'll get. And hopefully it will be enough for them to leave you alone."

"How the hell are we going to move all these drugs without Sam or someone getting suspicious? With all the threats on my life and the tunnels having been discovered? Sam's going to have someone watching me constantly," said Jess.

"I know that," Elliot said. He was so calm. So put together, despite being in a room filled with easily millions of dollars' worth of drugs. "Keep it together, okay, Jessica? I'll be in touch soon with a plan."

"Wait!" Jess grabbed his sleeve without thinking. She loosened her grip, immediately recognizing her mistake. "Where are you going? You can't leave me here with all this—"

His hands fell to her shoulders, and the weight felt reassuring. And the way he looked down at her, a bit of dark hair flopping subtly over his forehead—well, it gave her just the tiniest bit of hope that things might be okay. Even though she knew that likely wasn't true. "Relax. Have your chat with Dane. I have to go check on a client, but I promise I won't leave you in the midst of this confusion for long. I'll call you tonight and be back tomorrow with a fully formed game plan. You can count on that."

Her cheeks flushed. Was it fear? Anxiety? Or this stranger's hands on her body?

"Jessica," Elliot continued. "You can count on me."

And when he said it, she believed it. Jess believed it in a very different way than she believed Dane or Sam when they said it.

A snort came from behind them and Jess cast Dane a fiery look. With a squeeze to her shoulders, Elliot backed out of the half-sized door.

She watched as he disappeared, his footsteps growing fainter as he made his way down the stairs.

"*Please* don't tell me you're falling for his charms, too."
Dane's voice broke her trance and Jess rolled her eyes, turning
to face him once more.

"*No.* Not even a little. I just find him . . . strange. And unsettling."

Somehow in this tiny room, Dane looked even larger, standing tall with both hands tucked into his front pockets. Jess was
suddenly very aware of how much stronger he was than her.
Her back was nearly against the wall and as she glanced around,
the already small room seemed to close in around her. With
only one half-sized door as her escape, her throat tightened. "Is
it possible to get trapped in here?"

"No," he said. "This button can open and close the door
from the inside." He pointed to a small switch on the wall. "So,
if Cass wanted to close herself in to do some work, she could."

"And what if the button failed? Or there was a power outage
or something?"

Dane chuckled softly, and the sound was oddly comforting
in the midst of a very unsettling moment. "You're so much like
Cass," he said, and shook his head, moving over to the corner
of the room. He tugged on a ring, and the floorboards came up,
revealing a steep staircase. "These lead to the basement. That
way if she got locked in, she could always go down and then be
back inside her house."

"I didn't see any doorway in the basement."

"Of course not. That would defeat the purpose, wouldn't
it?" He paused, and his eyes flicked down her body for half a
second before he brought them back up to her face. "Wanna
see?"

Holy God, yes. But Jess only shrugged. "Okay."

"You still got Cass's skeleton key?"

"I—you know about that?"

"Cass trusted me, as well. Despite what Warner might tell
you. She always wore that key around her neck."

There was something in his voice—a hesitancy that left Jess uneasy and made her blood roll in her veins.

"Well, I left the key downstairs. Another time, maybe."

"I'm sorry again about stealing the prescription pad from you, Jess. I have a damn good reason, though. Those pills—"

"I'm less concerned with your drug habits these days and more curious as to why you lied to me. And Sam."

His eyebrows furrowed. "What?"

"The day I caught you in this house . . . the first day I moved in. You lied. You knew she was dead." Jess's voice cracked and she couldn't help the obvious emotion in it. "Why, Dane? Tell me why you lied."

Dane face flashed with anger and he stalked toward the exit. "I don't have to explain anything to you. You're not the cops."

She lunged for the button, and slamming her palm down on it, the door slid shut.

"What do you want from me?" Dane asked.

"The truth."

"The truth?" He cracked a bitter laugh. "You want to know if I killed Cass, right? Just like your boyfriend thinks I did. Well, I *didn't*. I have an alibi."

"Yeah? The supposed truck stop on your way to Boston, right? Except that the timeline of that doesn't quite add up. It's a two-hour drive to Boston . . . even less at one in the morning when you were claiming you were on the road. And the schedule you gave means that your trip to Boston would have been almost three hours. It doesn't make sense." There was a tense pause as Jess gave him a chance to explain. Only, he didn't. "Your alibi is thinner than lace. Now, why'd you lie to me?"

He sighed. "Because that day when we first met I was here in the house looking for *this*. For the drugs. And I thought it would look far less suspicious to just pretend I didn't know about her yet. But . . ." His voice faded away and he looked again to the floor, shaking his head.

"But *what*?"

"But you were so . . . so . . . kind. And you offered to bring me to Cass's headstone. I really did like you. And I don't like lying. It was the means to an end."

"Is that also what you were doing the night Cass died? Poking around the house?"

"If I said yes, would you even believe me?"

"If there was someone to corroborate your story, then yeah, I would."

"Everyone was drunk and no one would have noticed me poking around. And I wasn't the only one in this house looking. Lots of people are looking for this room. That mug you dropped when you first saw me? Do you ever recall Cass wearing that shade of red lipstick?"

Jess remembered the coffee cup with the scarlet lipstick print. He was right—it was so not Cass. "No," she said, and gulped as she also remembered the intruder she heard in her basement just after Dane left that afternoon. The police hadn't found anyone . . . something Jess could now chalk up to the secret passage in the basement.

"We had a cleaning service here the night Cass died. We have one after every party. Things are spotless by four a.m. That mug would have never been left by the service. Someone else— someone other than Cass was in here searching."

Dane held Jess's stare and she didn't even realize until that moment that his hand was on her arm. His grip was tight but tender at the same time and his thumb moved in little arches over her bare skin, firing little pulses of electricity off in her belly. Jess wet her lips as she searched Dane's face for the truth. For the honesty that she so desperately wanted from him. She needed friends. She needed people she could trust in her life and there was still a little flicker of hope inside of her that Dane was good.

"Hello?" a woman's voice called from the second floor. Both Jess and Dane stiffened. "Ms. Walters?"

"Oh my God," Jess whispered. "Someone's here!"

"Jessie!" Matt's voice echoed up her staircase. "Jessie, you home? The door was open."

"Come on." Dane grabbed her hand, hit the button opening the door, and tugged her out of the room, nodding to the keypad. "Type in the code. Quickly."

Oh, shit. What the hell was that code Elliot gave me? "Oh, God. I-I don't know. I can't remember."

Footsteps pounded against the stairs as Matt called out for Jess once more.

"Jess!" Dane said. "Focus."

She pressed her fingers against her temples, clamping her eyes shut as the banister just outside the door creaked against someone's weight.

"He's a cop, Dane. We're fucked if he finds this room."

Dane's head jerked between the keypad and the door before he ducked inside, slamming a palm against the inside button. The wall slid closed just as Matt, with Officer Rodriguez at his heels, entered the room.

7

"Matt! Laura!" Jess exclaimed, glancing nervously to the crooked sconce with the keypad still showing. As casually as she could, she nudged the sconce, sliding it back into place. "What the hell? What are you doing here, barging into my home?"

He scratched at his goatee, his eyes wandering around the room. "We were examining the tunnel and the wharf. I wanted to swing by and ask to see the basement where Sam was attacked." But even as he spoke, his attention was divided. "Why didn't you answer me when we called?"

"Why did you feel like it was okay to just walk in? You're a cop, Matt . . . you should know better." Her heart pounded inside her chest, a deadly cocktail of anger, panic, and adrenaline.

His face softened. "But I'm not *just* a cop, Jessie. Right now, I'm also your friend." He paused, looking around the room again. "Why didn't you answer me?"

"I-I only just heard you and . . . um, I was getting dressed."

"Up here?"

"Yeah. I mean . . ." Jess scanned the room, finding a rolled-up yoga mat in the corner. "I was doing yoga and just had to put my shirt back on."

"You do yoga topless?" Officer Laura Rodriguez asked.

Jess stretched her spine, standing a little taller and noticing Rodriguez's red lips. *Could she . . . ?* She and Rodriguez hadn't exactly gotten off to the best start. She had been one of the cops to arrive on the scene when Jess first heard an intruder in the basement. She knew Rodriguez was a rookie cop. How long had she been working with Matt and Sam? How well did they trust her? "Actually, I do yoga naked." Jess flashed them a coy smile. "It's very freeing. You should try it sometime."

Rodriguez sneered. "I'm more of a kickboxing kind of girl."

Matt's jaw dropped even more and he stuttered, looking away as though Jess were still totally nude right in front of him. "Oh, um, wow. Well, uh . . . no one else was up here with you?"

"I thought I heard a man's voice up here." Rodriguez didn't seem to be buying it and while Matt was looking around the room, the young female officer's dark brown eyes fastened directly on Jess.

Jess shook her head. "Nope. Just me. I sometimes talk to myself, though. You know . . . um, motivationally." She dropped her voice an octave. "Keep going, Jess. Come on!"

Matt and Rodriguez exchanged glances briefly and then Matt whispered, "If you're in trouble, you don't have to say anything. Just blink twice."

Jess paused, holding his stare without blinking. "I promise you, I'm fine. Could you come back tomorrow, though, to look in the basement? Today's a bit busy."

She started walking down the stairs and luckily they both followed her.

"Of course," Matt said. "I'm surprised you're still here. Sam seemed pretty convinced you had left to go home to Brooklyn."

"Not yet." Jess gripped the banister, anxiety roiling through her chest. Reaching her front door, she held it open for them.

"Good," Matt said with a slight smile.

"I wouldn't leave without saying good-bye, Matt."

"Really? Because you've done it before," he said, referring to high school when she had left town after graduation. "And I'm less worried about you saying good-bye to me—"

"I promise you, *this* time, I won't leave without letting everyone at least know."

"We'd all appreciate that, Jessie." He squeezed her arm, backing out the door with a very confused Rodriguez behind him. "I'll call tomorrow before coming over to have a look at the basement."

Jess closed the door behind them and then waited until they were down the stoop before she locked the door and rushed back up the stairs.

As she pulled the sconce back, the code rushed back to her mind. *Zero-four-two-zero.*

"Dane? You okay?" she called through the wall as she punched in the code.

The wall slid open and he hopped out, a grin on his face. She closed the wall once more, sliding the sconce back into place.

"Naked yoga, huh?" His grin stretched wider. "Wouldn't I love to be a fly on your wall for a day."

Jess smacked him across the shoulder. "Don't be lewd," she laughed as her phone rang from within her pocket.

"This is Jess," she said, answering the call.

"Jess?" a hushed voice echoed from the other line.

"Hello? I can barely hear you—"

"Jess, this is Zooey. I need you to come to the hospital right now."

Then the line went dead.

8

Rain stung her cheeks as Jess ducked underneath her jacket and barged through the hospital doors. After a quick check-in with the front desk, she rushed toward the elevators, hitting the button for the fourth floor as she stepped in.

"Hold the elevator!" a man called from the other side and Jess hit the *open* button just in time as Dr. Marc Moore slipped inside. He glanced quickly at Jessica, taking pause with narrowed eyes, sizing her up before pointing in her direction. "Jessica, right?" he asked. "You're working on my friend Richard Brown's murder?"

She nodded as Marc hit the button for the third floor. "I was. I mean, I'm just a photographer, so I don't really have much to do with the case."

He shook his head, shifting his hands into his lab coat pockets. "I heard it was Richard's girlfriend who did it? And that she's here in the hospital?" He grunted something that sounded like a mix between a laugh and a cry. "I didn't even know he was seeing anyone seriously. My wife, Nancy, tried to set him up with a girl from our church. I didn't think he even liked her."

"I'm really sorry, again, for your loss." He and Dr. Brown were good friends from what she and Sam had discovered last week. This couldn't be easy for the doctor. "Like I said, I don't really play much of a part in the investigations after . . . well, after the initial crime scene."

The elevator dinged, reaching the third floor. "Yeah. Well, sorry to have unloaded my questions on you. Just haven't heard much from the detectives on his case since last week."

He moved to step out of the elevator and Jess grabbed the elevator door as it started to close, jolting it back open. "I can assure you we—they're working on it. They'll be in touch soon."

He nodded, taking off down the hall and as she brought her hand back to her side, the elevator closed, going up one more level to the fourth floor.

Room 428, Jess thought as she walked down the hall toward Zooey's room. Thoughts swarmed her head like a too-busy hive of bees and the noise was almost as deafening.

Zooey had survived? It seemed so unlikely, based on what Matt had told her the other day. A suicide attempt, they had claimed—but Jess knew better than to believe that. Sure, when she'd found Zooey in Dr. Brown's office, Zooey had been scared and sad . . . but she didn't seem suicidal.

A large uniformed man stood guard outside Zooey's room. He was slumped over in a chair, rolls of several chins pressed against his man boobs. Jess fumbled, pulling her ID from her wallet as she approached the room. She held it out for him to see and placed her on hand on the doorknob, waiting for him to wave her through.

Instead, the man jerked to his feet, nearly dropping her ID in the process. "Ms. Walters," he said slowly, examining her picture.

The *rap-tap-tap* of her toe mimicked the sound of rain fall' against the windowpane.

"You don't have clearance to see Ms. Devonshire."

"What?" Jess said, grabbing her ID back from the officer. "What are you talking about?"

He jerked a chin toward her laminated ID. "It says you're a forensic photographer. That doesn't give you authority to talk to a person of interest. If anything, you're communicating with her could cost the DA his case."

"I don't need clearance if I'm here simply to talk to a friend. You can come in with me—"

"You're simply not allowed in there. I'm sorry." Only, he didn't sound sorry. He sounded smug. Her mind raced as she tried to think of something—anything—that she could use to get through that door, yet, not a single thing came to her.

"*She* called me. She wants to speak with me. Doesn't she have the right to request my visit?"

He shook his head. "Not unless you're family or there's an officer present."

"Well, couldn't you come in with me?" Sure, he was kind of a jerk, but she'd rather see Zooey alongside a jerk than not see her at all.

" 'Fraid not. Who would watch the door?"

Jess did a mental face palm. "If you're *inside* the door, no one needs to be standing guard, right?"

He bit a meaty lip, eyes rolling toward the fluorescent lights in thought. "Well . . ."

"It's okay, Acker. I can go in with her." The familiar rumble of a baritone voice somersaulted through her. Jess resisted squirming as the tingly shiver spasmed in her core. She knew that voice. She knew that voice far too well. She knew it back in high school, when it would still crack a little when he was excited, and she knew it now. Sam McCloskey.

She spun to face him and it was as though all time stilled with that pivot. Crossing her arms over her chest, she delivered the meanest scowl she could manage. Though only a few days had passed since the party, it felt like ages. Her gaze wandered the landscape of his face, taking it in like a dry sponge in need of water. She'd felt brittle, unengaged, and not like herself all weekend. And he was just the moisture she needed to be flexible once more. Only she didn't want his water. *She didn't need it,* she told herself. She swallowed the satisfied sigh she felt deep in her chest at seeing him again. That dark wet hair that was long enough at his nape to curl a little over his ears. The day-old stubble and fresh smell of Irish Spring on his skin. And the way that button-down shirt clung to his muscled physique, holding promises of tight abs and swollen, hard biceps. Her hand itched to brush over the swell of his pecs for just one moment. But instead, she balled her hands into fists at her sides. "I didn't realize they cleared you for duty."

His eyes connected momentarily with Officer Acker's. Otherwise becoming known to Jess as Officer Stickler.

"I'm here, aren't I?" said Sam.

"That's not really an answer."

He lowered his voice and Jess nearly jumped as his hand landed gently on the bend of her elbow. "Do you want to get in there or not?"

She let the silence answer for her and let Sam step forward, presenting his badge. "Matt is stuck at a crime scene, so I got the call she was awake instead," he said to Acker.

Acker nodded, jowls swinging with the movement. "Of course, go on in." He bent to his chair, grabbing a notebook and tapping his pen to the cover. "But I'll have to note it in the logbook."

"We understand," Sam said, smiling. Then he turned the knob and pushed through the door. Waiting until the door was shut behind them, he said, "And that logbook will likely mysteriously disappear tonight."

"Jess!" Zooey cried from the opposite side of the room. She jerked her arm, but the soft restraints rattled the hospital bed.

Jess rushed to her, mouth dropping in horror at the sight of Zooey tied to the bed.

"Oh my God! Is that really necessary?" Jess exclaimed to Sam.

"I had nothing to do with the restraints. You said it yourself; I'm not even back on active duty, yet."

Fury bubbled deep in Jess's belly like someone had turned on the boiler in her body. Instead of answering Sam, Jess turned to Zooey. "Are you okay? What happened?"

Zooey's eyes darted wildly around the room. Bandages were wrapped from her wrist up the length of her arm. "I-I don't know. One second, I was waiting in the hallway for you, opening Rich's letters . . . and the next I woke up here. Is this all because I pushed Rich? It was an accident, I swear. I shoved him during our fight, but I barely touched him when he lost his balance and hit his head."

"Shh," Jess said. "Don't talk about that now."

"No one has said anything to me. I don't even know why I can't move my hands! Jess, I'm totally freaking out."

Sam and Jess exchanged looks. Legally, neither of them should be talking to her at the moment. Sam held out a palm and as though responding to some sort of innate show of power, Zooey quit talking, chewing her bottom lip nervously. "You didn't try to run away? Attempt to take your own life?" he questioned.

Her eyes widened to saucers. "Take my own . . . ? *No.* And I didn't run away from you. Everything just went . . . dark."

Sam flipped through a chart at the end of her bed, which Jess read over his shoulder. The doctors had found an overdose of a whole bunch of drugs in Zooey's system. Sleeping pills, Vicodin . . . and Biophuterol. There were contusions on her head caused by a fall. And vertical cuts from her wrist to her elbow. Whoever orchestrated this wanted it to scream of a suicide.

"Zooey, did anyone read you your rights yet? Were you officially placed under arrest?" asked Sam.

"I don't know, I don't think so. I woke up and was already cuffed to the bed." She yanked at one wrist, causing the side of her bed to wobble.

Sam rested his hand on Jess's hip, heavy with implication and history. "This could be a good thing for her. She could get off on a technicality if she hasn't been Mirandized."

"Yeah. But at *our* expense. We could lose our jobs over this."

Sam shook his head. "You're here as her friend . . . not as a member of the Portland Police Department. And I'm here as chaperone because as of right now, they aren't allowing non-family members in here alone. But likewise, that probably means you won't be allowed near this case. Especially not now that Dr. Brown's murder is officially connected to Cass."

Jess's stomach turned. She'd known for a while that Dr. Brown was connected to Cass. She'd discovered as much at the crime scene and it was even further confirmed when his prescription pad showed up at the masquerade on Friday night. "That's okay," she said. "I understand." Then she turned back to the frail, ghostly girl in the hospital bed. "Zooey, I can't tell you what I know about the case—or why you're handcuffed. But what I can tell you is that I'm on your side. Okay? You have to trust that I'm trying to do right by you. Sam, too."

Zooey nodded, her eyes darting back and forth between Sam and Jess. Her black bob hung against her chin in stringy wisps. So unlike her normal sleek, silky cut. "I'm so scared." She held up her wrist in front of them. "I did not do this to myself." Red circles framed her swollen eyes. "And whoever did do it will probably not be happy that the job isn't finished."

"There's an officer stationed outside your door. No one will be coming in here except for doctors, police officers, and your family. You're safe here," said Jess.

"I wasn't safe here last time," Zooey said, referring to how her abduction had happened right on the third floor of this very hospital.

Jess squeezed Zooey's hand. "Do you need anything? Need me to call anyone for you?"

Zooey shook her head. "No. My mom will be here soon. I should get a lawyer, right?"

Jess paused for a moment before giving a jerky nod. "Most definitely," she agreed. "I'll be back to visit you soon, okay?"

Zooey flashed a weak smile. "Thanks, Jess."

Sam and Jess left quickly, with a nod to Officer Acker, both walking silently toward the elevators. The static quiet was painful and left an itchy feeling on Jess's nerves, not unlike steel wool being rubbed on her arms.

"You're still here," Sam said, diving his hands into his front pockets.

His deep azure eyes studied her as they walked. Each footstep was loaded with pure concrete as it grew harder to move. Why did he have to stare at her like that? Like he was cataloguing her every motion, as though he could see right into her thoughts.

"I am," Jess said. "You're feeling better?" She lifted her hand to the little corner of a white bandage that poked out from beneath his hat. "You look a lot better," she said, and damn if her voice didn't crack as the words came out.

"Thanks. The pain's going away slowly."

"Are you going to need any therapy? Rehab?"

His face scrunched and she could almost hear his *Jess, please* in her mind. "No, no rehab. Just some pain medicine until I'm back to one hundred percent."

Soft music played through a loudspeaker and the quiet beat of a drum in the background mimicked Jess's thrumming heart. She managed to look into those midnight blue eyes, fighting to keep her expression casual rather than reflect on how she really felt in the moment. "Be careful with those," she joked. "We can't have you pulling a Rush Limbaugh and getting hooked on them, now."

"Oh, please. If you must compare me a celebrity painkiller addict, at least let it be Elvis." Even though he joked, the smile was merely a quick flicker at the corner of his mouth before it straightened back into his brooding stare.

He was exhausting. She'd spent so long trying to figure him out, trying to determine why he had abandoned their friendship in high school after her parents died. And as he kept securing the walls around his heart, she swung her sledgehammer, constantly trying to tear those walls down, but never succeeding. At best, she made little cracks in the surface, which awarded her small glimpses as to what was behind. But just as she had made peace with the wall and learned to live with it, Sam set it on fire, thrusting her into the blazing inferno right along with him. And she couldn't breathe.

The longer she stood here in his presence, the more likely she was to get burned.

She slammed a finger so hard onto the elevator button that it hurt. But she didn't care the least bit. If she focused on the pain, maybe it could act as a reminder of this man and all that he brought into her life. He was bad for her. Terrible things happened when Sam McCloskey was around and dammit, Jess needed to remember that. Not the way his silky touch would float over her body. Or the tension that pulsed between her legs every time she was near him.

When she dared to sneak a glance in his direction, his eyes were locked onto her. As though he knew she was powerless to resist a peek at him. Hunger and pure sexuality swirled in his eyes and had her nipples pebbling beneath her shirt. Her sex pulsed and she squeezed her thighs together, feeling a dampness in her panties that wasn't there a moment earlier.

"Jessie . . ." *That rasp . . . that damn rasp of his.*

It was suddenly too damn hot in that hospital lobby. Jess

tugged at the scarf around her neck, clawing to get it off. She was hysterical, light-headed as the walls grew nearer, closing in with each passing second. She dove for the elevator button again, pressing it like someone with OCD needing her fix.

To the left was a doorway to the stairwell and as Jess eyed it, ready to make a break away from Sam, he closed the space between them, pressing his lips to hers.

Jess moaned into his mouth as the tears welled hot behind her closed eyes. Sweet, blissful silence echoed in her mind as all the thoughts that had been racing there receded into the erotic euphoria of Sam's tongue against hers. His strong hand scooped up her back until his firm grip cupped behind her neck, the tips of his fingers tugging the base of her hair.

His other hand weighed heavily on her hip. His circling thumb pushed at the hem of her shirt, revealing an open strip of soft skin. A sharp hiccup echoed in the quiet hall as Jess gasped to catch her breath between kisses. Desire had daggered her to the wall, rendering her completely useless, unable to move beneath Sam's capable hands. His two thick thighs flanked either side of her leg, pressing against the burning area between her legs. Dampness flooded her panties and she moved her pelvis against him; anything to ease that throbbing ache that grew heavier with every passing moment.

His erection pushed into her thigh, a promise and a reminder of all the things they'd shared a mere few days earlier. Without thinking, Jess gripped him through his pants, squeezing and running her palm along the outline of his shaft while grinding against his thigh.

It wasn't enough. She needed more. More of Sam. With fewer layers of clothing. Jess bit his bottom lip, sucking his tongue into her mouth and tasting all he had to give.

Her eyes fluttered open, meeting his, wide and glistening. As though he hadn't taken his gaze off her from the moment they started.

"Not here," Sam said, his voice heavier than before. He didn't let her go and instead moved the hand that rested on her hip around her waist and pulled her into the nearby stairwell. The door slammed behind them, the sharp sound reverberating, and then they were surrounded by cold, echoing silence once more.

"Sam, we can't—" It was a cry, a plea. Having him right here and now was everything she shouldn't be doing. He was everything she shouldn't want and couldn't have, but her body wanted him even when her mind screamed no.

He ran his tongue over his wide, full lips—his stare holding as much passion as his kiss had. "We absolutely can. Whether we should or not is a different story." His curse was muffled as he ran a hand down his face, pausing to scratch at the stubble on his jaw. "Why are you still here, Jessie? You should be far away from Portland. That's all they care about. That's all they want. If I had known you wouldn't have left I wouldn't have—"

"Wouldn't have what? Been honest with me?" she finished for him.

Silence. Again. Except for that alarm blaring in her head.

Jess stepped back, pressing her palms against the cool, painted cement wall behind her. It was a reminder of where she was, of what she was doing here and what the end goal was. None of which involved Sam. Not anymore. Not now that she knew the truth about this man. This man she thought she knew who had turned out to be her enemy.

9

Sam's heart slammed against his rib cage, his blood rushing between his thighs, torturing his cock. And it was all Jess's fault. But it was more than just the animal urge to fuck. He cared for her. Worried about her. Maybe even . . . loved her. He studied her as she pressed her hands against the wall behind her. Yeah, she was beautiful, but it was so much more than that. She made him laugh. She was tougher than nails and that was something he could respect in a woman. And she was smart; smarter than she ever let on in high school. The girl had gotten straight As but partied like a kid who was failing. He *loved* her. Holy shit . . . he, Sam McCloskey was in love. And if he didn't get to tell her soon, he thought he might burst.

But no. He couldn't. She needed space. For her own safety—emotional safety as well as physical safety—the last thing she needed right now was for him to profess his love. It would only serve himself. And he had no desire to further break her heart or watch as her soft brown eyes filled with tears. Right now, Jess's safety took priority and after they found this fucker, he could work on repairing the damage he'd created.

Sam's phone went off, echoing through the cement staircase, and he struggled to grab it from his pocket. "Hello," he said.

"Sam, how ya feeling?"

"Matt. I'm feeling a lot better. What's up?"

"I finally had a chance to review that security footage from the rest stop outside of Boston today. Don't know why I even bothered now that we've got Zooey, but you asked and I had time on my lunch break . . ."

Sam froze, eyeing Jess. "Oh, yeah?" He tried to keep his voice even, but it felt tight, like his throat.

"Yeah. I don't know what's going on, man, but I watched that video really closely. From what I can tell, Dane's truck pulled into the rest stop as he claimed. And a man wearing a hat entered the building. I didn't see any specific close-ups, but . . . I dunno. Something felt off. The guy . . . he didn't look like Dane. He was shorter and I could have sworn younger. With blonder, longer hair. I mean, to someone not really pay-ing attention, it could look like Dane, but I don't think it was him."

Check fucking mate. He knew that man was hiding more than he let on. He knew it before Jessie had told him about his lie in not knowing Cass was dead. That whole story about the job he had in Boston and his stop at the service area . . . it was all too damn convenient. It wasn't until Sam met Dane's assis-tant at the masquerade, "Mr. Fix-It," that he had confirmation. And the video footage would prove it. Dane had given the kid his truck to go down to Boston without him. So then where the hell was Dane when Cass was murdered? As though Jess could read his thoughts—or maybe she could overhear the phone call—she glared at Sam. He cleared his throat, leaning against the wall in an effort to appear casual. "That's . . . interesting."

"Interesting? Sam, what the hell is going on? I know you don't believe Zooey is guilty here, but you've been looking into Cass's death as more than just a robbery gone wrong long before you were attacked. Well, now we know it *wasn't* a robbery gone wrong—it was a crime of passion. A love triangle. And yet, you're still digging." His partner paused. "And I'll admit, the more I help you look into the details, the more I'm inclined to think something more is going on, too. I feel like a damn conspiracy theorist."

God, he hated keeping these sorts of secrets from his partner. Especially since he knew Matt could be a huge asset in a case like this. "Matt, we need to talk about this another time. Soon, but another time. I'll call you back."

"But—"

Sam hung up before Matt could say anything else.

"What was that about?" Jess sounded cold. Bitter. Untrusting. Not that he could blame her.

"Work."

"We both know better than to think I'll accept that answer."

Sam bit his cheek to stop himself from smiling. She was too smart for her own good. And though he loved that about her, it also made her a huge pain in the ass. "I don't want to lie to you, Jess. Never again."

"Then don't."

"You realize that I am not supposed to share case details with you?"

"I think we're well beyond that. For God's sake, I found my dead sister's cell phone outside of a secret tunnel from my house the other night. I'm involved in this whether you want me to be or not."

He took a step toward her and she backed up so quickly that she hit the doorknob with her lower back, wincing.

"Jessie," he said.

"Never mind, I'll find out myself. Whatever it is you and Matt know, I'll find out. Besides, I know things, too."

That gave him pause. "You do?"

"Oh, *now* you want to converse about my sister? Tough shit. That ship sailed."

Why did she have to be so difficult all the time? Why couldn't she recognize that this was his way—only way—of keeping her safe? They had tried doing it together and they both nearly got killed. But she didn't let him get another word out. Turning the doorknob, she shoved her way out the door and back over to the elevators.

He followed her, rushing out the door, and nearly slammed into her petite shoulder.

"Matt," she said as the elevator doors slid open and Sam's partner walked out.

Matt's eyes flashed with an emotion Sam couldn't quite read as they slid from Jess to Sam and back again. A grin spread slowly across his face. "Well, hey, you two. Jess, twice in one day . . . hell, twice in the course of an hour. Impressive."

"What are you doing here?" Jess asked.

"I got a call that Zooey was awake. I need to Mirandize her."

Sam slid a look to Jess as she fidgeted with the strap of her purse.

"You two didn't talk to her, did you?" When neither of them answered, Matt looked to the ceiling. "Fuck me."

"It wasn't anything," Sam began. "I didn't say anything—Zooey called Jess in as a friend and I stood by to chaperone."

"Dammit, Sam. You *can't* be the chaperone. You're not even on active duty yet. What the hell were you guys thinking?"

"We were thinking that Zooey is not a murderer. And she didn't try to kill herself. She just—she didn't do this, Matt."

"Maybe not," Matt said, scratching his goatee. "But you can't pull that shit again. Jessie, you can't even be on these cases anymore. Not with your link to—"

"I know," she interrupted. "I know that. And officially, I'm not on the case. But Captain Straimer has yet to pull me off, so I can only assume that I'll be called in for other cases that are unrelated."

Matt sighed, looking to Sam. "And you? What's your excuse? You of all people should have known better."

Sam grinned at his buddy. "You're the good cop, remember? I'm the bad cop."

Matt's scowl softened at that and he rolled his eyes, reluctantly fist-bumping him. "Tango and Cash. You okay? Should you even be out of bed?"

"I feel okay. I'll probably be put back on active duty soon." Though based on the way his head throbbed, it wasn't likely. Not unless they got hit with a heavy caseload and Straimer had no choice but to call him in.

"You guys better hope to hell that Zooey doesn't tell anyone you were in there. I'll do my best to sweep it under the rug, too." He paused, giving them each a small smile. "I'll let you get back to whatever you were doing. By the way," he said to Jess, "Your lipstick's smudged." Then he winked at Sam. "Yours is, too."

He walked in the direction of Zooey's room, then paused and spun around to face them. "Oh, Jess, I didn't get to tell you at your house. We swept the area outside of that tunnel. There was nothing. I mean, *nothing* we could use. Anyone can access that wharf from the dock. But thank you . . . for, uh, marking where you found Cass's phone."

A splash of red fanned across Jess's cheeks. "Please tell me it was just you who found it . . ."

"What's going on?" Sam demanded.

Jess cringed. "I needed something to show where I had found her phone and . . . and . . . the only thing I had on me to leave there was the um, gift you gave me that night."

The gift? Sam stiffened as he remembered the vibrating panties he had given her the night of the party.

"Wipe that knowing grin off your face, Matt, or I'll do it for you," he growled.

"Sure thing, partner." Matt tipped an invisible hat and took off in the direction of Zooey's room once more.

Sam watched him walk away for a second before turning to Jess. "I should probably go with him."

"But you're not clear—"

"I know, I'm not cleared for work. Even still . . . I heal through my job. It's just how I am."

She seemed to consider that for a moment before nodding and hitting the elevator call button once more. "Okay."

"But we're not done here."

"Sam . . ." she said, shaking her head. "We *are* done. Officially."

That familiar tightness squeezed his chest, but he walked over, cupping a hand around her jaw and tilting her chin up to him. Her eyes were glossy and goddamn did it wrench his insides. "When it comes to you and me, we're never done. And if you're staying in Portland, then you need me."

The elevator dinged, the doors creaking open. Jess slid away from his touch and got on the elevator, pushing the button for the lobby. "That's where you're wrong. I don't need you. I wanted you . . . before I knew the truth. Before you lied to me. But I don't *need* you."

And with that, the doors slid closed.

10

Jess walked numbly down the street, limbs tingling like she had slept on them wrong. Pins and needles cascaded down her arms and legs as the chill in the air cut through her lightly layered clothes. With each passing day, the weather was becoming crisper. More like autumn.

What she needed was a stiff drink. *Or maybe a stiff something else,* she thought, her mind wandering back to Sam and the nights they had recently shared. *Sex is therapeutic, right?*

No. When it came to her and Sam, sex was disastrous. Downright self-destructive. Alcohol was safer. She headed down the block toward her house. Normally, she'd just pop into a little hole-in-the-wall bar . . . something with peanut shells on the ground that was completely unassuming. But today she needed something to clear her mind. Somewhere Sam would never go . . . and likewise never suspect *her* to go.

Towering over Portland's skyline, she saw the outline of Top of the East, a swanky bar that overlooked the city at the top of the Westin hotel. It was a bit out of her league, but as long as it had alcohol, she was game.

A brisk walk and a few minutes later, she was riding the elevator up to the bar, feeling slightly underdressed, but on a Tuesday afternoon, she hoped she was a little ahead of the crowd. It was quiet and the sherbet-colored sun, sitting low in the sky, peeked in the floor-to-ceiling windows, casting a warm glow throughout the room.

The bartender greeted Jess with a warm smile as a couple of waitresses wandered around taking care of the few guests who were there.

"What can I get for you?"

"B&B on the rocks, please?"

He nodded and grabbed a clean glass from the stack beside him. A few minutes later, he handed her a full tumbler. Though the drink was cold, the brandy warmed her as she sipped it. A shiver began at her neck and tumbled down her spine as she felt that unnerving feeling of someone watching her. She wasn't about to take that feeling lightly anymore. Not after those photos were left on her car earlier.

Slowly Jess pivoted, scanning the bar. Her lips parted in shock at the sight of the darkly handsome man sitting in the opposite corner. He wasn't just any man . . . but Elliot. *Master.* His e-mails to Cass had been haunting Jess for the better part of a week and now it seemed he was everywhere Jess was. He had a glass of something in hand and was sitting in a club chair near the window, staring at her. Was he stalking her? Tracking her? Didn't he say he needed to run to a work thing? Then what the hell was he doing sitting at a bar during happy hour?

Even though she had been looking right at him for the better part of a minute, it wasn't until that moment that triumph flickered in his expression. She could feel his amusement in every part of her body.

The last thing Jess wanted to do was to sit and be social with a man who held some weird power over both her and her dead sister. But could she really just ignore him right now? Not likely.

Despite every little voice screaming in her head to run in the other direction, she gathered her courage and walked over to the chair across from him.

His eyes were steady on her every movement until she settled.

"Are you following me?" he asked her calmly.

"I was about to ask you that same question."

"If you were my sub, you'd absolutely be on the right track asking that."

"But . . . ?"

"But, no. I'm not following you. You're not my submissive. You're hardly even a friend at this point."

Wow. That was blunt. Then again, after the week she'd had, Jess appreciated the honesty.

"That's not to say we won't become friends or that I don't want to be."

"Hey, you don't have to backpedal on my account. I can call a spade a spade." After a pause, she forced herself to relax into her chair . . . or at least look relaxed. "So, if my sister was your submissive, did you have *her* followed regularly?"

"In the beginning, yes." He answered so simply. As if that *wasn't* psychopathic behavior.

"Wow. Just . . . wow. I can't imagine that she was okay with that," Jess said.

He chuckled to himself, swirling something clear and bubbly in his tumbler before taking a sip. "Yes . . . she made it very clear that she would walk out on me if I continued to have her followed. Even when I tried to explain to her that as a dominant, it was normal behavior."

Jess couldn't help the bitter laugh as it traveled up her throat. "*Normal.* Nothing about the way you live is normal."

His eyes shot up, as alert as if she had slapped him. He studied her for a long moment before he spoke. "Your sister said that exact same thing to me when we first met."

"Great minds."

"How much did she tell you about me?" His voice was sharp, demanding an answer that Jess wasn't quite ready to divulge.

Tension coiled in her gut and her spine stiffened as she distracted herself from the question with another sip of her drink. A server, dressed in a tight, black cocktail dress, approached them. "Can I get you something else, Mr. Warner?" She batted her webbed eyelashes over her large brown eyes and flipped her hair over her shoulder. *Subtle, lady. Real subtle.*

"Not for me, thanks. Jessica?"

The waitress blinked as though it was the first time she had seen Jess sitting there and though she turned in her direction, Jess couldn't help but think it was for the sole purpose of giving Elliot a better view of her butt.

But even as this supermodel waitress flaunted her assets in front of him, Elliot's eyes didn't leave Jess. He rested his elbows on his knees. When she didn't answer immediately, he lifted his eyebrows. "Do you want another . . . what is that, brandy?"

"With Bénédictine. And no, thanks."

"No problem. I'll check on you later," said the waitress, and she brushed her hand along Elliot's shoulder as she backed away from their table.

After she left, Jess's mouth turned up in a smile. "Does that happen to you often?"

"Hm?"

"The women. The flirting . . ." But as soon as the words left her mouth, she immediately regretted it. Heat spread across her cheeks and she dropped her head down, staring at the plush carpet beneath her feet.

"I don't know what you mean."

Jess rolled her eyes. "Okay, fine. Play coy. Makes no difference to me one way or another."

His eyes flashed. "Or maybe I'll answer your question if you answer mine. How much did Cass tell you about me?"

"Absolutely nothing."

His eyebrows shot up, almost hitting the base of his hairline. "And yet, you found me? Even knew me by the name she called me."

" 'Master,' " Jess scoffed. "Not like that's a tough nickname to figure out in BDSM circles."

"Alias," Elliot corrected. "And keep your voice down." His words were stern, but there was a touch of playfulness in the banter. In his authority. As though he enjoyed every second of the challenge. "And even still . . . you knew enough to realize she was in the lifestyle."

"I found Cass's e-mail account." Somehow, she managed to keep her voice steady with the admission. "Eventually it led me to you."

"A fact that I'm glad of. I think I can keep you safe, Jessica. If you let me."

A burning sizzled behind Jess's eyes and she crossed her legs. "Did Cass let you?" She didn't mean it to be a hurtful question. She was truly curious. How much had her sister let this guy into her life . . . into her heart?

"No, she didn't. And it was my fault for not pressing harder. Because I could have . . . kept her safe. But instead I honored her demands for independence, however misguided they were."

His expression was incomprehensible. This man was a walking contradiction. One moment, he was whispering to Jess proof of how much her sister trusted him with passwords and knowledge that she divulged. And the next, he was regretful— alluding to Cass not fully putting faith in his abilities. A burst of anger flared deep inside Jess. Anger not necessarily directed at Elliot. Hell, what could she possible have to be mad at him about? And yet, the darkness reared its bitter head inside of her.

"Excuse me a moment," Jess said, setting her glass down and standing up. "I'll be right back."

Elliot jerked to his feet as well, his eyes darkening. "Don't run from me, Jessica." It was almost as though he knew he had hit a hot spot within her.

She was taken aback when he gently wrapped his fingers around her elbow. "I'm not running. I'm using the restroom."

He nodded, but didn't seem to believe her.

"I promise," she added, dropping her jacket to the seat. "See? I'll be back in a minute."

Jess walked back to where the ladies' room was. Once inside, she shut the door and pressed her hands onto the cool, marbled edge of the sink. Turning the faucet on, she wet her hands, the chilly water refreshing her as it streamed over her heated skin. What was it about that man that unnerved her so much? It wasn't his money. She couldn't care less about that. It was *him*. His very essence and existence. He exuded authority and power . . . something Jess had struggled to claim from others her entire life. From her parents, from Cass . . . hell, even from Sam.

After drying her hands with a paper towel, she opened the door and stopped dead in her tracks as she turned the corner.

A tingling sensation danced in her belly as she recognized the broad shoulders sitting across from Elliot in her seat. She recognized that dark, messy hair. Across from her sister's lover—a man who she suspected knew all of Cass's secrets, or at least most of them—was Sam.

11

Sam was the opposite of Elliot in every way. While Elliot was debonair, a kind of millionaire sexy, Sam was all man, rugged, and hot. Was *he* following Jess now, too? First Elliot showing up here and now Sam?

Guilt pulsed in her core, more self-conscious than ever before, but she shook the ridiculous feelings away. What the hell did she have to feel guilty for? For not telling Sam about Elliot? Clearly, he didn't tell her everything he knew. Jess steeled herself for a battle and slowly walked toward the two men, listening in on their conversation.

"Elliot Warner, I see in our records that you were involved in funding a popular BDSM party that has been going on in Portland for several years," said Sam.

"And what records would those be, Detective?" Elliot stayed calm, his voice as even as a dealer during a rigged game of blackjack.

Jess cleared her throat, moving to stand next to Elliot's chair. "Since you're interviewing Elliot, should I assume that the doctor cleared you for work?"

Sam did a double take at the sight of Jess and, judging by the way he jumped to his feet, there was no way he had expected her to be there. "Jess? What the hell?"

"Well as lovely a greeting as that is . . . I could ask you the same question. What are *you* doing here?" Only, she knew what he was doing there. He had followed a lead on Cass's death that pointed him right to Warner.

"I'm looking into a case."

"The case of the masked dominant, perhaps?" Elliot quipped. He had a dry sense of humor, but damn if Jess didn't sort of like that about the guy.

"Don't get cute," Sam shot back. His cerulean button-down shirt was fitted over tight muscles, reflecting the blue in his eyes and his dark jeans were snug around his tight ass. Jess found herself wishing she could run her fingers over the soft cotton, bury her nose into his chest.

"What are you doing here?" Sam's commanding voice interrupted Jess's daydream, spiraling her right back into reality where Sam was still the guy who broke her heart and had lied to her for years. "You better not be working a case without—"

Elliot stood, claiming what little space was left between Sam and Jess. "She is not here on some interview. Well, maybe I take that back. It is an interview of sorts, isn't it, Jessica?" He slipped his hand into hers and lifted her knuckles to his lips. Her pulse jumped.

"*Jessica?*" Sam repeated as though her full name were foreign on his lips. "You're kidding me with this guy, right?"

Oh, God. What is he up to? Was he simply trying to get under Sam's skin? Or did he sense how unnerved Jess was around Sam and was helping in the only way he knew how. One side of Elliot's mouth lifted in an invitation and he squeezed her hand reassuringly. "We met online yesterday and decided to go for a drink," he said, enjoying toying with Sam way too much, based on the gleam in his eye.

"Jess?" Sam's eyebrows lowered, making those eyes of his dark, stormy.

"Um . . . yeah." Her voice was raspy, altered from what it usually sounded like. She was so not able to play it cool around Sam. "It's just a drink, Sam," she said.

"Well, isn't that just a precious story to tell the grandkids someday," Sam said, his lips edging into an insincere smile. He pulled a card from his wallet, handing it to Elliot. "I would really appreciate you setting up a time to talk to me about these parties of yours."

Elliot looked over Sam's business card before tucking it into his suit jacket pocket. "From what I've heard, you know all too well about my parties," he said with a grin.

Sam's flicked a quick look to Jess and panic surged in her chest. *Oh, God.* He thought she had snitched on him. "Sam, I didn't say a word—"

"She didn't need to," Elliot interrupted. "As you can imagine, even though I no longer run those masquerades, I still very much take part in the . . . scene, if you will. Clandestinely these days, as I have a new client with strict Christian values. But still, I learn things about the patrons of the parties."

"I see," Sam said. "Well, that is the sort of information we're looking for. There's only so much intel I can gather as an attendee. Your inside knowledge would be invaluable to a case we're—*I'm* on." He gave Jess a pointed look.

Jess took a step back, eager for Sam to leave. Though the room was spacious, with floor-to-ceiling windows and soft gray paint, Sam still managed to dominate any room he was in. And this time, there were two alphas clashing. It made Jess feel like the last banana they were fighting over. "Last I heard, you weren't on any cases . . ." she stated with chilly calm.

"Don't start," Sam said through gritted teeth.

She chuckled at that. "Don't start what? Telling the truth? That you have no right interrogating this man because you're not even on active duty at the moment?"

"Jessica, that's enough," Elliot said. And though normally she wouldn't have reacted well to any man hushing her, the look on Sam's face as she did what Elliot asked of her was too satisfying. His jaw dropped, eyes wide, as he studied Jess.

Sam raked a hand through dark hair, letting his palm trail down his neck and back to the dusting of dark brown stubble that shaded his jaw. Jess inhaled sharply, his scent the same earthy smell from the nights they had spent together. Woodsy. Masculine. And the effect of it was intoxicating.

"You've got to be fucking kidding me," Sam mumbled.

"In any case," Elliot continued, "I'd be open to discuss anything I know with the assistance of my lawyer. I'm happy to help Portland's finest in any way I can." It was hard to miss the sarcasm ringing in his tone. It was about as subtle as a parade.

"Great." Sam backed away, shaking his head. "We'll be in touch."

As he walked out the door, Jess couldn't help but snicker and Elliot joined her with his own throaty chuckle.

"That was fun," she said, taking her seat once more.

"I'm glad to hear you say that." Elliot's eyes twinkled as he studied her. "Because I think I know our cover to get your sister's things out of your house. We're going to pose as lovers."

12

"Lovers?" she coughed.

"Well, more specifically, you'll be my new trainee. I'll be your master and I'll be training you to be a submissive. It's the perfect excuse for why we would be together without raising any flags or unwanted attention."

"Why can't we just be . . . be . . . I don't know . . . *friends* or something normal?"

Elliot wiped his mouth gently with a cloth napkin before dropping it to the table in front of them. "I don't like that word. *Normal.* Society always wants to label things. Put them in a pretty box and either judge or persecute. Well, you know what? My box is covered in leather and nipple clamps and it's just as valid as one wrapped in a Talbot's cardigan."

Damn. "You're right. I'm sorry." Sometimes her tongue ran away from her mind before she had the sense to stop it. She stood, grabbing some money from her wallet.

He stood up as well, pointing a finger to the ceiling. "Lesson one. You never leave a table without finishing your drink or food and never without permission first."

Jess clenched her hand around the money. "We are *pretending* to be lovers. We are not really together. And I am certainly not really your submissive. Let's get that fucking straight as an arrow right now."

"Ah, but sweet Jessica. We need to be believable. And we only have a few short days to whip you into shape—"

"Whip?"

"Sorry, poor choice of words. In my community, people would be suspicious if I brought a non-trained submissive to a party as my partner."

"Partner. Right." She folded her arms, feeling the need to go on the defensive.

He stopped her before she could lock her arms across her chest and took one of her hands in his. Using his other hand, he brushed her jaw so lightly, she could have been touched with a feather and not have known the difference. "Yes, *partners*. While the titles of *dominant* and *submissive* suggest a hierarchy, it's quite the opposite. My submissives are my equals. Hell, maybe they're even above me. I worship them. I take care of them. And without one . . . I am nothing. Cass was my partner. You will likewise be my partner."

The blood drained from her cheeks. "I won't have sex with you," she declared.

That same amusement from before flashed in his eyes. "I don't expect you to. Sex is not the main focus of this lifestyle."

"Well, then. I guess I have a lot to learn."

"Indeed. And in a short amount of time, too."

"Why do we only have a few days?"

"Portland hosts a yearly masquerade that combines all the official parties in the state of Maine into one huge bash."

Jess gulped, tipping back the rest of her drink with a few heavy sips. Was that yearly party supposed to take place in Cass's house? It was a large enough home for a small gathering, but for a statewide party? There was no way . . .

"Don't worry. I have you covered, Jessica." He smiled, taking her money and tucking it back into her purse. "And the bill here has already been settled."

"I didn't see you pay it."

He offered her his arm, which she took, feeling strangely like she belonged in a Jane Austen novel . . . one that allowed for her to wear jeans and flip-flops. "There was no need. I own the place."

She suppressed the urge to roll her eyes at that. *Of course he does.* Tucking her purse under her arm, she allowed him to lead her to the elevator. "I'm surprised that you and Sam haven't crossed paths before today," she said. She wasn't exactly sure why the question surfaced, but it had been buzzing around her head.

"We have. He just doesn't remember it. I've known who Sam McCloskey is for quite some time."

"Where did you meet? At one of the parties?" Jess inhaled, catching the crisp scent of the aftershave on his skin.

"Where else?"

His chuckle dissolved and crackling heat buzzed between them as he looked down, meeting her eyes. This guy was so out of her league and yet his interest in her seemed to go beyond the explanation he'd given of her being Cass's sister. What the hell was she signing up for as this man's submissive?

But the moment of warmth, of intimacy was almost as fleeting as the excitement she felt and before she could define it, it was gone. He pushed the elevator button as a chill brushed between them and they stood in silence waiting. Very likely *both* of them were wondering what the hell they had gotten themselves into.

"How well do you know food?"

"Food?" Jess was caught utterly off guard by the question. "Um, I mean, well enough, I guess."

"Well enough to determine what garnish would go best with

a salmon fillet? Or what wine should be paired with crusted goat cheese?"

"Uh . . ."

"That's what I thought. Tomorrow evening, we'll do dinner at Hugo's and I'll teach you these things."

"Tomorrow night? Fine. Who am I to turn down dinner?"

"You can leave the snark at home. It will taste bitter alongside the five-star cuisine."

She didn't know exactly what his intentions were, but the guy was trying to help her. Even when she had barged into his office with a suitcase of money and a fake passport. Even when she accused him of knowing things about her sister's death. He was still here. The question was why? Because of some loyalty he felt to her sister? No, something wasn't quite adding up here. And Jess needed to find out what.

"Maybe instead of going to Hugo's, we could do something at your house?"

His eyes lit with surprise and what Jess thought was approval. "Oh?"

"I mean . . . would you usually be in public at a fancy dinner this early with a partner? Wouldn't you wait until I didn't . . . I dunno, accidentally pair port with salmon?"

His chuckle was an erotic rumble, deep and throaty. "Very well. My place, tomorrow night. I'll send a car for you at seven sharp."

13

The next day passed slower than molasses through a straw. Sam's eyes were getting heavy as he pulled his car into the hospital employee parking lot. Normally six p.m. wasn't the sort of time that he would be getting drowsy, but he'd had a long day ... a long week since his injury, and it was only Wednesday. The pain meds weren't helping with his alertness, either.

He moved quickly up the stairs to the neuro unit on the fourth floor and slid easily down the hall. He knew exactly where he was going. He also knew what Dr. Adams's schedule was that day thanks to a quick peek he had taken at the calendar on his office wall before leaving yesterday. And right about now, Dr. Adams would be finishing his last appointment of the day with just enough time to squeeze Sam in.

He got to the doctor's office and poked his head in. "Hey there, Doc. Got a minute?"

The older man had graying hair that was verging on becoming entirely white. He was startled, dropping some folders of paperwork onto his desk. "Detective, of course. Come on in. How are you feeling?"

"So much better," Sam lied, ignoring that throbbing ache at the base of his neck.

"Really? No headaches?" Dr. Adams grabbed his flashlight, holding it up to Sam's eyes. "Follow the light," he said.

"Nope. Weird, right?"

Dr. Adams said nothing, tucking the light back into his pocket and moving his hands to the base of Sam's neck. Sam caught his breath, praying that the doctor hadn't seen him wince.

"Very strange," Dr. Adams murmured.

Above his desk there was a framed family picture of Dr. Adams with a woman in her fifties and a large group of what Sam suspected were his kids and grandkids. Sam scanned the image. One of the younger women . . . he knew her. And beside her was Dr. Moore. They all sat on an old train like the one down near the water at the train museum. "Your family?" Sam asked, gesturing to the image.

Dr. Adams smiled, nodding as he turned to look at the picture. "Sure is. Most of my kids live down in Vermont or Portsmouth now. All except my daughter and her husband."

"Dr. Moore's your son-in-law?"

The doctor turned back to Sam, beaming. "He is. You know Marc?"

Sam shook his head. "Not well. We've crossed paths a few times."

Dr. Adams pressed his lips together thoughtfully. "Well . . . you can probably imagine that I'm more than a little surprised to learn you're having no pain. You're still taking the Percocets?"

"I am," Sam said, not wanting to lie about drugs currently in his system. "But less than I should. Since I haven't needed them, I didn't want to overmedicate."

"Hm." The doctor eyed Sam in a way that suggested he was onto his lies. Or maybe Sam's own paranoia was surfacing. "And why'd you feel the need to come tell me this?"

"I thought that since I'm feeling better, maybe I could go back to work?"

"I can't let you do that yet. Not without another CAT scan to make sure the swelling in your brain has gone down. And even then, I would suggest inactive duty for a week and a slow progression back into your field work."

"What about studying crime scenes and desk work?" Sam flashed the doctor a grin. Damn, that smile would go a lot farther if his doctor was a woman. He had a feeling his hundred-watt grin would have zero effect on Dr. Adams. "No chases or hunting down criminals. Just initial crime scene investigation and paper pushing."

Dr. Adams rubbed a hand along his wrinkled brow. "I can't authorize that. What if something happened? What if your blood started to clot while you were out working? Something as simple as you walking around can cause swelling. I would be liable. The city would be liable. It's four more days, Detective. Take it as a sign that you could use the break. Most of my patients are thrilled to have paid time off."

Fuck. He had expected this, but even still his mood darkened right along with the setting sun out the window. "I'm not most patients."

"I can see that. Look . . . stop taking the Percocets entirely for twenty-four hours. Come back tomorrow at four p.m. and we'll do another CAT scan. If you're really not in pain then and the swelling is gone, I'll clear you for partial active duty. That's the best I can do."

"Not ideal, but I'll take it," Sam said, and gestured to the door. "You leaving as well?" He knew the doctor had no more appointments—he could discern that much with a quick glance at the blank calendar hanging above Dr. Adams's desk.

The doctor hesitated, his foot nervously nudging a small overnight bag on the floor. "In a few minutes. Thanks for stopping by, Detective. And if any pain comes back, don't be shy with those Percocets. They'll work wonders and there's no shame in taking the extra time to heal."

Well, no one could blame Sam for trying. Most people probably would have been thrilled to have the time off work, just like Dr. Adams said . . . but most people probably didn't have the lives of others in their hands. Sam thought for sure that a doctor would understand that. He paused in the doorway on his way out. "Doctor, when you were in your residency—when you were young and ambitious—would you have let something like this keep you from getting the best surgeries?"

Dr. Adams's smile creased his face. "No. But then again, they always say that doctors make the worst patients."

"That's all I needed to hear."

As Sam backed out of the door, his shoulder connected with someone. "I'm so sorry," he said, spinning to finish his apology only to be met with Lulu, the submissive he'd met at the most recent masquerade. She was the latest submissive to Phantom—the alias of one of the masquerade's older and not so attractive dominants. Lulu's brown hair hung to her shoulders and contrasted with her pale skin. Her eyes widened, glossy with fear.

"Lulu," Sam said, gently cradling her bony elbow. He could feel how thin she was through the light fabric of her sleeves and he couldn't help but worry for her. If she was his submissive, he would want to be certain she was eating enough. But if her physique was any indication, Phantom didn't seem to give a crap about her health. "I'm so sorry. I wasn't looking where I was going," he apologized.

"It's fine." She dropped her chin, and even though he couldn't see her face, he could sense her nervousness.

"You sure? I slammed into you pretty good there," he said.

"Yes. I'm fine, thank you."

He hated the way she was so afraid—of everything. She'd been afraid to talk to him at the party. Afraid to drink or do anything without Phantom's permission. That wasn't what this lifestyle was about. It should be fun, playful. An exciting ride that you take together. "It's okay . . . you can look at me," Sam said.

He watched as she cracked her knuckles and slowly lifted her chin to meet his eyes. He gave her a smile. "See? Not so bad, right?" Red lipstick was smeared across her mouth, a distinct contrast with her fair skin. She was dressed up in a black dress, pantyhose, and heels. Fancy. Far too fancy for your typical doctor's appointment, observed Sam. "Well, anyway . . . I'll let you get on your way. It was good seeing you again."

She didn't say anything else, but gave a quick nod, pausing before entering Dr. Adams's office. As Sam turned the corner, just out of view of the office and around the corner from the elevators, every instinct he ever had as a detective buzzed to life.

"Sam?"

He swung around, tension straining his body at the sight of Jess. Her army green button-down shirt hung silky and loose to her hips, but not without first brushing over her breasts and outlining those damned tight nipples of hers. Nipples he wanted desperately to draw into his mouth and worship with his tongue. Desire blazed in his groin, tightening his dick to a full-on erection in seconds flat. It had to be a fucking record. "What are you doing here?" Without thinking about it, his hands went to her waist, pulling her gently back against the wall and out of the line of vision of Dr. Adams's office. Her smooth cheeks flushed and he quickly pulled his hands back and to his sides.

Jess straightened, her spine stiff, and watched him warily. "I stopped by to say hi to Zooey, but she was sleeping." Her voice echoed with suspicion as she glanced around. "Are you feeling okay? Did you see the doctor?"

"I had my follow-up appointment today."

She examined him for a moment, then gave him the look he'd come to know so well over the years. The kind of look that was a preamble to an eye roll. "I see. And did the doctor also advise you to press your ear to the wall like some sort of five-year-old pretending to be like a spy?"

Heat flared through his chest and Sam wasn't sure if he should be insulted, frustrated, or just damn exhausted with her. "Not like a spy, like a detective. Because unlike a certain childish woman who thinks she's bulletproof, *I've* been trained for this. This is what I do, and I'm pretty damn good at it, Jessica."

"Don't call me that," she hissed.

"Oh, right. Sorry, *Jess*. I guess my problem is that I don't have enough in the bank to order you around and call you by your full name, isn't that right?"

She stiffened defiantly. "No, your problem is that you're an asshole who's confused bedroom games with real life."

A shiver of crippling arousal tore through him. "I know you're pissed, but you're sexy as hell when you're mad at me."

"Back off, Sam."

"I tried that already. It's not going so well." Before he could stop himself, he wrenched her into his arms and pressed his mouth against hers.

He expected her to fight him, to push him away and maybe slap him—hell, he probably deserved it. But rather than end the kiss, she curled her arms around his shoulders, arching into him and moaning with need that could have split right through his chest and into his heart like explosive shrapnel. His own hungry growl tore through him and as he curved his palms around her lush ass, the flaming desire overtook all of his senses.

Her hands speared into his hair as her soft breasts stroked his chest, pressing against him with each heaving breath she took. He moved his tongue against the seam of her lips, pulling one hand reluctantly from her ass to stroke the soft, velvety skin at her neck.

He was absolutely drowning in Jess. She wrapped her muscular legs around his hips, grinding herself against him and moving her body counterpoint to his. The friction against his cock was so intense that it sent shocking waves of pleasure surging through his body.

"Tell me you don't want this as much as I do." he said, tearing his lips from hers, his hands and body still holding her firmly in place against the wall. What was it about Jess that tore through any ounce of patience he had? He'd never been able to control his feelings around her, not when he was fifteen and not now, over a decade later. What the hell was so addictive about her that he couldn't stay away—not even when it was for both his well-being and hers?

Whatever it was, Jess got into his head, his heart, his bloodstream, faster than the most potent liquor, and he craved the taste of her on his tongue. She gripped the collar of his shirt, her fingernails biting into the muscles leading from his neck to his shoulders. Lust tightened his balls and as she rolled her hips against his, his dick surged with a hunger so violent that he nearly lost all control.

He released her swollen lips, easing back and taking in her flushed face, expression tight with just as much of a need to orgasm as his. She ground herself against the ridge of his cock, once more pulling that swollen bottom lip between her teeth.

An announcement came across the hospital intercom in a static voice, calling for a doctor to go down to the NICU. *Shit, what am I doing?* Did the hospital pump some sort of aphrodisiac through the vents? "Jess," he said hoarsely, "We need to talk. But not like this . . . not out in the open." He dragged a finger gently down her cheek as a scowl contorted her mouth. "I'm not here as a patient right now. I'm here as a detective.

And honestly," he said, and paused, taking a deep breath. Honesty. He needed to be honest with her from now on. "Honestly, I have a hard time acting professionally when you're around."

Her eyes widened and she braced her hands on his shoulders, pushing his body away from her. "Are you serious? You're pulling that card? That I'm just too sexy for you to focus?" Her fists clenched beside her and she moved to shove past him. "I never thought you were one to victim-blame." She stopped midstride just a step beyond him and spun back to face him. "*Not* that I'm the victim in all of this."

"I'm not victim-blaming," he said. "And no one thinks of you that way, especially not me. I just shouldn't have kissed you. Not here, where anyone could see us. Particularly not when there are people actively trying to keep us apart and threatening our lives to do so. But the fact remains that you're a photographer, not a police officer. And apparently, you're also dating one of Portland's most renowned doms. Unless . . ." A moment of hope sparked in his gut. "Did that fizzle already?"

Anger blazed in her eyes, her voice throbbing with frustration. "No, it hasn't. I also got carried away just now."

"Just a couple of days ago, you were fighting me on nearly every aspect of the BDSM lifestyle. Now you expect me to believe you and this Warner character are a thing? It doesn't add up, Jess."

"Or maybe you don't know me as well as you think you do." She dragged herself away from him and left, getting onto the next elevator.

Fucking hell. He needed to patch this up, smooth things over with her. If she was determined to stay in Portland, they needed to find a way to coexist. But for now? For now he had to let her go.

Sam heard Dr. Adams's voice from around the corner. He

pressed harder against the wall, peeking out around the corner as Lulu and the doctor walked to the elevator together. "I hope you don't mind that I have to be on call tonight."

She shook her head, her brown hair brushing against her bare shoulders. "I don't mind. Will you be able to stay the whole night?"

Dr. Adams checked his pager before clipping it to his belt. "As long as I'm not called back in." With one hand, Dr. Adams slung the overnight bag over his shoulder while the other gently brushed Lulu's jaw. He gave a quick look around before he kissed her, curving his hand around the back of her neck. The elevator dinged.

"You go down first and I'll meet you at the hotel in a few minutes." *Shit,* thought Sam. He had almost liked Dr. Adams. Unfortunately it seemed that everyone had a damned skeleton in the closet.

Lulu nodded and stepped on the elevator. Sam waited for the door to close before stepping out and moving beside Dr. Adams. "Looks like your night's gonna be more exciting than mine," Sam said as the doctor's face went whiter than a sheet out of the dryer.

"Detective," he said, his eyes shifting between Sam and the closed elevator. "I'm not sure what you mean. I'll be working tonight, um, on call—"

"Save it, I've seen pictures of your wife and that woman you were kissing is definitely not Mrs. Doctor Adams."

The old man stuttered, gesturing nervously toward the elevator. "M-Michelle is no one. She's just a friend. An old friend—"

Michelle? Interesting. "She didn't look so old to me. Look," Sam said, "It's not my place to tell your wife about your . . . indiscretions with the lovely Michelle."

Dr. Adams lifted his brow in question. "What do you want in return?"

"Sign off on my active duty."

His response was met with a gruff, dry laugh. "I told you—I can't put you on active duty. I'll sign off on a partial return. But it'll have to be against my advisement. I could be sued for malpractice."

"Partial duty. With no mention of your advisement. You know the force wouldn't accept me if it was against your orders. And I want it in writing, now . . . before either of us leaves."

There was a coldness in his gaze, a firmness to his mouth, as the doctor snatched a prescription pad from inside his bag. He scribbled a note and signed the bottom. "You're a piece of work." Ice dripped from his voice and Sam couldn't help but notice the immense shift of Dr. Adams's personality. He turned from warm grandfather to cold and hard with anger glittering in his eyes.

You too, asshole, Sam thought. Dr. Adams finished signing his name with an aggressive slap of pen to paper. "Here," he said, shoving the note into Sam's hands. "No pain medicine while you're working. If you get nosebleeds, dizziness, or a migraine, come see me immediately. And I expect you to keep your CAT scan appointment for tomorrow. I want to make sure that swelling is indeed going down."

"You're the boss, Doc." Sam saluted him with two fingers and as the elevators opened, he stepped on, pausing to pivot back to face Dr. Adams. "Be careful with her. With Michelle . . . She's a sweet girl—and young."

"She's not *that* sweet."

Sam shook his head. "And you say *I'm* the piece of work? If that's true, then you're the damned *Mona Lisa.*" He slammed his hand against the closing elevator doors, to keep them open. "I mean it. Don't hurt her." He liked Lulu—or Michelle, it seemed. She'd been a huge help to Sam at the masquerade, helping him discover Elliot Warner. She was nice and it seemed like she was in desperate need for someone to look out for her best interests. He didn't quite know what her arrangement with Phantom was—but he knew dominant personalities. And they didn't usually care for sharing their submissives. That girl had better be careful.

14

Jess hugged her arms to her body and somehow fought the anger and tears that rose from deep inside her the entire walk back to her house. How was it that Sam could always knock her walls down? No matter how much time she spent building them, he always found a way to power through with one simple kiss.

She glanced at her sister's iPad sitting on her bedside table. She had over an hour to get ready for the dinner at Elliot's house tonight. Maybe a little reading would calm her nerves. Help her with what she could expect out of a night spent with "Master."

Jess grabbed the iPad, settling back on the bed and swiping open Cass's e-mail account. Scrolling to the bottom, she found some of the earlier e-mails between Cass and Elliot. One particular e-mail with the subject line *Indulgence* caught her eye and she tapped it open.

> Indulgence. That was the lesson last night, wasn't it? Learning to relish in the divine flavors and

pamper myself every now and then? I know the point of these e-mails—these lessons—is for me to piece the puzzle together without you feeding me the answers, but I have to tell you, sometimes I feel like you're throwing me blindfolded, with hands and feet tied, into the middle of a whirlpool and expecting me to swim to safety. How the hell am I supposed to learn when I'm not even sure what the lesson is? How do you expect me to swim, when you've set me up to sink? How can I learn when the lessons are so ambiguous?

In any case, to answer your question, I think last night was my favorite evening yet. While punishment and pampering were still a huge part of it, I loved how I relied on you for every need I had in the evening. Obviously, I was reluctant at first. I'm independent. Always have been. I've not only been on my own since eighteen, but I've been responsible for Jessica for years as well. Being bound to a bed with all my senses except touch and taste cut off was . . . difficult to say the least.

But you were gentle with me. The entire night. And I'm grateful for that. You were tender and made sure I was comfortable; warm, though naked. Satisfied, but not full. Hydrated. Everything that was a normal part of my nightly routine was in your hands. You gave to me without receiving anything in return. And by the end I was begging for you to take—and even then, you did not. Because, in your own words, it was about me. About my pleasure. But no amount of your lips between my legs could take the place of what I really wanted. I wanted to be filled with you— by you.

So, I guess in a sense, I'm still a little confused.
If the night was about me and indulging my every
desire—then why did you deprive me of the one
thing I wanted most? You.

Because he could, Jess thought. Because he wanted to maintain the control, the power. And it was the best way he knew
how. Jess squeezed her eyes shut and tossed her sister's iPad
onto the table beside her.

But if Elliot thought she was anything like Cass—willing to
be tied up around a man she barely knew . . . well, he had a lot
to learn about her.

Swiping her phone, she checked for any missed calls or messages. Nothing. Again. Not from Sam. Not from Matt. No
cases had come in since Dr. Brown's murder last week and Jess
couldn't help but feel a little resentful. Were they just ignoring
her? Or purposely not calling her for the cases because she and
Sam had broken up?

Ridiculous, she thought, and threw open her suitcase. Rummaging around, she held a couple of pieces of clothing up to her
body before tossing them to the side. She had nothing suitable
to wear. Without knowing how fancy this evening was going to
be, it was difficult to choose an outfit . . . but either way, she
decided to bring only three dresses with her to Portland from
her home in Brooklyn. Two of which she had worn for her sister's wake and funeral. Jess balled up the soft, black dresses and
threw them into the dirty laundry pile. She might as well throw
them directly into the garbage. There was no way she could
stand to wear them again. She had never again worn the dress
she had on at her parents' funeral, either.

She ventured into Cass's closet. There were rows of hangers
lined with gorgeous designer outfits that contrasted the simple,
tailored work clothes hanging next to them. Givenchy dresses.
Prada boots. Manolos. She'd never once seen her sister in an

outfit from anywhere other than Ann Taylor. Who was this woman? This version of Cassandra that Jess had never known. Her hand trailed the exquisite design of a Miu Miu fitted leather pencil skirt and sheer lace wrap top. It was perfect. Just fancy enough to fit in with whatever designer suit Elliot would most certainly be wearing.

Jess pulled the skirt off the hanger and held it up to her body. She and her sister were nearly the same size . . . except Cass was a couple of inches taller. Just as Jess was getting ready to pull her jeans down, she paused. That same paranoid feeling of someone watching flooded back to her. The photographs left on her car flashed in her mind and she suddenly felt sick to her stomach. Fear slammed into her body, crashing over her like an icy wave.

Rushing to the windows, she peeked out. No one was there. There were only a few parked cars in the street below and a couple of people passing by on their way home from work. Jess tugged the curtains closed, making sure the edges were pulled taut to the end of the window frames. Not even a sliver of window-pane could be seen. She would staple the curtains to the walls if she needed to. Even with the curtains pulled tight, she grabbed the pile of clothes and shut herself in the bathroom to change where there were no windows at all.

Nearly an hour later, Jess was dressed in her sister's de-signer clothes, wearing the Jimmy Choos Dane had given her for the masquerade. Her hair was knotted in a sleek French twist and her makeup was sultry, but still subtle. She wasn't exactly sure why she was trying so hard with Elliot. What was this desire to impress him? To please him? It was the same part of her that got a thrill when she would both obey and dis-obey Sam.

It was seven o'clock sharp. Jess paused in the foyer, grabbing her camera off the front table. Her camera bag didn't exactly go with her outfit and yet, she felt naked without it—and she'd been without it far too often these days. After locking the door behind her, Jess walked down the stoop, scanning the street in front of her house. A black sedan was parked right outside and she walked over, reaching for the door as the window slid down.

"Well, didn't you fall out of the pretty tree tonight?"

Startled, she pulled back from the car, confused for all of a second. *Matt?* What the hell was he doing here? She inwardly rolled her eyes ... *Sam.* He probably sent his buddy to keep tabs on her. "And hit every damn branch on the way down." She finished his statement with a wink. Bending into the open window, she draped her arms inside the car. "So, you're my ride tonight?"

He chuckled, shaking his head. "No, but holy shit, Jessie. I *could* be your ride! Where you off to?"

"I have a dinner thing. What are you doing here then if you're not my ride?" She gave him a pointed look, glancing at him through her inked eyelashes. "Sam sent you, didn't he?"

His expression softened. "I take it that means your dinner tonight isn't with Sam?"

"No. It's not."

Regret seemed to wash over him and his mouth twitched into a frown. "Sorry to hear that."

"Matt—I'm gonna ask one last time. What are you doing here?"

"Things got busy at the precinct today—work is piling up without Sam around. And I realized a little late that I hadn't come by to look at your basement."

"So ... you were going to have a look around at seven p.m.?"

He hesitated, scratching the back of his neck. "No. I mean, maybe. I was just gonna pop in and see how you were holding up. We've all just been sort of ... keeping track of you. Making sure you're safe." He paused, the hesitation in his voice mirroring the cringe Jess felt. "I have one guy stationed down near the tunnel you found until we can get it boarded up for you."

"Matt, come on. I know the attack on Sam was alarming, but I don't think the house needs a twenty-four-seven watch on it—"

"Respectfully, Jessie, that's not for you to decide. Not when one of our own was attacked last weekend."

She knew she wasn't about to win this argument. And she couldn't blame the Portland police for being extra vigilant on her behalf. With how shaky she'd been feeling in her own home lately, it was actually kind of reassuring. "Any leads yet?"

He shook his head. "Unfortunately, no. We've been grilling Zooey for two days. Sam seems to think it was a man who attacked him—"

"It *was* a man who attacked him. Zooey's the easy one to blame, but it wasn't her."

"All evidence points to a woman being down there. A woman being our killer."

"What? What evidence?"

"To begin with—the footprints are likely from a woman. High heels."

Oh, these idiots. She loved Matt, but there was a reason Sam was head detective, not him. "Matt, those are probably *my* footprints."

"No, these are big feet. Likely, a size ten female footprint. The exact size of Zooey's shoes."

"Really?" *Damn, the girl had big feet.*

He nodded. "Not to mention, Zooey's prints were found on the doorknob down there. And that's just the tip of the iceberg."

Jess gulped. "Someone's setting her up, Matt. They easily could lift her print and put it on a doorknob. And how hard is it to put on someone else's shoes and stomp around? Little Zooey could not have done the sort of damage that Sam is suffering from." Not to mention Jess had seen a masked man running from the scene. She chewed her bottom lip in thought. "Were there other footprints down there as well?"

"No, just Zooey's."

"There you go. I was in those tunnels, too. Where the hell were my footprints? Whoever set her up wiped the floors and then trudged Zooey's shoes through the tunnel."

"Look—" he said, dropping his voice even though they were the only two people in the street. "I don't think you're wrong. Even with all the evidence pointing to Zooey, she had to at least have had an accomplice. But things just aren't adding up with your sister's death. The robbery-gone-bad angle is dissolving by the second, even if Zooey isn't our killer. And this crime of passion idea doesn't work either because it doesn't appear as though Cass had any sort of romance with Brown." He sighed, stroking his goatee. "I shouldn't be talking about this with you. Anyway, that's why we're here watching. Hoping that the bastard returns to the scene of the crime."

Yeah, right. Whoever he was, he was too smart for that. He knew the tunnels had been compromised. He knew there was no coming back now. At least not in the way he usually did. Jess's spine stiffened. In fact . . . it was probable that they wouldn't want to host the parties at her house ever again, now that the access to the wharf was cut off.

"You know," Matt said, his voice hard, "If Sam could just stay here with you for a few nights, then we wouldn't have to post officers outside your home. And he could feel like he was on active duty even though he shouldn't be. You could help make him rest and he could still feel relevant—"

"Good night, Matt." Jess pushed off his window, backing away.

"Think about it!" he called after her as another black sedan pulled into her driveway. A man in a wrinkled suit rushed out, opening the back door for her.

"Ms. Walters," he said, breathless. "I apologize for being late."

She glanced at her phone, eyebrows furrowed. "You're literally three minutes late," she said with a chuckle. "It's not a big deal."

He offered her a gracious smile. "Mr. Warner doesn't stand for tardiness."

"What's your name?"

"Lyle, ma'am."

She slid inside, stopping the door before he shut it. "Well, Lyle, we'll just have to tell Elliot that *I* was the one running late. My hair just wasn't behaving," she said with a wink.

Lyle smiled. "That's very gracious, Ms. Walters. Thank you, but I can't lie to Mr.—"

"You don't have to. I will."

Lyle drove straight for the shore and pulled up to the Casco Bay ferry. With barely a pause, he pulled the car onto the boat and parked, shutting the engine off.

Jess blinked as Lyle opened the door for her. "You're welcome to wait in the car for the ride, ma'am. Or if you prefer to step out and enjoy the scenery, Mr. Warner left a bottle of champagne in the backseat for you. Either way, would you like for me to pour you a glass?"

"Elliot lives on one of the islands?"

"Yes, Ms. Walters. Peaks Island."

"And he commutes every day?" She unbuckled and slid out of the backseat, grabbing her camera before shutting the door behind her. The air was crisp and salty and stars flickered in the night sky. Jess took a deep breath, inhaling the smell of the sea. The scent was fresh and delicious. So different from the smell of hot garbage she was used to experiencing outside her door in New York.

"Well, he has an apartment on the peninsula, but he only uses it on rare occasions." Lyle grabbed the bottle of champagne and a glass. He held it up to her with a questioning tilt of his head.

Jess nodded and he popped the cork, pouring her a glass. "Mr. Warner doesn't take the ferry usually."

Steadying the camera against the railing for a long exposure, she zoomed out in a wide shot of Portland's shore they were leaving behind. *Click.*

"No? Then how—"

"He has his own boat."

Of course he does. Jess took the glass of champagne from Lyle's hand, sipping it, careful not to spill on her camera. The bubbles fizzled against her sinuses and tickled her brain.

Without waiting for her to ask, he took the glass back from her. "Here, let me," he said as she moved to reposition the camera, this time, angling it toward Peaks Island.

"Can we see Elliot's house from here?"

"Not from this far away. Not unless you've got a wicked long lens in that bag."

She didn't. And even if she did, they didn't tend to work that well in dark lighting. "But closer? And in the daylight?"

"You can see his property from the boat, but his home is mostly shrouded by the trees."

She took the glass again, this time her sip far less careful. She winced, the sweetness a little much.

"Is the champagne okay, Ms. Walters?"

She smiled, nodding. "Thank you. I just tend to prefer red wines and hard liquor in the amber family—scotch, whiskey, bourbon."

"Ah, a woman after my boss's own heart. And quite the opposite of your sister."

Jess's spine bristled. "You knew Cass?"

A moment of regret passed along his features, but it was gone almost as fast as one of the ripples in the water. "Not well. But on these drives, we became . . . acquainted." He covered the bottle and slipped it back into the liquor compartment of the car, tidying the backseat as Jess leaned on the railing. The boat picked up speed and she shivered, pinching her glass in one hand and hugging her body with the other arm. Though pretty, her lace top offered little warmth.

Lyle had his jacket off and around her shoulders before her shiver could travel from her head to her toes. "Your sister loved her champagne, though," he added with a wistful smile.

Jess didn't say anything more, but watched as his expression shifted from professional to something more personal. Just how much did her sister chat with this guy? He seemed . . . he seemed to miss her; he had a heaviness in his voice that wasn't present until the subject of Cass came up.

Just how loyal was this guy to Elliot? How much did he know about his operations—and her sister's as well? Did Elliot buy his trust? Because if so, there was no doubt that other people in this town had pockets just as deep as Elliot's. And for the right price, just about anyone would deceive.

She took another sip of her champagne and this time it went down easier. "I'm surprised," Jess admitted. "With Cass and Elliot working in the same building, I would think they'd mostly travel together . . . and that she wouldn't need a car service to transport her."

"Mr. Warner is a busy man with a lot of early meetings and late nights in the office. I was always happy to help and he wanted to ensure her safe travels even when he couldn't be there."

They sat in comfortable silence for a while longer. Waves splashed against the side of the ferry and though they weren't going fast by any means, the boat tipped a bit as the water surged. Jess turned to look at him, bringing her camera to her eyes. She studied him from within the viewfinder. His profile was highlighted by the smallest strip of silvery moonlight. His reddish brown hair took on a purplish tint in the inky night and though his features had a boyish playfulness to them, the beginnings of wrinkles flanked either side of his mouth and eyes. He was likely in his late twenties or early thirties, if she had to take a guess. A little older than herself probably; about Cass's age when she died. *Click.*

He seemed startled by the image and grinned, holding a hand up to block his face from the lens. "Sorry," she said, gesturing with the camera. "Force of habit. I can put it away, if you prefer?"

His dimple deepened. "No, it's fine. It's nice to be the focal point of anything for once."

Jess moved the camera for a close-up of his hands clenched on the railing of the boat, wakes of water providing a dark, blurry backdrop. *Click.* "How did you know Cass is—was— my sister?"

"The proper answer?" He glanced at her carefully. His hands were tucked into his pockets and he kicked a foot up behind him, his knee propped on the boat railing. "Mr. Warner told me, of course."

"And the improper answer?" She was almost afraid to ask. She'd had her fair share of creepers enter her life since her sister's funeral. But he didn't seem creepy. He seemed nice. Genuine. And she wondered if Cass had felt the same immediate kinship with him as well.

His grin widened, deepening that dimple. "You two have the same smile. If he hadn't told me, I would have assumed you were related. Besides, it wouldn't be hard to figure out. Same last name, same pink house to pick you up in."

"Ah, yes," Jess chuckled, "The infamous pink house." With the twinkle lights around the edge of the boat, she could almost see her reflection off the water—inky, but with the golden hue cast in its ripples. "And would 'Mr. Warner' approve of you hanging out so casually with me tonight? Hanging on the boat with me as I sip champagne and snuggle into your suit jacket?"

"It's my job to keep his guests comfortable on the ride to his home."

"And is it also your job to notice things like your boss's girlfriend's smile?"

His dimple disappeared. "Are you referring to *your* smile or Cass's?"

Though they were a good several feet apart, something sparked between them and Jess found herself taking an instinctual step back. Her phone vibrated from within her sister's clutch and she rushed to pull it out, thankful for the distraction. Sam's name lit up her screen with a text message: *We need to talk. Where are you?*

She hesitated before typing: *Can't tonight. Dinner plans. Besides, what is there left to talk about?*

She looked up to find Lyle's gaze still burning into her. "Mr. Warner won't like it if you've double-booked for the evening."

The phone buzzed again in her hand and she maintained eye contact with Lyle, tucking it back into her purse without reading it. "I don't double-book."

"You better hope not," he said.

"Is that a threat?"

"Not from me, it isn't."

"But from . . . him?"

A horn sounded from somewhere on the boat. Lyle pulled the keys out of his pocket, opening the door for Jess. "We're about to dock." She paused, hovering at his shoulder just long enough to get a whiff of his cologne. It was clean, fragrant, and nearly on the verge of feminine but with a spicy end note. Brushing by him, she slid into the backseat of the car once more, unsure of what to make of this nervous energy between Lyle and herself. He flicked a glance to the right, dropping his voice even lower before speaking.

"And . . . consider it a warning. Not a threat."

For the first time since she'd met Elliot, Jess had a forebod-

ing sense about him. What exactly was Lyle saying by not saying? Did Cass cheat on Elliot? That didn't sound like her. Then
again, she knew there was some weirdness between Elliot,
Cass, and Dane. And it was obvious there were a lot of things
about her sister that Jess had never known before. "Did Cass
get that same warning?"

Though his brown eyes darkened with something tumul-
tuous, he shut the door and got into the driver's seat. "Let's get
you to this dinner, Ms. Walters."

15

Once they were off the ferry, the drive on the dark, quiet island was fast and nearly silent. There was something unnerving about having dinner in a man's home when you were really, truly trapped there with no easy way off the island in the event that something went wrong.

Jess shivered, despite the fact that she was still nestled in Lyle's suit jacket. The car turned up a long driveway. It was steep, the incline feeling like they were climbing a mountain. As they arrived, Lyle turned the car off, the engine winding down like a cat's purr once you've stopped petting it.

Jess moved for the car door, tugging the handle only to discover it was locked. She looked up to find Lyle staring at her from the front seat. "Put my number into your phone," he said.

"Why?"

"Just in case you need me. For anything. I can be here very quickly and I'm typically in the area when Mr. Warner has guests. It's my job to keep his friends safe. So whenever, wherever, even if you've been out in the peninsula and you're afraid to walk home—call me."

"Seems a little extreme for a guy I just met." She slipped her arms out of his jacket and passed it over the console.

"It probably is."

She pulled out her phone once more, Sam's response from earlier blinking back at her: *You're with him, aren't you?*

Heat seethed through her body and she resisted the urge to respond, instead swiping away from her text messages and plugging in the numbers Lyle gave her.

"I doubt you'll need it tonight. But never hesitate to call."

She didn't want to be reliant on any man. And yet, she couldn't help but feel a little comforted by having an ally on this island. Someone other than Elliot who knew where she was and, if she disappeared, could trace her.

She pushed the overactive thoughts from her mind. Yes, it was good to be safe, but there was no need to be skeptical of everyone when they had done nothing to deserve it. She couldn't become that sort of paranoid woman who suspected everyone of everything.

The door to the brick mansion swung open and if she hadn't already seen Elliot in casual attire last night at the bar, she may not have recognized his silhouette. He was backlit with golden, ambient lighting, wearing a button-down shirt, slacks, and no jacket. His hands were tucked casually in his pockets. Her fist clenched around her camera, finger tickling the shutter. Lifting it to her face, she took the silhouetted image of Elliot standing in the doorway of his mansion. Through the viewfinder, she could see more clearly that despite his seemingly casual stance, there was a predatory alertness tight in his muscles. *Click.* She pulled the camera away from her face and he was back to being the casual millionaire.

"Let's get you inside, huh?" Lyle gave her one last smile before climbing out and opening the door for her.

The stony walkway was surrounded by manicured shrubs and a lawn. Everything about the home looked perfect; out of a fairy tale. And yet, for Jess, it was the sort of home that felt like anything but. It was a museum . . . not a home. The sort of place she would enter and immediately fret about breaking something. The sort of place she'd be afraid to walk around in for fear that her shoes were dirty.

As she got closer, she could smell the fresh scent of aftershave on Elliot's smooth jaw and neck. She could see that his starched shirt had perfect creases as though it was just ironed. He was so put together. Nothing was done without intent. And even though it had been her idea to have dinner in his home, she got the odd sense that this was all still orchestrated by him. Even her "ideas" and thoughts around this man were no longer her own. She didn't know how he did that—but she was certain this had been his plan all along.

"Jessica, I'm glad you made it."

"It's Jess," she said, even though she knew it was a pointless battle.

Her phone buzzed loudly in her purse as she entered the dramatic foyer.

He watched her carefully, his eyes flicking to her buzzing purse and then trailing to the camera bag. "Let me guess . . . your detective wants to know where you are?"

"How astute of you." She should have known Sam wouldn't stand for her ignoring his texts.

"I don't mind if you want to answer him." For a moment, Elliot's eyes looked soft—warm, yet still relentless in their intensity.

"No. It's fine. He doesn't deserve an answer . . . and I owe him nothing."

Elliot's mood seemed to shift. *He trained submissives as a hobby,* thought Jess. *He's more than just a connoisseur of wine and food. He's a connoisseur of women, too.* She told herself that any woman at all could be awarded that same type of look from him, and yet, she knew better.

"Did Cass ever tell you that I lied to her?" he said, utterly catching Jess off guard with his question.

"No. But then, she didn't really tell me anything about you."

"Well, I did. I hid many things from her but I only ever came clean about one thing. It was the most challenging moment of my entire life and now that she's gone I wish I had confessed everything to her."

"Why are you telling me this?"

"Because when I was finally honest with your sister, she didn't hesitate to accept my apology. Not even for a moment. She knew immediately how difficult it was for me to be candid with anyone. She told me she knew it was only one of many of my secrets and that when I was ready, she would be waiting and ready to listen."

Jess listened intently, running the heel of her stiletto into a crack in the foyer's hardwood floor. "Cass was always really great about forgiving and forgetting," she said.

"She was. Sometimes things are unforgivable, though. But it's important to remember that the most unforgivable secrets are the ones that take the most courage to be honest about. That was something Cassandra not only knew, but lived."

Jess's eyes slid closed as he purred her sister's name. Did he know about Sam's lies? Sam's secrets? "That sounds like Cass," she said.

"Just think about what I said." Jess opened her eyes, taking in the details of Elliot's house, searching for a distraction away from her situation with Sam. There were marble columns and a dramatic stairwell descended in a large curve to what she could only assume was one of many floors. "You know," Jess said, looking around the impressive entryway. "When I suggested dinner here, you could have mentioned that I would have to come by boat."

"And why would I do that?" His wispy tone from earlier was long gone now.

"Oh, I don't know. Maybe so that I would be ready for the chilly boat ride. Or just in general so that I could feel prepared."

"Everything you needed was inside the car. I was prepared *for* you. Besides, you were prepared enough to bring your camera, I see."

"Well, it's practically like an appendage to me at this point."

He moved to a cart that held a decanter of whiskey and poured two fingers worth in a cut-crystal bourbon glass. "Here."

"And *this,*" she said, sloshing the drink around. "Why don't you try asking what I would like instead of assuming?"

He didn't look fazed. His eyes flashed, ripe with the challenge of Jess. As though she was his next conquest, which simply made her want to dig her heels farther into his Ralph Lauren area rug.

He poured himself a glass and clinked the edge to hers before taking a sip. "You said at the bar last night that you preferred whiskey, scotch, and bourbon, did you not?"

"Yes."

"And so I took that information and anticipated your needs."

"And the champagne in the car?"

"While driving, there's an ordinance in the city that liquor has to be in the beer, wine, champagne family. I took a guess. Besides, one can never go wrong with champagne. You should have had everything you possibly needed in the car. There was water. Snacks if you got hungry. Didn't Lyle give you the blanket I asked him to put in there?"

Jess paused, remembering Lyle's jacket wrapped around her shoulders. He hadn't given her a blanket . . . but he had made sure she was warm. "He made sure I had everything I needed," she answered.

"Good," Elliot answered quickly, then placed a hand at the middle of her back. Her lace top came down low in a V between her shoulder blades and his palm sizzled against her bare skin. She was thankful for the long lace sleeves that covered her goose bumps. "However, not exactly the question I asked," he said. "Now, if you don't want whiskey, I have vodka, brandy, sweet vermouth . . . unfortunately, I'm all out of gin, which is a shame."

"Well, damn," Jess teased. "The one thing I wanted was a gin martini."

"A true martini is always gin, Jessica. If you're going to be cheeky, at least get it right. And don't even ask me to make you a vodka martini. I absolutely refuse. And unfortunately, as I said, we don't have a drop of gin left in the house."

"Are you sure? Did you check the bathtub?"

He paused, staring at her, a bemused smile just barely lifting at the corners of his mouth. That might be as much of a reaction as she'd ever get from him in the humor department . . . and she'd take it. When he didn't respond, she winked, sipping from her tumbler. "Just kidding. Whiskey's perfect."

An older gentleman in a pressed suit entered. "Appetizers are ready, Mr. Warner."

"Thank you, Simon." With his free hand, he gestured to the doorway. "Shall we?"

Jess moved through the impressive foyer into a parlor that was decorated almost entirely with '60s antiques. On the cherrywood buffet table were silver platters of goat cheese, almonds, bacon-wrapped dates, pâté, and miniature baked brie slices. "Where the hell are we? It's like we stepped onto the set of *Mad Men*."

"I have a thing for the nineteen-sixties."

With the dark furniture and polished wood floors, there was a regal quality to the house, and though it lacked a feminine touch, it was certainly not a bachelor pad. "You said you made your fortune in real estate?" Jess asked, bringing her attention to the hand-painted plaster ceilings.

"Yes, *made*. Past tense."

"I thought you were still in—?"

"I still dabble. I also run a consulting business."

"Consulting?"

"Businesses that aren't reaching their maximum potential bring me in to overhaul their books, cut waste—that sort of thing."

"And when a business is failing, they can still afford to pay you whatever exorbitant fee it is you charge?"

"It's not easy for them. But I manage to earn them that money back and then some almost every time. I have a wildly high success rate and hardly any of the businesses that follow the plan I lay out for them go bankrupt. The ones that do? I give them a full refund—so long as they prove that they implemented my strategies. If they ignore my suggestions, well, then I can't help them." He spread some pâté on a cracker, holding it up for Jess. "Here. Try this."

She scrunched her nose. "I'm not really a liver kind of girl."

His features sagged as though she were in for a scolding. "Just try it. It's foie gras with apple chutney on top. Paired with the whiskey I handed you, it should be quite delicious."

Jess pinched the cracker and gave it a sniff. Her stomach turned at the thought of what she was about to eat. But before she could think too hard about it, she popped it into her mouth and chewed quickly. The burst of creamy with the pop of sweet was rather nice. Still not something she'd go out of her way to order, but not altogether bad.

"Now take a sip." She did as she was told—perhaps for the first time in her existence. Most of her life she'd been told that whiskey went with two types of food—steak and bacon. She didn't exactly see it being paired with such a delicate appetizer. "The whiskey has caramel undertones," he explained, "and the sweetness of the apple should bring that out. Meanwhile, the smoked pâté mirrors the whiskey's smokiness just about perfectly."

She nodded, brushing the crumbs off her fingers. "That's probably the closest I'll ever get to liking goose liver."

"Well, I like an adventurous woman. At least you tried it. Here . . . wash it down with some bacon-wrapped dates. They're glazed with barbecue sauce and should also pair well with your whiskey, but in a much more bold and obvious way."

Jess rolled the piece of food between her fingers, its stickiness clinging to her skin. "Is this how you started teaching my sister? With food pairings?"

Elliot's eyes lingered on the floor for all of a moment before lifting and capturing Jess. "I don't like answering questions when the person asking clearly already knows the answer. But for the sake of being agreeable . . . no. Your sister and I didn't start this way. In fact, she already knew quite a lot about food and wine." His angular features softened, that cutting scowl lifting into something more melancholy. "Even if she was more of a champagne drinker. She knew her stuff."

Jess recalled one of the e-mails she had read. "And so you started by having her undress in front of you? That was how you saw fit to begin an introduction into this sorry excuse you call a relationship?"

That moment of softness—of vulnerability—was almost as fleeting as the foie gras on her taste buds. Anger flashed once again across his stunning features. "Don't get judgmental on me now, Jessica." Though his face flared with indignation, his voice maintained a state of quiet control. "What your sister and I had was consensual. Neither of us is broken. We didn't enter this lifestyle because we were damaged. What we got from it was pleasure. And with the right person, the right amount of trust . . . my kind of sex is mind-blowing. She knew she could leave at any time. She knew her safe word."

"Elliot—" Jess tried to break in with . . . what exactly? She wasn't about to offer an apology, even though maybe he deserved one.

"And if you dare to come into my house, after asking for my help and insult not only me but your late sister with accusations that have no foundation, you will not be invited back. Ever. Do I make myself clear?"

His eyes flashed and he waited, staring—more like hovering above her. Jess gave a panicked nod, not knowing quite what else to do. "Good," he grumbled, and, grabbing a small bell beside the appetizers, rang it.

Jess stood there stunned. *Ringing a bell? To call a butler?* She thought that only happened in movies. Simon entered. "Yes, sir?"

"Bring Ms. Walters to the dining room. I'll be there shortly."

Without waiting for a response from Simon or an objection from Jess, Elliot turned and went through a door to the right. It didn't slam shut behind him. He didn't need it to. For the same reason that he didn't need to raise his voice. Elliot Warner was in control. Constantly. Nothing was without intent with this man. And yet—storming out? Holing away in some room? It didn't seem like the sort of actions from a man in control. But Jess wasn't about to let that fool her.

"Follow me, Ms. Walters," Simon said, holding open a door into a very elaborately decorated Victorian dining room. There were two place settings on the table. One at the head of the table and one just beside it. For a table as large as it was, Warner had planned on getting awfully cozy with her that evening.

"May I start you off with some wine?"

Jess looked over at the doorway Elliot had gone through. An empty, ominous feeling settled low in her belly. She didn't like that things had been left so heated between them. Without her having a chance to explain—or even apologize. Not that she was about to. She didn't get the relationship between Elliot and her sister. Nor did she want to. Even still, she hadn't wanted to insult him. Or Cassandra. Whatever the two of them did together in the bedroom was only her business if it somehow involved Cass's death. And though she wasn't ruling that out entirely, it still wasn't her place to judge what they enjoyed consensually. Everything she had learned about him and her sister via their e-mails had been affectionate. Perhaps even loving . . . in their own offbeat way.

"He just needs a moment to cool off," Simon explained, noting how her attention was still locked onto the door.

"Shouldn't I go apologize?"

The older man shook his head. "Oh, no. When Mr. Warner gets this way, he needs some time. He holes up in his study when he needs to think. It's best to let him blow off steam first."

It went against everything in her nature to allow the contentious feelings to simmer; it would only make it all the harder to stumble through an apology later. "Could you point me in the direction of the restroom?" She held up her hands. "I just want to wash the stickiness off my hands from those appetizers."

He nodded, showing her back through the door. "Of course. It's right through here, down the hall and on the right."

Jess moved in the direction of the bathroom, waiting until Simon had closed the door behind him before she pivoted and slipped into Elliot's study.

She was met with the immediate smell of candles. Hot wax. And a smoky scent—cedar, maybe. There was a huge lacquered wood desk and dark wood-paneled walls lined with bookshelves. A plush area rug. The complete opposite of his office building's modern black-and-white interior.

His back was to her, his hands in his pockets and though Jess was certain he must have heard her barge through the door, he didn't turn around. Didn't even twitch. Her eyes scanned his strong, bold body and landed on the wall above his desk where he was staring. A giant black-and-white photograph of a woman gagged and bound to a bed.

Jess's throat tightened. No—not just any woman. Cass.

16

The slow tremble started at her toes and crawled up her body until she was shaking entirely.

"You shouldn't be in here." Elliot's voice was dark and dangerous. Fierce but quiet, like the low trill of a panther before a kill.

"I do a lot of things I shouldn't." Jess did her best to put on her bravest voice. And yet, she could feel the fear. Hear it in her own shaky voice. "Did—did you take that photograph?"

"Have you ever heard of shibari?"

Of course he wouldn't answer her question. She should have suspected that. Jess tried to swallow, but her throat felt swollen and dry. "Are you changing topics so that you can maintain control of the conversation?"

With that, he turned around to face her. "Yes," he answered simply.

That stunned her nearly as much as the image of her sister on his wall. "Oh."

"Have you ever heard of shibari?" he asked once more.

"No," she said, averting her eyes from the image of her sister. It felt intrusive to see her this way. And she knew Cass would never want her seeing her in such a sexual, vulnerable state.

"In Japanese, it literally translates 'to tie' or 'to bind.' Yes, the ultimate goal is to immobilize, however to do so elegantly and beautifully. As seen here." He gestured to Cass's picture. "It's an art form."

Jess forced her eyes back to the photograph, focusing on her sister's face. She didn't look to be in pain. She looked peaceful. Her arms were bound behind her back at the elbows in intricate, small knots. She was sitting up on her knees, ankles bound, mouth parted—as though awaiting a kiss. From her master. From Elliot. "Is it painful?"

Elliot shook his head, moving closer to Jess. "Not really. An understandable question, though. To an outsider, it could look barbaric. But the act of shibari is intimate and erotic and actually quite gentle. Hold out your wrists."

Jess jerked away from him as though his touch could burn her, brand her as his own. "Absolutely not."

A smile tugged at his lips. "I promise you—no knots. I just want you to feel how soft the rope is. What it feels like."

"One wrist," Jess said, gathering courage and stepping forward, pushing her sleeves above her elbows.

"Very well."

"You conceded that easily?"

"Bondage and dominance is all about comfort levels. I may push boundaries, but I never cross them. If you say one wrist . . . one wrist it is." He gestured with a twirling finger. "Turn. I don't want you to see what I'm doing. I want you to *feel* it."

Oh, she could feel it, all right. She could feel it without him laying a hand on her. The velvet in his voice. The smolder in his eyes. There was a reason her sister fell and fell hard for this guy. "Elliot—" Jess's voice was raspy as the words stumbled past her tongue. "I'm sorry. For what I said earlier. I'm sort of skeptical about everyone and everything these days . . ."

"I understand," he said, and his gaze lingered on her mouth. "You have every right to be cautious. I just hope that soon enough you'll learn that I am not the person you need to be afraid of."

With that, Jess turned around, holding her wrist out behind her. "Actually—" She spun back to face him, misjudging how closely they were standing and her breasts brushed against his chest. He caught her around the waist, steadying her as she swayed, perched atop the Jimmy Choo heels Dane had given her. Her hand rested on his chest, hard muscle pushing through the high thread-count cotton.

"Yes?"

"I was going to say—well, that statement alone makes me trust you even more. Go ahead. Tie up both wrists."

Surprise and maybe a bit of triumph washed across his face, but as quickly as she thought she saw it, it was gone. "Very well." Loosening his tie, he pulled it from his collar and tied it around her eyes. With her sense of sight gone, she felt naked and her body buzzed to life. Her sight was her lifeline. Her very existence, job, and passion with her camera. She felt his hot breath against her ear, close, but his lips not touching her. "Just in case you're a peeker." She could hear the smile in his voice.

The rope was silky—not itchy or frayed like how she imagined it feeling. It wound around her wrists up to what felt like her elbows . . . or just below and then back down again. One by one, he slipped it between her fingers, around her palms. But what was most notable was how gentle his hands were on hers. Caring. Attentive. And his touch registered in every part of her body, firing off synapses in her brain. With her sight gone, she never knew where his hands were about to land and it was like a mysterious little game. Even with both of them fully dressed, she was his erotic playground and he was attentive and careful.

She sighed, relaxing the weight of her arms onto his hands even more. As his fingers gently swiped her skin, she thought of Sam. Missing the way his hands would grasp around her waist. The way he would claim her lips, her tongue, her mouth as his. Her breasts grew heavy within her lace blouse, pulling toward those hands that bound her wrists. Wanting Sam's hands on her, kneading the tension from her tight nipples.

Moments passed and she hadn't felt his hands on her in . . . how long had it been? Ten seconds? Twenty? Time passed slowly in this state. She opened her mouth, Sam's name nearly slipping past her tongue before she stopped herself. "Elliot?"

"I'm right here," he answered, and his voice sounded as tight as she felt inside. "Admiring my work."

"May I admire it with you?"

"First, tell me. How does it feel?"

For the first time all night, a peace had fallen over her. A calmness. One she couldn't quite explain. "It's . . . surprisingly comfortable."

"Go on."

"Not just comfortable. But . . . *comforting*. But this is crazy. How can I feel so at home being tied up?"

She felt the tie slide off from her eyes and though the first thing she should have looked at was her bound arms, Elliot's stare was the first sight she locked into. Those sharp eyes were on her, attentive and curious. "An interesting observation. A hug is restrictive of movement and yet, we find comfort in it. Spooning is the same thing. And as you get more comfortable with shibari, the bindings get tighter, more restrictive, depending on whether you prefer a little pain in your lovemaking. Think of shibari as taking your average spooning to the next level."

"I'd say the two are extremely different."

"And yet, it feels good?"

Jess paused before nodding, not daring to take her eyes off him. His smirk lifted. "Sometimes, those of us who have fought the hardest to remain in control of our lives are the exact ones who find the most comfort when we let go and allow someone else to be in control. As if the reason for the struggle was that we were fighting to be something we aren't."

"Are you saying that I'm a natural submissive?"

"I didn't say that. But the fact that you connected those dots should say more than my words."

She rolled her eyes, unable to help the annoyed shake of her head. "And you think you're going to be the one to break me, right? That you're going to be the all-powerful dominant who sweeps in and saves me?"

His brows knitted between his eyes and he shook his head. "No," he answered. "You don't feel that way about me. Nor I, you. And I don't think our . . . styles would mesh well. Lord knows your sister and I butted heads on many things." After a moment, he gestured down to her arms. "You haven't even looked at my art yet."

She looked down and was met with a beautiful design. In the center near her wrists, the knot formed a sort of flower. "A flower?"

"A daisy, specifically. Your sister's favorite. Had I known yours, I could have—"

"Peony," she answered quickly before she could stop herself. "Peonies are my favorite."

"Good to know. Now. I'm famished. You good to eat like that?" Her mouth dropped as his grin spread the length of his face. With a quick flick of his fingers, he untied the knot. "Just kidding."

"You're an ass," Jess said. And yet, she found herself laughing along with him.

17

Sam loped up the steps to Matt's front door just after seven-thirty, a bundle of flowers clenched in one hand and a teddy bear in the other. Dr. Adams's work release burned a hole in his back pocket. He knocked twice.

Kelly came to the door with cooing baby Grace in her arms. "Hey, stranger," she laughed, leaning in for a hug. "I'm so glad you finally took us up on this offer to host dinner."

Sam pecked her on the cheek, a bit of blond hair from her ponytail clinging to his stubble. He brushed his hand down Grace's ruddy cheek. "Thanks for having me. And for all the food you sent me. These are for you," he said, holding up the flowers. "And this is for baby Grace." The five-month-old gig-gled, stretching out her arms toward the bear.

"You didn't have to do that, but it was very sweet. Come on in," Kelly said as she stepped to the side. "How ya feeling?"

"Much better."

"Good, we've been worried about you." She squeezed his arm, giving him a sweet smile before climbing the stairs. "Let me put the munchkin down for bed."

"There he is!" Matt said, rushing in from the kitchen and reaching out to clasp Sam's hand.

"Sorry I'm late."

"It's okay. Where the hell's *my* gift? Kelly gets flowers, Gracie gets a teddy bear . . . ?"

"Actually," Sam pulled the piece of paper from his back pocket, handing it to Matt.

Matt held the paper closer to the light, reading. "What's this?"

"Use your eyeballs and read, man. Unless you never passed the third grade. In which case, I can wake Gracie up and have her read it to you."

Matt punched Sam's shoulder, still grinning. "You're such a dick sometimes, you know that? You're cleared for work again? So soon?"

"That's why I was late. Got caught in a late appointment with my doctor."

His partner's eyes shifted back and forth between the bandage on Sam's head and the sheet of paper in his hands. "But—but, are you sure? I mean, I just saw you yesterday and you were in so much pain still. Wait—this 'appointment' with Dr. Adams . . . is the department going to get hit with a harassment suit because of it?"

Sam chuckled, taking the paper back from him and tucking it into his pocket once more. "Be careful with that. It's valuable." He winked and threw an arm around his longtime best friend. "Come on, relax. Let's celebrate the win."

"Dude, if you're still in pain, you could really hurt yourself—"

"Matt, seriously. I'm fine. I know the warning signs to look out for. Nosebleeds, dizziness, headaches. If any of those things persist, I promise you, I'll stop and take it easy. For now, can we just toast to you getting the best partner in the world back?"

Matt grabbed two bottles from the fridge and popped the

caps off. "Here you go. To the best damn partner—wait, are you even supposed to be having alcohol?"

Sam tipped his head back, taking a swig of the beer. "Dunno. I'll just have the one and see how I feel."

"Jesus Christ," Matt muttered as he took another sip.

"Hey now," Kelly said, grinning as she came back in the kitchen. She sidled up beside her husband, grabbing his bottle and drinking from it before handing it back. "God that feels good. I cannot wait to be done with breast-feeding so that I can eat and drink whatever I want again."

Matt eyed his wife's cleavage and sent Sam a few eyebrow wiggles. "I on the other hand will absolutely miss the girls when they're gone."

"Will you also miss milk splattering everywhere during sex?" Sam cringed. "Okay, I love you guys, but please stop."

Matt kissed Kelly before setting his beer down and jerking his head toward the front door. "Come here, let me show you what I found today."

"No," Kelly pouted, jutting her bottom lip out. "No work talk. Matt—you promised."

He slid Sam a look before dancing back over to her and dipping her in his arms. "Five minutes," he said, kissing her. "I promise."

"Your promises mean nothing! Five minutes!" she called after them, but they were already out the door and standing in the garage.

Matt glanced back, shutting the door behind him so that Kelly couldn't hear. "Weren't you and Straimer talking about that new drug on the streets?"

Sam gulped. He and Straimer had been working on the drug case. Along with Cass. "Yeah, Biophuterol. There's not a whole lot to know yet. Just that up here we think most of it is coming down from Canada. We've heard from other areas that they're getting it in from Mexico as well."

"Rodriguez and I booked this kid today. He tried to rob a convenience store and we found this on him." Matt swiped his phone, pulling up a picture of pills in a small baggie. "He kept calling it 'O' which we thought was Oxy at first, but I had Oxycontin when my back went out and these pills are definitely not them."

Goddammit. Why hadn't Straimer called him? Sam needed to grill this guy as soon as possible. Before he got released on some sort of technicality. "How long can we keep him in custody?"

"He hasn't lawyered up yet and we totally have him on the small robbery. We tried, but he's not talking about the drugs."

"What about his parents? Is he a minor?"

Matt shook his head. "He's eighteen. Lives with his mom, but it looks like he may not have a reliable family situation at home. He didn't even bother trying to call either of his parents."

Sam thought back to his own childhood—if you could call it that—with his drunk of a mom. He had always been the same way when he got in trouble, avoided contacting her at all times. Not because he feared punishment, but because he knew it'd be a waste. In the rare case that she was sober, she was usually too wrapped up in her own life to be bothered. At least until she married his stepdad. For those few years that those two were happily married, she straightened up her act. In fact, it was the car wreck with Jess's parents that had made her go straight for a while. She met Sam's stepdad soon after that. Sam shook the memory from his head. "So because of the robbery we've at least got him for twenty-four hours or until he or his parents get wise and lawyer up?" Matt nodded. "I want to take a stab at him first thing tomorrow morning."

"Sure thing. Pick me up early . . . around seven? We can grab Tim Hortons."

Sam rolled his eyes. "Just like old times. You know . . . all of four days ago." Matt smiled, but it quickly faded. "Matt . . . what is it? What aren't you telling me?"

"It's just . . . I swung by Jess's house. . . ."

Every muscle in Sam's body bunched beneath his clothes. "And?"

"And . . . she's fine."

"Okay."

"Okay." He paused. "But . . ."

"Matt, I swear to God if you don't spit it out . . ."

"Fine. She got into a car. A really nice car-service type of limo. I mean, not *really* a limo. Not like what we took to prom—"

"Get *on* with it." But Sam knew where this story was going. He hadn't met too many people in this town recently who would be so flashy.

"I followed them to the ferry to Peaks Island."

"Goddammit, Jess."

"I'm sorry, man. She was all dressed up. It looked like a date or something."

The pounding in his head was back, only this time he could attribute it to one petite brunette who was constantly getting under his skin. "It's okay, Mattie. Thanks for checking in on her. And for telling me."

Matt jerked his head back toward the house. "Let's go have some dinner, okay?"

"Sure thing. You go on in . . . I'll be right behind you."

18

Jess sighed in contentment as she finished her last bite of mashed potatoes, smiling when Simon whisked her plate away. Dinner had been delicious and Elliot was surprisingly good company. There was a calmness to his dominance. A resolute acceptance about who he was versus Sam's constant need to push her away. Then again, she realized that had less to do with his deviant sexual side and more to do with his guilt all these years about her mother and father. Even still, Elliot controlled with a light touch while Sam bulldozed his way through life. But maybe that was the difference in their jobs, in their lives. Sam's bulldozing way of living was how he potentially made head detective. How he survived his upbringing. Whereas she had no doubt that Elliot's calm control is the reason why businesses trusted him to go behind the curtain and restructure their entire company.

"So," Jess said, "Care to explain why you think it's necessary for us to pretend to be in a dom and sub relationship?"

"I would love to explain," Elliot replied. "Other than now owning your sister's house, you have no ties to this community.

But as my lover, it won't be odd for you to be a part of the big upcoming party this weekend. Furthermore, we can work together—and potentially with Dane should he be willing to help—to get those drugs out of your possession. Once they're returned to the people threatening you and these men are off your back, you should get out of town . . . even if just for a little while. I can care for your house. Even put it on the market for you."

"Oh, I don't need you to do that. I had an offer I'll probably accept."

"I promise you I can get you a better offer," Elliot said, hardly looking at her. As though he simply assumed she didn't know what she was talking about.

"Really? You can get me a better offer than one point two million dollars?"

Elliot nearly choked on his wine and she couldn't help but chuckle at the sight of this guy who always had it together almost doing a spit take. "Who offered you that?"

"Gilles, from Cass's office. Apparently, he wants a home here for when he's in town on business from . . . Canada." Jess paused, nerves jolting in her belly as she realized the strange coincidence. "You don't think . . . ?"

"No," Elliot answered quickly. "He has nothing to do with this. The drug ring wouldn't be run by someone living up in Canada. I think it's someone local. Someone who also has a hand in these parties."

"How are you so certain?"

"I just have a sense. I've met Gilles in the building before and he doesn't seem the type." The little flare of hope Jess had experienced deflated as quickly as it had come on.

"In any case," Elliot continued, "If I were you, I would think twice before selling your house to him. But we can worry about that later. For now, we need to focus on those pills and getting them out of your house."

"And putting them where? I don't want them back in the hands of the dealers. They shouldn't be on the streets at all."

Elliot sighed. "Then what do you want? You want these men off your back, yes?"

Jess gave a tight nod.

"But you don't want to give them what they want?" There was an annoying condescending tone to the question that made Jess wince.

"Well, we don't *know* that's what they want. What if it's just about the money? We could return Cass's money to them? Then just claim that there were no drugs in the house."

"They're smarter than that. And suppose they want both the money *and* the drugs . . . what then?"

"You said yourself that money is mine to do with as I wish. And I wish to give it back to them and then throw the drugs away."

"That's incredibly stupid. Even if you give the money back, they still would likely want the drugs—drugs are more valuable than money. These are people who are willing to kill to get what they want. And you're going to withhold from them? Not to mention, what exactly do you propose we do with all those pills if we're not putting them back into the hands of the dealers?"

She hadn't really thought that far ahead. "You said you know who these people are, right?"

Elliot held up a finger. "That is not what I said. I said I know they are involved in the masquerades and I bet we could get a message to them that we have what they want."

"Couldn't the drugs just . . . appear on the steps of a DEA officer's home or something?"

"You don't think that it would be priority number one to find out who dropped cases and cases of drugs onto their doorstep?" Elliot stared at her from over his espresso. "Okay, I have one other idea. And it only works if you're willing to part with your sister's money—as it obviously and stupidly seems like you're willing to do."

"Absolutely."

"Instead of holding this year's ball here in my home, I could have it on my yacht."

"Okay."

"And we can sail it up the coast of Maine to the Canadian border where you and I will find a way to drop the drugs into the country where they likely came from."

"Don't you think the Canadian border patrol will find it?"

Elliot nodded. "And then it will become their problem."

That could work, Jess thought, sipping her coffee. "But if you have a yacht, why can't we just take it now—tonight—and drop all the drugs? Why do it during the party?"

"A couple of reasons. We need alibis. If Canadian drug enforcement traces the drugs back to my yacht, we have a huge party of people to blame it on. Proving it was us will be much harder for authorities."

"And the second reason?"

"If the drug dealer is at that party, on that boat, we can deliver them Cassandra's money and hope it's what they're looking for in your house. Hope it's enough to get them to leave you alone. Again, it's a risk. But if they have their money back, I think you're correct that they'll consider everything settled."

It *was* risky. These people wanted her dead for how she'd been sticking her nose into their business. But if she went directly to Sam or turned the drugs into the police, she'd be a dead woman anyway. And she couldn't just do nothing. Not now. Not knowing that her sister's death was no accident. "I'm in. But I still want to look these bastards in the face. Meet the man who killed my sister."

"I already told you—I'm not going to take part in vigilantism . . ."

"It isn't that. I just want to know. I want to see him." Jess paused, shocked that Elliot had nothing to say to that. "Don't you? Don't you want to know who killed your girlfriend?"

"Of course I do," he hissed. "But that can't bring her back. I knew this robbery-gone-wrong story was complete bullshit. But what good will the truth do now?"

Jess crossed her arms, observing the way he chewed the inside of his cheek, awaiting her answer. "It'll make me sleep easier. Wouldn't it for you?"

"Sleep didn't come easy when Cass was alive. It certainly won't now that she's gone," he said.

Jess pushed her chair back and stood up. "I should really get home. Besides, having gotten to know you a bit better, I'm gonna guess you've probably paid Lyle to wait around, haven't you?"

The warm lighting danced in his amused eyes as he stood, walking her to the foyer. With another ring of the bell, Simon poked his head in. "Simon, could you get Ms. Walters's things?"

"Yes, sir."

Silence settled between Jess and Elliot as they stood in his impressive hall. Usually Jess was totally comfortable with silence. In fact, in many instances she preferred it. But with Elliot it felt itchy, uncomfortable. And she hated the way he seemed so at ease while she was twitching like a cheerleader after three espressos. "You know," she said, her voice sounding loud now, cutting through the quiet. "If they find out we're lying, they'll probably kill us both."

"I know," he answered.

"Then why are you helping me?"

"I thought we established this already? I feel responsible for you now that Cass is gone. And I feel like it was partially my fault that Cass died. I want to help. Besides, my life is empty without her anyway."

Simon reentered with Jess's purse and a long, black cashmere cardigan that Jess immediately recognized as her sister's. "Here you go, Ms. Walters. The other Ms. Walters left it here."

"Just in case Lyle forgets to give you that blanket again," Elliot said as he brushed his lips across her cheek. "Call me when you're home."

Elliot helped Jess into Cass's cardigan and then opened the front door for her. She felt numb. The sweater still smelled like Cass. It was cozy and soft; it had been her sister's favorite cardigan for as long as she could remember. Growing up, Cass would wear it around the house constantly and in those rare moments that they would curl up on the couch and watch a movie together, her sister had always worn it. If she closed her eyes and wrapped her arms around herself, it would almost feel like Cass was there with her. Holding her. Surrounding her.

The door closed behind her and the night air was cold, but the memories kept her warm. The memories and Cass's cardigan.

"Ms. Walters?" Lyle stood in the driveway, his eyebrows twisted in concern.

"Just a minute." she said, rummaging inside her purse for a tissue. *That's weird,* she thought. The keys that she always kept in the outside pouch of her purse were now in the main bag. And her silver business card case was open.

"I need a minute, Lyle." She dug around further, making sure everything was inside and nothing was missing from her wallet. It almost seemed like someone had been looking through her stuff. She pulled out her phone. *Four missed calls? Six text messages? Holy hell, who is trying to reach me?* She groaned as Sam's name came up with every missed alert.

Oh, crap. Elliot had said to call him when she got home. And yet, after all this, she still didn't have his number. She started to turn to go back to the house.

"If you know what's good for you, you will not knock on that door." Sam's voice sent chill bumps skating down her arms.

Before she could respond, her phone buzzed within her hand. She looked down to an unknown Portland number lighting up her screen:

Please call me when you get home ... this is my cell. Use it any time. Your detective friend has been waiting for you in the driveway. If you need me out there use the word pancake *in conversation and Lyle will call me instantly.*

19

"Did you forget something inside?" Sam asked.

"Apparently, my independence. What the hell are you doing here, Sam? How did you find me?"

"I was given an anonymous tip that you were in a vehicle with a broken taillight. Very dangerous, you know," he said, directing the last sentence to Lyle.

Matt. Of course.

"This taillight's not broken," Lyle interjected, immediately rushing to the back of the car.

"Lyle, it's fine. He's just being—" Jess started to explain.

"Protective?" Sam interrupted.

"I was gonna go with 'an asshole.' But sure. 'Protective.' Whatever."

"Ms. Walters?" Lyle said. "I hate to interrupt this . . . tête-à-tête, but the last ferry leaves in ten minutes." He opened the door to the backseat, waiting for her to enter.

"Thank you, Lyle."

"Yes, thank you, Lyle. I appreciate any man willing to get her home safely. But I can take it from here," said Sam.

Lyle shifted uncomfortably, his attention steadied directly on Jess. "I'm being paid to ensure her safe delivery home. Ms. Walters, if you prefer to ride with him, you may. I'll be following behind you the whole way."

"You don't have to do that—"

"Yes, I do. Besides, I don't live on the island. I have to take the ferry to get home regardless."

Sam's blue eyes cut through the dark night, leveled at Jess. "Well? Who would you like to ride with?"

He was actually asking her? That was a change. A request for her decision rather than a demand that went against her will. And above all else, she wanted to ride with Sam.

The most unforgivable secrets are the ones that take the most courage to be honest about. Elliot's words from earlier buzzed in her mind. Sam reached his hand out, brushing it down her arm. The friction between his touch and the sleeve of her cardigan sparked and though she knew better, it felt like a sign.

"Jessie," Sam said.

She wanted to talk with him. She wanted him to hold her and kiss her and maybe tie her up like Elliot did. But any time spent with Sam was detrimental to both their lives, regardless of the fact that this lie hung over them like creaky scaffolding, ready to collapse and destroy them at any moment.

"I appreciate your concern, Sam. As always. But I'll have Lyle take me home tonight."

A shadow crossed over Sam's face, darkening his already grim features. "Wait . . . I just . . . I need to see you. I need to talk to you." Awareness tingled over her shoulders and down her chest until the feeling resonated at her nipples. The spread of warmth surged through her body and she wasn't sure if it was because of the very charged evening, or because she'd just experienced shibari for the first time, or if it was because this was Sam. The very man that she could never quite let go of.

If Sam ever found out that she allowed Elliot to tie her up

like that . . . her focus drifted to his gun, holstered at his hip, and she tilted her head. "Your gun . . . you're not supposed to have that on you until—"

"I'm back on active duty. I was released for work earlier this evening."

Her eyes traveled over his body, hard and masculine in all the right areas. And in his presence, she felt feminine. Soft. Maybe that's why being around Sam was so unnerving. It was like what Elliot had described—she'd spent her whole life trying to fight for control of her life. But with Sam, it felt more natural to let him take care of her. Even though she still fought him for her independence, he was the one person with whom she could see herself letting go.

Her gaze landed on the bandage still peeking out from underneath Sam's baseball hat. "But . . . but your head is still bandaged. Sam, there's no way you're ready for fieldwork so soon."

"The doctor signed off—"

Realization slammed into her and Jess shook her head. "What did you do? Did you force Dr. Adams to let you go back to work?"

"I—"

"Never mind." She held up a hand, shaking his explanation off. "It's none of my business. Not anymore." She placed a hand on his arm. "We can't talk here. Out in the open like this. It might feel remote but it's not." She glanced around and back at the car. Lyle was leaning against the trunk, his eyes glued to his phone. And yet, she had no doubt that he was hanging on to every word she said, on the orders of Elliot Warner. "Let's talk later." Then, backing away toward the limo, but still looking directly at Sam, she said. "Take me home, Lyle."

Sam nodded, backing away, and Jess was glad that he understood and didn't fight her for once. She could go home, have a hot bath, and give him a call in the morning. "See you around,

Jess," Sam said, pulling out his keys. With that, he got in his car and drove off to the ferry and she did the same with Lyle.

On the ferry ride back to the mainland, Sam stayed in his car and Jess stayed in hers. For Jess, it wasn't the same magical ride over the water that it had been coming there. It was tense and Lyle seemed to pick up on that immediately.

"That guy doesn't like to hear the word no, huh?" Lyle asked.

"No. He doesn't," Jess answered. The half-empty bottle of champagne sat next to her in a bucket of fresh ice with a clean flute beside it. Whereas before it was a lovely gesture meant to make her feel cared for, now it simply mocked her. Sam was going to get himself killed if he wasn't careful. Even aside from the drug dealers and their warnings for them to stay apart, he was going to kill himself. *You don't mess around with head injuries,* thought Jess. *If a doctor says to stay off your feet, dammit, you need to do just that.* And that's exactly what she planned on telling him tomorrow.

As soon as their cars pulled off the ferry Sam took a left turn, heading down to the wharf. Jess released a relieved breath. She only hoped he was on his way home to get some rest.

Though the drive from the water to Jess's house was a short one, it seemed to take forever. When Lyle pulled into her driveway, he popped out of the car to open her door before she could stop him. "Unnecessary," she said, smiling up at Lyle. "But thank you. Again."

He tipped his hat and even though it seemed genuine, there was a hint of playful mockery to it. "It's my job, Ms. Walters."

"Seriously, it's Jess. Call me Jess."

He smiled, revealing that dimple once more. "As long as Mr. Warner isn't around . . . Jess it is. I'll wait until you're safely inside before leaving."

Jess walked up the steps of her house, taking note of Cass's ceramic frogs, all facing front. No Dane inside. She would hope not, considering it was after eleven. She slid her key into the lock, and the door creaked open. She gave a wave to Lyle before closing and locking the door.

She couldn't wait to sink into a hot bath with a good book . . . or at the very least, get out of her restrictive dress. It was gorgeous, but the lace sleeves were itchy and the waistline tight. She and Cass were almost the same size, but it seemed Cass had lost some weight since Jess had seen her last.

As she turned to go up the stairs, the light beside her couch clicked on and a deep voice crooned her name.

"Jess . . ."

All the organs in Jess's gut seized up into her throat and she let out a bloodcurdling scream as a hand came down over her mouth.

20

Someone was saying her name over and over, but the sound was murky in Jess's head. All she could feel were the strong arms pinning her against someone's hard-muscled chest. His hand pressed into her mouth, but she kept screaming. The sound was muffled, but she could only hope it was still loud enough for one of her neighbors to hear. His palm dipped into her open mouth and Jess bit down hard on the space between his thumb and forefinger. Tangy blood pooled in her mouth and she spat before throwing her elbow into his gut and rushing for the door. But his hands held on strong around her waist and he kept calling her name. Her name and someone else's—Sam's.

"Jesus Christ, Jess, it's Sam! It's Sam, relax!"

"Sam?" She panted his name, out of breath from the fight.

"Yes! Fuck, I think I'm bleeding. I have your goddamn tooth marks in my thumb!"

Tears brimmed her eyes from the adrenaline rush and she dropped to a seat on the bottom step of the stairs. "What are you doing here, Sam?" she said, shaking.

"You said you wanted to meet here!"

"No I *didn't!*"

"Yes, you did! You said 'Let's talk later.' And then you pointedly asked Lyle to take you home."

"Oh, for God's sake . . . I meant let's talk tomorrow!"

A knock pounded on her door. Jess put a finger to her lips, shushing Sam, as he backed himself against the wall so he would be hidden from view.

Cracking the door open, she found a very concerned-looking Lyle standing there.

"Are you okay? I heard screaming." He glanced behind her, frantically looking for any signs of a struggle.

Jess relaxed, resting her head on the door. "I'm fine. I . . . I saw a spider and freaked out a bit."

"A spider?"

"Uh-huh."

"Do you want me to come in and kill it for you?"

"No! Um, no, that's not necessary. I killed it already."

"Did you now?" The timbre of his voice had dropped considerably. "Are you sure you're okay?"

She gave him a tight smile, but it was the best she could muster with her heart still pounding from the earlier scare. "I promise."

His eyes drifted behind her one last time, scanning the foyer before he stepped back. "Good night—" said Jess. As she moved to close the door, he shoved his foot inside, stopping her.

"Just one more question. I forgot that Elliot wanted me to ask if you wanted pancakes tomorrow for brunch?" His eyes glistened and she could see the twitch of his jaw as the unspoken passed between them—Elliot's text flashing into her mind: *If you need me out there, use the word* pancake *in conversation.*

She gave Lyle a small smile once more. "You know, I don't. I'm more of a waffle girl, myself."

He relaxed and backed away. "Okay, then. Call if you need anything Ms. Wa—" Jess held up a hand, stopping him before he finished. That boyish grin widened and he nodded in her direction. "I mean . . . *Jess.*"

She waited until Lyle was inside his car and the headlights came on before shutting and locking the door. Moving to the stairs, she found Sam there, applying pressure to his bleeding hand.

"You and your spiders," he said.

She rolled her eyes and held out a hand. "How's your thumb?"

"Bleeding," he grumbled.

She sighed and jerked her head up the stairs. "Come on. I thought I saw some hydrogen peroxide and Neosporin in Cass's bathroom upstairs. Let's clean you up."

To his credit, Sam followed her and though it may have been begrudging, he didn't show it too much. Once they were in the bathroom he dropped to a seat on the edge of the bathtub, holding his hand out as Jess grabbed some gauze and Band-Aids from the medicine cabinet.

Cradling his hand in hers, she dribbled the hydrogen peroxide on. It fizzed around the cut and she had to admit, she'd bitten him pretty damn hard. He breathed in sharply through his nose, though if he was in pain, it didn't register on his face in the least.

"I'm sorry I bit you," Jess said, looking up at him from where she knelt. Kneeling before him, like his submissive. Unease tore through her core and she pushed to her feet and instead sat next to him. Level. On even ground. "But not *that* sorry," she teased, a smile touching her lips.

"It may suck for me that you bit so hard, but I'm glad that you did. I'm glad you were of sound enough mind to fight off someone you thought was an intruder." His jaw tensed and his eyes sparked with something alive and heavy. "I'm sorry I was the one to scare you. I thought you were expecting me—"

"I know. It was a misunderstanding." She wiped away the remaining blood around the cut.

"How did you get in?"

Sam jerked his head towards the basement. "The tunnel. They had someone stationed down there, but I used my badge and got in that way."

When Jess was finished cleaning the cut, she then spread on some Neosporin and put on a bandage. She lifted her eyes to find Sam's steeled onto her, unrelenting. Demanding things she wasn't sure she had it within herself to give anymore. Not to Sam. Maybe not to anyone. Nerves fluttered through her belly and the rush wasn't entirely an unpleasant feeling. As she moved to pull her hand back, Sam held on, the gentleness of his touch contradicting the fierceness of his stare. Jess inhaled that musky scent that was purely Sam and the smell resonated deep inside of her. It felt warm and reassuring in a way that she needed more than anything and yet had been lacking the last few days. "Jess—" With the mere mention of her name, it was as though he pulled the supporting piece out of a Jenga tower, sending all the pieces of her life crashing to the ground.

"Please, Sam. I don't want to talk. I'm so *sick* of talking."

He paused. "You want me to go?"

The quietness of the house spoke louder than she ever needed to. "I didn't say that, either."

That was all the prodding he seemed to need. His mouth came crashing down onto hers, his hands scooping her onto her feet with him. Her palms were cold against the warmth of his skin as she slid them beneath his shirt. His chest was a landscape of soft skin stretched over taut muscle. She could taste how much he wanted her and his urgency was as potent on her tongue as the whiskey from earlier that evening. As she arched into him, his body encompassed hers, holding her, cradling her into the kiss.

A grim feeling rose from her stomach—a reminder of all the lies. It pushed past that warm uncoiling passion, but Jess shoved it back below the surface. Buried the uncertainty and darkness and doubt down below the desire. For tonight—for now—she didn't want to remember. She didn't want to address the lies and the pain. Instead, she focused on the moment. The slick heat spreading between her legs and Sam's hot tongue sliding inside her mouth. Nothing other than the feel of his hard muscle against her hands. Nothing other than his erection pressing against her, claiming her body as his. Just for this one night.

A rough sound of pleasure rumbled through Jess's mouth from deep in Sam's chest and she relished in it as though swallowing this groan could bring them closer. She wanted all that he had to offer. Every bit of it. She wanted his pleasure. And his pain. She wanted Sam.

It was comforting to know he desired her as much as she did him and as his hands roamed down her back, he paused at her ass, pulling her hard against his cock.

Something inside of her cracked. She didn't care who Jessica Walters was tonight. Or who she would be tomorrow. Because for now, she wanted to just enjoy. And relish in the feel of letting go, putting her pleasure in Sam's hands.

Her fingers dipped into his soft head of hair, careful to avoid the bandaged area. Gently, she tugged his neck back but she couldn't pry her lips off his skin even if she wanted to. And she definitely didn't.

She gasped as Sam tore his mouth from hers, pushing her to arm's length.

"Jessie, what the hell—I thought—"

"Shut up," she rasped, and her voice was low and sultry, nearly unrecognizable from what she normally sounded like. "Take me. Do with me what you do. Be my master—"

"Jessie, I'm not your master. I'm no one's master."

"But—"

"I don't want to control you. I just want to feel good with you."

Heat rushed through her body, swirling, and her head grew light. "But I thought that's what you do. What this lifestyle was about."

Sam shook his head and brushed her hair from her forehead. "For some." His eyes glinted, and the dim lights of the bathroom hid the deep blue of his eyes. Cupping her jaw, he pulled her in slowly for a kiss that lingered, his tongue nudging her lips wider. "But I don't want to own you," he said. "Not in that way. Wanting control in the bedroom is different from wanting ownership."

Long seconds ticked by and Sam's gentle touch brushed down her neck, pausing between her breasts before cupping one, rolling his thumb over her nipple. Friction from his touch sent jolts of electricity shimmering down her body and Jess let her head fall back against the wall. It was impossible to hide how affected she was by him. Sliding her knee between his legs, she stopped short of his groin.

"Show me," she managed to choke out. "Show me what you mean by that. Take me into the world you explore again. I miss it. I miss *you*." His lips brushed over her neck, moving slowly up her jaw and landing on her mouth. It was possessive yet maintained a softness that so perfectly defined Sam. To the world, Sam exuded a hardness. A roughness. He was a brick wall, impenetrable. But with Jess? He was malleable . . . he was changing. Growing. Where he used to be stubborn to a fault, he now made compromises.

"Nothing would please me more," he growled, and he lowered his mouth to hers once more. His kiss was fiery and demanding and it was all the distraction Sam needed to slip Jess's dress off her body. He backed her, dressed now in just her bra and thong, toward the bedroom, his lips never leaving hers.

The back of her knees brushed against the bed and Jess gasped, a light-headedness taking hold of her. She panted, stretching her head back to reveal a strip of her neck, but Sam was relentless, wanting more than she was offering. He unhooked her bra and the chilly air brushed over her nipples. A whimper splintered her lips and her body clenched at that low, sexy chuckle Sam had. It ripped through her body, vibrating.

Scooping his hands into her hair, he tugged her neck back even more, stretching her muscles tight, but not so that she was totally uncomfortable. His hands traveled down her body as he lowered in front of her, pausing at her breasts and taking a nipple into his mouth, while fondling her other breast with a gentle hand. She hissed as his teeth grazed her sensitive nipple and he moved to repeat the sensation on her other breast.

Dropping to his knees in front of her, he hooked his fingers into her panties and scraped them down her thighs until they banded around her ankles. Desire sizzled in her chest as he pressed a tender kiss to her stomach, dipping his tongue into her navel.

Rather than use his mouth immediately, he teased her, running his nose gently up her sex and inhaling deeply. Her body bucked against the barely-there tingle and tease of a touch. Just enough to let her know something was coming, but not enough to give her a true jolt of pleasure.

"Screw you," she said playfully, peeking one eye open at him kneeling in front of her.

She could feel his smile against her skin. "That's the idea," he said, casting her a heated look. And that smile, now directed up at her, was dazzling, nearly taking her breath away. His fingers trailed against her swollen lips and Jess bit down on her bottom lip to suppress a pant.

A slice of his irresistible tongue darted out, licking, exploring, and circling her. His finger continued its slow stroke back and forth against her pussy, now and then switching places with where his mouth was. He paused, circling his tongue slowly around her clit in tortuously luscious licks before he delved two fingers inside of her, pressing and stretching, just where she ached for it most. His fingers pumped in and out as he increased the speed of his tongue against her clit.

Jess scooped her fingers into his dark, soft hair. Every muscle tightened as her pleasure increased and her legs trembled with the simple task of remaining standing in front of him.

His fingers and tongue worked perfectly together, driving her faster toward the edge. The roaring sound of blood deafened her and nothing existed in the moment except for this. Except for Sam and this pleasure. Her mind drifted to the soft feel of being tied up. The excitement of the blindfold and not knowing what was coming next.

His teeth scraped along her clit and his fingers retreated, only to be replaced by the darting thrust of his tongue inside of her. "Oh," she gasped, and Sam was there to catch her as her knees buckled, his hands gripping around her ass. "Oh, God. Sam—"

Her muscles contracted, beginning with her toes curling, and it rapidly swept up to her sex and over her stomach and chest. Quiet moans that she couldn't contain anymore strangled in her throat and she sighed as the feelings released. Like snipping a stretched rubber band, Jess snapped. That heat that had been slowly warming her body flared to a smoking blaze and she wilted in his arms, curving her back as she pumped her hips against his mouth. That first spasm was the largest and jerked her body back as pure bliss erupted through her so deeply that she could feel the contractions within her bones.

Sam braced her weight as though it were nothing, releasing her onto the bed and stripping his own clothes off. His hot body, slick with sweat and moisture, pressed her into the soft mattress. His erection nestled between her legs, putting rock-solid pressure just where she needed it. Despite the mind-blowing orgasm she'd just experienced, she craved more.

Needed more. Tingles cascaded down her body, some lingering just long enough at her breasts to peak her nipples into two solid nubs.

Sam rocked his hips against her. "You think you're ready for more? Or do you need a break?" he challenged, eyes glistening.

Cupping his face, Jess kissed him, rolling Sam onto his back and straddling him. Even in the darkness, she could see his gaze sharpen and his large hands settled on her hips, cradling her body. He grinned up at her. "You know, I don't usually let my subs flip me onto my back."

The memory of shibari once again invaded her thoughts and she squeezed her eyes closed, trying to rid her mind and body of the thought. Yet, wetness pooled between her legs and over Sam's erect cock.

When she opened her eyes again, his questioning gaze locked onto her. "What is it?"

What did it say about herself that she wanted to try this? What did it say about Sam if he was willing to as well? "There's something I want to try."

"Oh?"

"I-I want you to tie me up. Gently, but—" His grip on her tightened and she could feel his dick harden and pulse against her wet heat. "Would that turn you on?"

His thumbs circled her hipbones, burning a spherical path, leaving heat tingling in the wake of his touch. "More than you can know or understand. It turns you on as well?"

She jerked a nod, nerves dancing in her belly.

He glanced around the room, his eyes settling on the gold cord tassels used to tie Cass's curtains back. Jess rolled off him, pulling her knees to her chest and watching him in all his masculine glory as he stood, untying the tassels from the windows. It didn't take long until he had one long rope held together by several knots.

Jess gulped. "Have you done this before?"

Sam sat on the bed, smoothing Jess's hair with his palm. "What answer would freak you out the least?"

"The honest one."

He nodded. "Then, yes. I've tied women up in the past."

Oh, hell. She thought she wanted the honest answer, but maybe she *didn't* want to know some things.

"Some women want to be tied up really rough—restricting blood flow to certain areas. Others simply want their movement restricted. You remember your safe word?"

"Sapphire," she noted, staring into his deep blue eyes, which always reminded her of her favorite gemstone.

"Have you been tied up before?" There was a challenge within the question, but Jess didn't want to lie.

"Yes, but not during sex."

There was a static shift of energy within the room. "When?" he demanded.

"Why does that matter? It intrigued me. And you're the one I want to experiment with. Why can't you just give me what I desire without questioning and needing to control my past?"

His expression softened, though not quite as much as it had been earlier. "On your knees," he said with quiet command.

Her body clenched, clit swelling as she did as she was told.

He moved gracefully as he took one wrist, pulling it behind her back, followed by the other. "Spread your knees." His voice was rough with a rawness that hadn't been there before and it raked across her skin. She scooted her knees apart. "Wider," he growled, and his voice sounded almost as dry as her throat felt.

He didn't possess the tender precision that Elliot did, but this wasn't about comparison. It was about trying something that caused her body to react. And react in ways she wasn't used to. Winding the drapery tassels around her, he coiled her arms together behind her back, finishing at the wrists.

"Is it too tight?"

She shook her head. It was tight, but not painful. "It's perfect," she said, and wet her lips, looking at his blazing eyes.

He advanced on her, pausing at her mouth before sucking her bottom lip and tongue into his. Scooping her body up, he rested her on her back. "Keep your knees bent open and put the bottoms of your feet flat against each other."

Her pulse fluttered, heart racing, slamming into her rib cage, but she didn't fight him. He grabbed the only tassel left from the last curtain and wound the cord around her ankles, tying her feet together. When he finished, he stepped back, admiring her. Or she thought he was admiring—it was hard to tell with his impassive expression.

"Don't you like it?" she asked after another painfully silent second.

His erection jutted toward her, thick and hard and completely ready for her. "I love it." She could feel that hoarse whisper in the depths of her body and they stood there, eyes locked for a moment longer.

"What now?"

His smirk twitched. "You sure about this? Wanting me to be in control?"

"Well, one of us is tied up and the other isn't."

A vibration grumbled in his chest and he closed his eyes thoughtfully. "With that sarcastic answer, you're lucky I don't have my crop here," he said.

His eyes darkened, dipping the length of her body. Her knees were still open, her vagina wet and spread. "And if you did?"

Bending at the waist, he brushed his fingertips over her pussy. "I'd spank you here. Not too hard . . . but enough to warn you that I didn't approve of your tone."

"I think I might enjoy that."

"Then you should disobey me more, apparently." He stepped forward, sliding Jess so that her head was at the edge of the bed, and positioned his cock at her lips. Her throat moistened immediately at seeing him up close like that and she opened up, taking him deep inside her mouth. He groaned and pumped his hips against her face before lowering his lips to her pussy once more. He dove his tongue inside her, pumping with a ferocity that mirrored her own.

His dick grew with each slurp and she curled her tongue around the head, nibbling the ridge and stroking the vein that pierced forth from the skin.

Another sweet release was right there as his tongue flicked skillfully against her clit. It was within reach, seconds away, and yet even if she tried, Jess couldn't get there on her own. And just as she thought she might explode, he stopped, removing his tongue from her as that orgasm faded into the darkness growing further out of reach with each passing second.

Jess whimpered as her nerve endings zinged alive.

His hands were on her again, fondling her heavy breasts, teasing her clit, pumping his fingers in and out of her tight pussy before he flipped her onto her stomach, nudging her hips high in the air. She heard the sound of a condom wrapper ripping and watched over her shoulder as he rolled protection over his solid length.

With a hard thrust, he buried his erection deep inside of her. He seemed to relish the feel of being deep and he paused, rolling his hips and hitting that sweet knot deep inside. Then he pulled back, his cock stroking its way back and out of her before repeating that same hard, pounding thrust, speeding up with each pumping motion of his hips.

With one hand, he spanked her ass hard and out of instinct that she didn't even know she possessed, Jess arched into his hand on her backside. His dick, hard and veined, stretched her, molding her body around his and he slipped his hands around her wrists, using the tassels as leverage to pull her body back against his even more firmly.

Reaching around, he fingered her clit, pinching and stroking until pleasure was spiraling and spreading through her body. "I won't come until you come again," he said through heavy breaths, and his body was sweaty against hers. "Come for me, baby."

A low, guttural sound escaped from somewhere so deep that Jess didn't even know it existed. She felt as if she were outside of her own body as her spasms took hold. She clamped around Sam's cock, releasing with each contraction. His release came quickly after hers, his cock pulsing as the tension in Jess's body eased.

Curling his arm around her waist, his hand settled on her stomach and he rolled onto his back, taking Jess with him, still tied up. Her legs flopped open, his half-flaccid erection still wet and pressing into her ass. She sighed, utterly satiated, and felt his lips land at the curve of her shoulder. Her bound arms served as the only barrier between their bodies and the pull against her muscles wasn't entirely unwelcome.

Questions swirled in Jess's mind. *What the hell was Sam talking about—not wanting to be my master? Isn't that the whole purpose of this lifestyle?* Waves of pleasure tingled down her body as his fingers stroked her torso up and down. He was tender in the movement, a sweet caress that wasn't meant to be sexual. And yet, it was. Jess wasn't sure she could be with him for life. She wasn't even sure she could forgive him for the past and all the lies. In fact, she was certain they were a long way from reconciling. And yet she wanted him here. She wanted to be in his arms. In his bed. In his life. And that desire to be near Sam was too strong to ignore.

She sighed, inhaling his woodsy scent. "You should untie me before I fall asleep like this."

He gently rolled her off him. "Only if you promise not to run."

"It's *my* house."

"Very well. Only if you promise not to kick me out." He slid his mouth over hers, his tongue parting her lips.

"Mmm. You win. You can stay . . . for tonight."

"Good." He slid down the bed to her feet, working out the knot at her ankles. "Because I had more of this in mind before we fall asleep."

21

The next morning, Sam's phone alarm blared from the pocket of his discarded pants. Jess flung her body to a seated position in bed, seemingly disoriented as Sam scrambled, reaching for the phone that was just an arm's length out of reach. Turning it off, he smoothed her hair and pressed another kiss to her temple as he guided her onto her back once more. Her hair fanned around her, the dark brown ripples draped across her white pillow like a painting.

"Sorry," he said, nuzzling into her for just a moment more. Was it possible? Had she already forgiven him for the horrible reasons he had pushed her away all those years in high school? It didn't seem likely and yet, here they were. In bed together, spooning as though no rift had ever separated them.

She moaned, throwing an arm over her face, shielding her eyes from the encroaching morning sun. "What time is it?" she croaked, and despite the fact that he hadn't brushed his teeth yet, Sam slid his lips up her jaw.

"Just after six. I have to be down at the precinct by seven, unfortunately."

Her eyes opened wide at that and she spun to face him. "The case?"

He didn't want to lie to her anymore. Never again. But he knew that by talking about her sister's case, he was putting both their lives in danger. After a heavy sigh, he nodded. "Maybe. I don't know. Your sister was involved in this new drug that's illegal in the US—"

"Biophuterol," Jess said, and a flash of regret passed across her features. Something unspoken tightened between them. *Shit. How did she know the name of the drug?* wondered Sam.

"What have you found out about it?"

She chewed the inside of her lip, but to her credit, she didn't shrink away from their eye contact. She held her own, even naked in bed.

"Not much. I just came across it and put it all together. So, this case you're going in for this morning—you're not sure it has to do with Cass, but it involves her drug?"

"Pretty much, yeah." Sam pushed off the bed, grabbing his pants and sliding them on. "Just a teenage user. He robbed a gas station and we found the pills with his arrest. I'm hoping I can trace the drugs back to where he initially got them and then maybe the path will lead to whoever is the boss of the ring— and also Cass's likely killer."

"Maybe I could come with you—"

"Jessie, no. Jesus . . ." He tucked his shirt in, sitting on the edge of the bed and doing his best to explain calmly. "You get why that's a bad idea, right? You *have* to get why we can't do that. You said yourself last night, we're not even supposed to be seen talking to each other. It's one thing if we're both called into a crime scene. But ultimately, they want you out of town and away from me. They want you to stop shoving your nose where it doesn't belong." He cupped her jaw and traced his thumb down the edge of her ear to her chin. "I'm good at my job. Let me do this."

"But—"

"You coming in with me to the station? Us leaving this house and driving together? It's a terrible idea. I *know* you know that."

"I know," she said, aiming her eyes at the bedspread and picking at invisible lint. "I just really want to catch this bastard."

Those brown eyes were velvety soft, like milky chocolate. They tore into his heart. "I know. We want the same thing. We just have to be smart about this."

She pushed onto her knees, still nude, skin soft, and wrapped her arms around Sam, tugging him against her body in a kiss. His erection came on swiftly, pushing into her belly. "Does this mean you forgive me?" he said, nipping at her earlobe.

She sighed, falling even further into his arms and resting her cheek on his shoulder. "Almost."

"Anything I can do to speed it up?"

She pulled back, peering up at him and Sam couldn't help himself. He ran his hands across her nude flesh, softer than satin and even smoother pressed now against his body than it had been in his memory. When she didn't answer his question, he pulled back, grabbing his wallet and stuffing it into his back pocket. He kissed her once more. "I understand you need more time. Take as much as you need." He squeezed her hand and as he turned to leave, she held on, tugging him back into her as one side of her mouth lifted into a mischievous grin.

"Uh-oh," Sam said, tossing his keys back to the floor. "I know that look."

"What look?" she asked in mock innocence.

"On your hands and knees, Walters," he demanded, but softened the order with a smile.

She licked her lips and dragged her own hand down over her breast, landing at her damp sex. "Make me."

"Oh, babe. Don't say things you don't mean."

* * *

Ten minutes, a shower, and two orgasms later, Sam left through the back door, making sure it was locked behind him. Whoever was after her clearly wanted Jess nowhere near him or the case involving her sister. And that's all they needed to see—him sneaking out of her house early in the morning. Luckily, he had parked down by the street near the wharf, only a five-minute walk away.

Sam scaled Jess's fence—which admittedly wasn't all that tall to begin with—and landed in her neighbor's yard. To be safe, he ran the back way around—an extra two blocks—so as to not attract attention before getting in his car and going to pick up Matt.

He pulled up to his friend's house on the outskirts of the city. One of the reasons Matt and Kelly had chosen their house was specifically because of the infamous jogging path around the Back Bay—a six-mile loop that Kelly was convinced living near would get Matt to join her in runs.

Sam snorted at the thought as he pulled into their driveway and gave his horn a quick honk. Kelly knew Matt almost as long as he had. The kid had barely run when he was in high school. Why she thought he would take up running in adulthood was beyond Sam.

Matt came out his front door and Kelly was there with baby Grace in her arms, her hair piled in a messy bun on top of her head. She gave Sam a wave and kissed Matt before he got in the car.

Matt gave Sam a once-over, eyebrows nestled low over his eyes before they lifted along with his grin. "Same clothes as yesterday, huh?"

Sam ran a hand through his wet hair. Thank God he had thought to shower at Jess's quickly before leaving. If he'd come to pick Matt up smelling like her perfume, he never would have heard the end of it. "Laundry day," he muttered, and skidded out of the driveway.

"You're also late," Matt said, buckling up and settling into Sam's passenger seat.

"Look in the backseat," Sam said, speeding toward the station.

"Doughnuts!"

Sam smirked. *Do I know my buddy or what?* Even though he knew Matt would still likely see through his "laundry" excuse, the powdery doughnuts were the perfect distraction to draw attention away from him. "Just a little celebration for getting our duo back together."

And just like that, Matt let the Jess conversation drop. By the time he had finished his doughnuts and coffee, Sam was backing into a spot right outside the precinct. That was the nice thing about getting there hours early.

Sam grabbed the extra coffees and the hidden bag of doughnuts he had tucked under his seat so that his partner wouldn't find them. He locked the car as Matt wiped the powder from his goatee. "You tell Rodriguez I was coming back today?"

Matt nodded. "Yeah. She might still shadow the both of us, though, if that's okay. Straimer wants her to get more experience on the job."

Sam held the door open for Matt as he walked in. "It's okay by me."

Matt led the way down to the holding cells on the lower level, providing Sam with info as they went. "Dylan Delansky. We've still yet to get Delansky's parents on the horn." The elevator opened and Matt passed Sam the files. "There you go. Work your magic."

Sam stepped out of the elevator, eyeing the kid asleep in his cell.

Before he woke up, Sam slipped inside the interview room and set up the coffee and doughnuts for Dylan. He hit the temperature on the thermostat, making it warmer, more comfortable, and pulled over the cushioned chair that was softer and more plush than the others. Sam paused, looking around the room. Two-way mirrors were on each wall for the two separate observation areas and Sam dragged a chair underneath the video feed, turning the cameras on.

Sam quietly opened Dylan's cell, gently waking him. The boy's eyes were bloodshot and he jerked awake. "Hey, Dylan," Sam said, leading him into the interview room.

"Hi," Dylan grumbled as he pulled his faded T-shirt up to his face, wiping the sweat off his forehead.

He blinked, rubbing his eyes, but became immediately more alert as he took a seat in front of the assembled breakfast. Dylan licked his lips, eyeing the food as though it was some sort of trap and ran his hands through russet-colored hair.

"I thought you might be hungry." Sam gestured to the breakfast. "Go ahead, eat."

"R-really?" But the question was barely out of his mouth before he was stuffing a doughnut into his mouth.

Sam sat back in his chair, reading through Matt's and Laura's notes on Dylan's arrest while he ate. Sam hated watching kids like Dylan come in . . . kids whose parents had failed them. It was a bitter reminder of Sam's own childhood.

Dylan gave a satiated moan and he sipped the coffee. "Hey—why am I still here?" he asked through doughnut crumbs. "I already told you I did it. I robbed the gas station."

"Yep, you did. You confessed." Sam tapped the legal pad with his story written down on it in messy, hurried cursive. "But there's something we need to know even more than the Irving robbery."

"What's that?" Dylan licked his lips nervously, eyes darting back and forth at the observation mirrors that led to two different rooms for viewing the interrogation.

"Look, I know cops always say this . . . but it's just you and me here. No one's back there. I want to get you out of here. *You* want to get out of here. But I need your help." Sam rested his elbows on the table, tossing the blank legal pad to his side.

"What do you want to know? It's not like I got much from that stupid robbery. Some cigarettes and a hundred bucks."

"Yeah. Exactly," Sam said. "And that little robbery is enough to send you away for a few years and fuck up your whole life. You get that, right? You got someone I don't know about who's willing to cover your lawyer fees? Because trust me, they don't come cheap."

Dylan's eyes settled on a spot on the wall somewhere behind Sam. "I'll figure it out," he said, but his voice was hollow.

"Yeah. You'll get appointed a city defender who has too many cases just like yours. You'll get ignored until your trial day and he'll read about your case on the commute in over his morning cup of joe. He'll barely have enough facts to stumble through your trial—"

"What's your point?" Dylan said, heated. He sat up straighter.

Sam felt the urge to smile but repressed it. He was getting to him. *Well, good.* He was saying exactly what he needed to get information, but that didn't make it untrue. "My point is you will go down for this. It'll be more than a little community service this time. You're no longer a minor. You're not a first-time offender—"

"They can't use my juvy record in the trial—"

"Doesn't mean they won't try to," Sam said. "There's a chance I can get these charges lessened though. If you tell me where you got your Biophuterol."

"My what?"

"Your drugs, Dylan. The O. Where'd you get your O from?"

Dylan fell back against his chair. "Man, if I tell you that, I'll have a target on my back as soon as I step out of here. They don't let snitches walk away. And that stuff's harmless. I don't do the bad shit—never touched cocaine or heroin. Don't mess with meth. Just some pot and some O. Feels fucking good, but no worse than a few cups of coffee."

"Who's telling you that?"

He shrugged, avoiding Sam's glare. "Everyone. It's just red tape keeping it from being a legal prescription drug here. You can apparently get it easy in Canada."

"Oh yeah? Guess they didn't tell you that we've seen a handful of OD's on Biophuterol lately, huh? About how the increased oxygen to your brain and organs causes your heart rate to increase to dangerous levels?"

"What? No—"

"Yes. It's a drug meant for people whose hearts aren't working properly. But if healthy people use it, it's dangerous."

For a moment, Sam thought he was getting through to him, but then Dylan shook his head, crossing his arms. "You're just trying to scare me."

"Dizziness. It starts with dizziness and escalates from there. It's *not* as safe as a cup of coffee. Unregulated and in the wrong hands, this is dangerous. And people are dying. You tell me where you're getting it and I'm sure I can get these charges lowered to a misdemeanor. Some community service and that's it."

Dylan stared at the ground, scuffing his toe against the linoleum. "And no one would know I told you?"

"Just me and a small group in my team. That's it."

"Would I have to testify?"

"Let's take it one step at a time. We're not looking for a pusher on the street. We're looking for the head of the operation. We wouldn't put you in danger to testify for someone small."

There was a long moment of silence that settled densely between them. Dylan stretched his neck, wiping at his face with both hands. "Okay."

Sam waited, not saying a word for fear that the kid would get cold feet. "I get the stuff down at the free clinic."

"The free clinic?"

"Yeah. I really don't know from who. You just go there and say you're feeling tired. You have to say the code: 'It's like I'm carrying a watermelon on my back.' When the doctor leaves and you're alone in the room, you put your money under the exam table. Then when you check out after, the pills will be behind the clinic, taped to the side of the Dumpster."

"How much do you leave under the exam table?"

"Two hundred dollars gets you a small bottle of pills."

Sam paused, chewing the edge of his pen. "So . . . the doctor you see. He's your dealer?"

Dylan leaned forward, a sudden urgency in his eyes. "That's the thing. I don't think so. The last two times I went there, the doctor had no idea what I was talking about. Even said, 'What the hell are all these kids talking about watermelons lately?' He had no fucking clue."

"Do you remember his name? That doctor? Or any doctors."

"Dude, I've got no clue. He was young for a doctor, I guess."

Young. Sam dove into his pocket, retrieving his phone, and did a quick image search. "Was it this guy? Dr. Moore?"

He held his breath as Dylan squinted, examining the picture. "Nah. I don't think so. Around that age, though."

Sam's blood ran cold. "One more question." He did another image search for Dr. Richard Brown, finding the same photo they'd been showing around during his homicide case. He held up the phone to Dylan. "Is this the doctor?"

"Yeah! That's him. Look at those fucking chompers. Whiter than the goddamn snow."

Dr. Richard Brown. He must have found the drug operation going on in the clinic and that's why he died. It had nothing to do with Zooey. Jess was right—Zooey was being framed.

Sam glanced at the picture on his phone before tossing

it onto the table. "You're certain this was one of your doctors?"

"Yeah, that's the guy," said Dylan.

"And he had no idea about the selling of O at the free clinic?"

"Man, I don't know. I mean, based on his reaction, I doubt it."

That's about as good an answer as he was likely to get. Sam slid a notepad over to Dylan. "Can you write all of that down and sign it for me?"

The kid nodded, taking the pen. Sam stood and Dylan's eyes followed him as he got to his feet. "You did good, Dylan. Thank you. I'm gonna work on getting you out of here—just sit tight, okay? Need anything else for now?"

"Nah. I'm good." Dylan shook his head and sunk back into the chair.

Sam left the room, locking the door behind him. As he moved to pull out his phone to text Matt, he looked up to find his partner and their captain walking right toward him. "Hey, guys," Sam said, dragging a hand down his face and over his stubble. Damn, he needed to find time to shave before he saw Jess next.

"McCloskey, what the fuck do you think you're doing?"

Sam steeled himself for a battle. He knew this would happen. Knew he broke protocol by coming down here alone. He also knew he could get the information they needed. And with a mole in the precinct? The fewer people listening in on his interviews, the better. "Getting the break in the case we needed," Sam said, handing over his notes from the interview with Dylan to them. "Brown's death is definitely connected to the O that's been on the streets. And Dylan gave us the information we needed to break it open. Can we cut him a deal for his cooperation?"

Straimer quickly flipped through the notepad. "Please, at least tell me you hit *record* on the cameras in the rooms?"

Sam nodded. "I'm not a total moron."

"No, you're just a James Dean wannabe," Straimer muttered, and Matt stifled a chuckle from beside him.

"Except I've got a cause. A damn good one."

"I think we can get this kid off lightly, maybe charge him with a misdemeanor. As long as the Irving gas station's owner isn't pressing charges I'll have Rodriguez start his release."

"Can we trust her?"

"You worked with her. What's your take?" Straimer asked Matt.

For the first time in years, Sam saw a darkness shadow Matt's features. Matt's jaw clenched and his cheeks turned a fiery red as he shook his head, not answering.

"What's up, buddy?" asked Sam.

"Is *she* trustworthy? Is she? Are you seriously going to let her in on whatever the fucking mystery is before you tell *me*? Your own goddamn partner? What is going on? If you expect me to be of any help on these cases, I need to know everything. Especially with how often Sam is landing in the emergency room these days."

The doughnuts from earlier turned in Sam's stomach as he looked to his captain. "He's right. Matt deserves to know."

The captain gave a tight nod, turning on his heels and backing toward the elevator. "You're right, Matt. You've earned our trust. Earned it long ago. Don't blame McCloskey. He was following orders by keeping the case a secret. Go take a coffee break, you two. Sam, fill Matt in on everything. And let's arrange something at the clinic for as soon as possible. Try to find whoever is in charge of getting this O on the streets." He turned, hitting the elevator button. "Oh, and Sam? Did you check the observation rooms to make sure they were empty before you started?"

Sam froze and a chill skittered down his body. He hadn't. He had completely forgotten to make sure they were locked up.

But it was really early in the morning. No one had known he was coming in today. "Of course," he answered. There was no need to worry the captain unnecessarily. But the words nearly got caught in his throat as he spoke. "What am I, a rookie?"

Straimer nodded, stepping in the elevator. The doors closed and silence buzzed between Sam and Matt when they were left alone. "You didn't check shit in either room, did you?" Matt asked, a playful grin sliding across his face.

"Totally fucking forgot." Sam dove a hand into his hair, his lack of sleep catching up to him.

"Well, let's check now, huh?"

Sam couldn't help but worry the inside of his cheek as they moved toward the side door off the interview room.

Matt's hand hovered over the doorknob to the first private room and he swiftly turned the knob, swinging it open to reveal an empty room. A smile flicked up at the corners of his mouth. "See? Nothing to worry about."

Sam peeked in around him, relief initially taking hold where stress had been moments before. But just as he was about to relax completely, his body stiffened. On the corner of the table was a white paper cup with a coffee lid on it. Matt followed the direction of his glare, landing on the cup.

"Dude, that could be from anyone yesterday who just forgot to throw it away."

Sam slid past Matt's shoulders and gripped the cup, inspecting it. "It's still warm." Matte red lipstick stained the lip of the coffee lid and he pried the plastic off, peeking inside, smelling. Sweet. Chicory coffee. With cream.

Sam peeked out into the open area where the cells and the elevator were. This section of the Portland Police headquarters was small. Not a lot of places to go or hide. And not many people were bustling around. Whoever had snuck down here wouldn't last long in the shadows.

"Maybe they moved into the other room?" Matt said.

Sam gave a quick, jerky nod, pressing a finger to his lips as they slipped out and moved in front of the second door. His hand hovered at the doorknob and he took a deep breath before giving it a quick twist and shoving the door open. A sharp yelp came from inside the room and he nearly slammed into a stunned Jess.

22

Damn. She should have known he would find her. To be honest, Jess was prepared for Sam to walk in and find her in the observation room the whole time. But when his interview with Dylan ended, she had thought that maybe—just maybe—she had gotten away with her flimsy attempt at espionage.

After he left her earlier, Jess knew Sam had to pick Matt up and that they would inevitably stop for doughnuts or coffee, so she had dressed quickly and rushed to the precinct.

Apprehension trickled down her spine and she ignored the impulse to shiver, instead standing tall as she faced Sam. She'd expected him to be livid, but he looked amused more than anything.

"You're lucky it's just me," she said.

"I am lucky, aren't I?" Sam said, his eyes crinkling in the corners.

"Well," Matt said, and cleared his throat. "I'll go check that Rodriguez is on top of the release papers." He backed out of the room, also hiding a grin as he gave a quick nod hello to Jess. "See you upstairs in a minute?" he said to Sam.

"Sure thing."

When they heard the elevator ding, Sam checked to make sure they were alone. Once Matt was gone, Sam rushed to her, closing the space between them and claiming her lips, pressing her body against the wall. His tongue curved into her mouth, a seductive caress, and his hand brushed over her nipple and down her waist.

Without thinking, Jess responded, her legs parting for him as his thigh found its way between hers, adding pressure and a delicious tension.

He pulled back, smoothing her hair behind her ears. His eyes traveled her face, settling on her lips. His soft gaze quickly crumpled into confusion and he brushed his fingers across her bare lips.

"You're not wearing lipstick."

She shook her head, confused. "No."

"Were you earlier? Did it wipe off?"

She shook her head again. "I just put on some ChapStick earlier."

"Did you bring coffee with you this morning?"

"Coffee? Sam, what are you—"

"I'll explain in a minute—just please answer me! Did you bring coffee?"

"No. I was rushing out to beat you here."

"Fuck," he cursed, backing out the door and ran into the opposite observation room. Jess followed behind him as he lifted a cup from a table inside. Without looking at her, he shook his head. "Someone else was in here listening, then." He turned, holding up a cup with lipstick staining the rim.

Jess walked forward, careful not to touch the cup. "Fingerprints," she said. "Have it swept for prints."

"Easier said than done. The amount of red tape involved is crazy. They'd want to know why and for what case. Not to mention I'd have to admit to Straimer that I fucked up and lied about checking the rooms."

Tension bristled in Jess's back. *Lied.* Sam lied. He was a liar. Not only to her, but to the community. To his boss.

She could feel herself pulling away again, but before she could, he said, "I might as well get it over with, then, huh?"

That same stress that was weighted against her shoulders released briefly. "You're going to come clean?"

He studied her for a long moment. "Yes. I told you—no more lies. I don't want to be that guy anymore."

Warmth spread in her chest and she launched forward, wrapping her arms around his neck as hot, salty tears filled her eyes. "Even though I lied to you this morning?"

"Yeah," he said. "That kind of sucked, but I understand why. I'm more concerned that someone saw you coming here. You need to be careful. They can't think you're still looking into this."

"I know, I know. But I'm still a photographer for the Portland Police. It would make sense that I'm here."

"Not down here in the interrogation area. And someone else was already here and maybe saw you arrive."

Damn, Sam was right. Whoever was stalking her seemed to always be one step ahead. Jess picked up the coffee cup, inspecting the rim.

"What are the chances you got here before whoever this is?" he asked, disrupting her thoughts.

"Not likely. She was here first. When I arrived this room's viewing area was already locked. I just figured they were always locked and I got lucky that the other wasn't."

"They *are* usually locked. Whoever this is probably unlocked both doors before I got here so she could easily hide from me. But then you arrived and she couldn't slip into the other room."

The shade of red lipstick was so familiar to Jess. An eerie feeling passed through her as she remembered the scarlet lipstick she had seen on one of Cass's mugs the day she first arrived at the house.

Sam squeezed her arm, pulling her back to the present. "It's possible that she left early when she knew you were down here, too. Too much risk of getting caught—maybe she heard nothing about the free clinic."

Jess gulped. "Maybe."

A few more seconds of silence ticked by and as Sam removed his hand from her arm, Jess couldn't help but feel empty without his touch. "So . . . is Cass's murderer a woman?"

"It doesn't seem to fit the pattern. But she could be our mole here at the station."

"Or it could be a smart man, using lipstick to throw you off." Sam seemed to consider that a moment as Jess lifted the cup again. "It's one clean lipstick smudge. On a coffee cup. A cup that's two-thirds of the way empty," Jess said, thinking out loud. "Have you ever seen one of these lids after a woman with lipstick finishes a cup of coffee? It's smudged everywhere. Unless you have perfect precision with each sip, drinking a whole cup of coffee will never result in one mark."

"Huh," Sam grunted, taking the cup from her and turning it over in his hands. "But a smart person wouldn't have left the cup at all. They're fucking with me, maybe," he said, slamming the cup onto the table.

"But why? What the hell is the point of that? Why risk it?"

"These people don't act rationally, Jess. It's a game to them. It's fun. I should get back to Dylan. Get him out of here. But—can I see you tonight?" There was a hopeful gleam in his eyes as he dragged his knuckle across her cheekbone.

For a moment, a spark ignited inside of her at the prospect of seeing Sam again this evening. "I—" *Shit. No.* She had to see Elliot tonight. "I can't," Jess sighed. "I have plans."

Though he nodded, disappointment washed across his face. "Okay."

Okay? Where were the questions? Why wasn't he grilling her about where she would be? Where was the demanding Sam that she knew so well?

"Besides," she continued, testing her boundaries. "I'm not sure I've forgiven you yet."

Emotion twisted inside of her. She hated making him feel guilty. And she did love him. But because of Sam's mom, her parents were dead. How was she supposed to just move on from that?

"I know," he answered, lacing his fingers into hers. "But it seems like you're trying to find it in yourself to." That ghost of a smile flickered before fading once more. "And I'll spend forever trying to earn your forgiveness again."

Forgiveness is easy. Trusting him again is the hard part, she thought.

"In the meantime," he continued, "we just need to keep you safe."

"You mean alive."

"Preferably, yeah." He moved past her, where his bag was, and pulled out a burner phone. "Alive and uninjured. Call me on this if you need me. We know it's not tapped. And I check my cell several times a day for bugs, so I know that's safe, too."

"And what about Cass's house? What if that's bugged?"

"I can't be there to check every day. Just text me. That's your safest bet. And we can always find somewhere near here to chat." Gently, he brushed two fingers under her chin, tilting her head toward his lips. "In the meantime, here's something to ponder for the rest of the day, along with my unending apology." Jess's eyelids fell, her lips tingling even before Sam touched his mouth to hers.

He finished the kiss and led her out toward the elevator.

"When did you get to be such a softie?"

"I've always had a chocolate center. You're just melting it."

Jess couldn't help her laugh. "Excuse me while I examine the inside of my brain while my eyes roll in that direction."

He returned her smile with a wink, still holding the mole's coffee cup. "You stay here for a few minutes," he said, backing onto the elevator. "We shouldn't go up together." Then, darting a hand out, he stopped the elevator from closing. "Unless you want to go up first?"

Jess shook her head, shocked that he was asking her opinion. "No, you go. Matt's waiting."

His jaw ticked and she knew how hard it must be for him to leave her unattended in an area where someone wanting to cause her harm had just been. "Okay. I'll see you."

The doors closed in front of him, leaving Jess alone with Dylan locked in his interview room.

23

Jess waited ten minutes before slipping down the hall. She'd started at the precinct less than a week ago and its layout was still foreign to her. As she exited the elevator, she sighed, relieved that Sam and Matt were already gone.

Her phone buzzed and she reached into her pocket to check it. *Elliot.*

Tonight. I will pick you up at five. We will have a reveal of you as my new submissive at a small gathering of local folks in the community. Be dressed to dazzle. Consider this to be a soft opening of sorts.

Jess typed her response.

I'll be ready. As should you. It's the closest you'll get to any soft opening of mine.

"Walters!"

Jess froze. *So close.* The revolving doors were just fifty feet ahead and yet so far away. She spun to find Captain Straimer walking toward her, his mouth set into a stern line.

"Captain?" she said.

With a flick of his finger he motioned her to follow him as he walked. "My office."

He looked pissed. And there was any number of things he could be mad about. Her sneaking into the observation room. Not disclosing the information she had about Cass and Dr. Brown's connection. Cass's drug room—*oh, God. He couldn't know about that, could he?*

That feeling of dread flopped in her stomach, rolling around like a marble on a slick surface. She followed him into his office.

"Captain? Should I be nervous?"

"You talked to our suspect." Though his words were quiet, there was a dangerous undertone to them. A warning.

Zooey. He meant Zooey. Instead of admitting her guilt immediately, Jess played dumb. "Our suspect?"

"Zooey Devonshire. Our main suspect in the Richard Brown case. And don't play it so innocent. You were no good at pretending you didn't run your bike through my rosebushes when you were ten and you're no better at pretending now."

His hands were clenched tight, white knuckled, matching the same blanched silvery hue of his hair.

Jess sighed. "Fine. Yes. I saw her. She called me, asking me to come as her friend. I was going to be taken off the Brown case regardless, wasn't I?"

"I'm supposed to take you off the case, yes. With Brown's connection to Cassandra, it would be completely immoral for me to allow you to continue. But as our forensic photographer, technically, outside of another crime scene, your work with the case is done anyway. I know you know that. Your record in Kings County is flawless. And yet . . . I get the sense you're taking it on yourself to, let's say, continue your job beyond its scope."

The hairs at the back of her neck stood on end. *Damn.* He was astute. Of course he was—he had been a detective once himself. "Not really, sir."

His face softened at that and he gave her a small smile. "Sir," he repeated. "It's still weird hearing you call me that."

Jess smiled in return. "You prefer Uncle Fuzzy here in your office?"

His smile spread farther and he dropped his head, laughing. "No, please, no. The last thing I need the guys here knowing about is the nickname my best friend's daughter used to call me because of my chest hair. How ya doing, kid? As your friend— as Uncle Fuzzy—I'm worried about you."

"I'm hanging in there."

"Maybe you should take time off."

She shook her head rapidly. "Absolutely not. If I have free time, I'll spend it obsessing over every detail of Cass's death."

He studied her a long moment before nodding. "I understand that. Sam tells me you've learned some things about your sister on top of all this."

"Yeah. She was . . . well, something was going on. I just don't know exactly what or why she got so involved with Bio-phuterol."

"If it's any consolation, no drugs were found in her system. It doesn't appear that she was using."

"Great. So she was only *dealing.* Lovely."

She ducked her head away from his searing eyes and felt his hand land on her shoulder, giving it a gentle squeeze. "I'm sorry I failed you two," Straimer said.

"You didn't fail us—"

"Yeah, I did. I should have been firmer with Rose. I should have insisted that we adopt you. It's what your parents would have wanted. Then maybe Cass wouldn't have felt such pressure to take over as your guardian."

Jess shook her head. "You can't know that. We never found their will."

"I do know that." His voice sounded garbled, like he was talking through a fistful of gravel. "Your mom told me once. Asked me if anything happened to them to watch out for you two."

Jess had always suspected as much. She had never understood why her parents' friends had never stepped up to help them more. Oh, they helped in the usual ways. Sending food, checking in, helping monetarily as they could. But when Cass needed them—when she needed character witnesses to prove she was able to be a guardian, Straimer's phone line went dead. He and Rose had never returned their calls and never filled out the affidavit. And that hurt like hell, though Jess didn't want to guilt-trip the man. "Rose didn't want to help?"

She'd always suspected Straimer's wife wasn't as into the friendship with her parents as he had been. Straimer and her mother and father all went to college together. Rose had entered the picture later.

"No. Not because she didn't love you both. But because you were a constant reminder of the baby we could never have." Straimer cleared his throat and it was almost like watching a mask being put on. Jess could see him transform from Uncle Fuzzy back into Captain Straimer. "Anyway, I just wanted you to know that you can come to me. You can trust me with any discoveries you find about your sister. There's a mole in the precinct—myself, Sam, and now Matt are working on finding who it is. I don't even want you telling the force psychologist about what you find in case he's the leak—however unlikely that is. But if you need to talk, I'm here. And it won't affect your job. I promise."

"Thanks. So . . . for now, my job . . ."

"For now, you still have it as long as you want it. I put in a call for another photographer to be on call, in case another crime related to Cass's death pops up, but in the meantime you're all we've got."

"Such high praise," Jess said, and rolled her eyes.

"Hopefully, we won't need you for any more deaths related to this case. Hopefully all that's over."

"I hope so, too." But she didn't think so. It felt far from over. "You know Zooey's innocent, right?"

"I don't *know*. But I do think she's being framed."

"And you want me to stay away from her?"

"I can't tell you what to do. I can tell you that I think you're making yourself a target, the more you talk with her. But I can't tell you who to be friends with. Just use your head. And if you talk with her, you cannot reveal any details of the case."

"It's not like I have any, anyway."

Straimer walked to his door and paused, his hand on the doorknob. "I think you do. I think you know more than you let on, Walters."

Jess held strong, maintaining eye contact as he attempted to read her thoughts and body language. "Thanks for the talk," she said as she moved past him and out the door. Stopping just past him, she added, "Uncle Fuzzy."

24

Sam took another sip of coffee before putting it carefully back in the cup holder of his car. "So, that's about it. The night Cass was shot, I had seen her earlier at the party. I know it has something to do with the drug ring, but I still don't have a lock on who is in charge."

Sam shifted in his seat once more, studying Matt's pale face beside him. He couldn't risk telling Matt all the details at a restaurant or some other public place where they could be overheard. So as cramped as it was, they were eating their lunch in his car while he filled Matt in on everything.

"Cassandra Walters, a drug mule? That makes no sense," said Matt.

"Tell me about it. She was terrified of something. More accurately, *someone.* And it seemed like the closer she was getting to me, the stronger the threat against her was."

"Shit, man. You can't blame yourself, though. You didn't push her into that life."

"No, I didn't. But something did. And it makes you think— if Cass could get swept up by all this, just about anyone could."

"She didn't tell you why she started?"

"No idea. She had a good job, no debt that I can find, so it couldn't have been the money."

Matt's eyes widened. "Does Jess know any of this?"

A winding coil tightened in Sam's gut. He didn't want anyone to know Jess had knowledge of this stuff. He trusted Matt; he truly did. And after he and Jess had talked outside the interrogation room, he'd gone straight to Straimer, telling him everything, about how Jess was aware of her sister's situation and that neither of them believed Zooey could be the killer. And yet, he couldn't ignore that whisper of uncertainty. "She knows her sister wasn't squeaky clean before she died. But I think fear is winning out over her curiosity."

Okay, so it wasn't the entire truth. Jessie Walters never let fear win out over any aspect of her life. And based on the suspicious look Matt awarded him with, it didn't seem like he bought that entirely, either. It was easy to forget that Matt had known Jess for almost as long as he had. Had grown up alongside both of them. Lying to Matt was like trying to convince a parent that you were sick on the day of your final exam.

"So . . . she's just letting it go? Her sister's unsolved murder?"

Sam gave his best shrug. "For now, at least."

"Why doesn't she just leave Portland until we catch this guy?"

Damn good question. "You'll have to ask her that. I'm the last person she wants to talk with lately. Especially about this stuff."

"So, then how can you be sure she'll stop snooping around?"

"I suppose I can't be sure. I just have to trust her."

Matt crumpled up the paper bag holding the trash from their lunch and tossed it down by his feet. "This is a lot to take in."

"Unfortunately, we don't have a lot of time to dwell on it. We need to plan this undercover thing with the free clinic. And we need to do it soon."

Matt sighed and Sam watched as the doubt faded from his face. In its place was a steadfast determination. "You're right. It can't be one of us. We're too well known in this area. We'd be recognized right away."

Relief spread through Sam, mimicking the grin that spread on his face. "Glad you're on board, partner. So, what about that big guy going in instead of us—the kinda oafish one? Donnelly, I think."

"That guy? To go vice for us?" Matt snorted. "He's dumb as a pile of bricks. No way. He'd blow cover almost immediately."

"Jesus, Matt. Have an opinion, already. What about Laura? She already knows a little with us releasing Dylan on a misdemeanor."

"Rodriguez? I dunno. She's kind of green."

"That's good, though. The fact that she's new to the force. No one in town will make her as a cop."

"That's true."

"What did your gut say while you were working with her? That she's trustworthy?"

"Yeah." After a long pause, Matt nodded. "You know, I think she'd be good. She's a little too perfect sometimes—and that unwillingness to break the rules may be her biggest flaw. But for the sake of this case? Someone like that may be just what we need."

Sam chuckled. "I give her a year before she breaks protocol." He put his key back in the ignition and started the car. "Let's go see what Straimer thinks. If he agrees she's a good match, we'll get started. Maybe we can even have her prepped and ready to go in by this afternoon."

Matt slid his partner a doubtful look. "It would be the first time in Portland PD history that we got an undercover operation going in under twenty-four hours."

"True." Sam pulled out of his spot and eased onto the road. "But since this will be so small and concentrated to only four of us, I think we could manage it. Plus we've got Straimer on our side. He can call in and get equipment almost immediately."

"Yeah, I don't know how that guy pulls it off, but he can move mountains with a snap of his fingers."

Jess pulled into her driveway. Before she could even get out of her car, her phone buzzed in her purse. She scrambled to find it, putting it to her ear. "Hello?"

"Ms. Walters, it's Ernie Kemp, your sister's estate lawyer. I received some bad news today—the prospective buyer pulled the offer on your house."

"Gilles pulled his offer?" she repeated.

"One point two million was very overpriced—even for a home in the historic district."

"No, I know."

"Even still," Ernie continued, "it's a great home. I don't think you'll have a problem selling once you put it on the market."

She looked up at the giant pink house towering over her like some sort of castle. That would be true if it wasn't for the damn Easter egg color. "Thanks for letting me know, Ernie." She hung up, climbing the steps to her front door and stopped, midstride, her eyes landing on the frogs facing backward on the middle step. *Dane.* She looked around over the banister and sure enough, a few hundred feet down the street was his truck, parallel parked between a Toyota and a Ford.

With a quick glance at the time on her phone, she unlocked the front door, peeking her head inside. She only had an hour until Lyle would arrive to pick her up for the next Elliot submissive lesson. She entered, dropping her purse on the table beside the door. Dane sat on her couch and quickly flipped his arm up, covering his eyes. "Don't shoot," he said, grinning from behind his tanned forearm. "My eyes can't take another blast of pepper spray."

"Don't worry," she said, holding both palms out. "I'm un-armed."

Dane pushed off the couch, but Jess waved him to sit back down and plopped down beside him, being sure to keep a couple of feet between them. "So, to what do I owe the pleasure of your little visit?"

"You went to dinner with Elliot the other night." It wasn't a question. He wasn't even attempting to disguise it as one.

Jess's muscles bunched beneath her blouse. "Yes . . ."

"At his house." Again, not a question.

A furious heat sprouted from deep in Jess's stomach and, like a fireball, rose up into her chest with a ferocity she couldn't control. "Have you been following me, too?"

"Too?"

Jess shook off his question. "No. Don't change the subject. Answer me, Dane." She paused, crossing her arms. "Or should I start calling you *Daniel*," she said, remembering the way Elliot had used his full name to get under his skin.

Dane's face softened. He reached out and took a stray curl that had slipped from her bun and twirled it slowly between his fingers. Though their faces were far enough apart that it shouldn't have been intimidating, there was an intensity in him that caused a shiver to run through her. "Don't play the game if you haven't read the rule book . . . *Jess.*"

"And you still haven't answered my question."

"I didn't follow you," he answered. "I don't play that way."

Jess arched her eyebrow, not quite responding, but also not knowing what to say just yet. "So how did you know that I went to his home?"

"Lyle is a friend."

Jess dropped her arms, simultaneously letting her armor down. For now. "Why would he tell you that?"

"He's loyal to Elliot. The man signs his paychecks . . . he has to be. But he—well, we all know there's something that Warner is hiding. Something huge. And he was bad for Cass. Despite what he will tell you. She changed when they met. She became something else entirely under his tutelage. I'll never forgive myself for introducing them."

"You think he's why she got into drugs?"

"Believe it or not, this is about more than the drugs. This is about who she was. She used to have such joy. She laughed. She smiled." Dane's voice cracked and he grunted a curse. After taking a moment to compose himself, he continued. "She would literally skip down the sidewalk when we would go to dinner. But after Elliot . . . it was like a darkness took hold of her."

Jess found herself looking at a framed picture of Cass and Dane that sat on the mantel. They were hugging and seemed to be laughing, each holding a hammer. Jess couldn't imagine her sister skipping anywhere. "Maybe the joy was all a farce. A guise to get through life and hide the darkness."

"Maybe," Dane said. "But I doubt it. You didn't know her like I did."

Though that statement was true, it still hurt like a kick to the chest. "No, I didn't," Jess admitted. "Are you afraid Elliot will suck the joy out of me, too?"

"No. I'm afraid he'll stop you from finding joy and light. You're already consumed by darkness."

His knuckle brushed across the back of her hand and couldn't help the jolt she felt as his gaze seared into her. He stood, pulling his keys from his pocket and reaching for the door.

"Dane," Jess said, stopping him. "Tell me where you were the night Cass died? The truth this time."

His grip on the doorknob tightened. "I was at a gas station outside of Boston."

It was a lie. He knew it. She knew it. And he knew she knew it.

"Why won't you tell me the truth?"

"Let this go, Jess. I can't tell you anything more—"

"Can't? Or won't?"

He looked at her, darkness clouding his expression. "Won't. Because it would get you killed for sure."

25

Sam looked at his watch, sitting in the van across the street from the free clinic. Three-thirty p.m. Not bad for putting together a last-minute sting. They had Rodriguez's fake ID ready within an hour of confirming that she was willing to help out. Other than that, Straimer just had to pull a few strings to get the van with all the recording equipment. Matt now sat beside Sam and Straimer was across from both of them. Rodriguez was equipped with a microphone and a small camera. The three men watched intently as her video feed played on the screen.

Sam tapped his fingers against his bouncing knee. The muscles in his back were so tense that they were cramping between his spine and shoulder blade. "I should be in there," Sam grumbled.

"Are you kidding? They know both of us way too well these days. You'd be made before you wrote your fake name down on the waiting list," Matt said. "Give Rodriguez a chance. She might surprise us all."

Inside the clinic, it wasn't very busy. A handful of people sat around, coughing quietly into their fists or sniffling.

Sam took a deep breath and stretched his neck to each side. "You're right, you're right. I need to relinquish the control to her. You trust her, so I should, too."

But trust wasn't something you could just throw out there and expect to come easily. It was earned. And Rodriguez hadn't earned it yet . . . not from Sam, at least.

A man stepped out into the waiting room, wearing scrubs and carrying a clipboard. "Diaz. Maya Diaz," they heard him say via Rodriguez's microphone.

"Here we go," Sam said, as Rodriguez stood and walked over to the physician's assistant. He could feel Matt and Straimer stiffen around him as well. At least he wasn't alone in his concern. If they fucked this up, whoever was behind the distribution of Biophuterol would know to pull operations and run. He couldn't let that happen. This bastard, whoever he was, was most likely responsible for Cass's death. Wherever he went, Sam would track him down. He may run . . . but Sam would sprint to catch up.

"I'm Maya," Rodriguez said, keeping her movements sluggish. As she walked behind the PA, the men got a view of the clinic. It looked like your typical well-run free clinic. It was new to Portland, erected in the last three years and the latest project by Mercy Hospital to get medical care to more people. The PA opened a door to an exam room and let Rodriguez walk in first.

He took her blood pressure, pulse, checked inside her ears and throat before typing some things into a computer. "So, what's the problem today?"

Rodriguez repositioned herself on the exam table and the crinkling of paper beneath her was like thunder in the microphone. They could barely hear her speak over it. She stilled immediately, seeming to know her mistake. "I'm just so, so tired lately. Sluggish. No amount of rest seems to help."

The PA turned to face her, concern on his face. The detectives watched as he reached out, feeling her lymph nodes around her neck and jaw. "Any other symptoms? Fever? Nausea?"

Rodriguez shook her head. "Nope. Just exhausted. It feels like I'm carrying a watermelon on my back."

Sam's breath froze in his chest. They had the perfect shot of the PA's face. He looked confused. "That's weird," he muttered, turning to the computer and typing it in. "You're the second person today to come here with that symptom."

"Exhaustion?" she asked, innocently.

"Yeah. But specifically, the watermelon comment."

Rodriguez sat forward, bringing the computer screen into view of her hidden camera. *Atta girl,* Sam thought. For a brief moment, they could see what the PA was typing. Sam saw a glimpse of the word *watermelon. Bingo.*

"Must be something going around," Rodriguez said with a shrug.

The PA continued typing, staring at the computer screen. "I haven't seen any mono diagnoses lately, but we'll test for it anyway. Untreated, mononucleosis can be really dangerous."

The camera panned down to reveal Rodriguez's elbows pushing her breasts together and up as she moved closer to the PA. "I've always wondered . . . what do you write in our charts for these things? Is it like a transcript of what patients say?"

The PA glanced back at her, his eyes dipping momentarily to her cleavage. He licked his lips and then forced his attention back to the screen. "Uh, yeah. Pretty much. It's a policy we have here. I have to type what the patients say almost verbatim."

He stood quickly, nervous, and pushed his glasses up higher on his nose. Turning for the door, he walked into a jar of tongue depressors, knocking it over. "Crap," he said, bending to pick them up. Matt snickered from beside Sam at the scene.

"It's like he's never seen a pair of boobs before," he said.

The PA finished cleaning up his mess. Grabbing the clipboard, he moved for the door, mumbling, "Dr. Moore will be in to see you in just a moment."

Sam let out the breath he'd been holding, rubbing his hands over his thighs.

"So far, so good," Straimer said, his eyes still locked onto the video feed.

The camera jostled as Rodriguez bent down and she whispered into the microphone. "Taping the two hundred dollars now," she said as she bent to put the money under the exam table.

Just as she was back to sitting on the table Dr. Moore walked in. "Ms. Diaz," he said, "nice to meet you. So, you're feeling tired lately, huh?"

"Yeah. It's like no matter how much I sleep, I'm carrying around a ton of extra weight. My muscles are tired—like I'm walking around with a watermelon on my back."

Good, Sam thought, *Say it again in front of the doctor.* Sam wanted to see Moore's response to the phrase.

Dr. Moore paused as he locked eyes with Rodriguez. "O-*kay*. Well, let's have a look." He pulled his stethoscope from around his neck, placing it in his ears. "What do you do for a living?"

"I'm a barista."

"You drink a lot of coffee on the job?"

"Some."

"Well, there you go. You're on your feet a lot of the day. You're probably over-caffeinated and not getting enough REM sleep."

"I don't know. I'm sleeping through the night, but I just wake up so sluggish and it stays like that throughout the day."

"Tell you what. We'll do a strep test and a few other swabs to see. I doubt it's anything serious. Lay off the caffeine for a day or two and see if it changes your restfulness. I can prescribe you some sleeping pills if you think you need a little help."

"Nah. Sleeping pills make my head all foggy."

"Have you ever tried meditation?"

"No."

He did a few more tests before clicking his pen and writing something down on a pad. "Here. Let me refer you to this meditation center. I think it could help you relax and wind down after a long day." The music playing in the background changed and Dr. Moore paused, holding up his pen in the air. "Ah, I love this song. 'Witchy Woman,'" he said. "You know it?"

"Uhhh, no. Can't say I do."

"It's great. You should listen to it sometime." After tearing a piece of paper from the pad, he handed it to her. "Sometimes things like mono lay dormant for a little while so if in a week, you're still feeling this way, feel free to come back. It could be something more serious and maybe you'll change your mind about those sleeping pills. I can walk you out to the front. It sometimes takes a few minutes to get patients discharged and checked out of here." He paused, holding the door open for her and his eyes flicked to the exam table. "Unless you need some extra time in here."

Sam's grip on his knee tightened and he focused his eyes on Dr. Moore's face.

"Time?" Rodriguez asked. Her fingers tapped a few times against the edge of the table.

Dr. Moore's brittle smile seemingly relaxed. "You know, to gather your things or use the restroom, what have you."

"He's our guy," Sam said.

"Maybe . . ." said Matt.

"It's not enough. This video isn't enough to arrest, let alone convict," said Straimer.

"Nope," Rodriguez said on the video feed, and the camera angle moved as she stood up. "I'm all set in here."

"This alone may not be enough . . . but that's the guy. We need to poke around in his life more," Sam said.

Straimer grunted. "It's not even enough to get a search warrant, McCloskey."

Sam turned back to the camera feed and watched Dr. Moore hold the door open for Rodriguez as she walked back toward reception. "Nice to meet you again, Ms. Diaz. We'll have you in tip-top shape soon enough," the doctor said.

"Laura?"

Everyone in the van froze. Sam could feel even Rodriguez tense up through the screen. Sam knew that voice. But not as well as Matt did. When Rodriguez turned to face the voice, the camera captured Kelly, Matt's wife, holding baby Grace in her arms.

"Fuck me," Matt said.

26

Sam was on his feet so fast that the top of his head slammed into the roof of the van. He was fast, but Matt was faster, on his feet and rushing for the door. Straimer bolted ahead of them, blocking their way. "Give Rodriguez a minute!" he boomed, looking beyond them toward the video feed.

"What's she even doing here, Matt? Don't you guys have a family doctor?" demanded Sam.

"We do. Grace was running a fever last night—sometimes if Kelly can't get an appointment, she comes here for their urgent care facility."

"Laura," Kelly's voice echoed through the van once more, her smile friendly, lighting up the screen. "I'm Kelly. We met at the picnic this past summer—"

Despite Rodriguez's short red wig, Kelly had still recognized her, even remembered her name.

"You must be thinking of my sister," Rodriguez answered calmly. "I'm Maya."

Grace cooed, reaching out for Rodriguez just before unleashing a hacking cough. Kelly covered her daughter's mouth, giving an apologetic look at their undercover cop. "Sorry. Guess I have mommy brain."

"It happens all the time. We look a lot alike."

"Well, Ms. Diaz," Dr. Moore's voice came from her right side, and Rodriguez shifted so the camera was back on him. "Let's get you out of here and back to being energized, shall we?"

"Thank you."

"They'll take good care of you up front here. Be sure to drink plenty of fluids and eat well. No Dumpster diving, okay?"

Sam jerked his gaze back to the captain, holding a hand out. "Straimer, come on! Dumpster diving? It's gotta be him."

"If it is him, the video feed near the Dumpster will prove it."

Sam looked at the second camera feed, which so far had shown only three people since they'd first set up. One was an orderly, dumping some garbage. The other two were staff members smoking cigarettes.

The PA who had checked Rodriguez in came up to the group and spoke to Kelly. "Mrs. Johnson? We're ready for Grace."

"Nice to meet you, Maya," Kelly said, walking past them and following the PA to the back. Dr. Moore gave a wave and then also headed back.

In the van, the detectives gave a collective sigh, Matt dropping his head into his hands. "Thank God."

"See?" Straimer said. "I told you Rodriguez would cover it."

"If it was *your* wife walking into a potential crossfire, you would have run in there," Matt said.

"You've clearly never met my wife."

On the second video feed, the back door of the clinic opened and Sam stretched out his hand, shushing them. "Here he comes." Dr. Moore appeared, sipping a cup of coffee and chatting on his cell phone. "Fuck, why didn't we put a mic out there, too?" Sam asked.

"Relax," said Straimer. "We'll get him."

Dr. Moore moved toward the Dumpster and stood beside it.

"Who the fuck takes their coffee break right next to a smelly Dumpster?" Matt said.

The doctor bent down, pinching his phone between his shoulder and ear, and appeared to be tying his shoe.

"What's he doing now? Is there something in his hand?" asked Matt.

Sam shook his head. "I don't know. I can't fucking tell. What are the chances that the tech guys will be able to enhance this video?"

"It'll be worth a shot."

Dr. Moore's hand went out, just barely touching the back of the Dumpster before he stood back up, finished his coffee, and tossed the paper cup inside. After ending his call, he opened the back door and headed back into the clinic.

"Straimer, that's gotta be it. That's gotta be enough to at least arrest him, right?"

"Wait." Pulling the microphone toward him, Straimer clicked a button. "Rodriguez, can you get out of there? We need you to check if the drugs are at the Dumpster."

On the screen, Rodriguez was standing at the front signing some papers and very quietly, she murmured, "Mm-hm," into her microphone. "There you go," she said more loudly, handing the papers back to the receptionist. Then she moved swiftly through the front doors and around the side of the building until she came back into view on the second screen. She paused, checking to make sure no one else was around before running to the Dumpster. As she got closer and closer, a song started to play over her microphone. It was "Witchy Woman," by the Eagles.

Rodriquez got down on her hands and knees, feeling around, and yanked out a mini Bluetooth speaker.

"What the—it's not here," she said. "It's not fucking here. It's a speaker!"

Anger burned in Sam's gut as he pushed to his feet and

kicked the side of the van as hard as he could. "That son of a bitch. He was fucking with us the whole time. He knew we were watching."

"What does that song have to do with anything?" Matt asked.

"Raven hair and ruby lips..." Sam said. The lyrics were about dark hair and red lipstick—like the kind that stained the coffee cup.

"We don't know that Moore had any knowledge of us being here. It may be coincidence—" began Straimer.

"Are you kidding me?" Sam whirled around, nearly slamming into his partner and pointing to the video footage. "He specifically mentioned the Dumpster. He waited to make sure she had put the money under the table. He mentioned the song and then delivered a speaker out there just to fuck with us! He's our guy! We just need to get the proof."

"And we'll get it," Straimer cut in, packing up the equipment. "They all screw something up eventually. And when he does, we'll get him."

"I want someone watching him constantly. Twenty-four-seven," Sam demanded.

Straimer nodded. "We can arrange that. I'll run his plates real quick. You and Matt can take the first shift until I can get another team here to relieve you. Probably an hour or two."

Sam rewound the video footage, pausing at the moment Moore bent down next to the Dumpster. He spoke to the image on the screen.

"You're going down, fucker."

27

Even with Dane's unexpected visit, Jess was still dressed and ready by 4:50. *Pretty impressive, if I do say so myself.* She was armed in another one of her sister's dresses, a midlength deep purple gown adorned with a black pashmina, when the doorbell rang. After slipping her toes into her heels, she took the stairs quickly but carefully, and opened the door.

"Elliot," she said, shocked to see him.

"I'm only two minutes early . . . you shouldn't be so bewildered." Without waiting for her to invite him in, he brushed by her and into the foyer, rolling two enormous suitcases behind him.

"Well, yeah, but I-I just expected Lyle." She looked at the bags he was wheeling behind him. "Are you moving in?"

"Are you offering?"

She frowned at him.

"I'll take that as a no," he answered for her. "These are for the pills. We're going to move them."

"Now? Tonight?"

"Yes. We'll act as though I want you to bring some of your

things to my place after dinner, which is pretty standard for BDSM tutelage, and we'll throw a few of your clothes on top just in case."

"In case of what?"

"In case we get stopped." He didn't pause for her to soak it all in and instead made his way up the stairs. "And you should plan to spend the night at my house. To keep up appearances."

"I work for the police department. I cannot get caught carting around illegal prescription drugs."

"Yes, well, you also cannot get caught holding them in your home either, now, can you?"

Shit. He's right.

"But ultimately," Elliot continued, "it's your choice. I won't force you one way or another."

Jess took a deep breath, grabbed one of the empty suitcases from him, and carried it up the stairs. "Okay, fine. Only because I can't think of any other way to make this happen."

It took them a little less than thirty minutes to load up the luggage with almost all the drugs while also tucking in some of her clothes.

"Perfect," Elliot said, sizing up the now almost empty room. He snapped his glove higher on his wrist and grabbed the last of the drugs. "We should be able to squeeze the rest of these into a smaller bag and be done with it. Jess grunted as she hoisted the suitcase onto its wheels, pulling it behind her down the stairs. Before she even got two steps down, Elliot took the handle from her, lifting it along with his bag as though it weighed nothing. "Ready for tonight?" he asked, and despite the ease on his face, his voice sounded a little strained.

"How can I be ready when I have no idea what you're up to?"

"I told you. There's a small dinner party planned with a few other couples in the community."

"And you want to throw me in the ring? See if I float or sink?"

"Better to find out tonight than on tomorrow at the masquerade, wouldn't you say?" They made it down the first flight of stairs and Jess popped into her room, grabbing her camera as well as her sister's paperwork that she had taken from her office at Holtz Health Sciences and Pharmaceuticals. If she would be staying the night out on a quiet island, the least she could do is get a little more research done. Maybe there was something in the paperwork that would lead her to the right people.

She turned to find Elliot standing in the doorway, staring at her. Stuffing the paperwork and her camera into a duffel bag, she avoided his glare. "I have some work to do later."

"I see." He took the bag from her, placing it on top of the suitcases, and waited for her to lead the way.

When they got to the bottom of the steps, Jess grabbed her keys and purse. "So what are they going to be looking for me to do tonight?"

"They know that you're new and in training. It won't be as big of a deal if you do something outside of what a typical sub would do. Yet, something tells me this will all come rather naturally to you."

"Oh, really? Another one of your instincts?"

His lips tilted into a smile and, almost as though he had timed it, a lock of his dark hair fell onto his forehead. "Mock if you like, but I think you know I'm right. I was right when I knew your sister was a natural dominant. And it was the reason I was so reluctant to fall for her. Two dominants do not usually fit well together. In life or in the bedroom."

"So why the change of heart?"

He paused, his gaze tipping beyond her shoulder and up toward the ceiling. "It wasn't my heart that needed convincing. And eventually my mind lost the battle. As hard as I tried to fight it, my love for your sister far outweighed any desire I had to be dominant."

"But isn't your dominance one of the things she loved about you?"

He nodded. "Perhaps. And likewise, one of the aspects I

loved about her. I believe your sister was more of a switch dom—one who can go back and forth. And though I started as a submissive, dominance was always more natural for me. It wouldn't have been easy, us together, but I was willing to try."

Questions swirled in Jess's head like water whirling down a drain. She longed to know more about her sister. About this life. About how Cass first entered the scene. But as she opened her mouth to ask more, she chickened out and instead asked, "What do I need to do tonight? Will I be bound to a pole or something during dinner? Be on my hands and knees as your human chair?"

"All you need to do is obey me. Don't sit until I sit. Don't drink or eat unless I give you permission."

Jess snorted. "Can I speak? Will I get a cookie if I do well?"

"If by cookie, you mean orgasm, then typically speaking . . . yes."

Jess choked in indignation. "You will *not* touch me—"

"Calm down." His voice was quieter than normal and there was a glint of humor in his eyes. "You won't be rewarded like my typical submissives. Even if you wanted to . . . I couldn't. Not with Cass's sister."

Her throat was suddenly parched, her tongue like sandpaper gliding across the edge of her teeth. Before she could say another word, Elliot opened the door for her. "Shall we?"

Jess walked out first, dragging one of the suitcases behind her as Elliot lagged behind. Her heart stammered in her chest, fluttering with her quickening pulse. For there, walking up her front steps, was Sam. He took in her gown from head to toe and his smile was enough to melt any doubt or lack of self-confidence she had about wearing her sister's clothes.

"Let's hurry it up. My type of people are not the kind who appreciate the sentiment of 'fashionably late'—Oh." Elliot stiffened beside her and Jess watched as the pink flush in Sam's cheeks drained. Elliot cleared his throat and placed his hand on her hip. Though meant to be a comforting gesture, it felt like five blades slicing through her skin.

"Sam—" she tried, only it came out as a croak.

"Jessica," Elliot cut her off, glancing at her through the corners of his eyes.

Shock, then pain, marred Sam's gorgeous face. Moonlight cloaked him in a silvery blue sheen, the light from the front porch casting deep shadows in the hollows of his cheeks and beneath his eyes. All the noise from the street and the sidewalk faded behind them. Elliot's presence, as invasive as it was, seemed to melt away. All that was there was Jess and Sam, eyes locked.

After freezing for a second, he shook his head, breaking their bond, and backed down the steps. "Sorry," he spat. "I shouldn't have come." And with that, he got into his car and drove off so quickly that he left tire tracks in her driveway. Jess rushed down the steps to chase after him, but movement from across the street caught her attention. A hooded man was in the shadows, facing her, a camera obscuring his face.

Adrenaline swirled in her belly and soon spread like a massive wildfire throughout her limbs. Whoever that was—he was the guy. She could feel it. He was the man who killed her sister. Who'd been threatening her life, photographing her. The man who'd attacked Sam.

And as quickly as she saw him, the figure turned, running in the opposite direction.

Without thinking, she dropped the suitcase and, heels and all, sprinted after the man with the camera.

Before Jess got even ten feet down the driveway in her heels, she felt two massive arms grab her around the waist, pulling her back toward the house. "No," she moaned, kicking her feet out.

"You have to let him go," Elliot grunted in her ear.

"I'm not running after *Sam!* There was a man with a camera, photographing us from across the street!"

"What? Why didn't you say anything?! Where?" he said, rushing to the edge of the driveway.

Jess followed, looking around. "Goddammit! He's gone. He was right over there. He had a camera." They both ran in the direction she pointed, looking around them. "Shit. He was here. He was *right here*. We could have had him," said Jess.

This time, Elliot's touch on her hip was comforting as he pulled her back toward the house. "Come on. We shouldn't leave those bags unattended."

Reluctantly, she followed him. The man was gone. And Sam was gone, too.

She wanted to scream out. Shout that this wasn't what it looked like and run after Sam. Tell him that she had no intention of ever being with Elliot. That there were no feelings there other than a small respect for the man her sister had loved. But she couldn't do that. Not without explaining their plan, explaining the mountain of drugs in her sister's closet, admitting that she was now the *liar* and the fact that she was still determined to find the man responsible.

Elliot opened the passenger door to his BMW. "Get inside, Jessica. It's chilly out here." She hesitated, eyes still scanning the sidewalk. "*Jessica*," he barked. "Inside. Now. I'll take care of the bags."

Only a few minutes into their evening and Elliot was already barking orders at her. It was going to be a long night.

28

Sam sped away, leaving Jess in Elliot's arms on the steps to her pink house. He gripped the steering wheel so tightly, he thought he may wake up with blisters the following morning. How could she do this? How could she fuck him the night before and then go off on some date with Elliot Warner? The alleged master and organizer of Portland's largest BDSM party to date? Her needing time to forgive him, that he could understand. But sleeping with him and then turning around to date someone new . . . that was low. And if her goal was to break his heart—*well, mission fucking completed.*

He remembered back to when he and Jess had made love last week—how reluctant she had been to dabble in the BDSM world. His world. *And now?* Now it appeared that she was off with Warner as a submissive in training.

"Fuck!" He slammed the heel of his hand down on the steering wheel, something crackling behind his eyes and in the back of his sinuses. The light turned red, but he flipped a button on his dashboard, putting his police lights and siren on so he could blow through the light.

He grabbed his cell phone and dialed the one person who might know where Elliot might be taking Jess. The one person who might be able to get him in. It rang twice before her husky voice purred on the other end.

"Sam? As I live and breathe—"

"Mary." He cut her off before she could waste any time flirting with him. He and Mary, one of the few local female dominants in Portland and the owner of the best chowder house in town, had known each other for quite some time. Though they had never been together sexually, they shared a mutual respect. A mutual attraction that had always proven helpful. "Elliot Warner—he's going somewhere tonight. I need to know where."

"Warner?" she repeated in mock confusion.

"Do not fuck with me tonight, Mary. I know you know. You know everything in this town when it comes to BDSM parties. Tell me where they are going."

"I don't know what you mean, Detective." Sam hung up the phone as he pulled into a parking space outside Mary's restaurant. He slammed his car door shut and took the steps two at a time up to Mary's apartment above the restaurant. He pounded on the door.

Mary answered the door and if she was at all surprised by his presence at her home, she didn't show it. But that was Mary for you. Seemingly in control, even when she clearly wasn't. Her jet black, cropped hair was spiked up in back and smooth over her forehead in the front. Though she always wore heavy makeup, her eyeliner narrowed out at the edges in a thick line and her lips were painted a dark shade of red. Something Sam normally wouldn't have really noticed except for a lipstick stain on a coffee cup. He placed each of his hands against either side of the doorframe. "Wanna try that again?" he said, taking in her sleek evening gown, highlighting her svelte curves.

She clicked her tongue and sighed. "Oh, yes. I do recall a small dinner party of sorts for a few local dominants. Unfortunately, you weren't invited, it seems."

"Fuck."

"Unless you were willing to go as my sub tonight, I'm afraid I can't help you—"

"I'll do it," Sam blurted out before he could stop himself.

And for the first time since he'd ever met Mary, she looked surprised. "You'll what?"

"I'll be your sub tonight."

"You'll let me order you around? Force you on your knees?" She gripped his lapel, pulling his face nearly flush against hers. Her breath was minty and her lipstick glistened in the soft light streaming around her from inside the house.

"I won't fuck you," Sam said. "But yes, you'll have control over my actions throughout the dinner."

Her smile sent a chill tumbling down Sam's spine. He didn't like that look. Not one bit. But if he wanted to keep an eye on Jess tonight, this was the only way.

"Well, then, Private Dick . . . let's get you suited up."

The leather seats in Elliot's BMW were lush beneath Jess. More comfortable than her bed back in Brooklyn. Pulling the mirror open, she inspected her makeup to see that it was still in place.

"So, where are we going?" she asked him when he slid into the driver's seat after loading the suitcases into the trunk.

"It's a dinner party at Hugo's. We've rented the wine cellar for our private dinner party."

"They allow that?"

"With enough money fanned out in front of them."

It wasn't a long drive and after about ten minutes, Elliot pulled up to the front of Hugo's, where a young man in a suit was waiting out front. Elliot got out, came around to Jess's door, and opened it for her.

As Elliot held open her door, she asked, "Are we just gonna leave my luggage in there? Unattended?"

He lifted a brow, but it wasn't a judgmental or condescending look. "What do you propose we do? Bring the bags inside with us?"

She gulped. "No. Hell, if they were taken off our hands, maybe it would even be a blessing in disguise."

Elliot chuckled, handing his keys to the valet before placing a hand at the small of her back and guiding her through the door of the restaurant. Jess watched, fascinated, as he showed identification to the hostess. It seemed that they took this whole private-party thing very seriously. The hostess nodded and led them down to the wine cellar.

Downstairs, the floors were a cool stone that also lined the walls. Bottles of wine adorned cubbies in the stone walls and the room was encased by warm lighting and decorated with copper pots, hanging fruit, and garlic. The room was rustic and beautiful, with candles lit in old copper candleholders—the exact kind that Jess imagined Dickens had written his books next to. It was a wonder that the restaurant didn't rent the room out more often.

"Absolutely gorgeous," Jess gushed to no one in particular.

She felt Elliot's hand land on top of hers and he curved it around his elbow, offering her a smile. "Isn't it? Wait until you try the food."

"Well, well, well," a baritone voice boomed beside her. "If it isn't Mademoiselle Pas Sûr."

A large man from Jess's first masquerade party stood in front her, dressed in a tuxedo. His submissive, Lulu, was standing just slightly behind him, staring at the ground, her mousy brown hair falling in front of her face. As Jess opened her mouth to say hello, Elliot cut her off.

"Phantom, it's great to see you again." Elliot used the man's code name for the BDSM parties.

"Master X," Phantom said, and nodded in return. "You haven't been around the last couple of weeks. We thought we had lost you."

"Not exactly." Elliot turned, addressing Jess. "We may have to reconsider that title of yours now that you're becoming surer of your role in this world," he said, referencing the French meaning of her alias Dane had entitled her with.

Phantom's face lit up at that and his gaze sliced down Jess's body. If he had X-ray vision, Jess had no doubt he would be peeking behind her dress right then. "Are you, now? That's quite interesting. You seemed so uncertain at the party just a few days ago."

Elliot brushed an errant curl off her neck and tucked it into her French twist. His touch, though light, caused her pulse to kick up a notch and she couldn't help but flinch. "She just hadn't been introduced to the right dom, yet."

She took a deep breath, trying to relax into his touch. *We are supposed to be sleeping together, for God's sake.* His fingers on her neck should not have sent her into full panic mode. Her nerve endings zinged and she clenched her eyes shut, dropping her face into Elliot's shoulder for a moment. She'd been here two minutes and already she was overwhelmed. Peeking out from behind his suit jacket, she was met with Phantom's leering gaze. A shudder jolted down her body. She hated the way he looked at her. How he looked at Lulu, his submissive. And she hated how he treated Lulu like a pet, not a person. She wouldn't even look anyone in the eye.

"Lulu," Jess said, "It's nice to see you again."

The girl's pale face became an even more ghostly white and her eyes darted from Jess to Elliot, then back to Phantom before returning to that same spot on the floor.

"Excuse me, Phantom . . . it seems my girl has forgotten her role." Elliot's grip on her hand was tight—too tight—and Jess winced as he yanked her into the stairwell from which they had arrived. "What are you doing?" he said, fury dancing in the steely depths of his eyes.

"I was saying hi to Lulu. We met at the party—"

"You do not speak to other submissives. Not at a function like this. You may speak to another dominant if they address you first. That is all."

"Do you need me to massage your feet while I'm at it, too? Perhaps fix your drinks? Blow you beneath the table?"

"Don't get cute. And if you were my real submissive? Then, maybe yes. Maybe I'd have you suck me off right here, right now, in front of everyone."

Jess gasped, seeing the truth in his eyes. It was no exaggeration. This was his life. What he did on a normal occasion. Maybe even what her sister had done. She gulped, her throat dry. "You would not—"

"I would. And you as my submissive would fucking love it." The hard line of his scowl softened as he noted the look of horror on her face. "That's not likely to happen to any of the subs here tonight, though. This is a dignified dinner. We abide by rules of decorum—they tend to come first, above all else."

Jess nodded, but her throat felt tight. Elliot glanced back at the room where Phantom and a couple of the other local dominants were staring at them. Putting his hands on Jess's hips, Elliot turned her away from them against the stone wall. "They're all watching," he whispered. "If I don't punish you for committing such an offense, they will be curious as to why."

"What?" Jess hissed, her forehead pressed to the roughly textured wall. "I thought you said—"

"I *said* there would be no oral sex with dinner. I didn't say there wouldn't be power play."

"Wh-what are you going to do?"

"I'm going to spank you." He answered so simply, as though it's an everyday practice. *And hell, with him, it probably is,* thought Jess.

She clamped her eyes shut. This was nothing new. She'd been spanked before—but in the privacy of her own bedroom with a man she loved. And certainly not with an audience.

Elliot slid his jacket off and hung it on a rack beside them. Slowly, he rolled his sleeves to the elbows. "It will be three strikes. On top of your clothes," he said. "You will count them out loud—loud enough for everyone to hear, okay?"

She couldn't answer. How could she respond to that? She was a grown woman and she was about to get flogged publicly. And for what? For speaking out of turn? What decade was she living in? Hot tears sprang in her eyes and she looked up to the candle burning in a sconce above her. "Okay," she managed to squeak.

"Hands on the wall. Spread your legs and stick out your ass. It hurts less if you don't clench." He paused as she did as he asked. "And pull your forehead off the wall. I don't want you to hit your head."

Anxiety and pure mortification percolated low in her belly, her knees trembling with nerves or anger—she wasn't sure which. Maybe a strong elixir of both. She took a deep breath and, with closed eyes, gave a nod. "Okay."

His hand came down hard against her ass and she was thankful that her dress had ruffled layers. And yet it still hurt. It hurt like a bitch and she yelped, throwing her head back.

"Count, goddammit," Elliot muttered in her ear.

"One." The number was a strangled cry, and her sinuses burned with imminent tears.

She'd barely gotten the word out when his hand came down a second time.

"Two."

The third was the worst, landing hard in the center of her backside. "Three." She took a shaky breath, composing herself as his hand rested gently on her hip.

"Are you all right?"

She sniffled, hands still pressed against the stone, only now it felt heated beneath her palms. And rough, like her heart. "Humiliated," she mumbled.

"I need you to pull it together and turn around."

She did as he asked, slowly opening her eyes. The low-lit room came back into focus as she pivoted to face Elliot. His mouth was set into a stern line, but his eyes—those eyes were soft. Concerned for her. Over his shoulder, the room watched, all eyes on them. Phantom particularly seemed a little too interested and even Lulu seemed to pull her gaze away from the floor to stare at her dully.

Someone cleared her throat on the staircase to Jess's left. She turned to find Sam staring at her, his mouth agape, with a stunning woman leading him by his necktie down the steps.

29

He was numb. Sam was completely numb, from the tip of his head to the bottoms of his feet. No amount of abuse or punishment from Mary could top the pain he felt right then in that moment, watching Elliot spank Jess. Another man's hand on her. Hitting her. Humiliating her. That wasn't what Sam did. It wasn't what he was into . . . sure, he loved spanking in privacy, but not like this. But apparently, she *was*. For Sam, the lifestyle wasn't about asserting power in public. It was for them, alone, in the bedroom.

God, he was a fucking moron. Coming here, wanting to protect her. And from what? From the very life he had pushed her into? If this was what she wanted, maybe they weren't right for each other after all.

Only, he didn't believe that. And he didn't want it to be over. Flushed, Jess lifted her head as Warner finished and time stilled as their eyes met. Mary tugged Sam's tie, pulling him down the stairs like a dog on a chain. Sam gnashed his teeth together. He hated this. He hated being in a roomful of his fellow dominants and being forced into a submissive position. But above all else, he hated watching Jess be put in the same position. He would endure ten times the punishment if it meant she didn't have to. *But she wants to do this. She wants to be here,* a small voice somewhere in the recesses of his mind echoed. And that little voice was right. Jess was strong and opinionated. If she wanted to leave, she would . . . and she wouldn't look back. He knew that all too well.

Mary reached the bottom of the steps, pausing by Jess. Even though Mary was a couple of inches shorter, her presence towered over everyone. With a slow pivot, she looked back at Sam, green eyes sparkling with an understanding that wasn't there earlier. "Ahhh, Mademoiselle Pas Sûr," she purred. "It's lovely to meet again. I believe you know my sub for the night— Private Dick."

Jess pulled herself off the wall to a standing position, glancing quickly at Elliot, who gave a slight nod. *Permission. He was giving her fucking permission to speak.* A few strands of dark, curly hair fell from the base of Jess's updo and she nervously wrapped her finger around a stray strand. "Yes, we've . . . met."

Sam huffed a laugh. He didn't get far in his chuckle because Mary pulled his necktie harder, making it so that he was bent at ninety degrees, his face near her hip. "On your knees, Dick," she ordered, her deep-red lips curling back over her white teeth, revealing a wicked grin.

Sam cleared his throat, dropping to his knees at her side. From inside the room, he heard Phantom's chuckle and he darted a glare in the dom's direction. Instead, his gaze connected to a terrified-looking Lulu. Her eyes darted back and forth between Sam and Phantom and suddenly Phantom's chagrin at Sam's current position wasn't so humiliating. Sam knew that Phantom's submissive was fooling around with Dr. Adams behind the dom's back. The look on Lulu's face when she saw Sam confirmed that Adams told her he knew and that she and Phantom did not have an open relationship. Sam cringed at the thought of her in bed with either Phantom or Dr. Adams.

"Come, Dick," Mary stated, walking as though she wasn't still gripping his necktie like a leash. "Let's find our seats."

She dragged a long, leather riding crop along the floor. The rest of the party seemed to follow suit behind Mary, everyone taking their seats as well, with Elliot and Jess dropping across from Mary and Sam.

A server stepped to their end of the table and Elliot put in an order in for a gimlet and Chivas on the rocks with a splash of water. "She likes Woodford," Sam said to himself. But before the words could reach Jess's ears, Mary had a fistful of his hair, pulling his attention back to her.

"My goodness, you are chatty tonight, aren't you?" A rumble of chuckles rolled like a wave across the table. Mary looked at the waiter. "I'll take a Tempranillo and Sam here will have . . . hmmm, let's see . . . he'll have a daiquiri. Strawberry. Please be sure to put one of those little umbrellas inside."

"I'm sorry, ma'am, we don't have blended drinks—"

She clicked her tongue, looking back at the menu. "Pity. A cosmopolitan, then."

Sam inwardly groaned and from across the table, Jess's eyes were wet and watery. Something electric passed between them. An apology, perhaps? One that Sam didn't care to hear from her. If she was seeking revenge for all he had done to her, she had won. She did it. He didn't know how much more his heart could take.

Dinner was about as smooth as a cobblestone street. Mary kicked Sam's chair out from beneath him and made him eat on the floor on his hands and knees. He tried to put his own humiliation aside, eyeing Jess carefully whenever he could. She didn't seem to be enjoying being dominated any more than he did. In fact, if anything, she looked trapped. Broken. She was looking more and more like Lulu as the night went on. The vision made his heart ache even more than when he had watched Elliot put his hands on her. It wasn't that Elliot was an unkind master—no, quite the contrary. He seemed attentive and forgiving. He took his time to teach her rather than beat her into submission like he'd seen some dominants do at these parties.

But that was the difference between Elliot and Sam. For Elliot, this was life. He was cool and calm in his dominance, but it extended throughout his everyday life as well. Whereas in Sam's industry, even when he wanted to, he wasn't allowed to assert that sort of dominance. Even though there were times he wanted to. Still, he'd never had the urge to bring a woman into a restaurant and force her to eat what she didn't want to.

But if that was really the life Jess wanted . . . if Elliot was really the man she wanted, he would respect that. As much as Sam wanted to rip the necktie off his throat and throw her over his shoulder. It wasn't his place. Was never his place, really. He loved her, but at some point he had to let go. Not that he would ever stop protecting her, but he could do that from afar.

He'd finished his meal. While everyone else dined on the best steaks in Portland, Mary had ordered him steamed spinach. He sat up on his haunches, watching the table. A bit of movement caught his eye and he saw Jess say something to Elliot, her mouth brushing his ear.

Elliot nodded, standing up in a moment of old-fashioned manners as Jess rose from the table. He gestured up the stairs and to the left. What were the chances Mary would allow Sam to go to the restroom alone? With her bitchy attitude tonight and her propensity for embarrassing him, she'd probably force him to pee on a fire hydrant outside.

He waited another moment before speaking. "Epoly," he said, using her main alias, "I need to use the restroom."

Her gaze settled on the empty chair across from him before she turned to look down at Sam. "Of course you do," she said, her smile a little too polite for his tastes.

Sam gave her a nod, rising to his feet. "Thank you."

"Master X," she said louder. "Would you be a dear and escort my submissive to the restroom for me?"

Elliot's eyes flared like a wild animal as he glanced at Sam, then back to Mary. "Is that really necessary?"

"Whether or not it's necessary isn't really your choice to make." Her smile turned even more saccharine. "Now, if you're not comfortable, I can ask another man here at the table to escort him."

"It's fine," he answered quickly, dropping his napkin beside his plate. "I needed to go, anyway."

Fuck. Sam followed Elliot and he swore he could feel his balls shriveling with each step. Once they got to the top of the stairs, Elliot grabbed his elbow and led him to the bar. Sam looked around the restaurant. It wasn't packed, but for a weeknight at one of the most expensive restaurants in Portland, there were a handful of patrons enjoying their meal with no idea about the kinky party going on just below them in the wine cellar.

"Two Lagavulins," Elliot said to the bartender.

With a glance at Sam, he offered a smile. "You're no sub, Detective." It wasn't a question and yet, Sam felt the need to answer him.

"Well aren't you fucking brilliant? Planning to take that skill on the road? Get yourself on *Jeopardy!*?"

Elliot ignored his sarcasm as the bartender slid the two tumblers their way. Elliot nudged one toward Sam. "Nothing is as difficult as watching someone be beaten into submission who doesn't want to be there. Here. Have a drink."

"Is that so? Have you watched who you're sitting next to at all?"

Elliot's smirk flickered from behind his glass. "She's here with me voluntarily. She knows that she can leave at any moment. She's a quick study. Something tells me you knew that already, though." He paused, eyeing Sam's untouched drink. "Come on, Detective. Don't make me drink alone."

"You are not my master."

"And yet, I'm fairly certain that if I were to go tell Epoly you ignored an order . . . even from me, she would make your night hell."

"She'll make my night hell if I drink it or not."

"Suit yourself." He tipped his head back. "Now, I actually do need to use the restroom. Would you mind going into the ladies' room to check on Jess for me?" He moved for the door, pausing. "She's been in there a while and I'm getting worried for her," he said pointedly, loud enough for any passersby to hear. With that, he slipped into the bathroom.

Son of a bitch. He was giving them a moment. Sam kind of hated himself for it, but he was starting to sort of like the guy.

30

Jess stood in front of the bathroom mirror, staring at her reflection. She still looked like herself. Everything was in place, her makeup exactly as she had applied it earlier. And yet, she couldn't help but feel that she should look different somehow.

Grabbing some of the bobby pins at the base of her French twist, she pinned some stray hairs back in place. What the hell was Sam doing there? Getting publicly emasculated and for what? So he could keep tabs on her?

The bathroom door creaked open, but Jess didn't bother looking over. She kept her eyes down at the sink, rinsing her hands. The door lock clicked, causing the hairs on her neck to stand on end.

Slowly she shifted her gaze back to the mirror and gasped to find Sam standing behind her. "Jesus, Sam," she said. "What the hell?"

"Your master asked me to come check on you," he said, his voice deadpan. "Is anyone else in here?"

She shook her head.

"I don't know why I'm here, Jess. Why am I here when you so clearly want to be with him?"

She wanted so badly to correct him. Tell him that wasn't the case, but then, the whole thing would be blown and she and Elliot would be back at square one. "I don't know what I want right now, Sam."

"Is this to punish me? Are you trying to get back at me—"

"No!"

"So, then . . . you like that? You like being berated in public? Spanked for all to see? Do you know what goes on in the more hardcore groups?"

"I'm not totally naïve, Sam. Yes, I know."

"Why would Warner send me in here to be with you? He must know about us. He must see the way I look at you."

Jess gave a noncommittal shrug. "Maybe he's testing me?"

"No," Sam said, pacing the bathroom. "No, that's not his style."

"And you know him so well?"

Sam froze midstep and spun, pulling Jess toward him. "I know him better than you do."

Her nipples pushed against the thin bodice of her dress. Pressed flush against his chest, her hand fell naturally just below his shoulder, her thumb circling beneath his lapel. A flash of heat spread through her body and before she knew what she was doing, her legs were spread, flanking his massive thigh against her pulsing sex.

She parted her lips, looking up at him, and he moved his leg, stroking the very ache that throbbed for him. He studied her face as he picked up the pace, shifting his hand beneath her dress and pushing her panties to the side, stroking her wet seam, soaking the tip of his finger before circling her clit.

"Oh, God," she panted.

"You're fucking wet." He pushed an index finger inside her and she gasped, as though all the air had been sucked out of the room. "But for who?" he growled, cupping the back of her neck. "For him?" He swirled his finger inside of her, teasing the hard knot at her G-spot.

She shook her head. "No. Never for him. It's always been you, Sam."

He crashed his lips against hers, his teeth scraping her bottom lip. She dove her tongue into his mouth, wanting more of him. Every bit of him that he would offer. He pulled back, the look on his face delicate despite his masculine features. "Then why are you here? Why are you with him and not with me?"

It was a fair question. And one she still couldn't answer. With one finger still inside of her, he positioned his thumb at her clit, with a steady pressure that sped up in rapid flicks. "Make a choice Jess," he said, licking her ear, sucking it into his mouth. "Come home with me tonight. I'll do this to you all night long. I'll worship you."

Her body clenched around his finger, spasming, erupting like a Fourth of July fireworks display. She clutched his arms, his biceps flexing beneath her fingers. She pushed onto her toes, kissing him again. "I can't," she said. "But believe me when I say it's for us that I can't."

"What the hell does that even mean?"

"Think about it, Sam. Go home tonight and mull it over. Why would my 'master' send another man—a man whom I've clearly had a past with—into the bathroom with his submissive? Why would he allow me to be alone with you right now?"

Sam's face softened. "Because it's not a real relation—"

Jess kissed him, stopping his thought midsentence. "Don't say it aloud. Just know it. Know that what we have is real. And what he gets of me is not."

With that, Jess pushed off Sam's body, unlocking the bathroom door and peeking to make sure no one was watching before slipping back out to where Elliot was waiting.

Sam waited about thirty seconds before he opened the ladies' room door and walked out—directly into one of the other diners. The older woman yelped as he ran into her. Her eyes flitted between his face and the LADIES' ROOM sign on the door behind him. Sam stumbled against the wall. "Sorry," he said, making sure to slur the word for effect. "Walked into the wrong one."

He purposefully tripped over his own feet, landing hard against the wall beside him. The woman quickly fled into the sanctuary of the ladies' room. He straightened his jacket, and the ache in the pit of Sam's stomach grew as he moved closer to the entrance of the wine cellar. *What the fuck am I doing here?* Jess didn't seem to be in any danger at the moment. Elliot was the sort of dominant that every sub begged to have. Other than that initial spanking, he seemed like an attentive and very controlled dominant.

It wasn't a real relationship. *But why?* Why would Jess and Warner be pretending? For the same motivation Jess had had since she arrived. It had to do with Cass's death. Was it a front to convince the killers that Jess was no longer interested in him? Then why not just let him in on it? Let him know so that he wasn't going fucking nuts every time he saw them together.

His body went cold with that thought. But he had to put on a show. No one would believe that Sam just allowed Jess to walk away and be with this new dominant without putting up a fight.

He did put up a fight. And now he had to admit defeat—do his part for the audiences. He fought for her and lost—even subjected himself to Mary's humiliation in battle. He couldn't go back down there. And yet, he couldn't just leave. Not without Mary. So, instead, he took a seat at the bar and waited. He wouldn't order. That was against the rules. She would come for him.

And within a minute, he was right. Mary barged through the door into the restaurant, her eyes sparking with challenge when she saw him sitting there. But the fire in them quickly receded to a low flame as she moved to sit beside him.

"May I please have a scotch, Epoly?" Sam asked, careful not to look at her.

There was a rustle of leather as she sat next to him. "Two Glenfiddiches, neat," she said to the bartender. Then she spoke to Sam. "Private Dick, look at me."

He did as he was told, watching the slight nuances within Mary's expression shift as she attempted to read him. Even after the bartender put the two glasses of scotch in front of them, neither of them reached for it, continuing their stare down. Mary took hers, lifting it, her eyes flicking to his glass as well. Sam lifted his own glass. "You know, I've had a lot of subs in my reign as Epoly," said Mary. "Even though the things I make them do are on the grittier side, I can tell they enjoy it. Some love to be my pony for the night. Others get off on the power trip of serving my every whim. And there are a few that just love being tortured. Being emotionally shred into a pile, just so that it feels so fucking good when I finally satisfy them sexually. It makes their release that much sweeter." She took a long sip and Sam matched hers, the alcohol stinging the back of his throat. "But the common denominator is that they love it. And they always come back for more. You are the first to never come back."

"But I didn't leave," he said. They both knew he could have. And that in the grand scheme of things, it wouldn't have mattered two fucks if he had. It wouldn't ruin his standing in the community. He wasn't a sub and had no plans of ever being one again after this night.

"That's right," she said. "You didn't. That's honorable, considering I did the unthinkable to you."

Sam tried to think of what she was referencing exactly. She had put him through a lot so far.

"Making you drink a cosmopolitan," she clarified with a grin.

"That was pretty fucking evil," he agreed, swirling his tumbler.

"In any case, you're the first to not enjoy my tactics. And

when my sub is not enjoying himself, then I am not enjoying myself. Okay, well, I enjoyed it at first. But nonetheless, you're relieved of your duties for the night," she said.

Sam released a heavy breath and took a long, burning swig of the scotch. "Thank you."

With that, his tumbler was almost empty and Mary gestured to the bartender for two more.

"I shouldn't. I have to drive home and you have to get back to the party," said Sam.

She waved a hand dismissively at the door and rolled her eyes. "In a minute. I'm in no rush to rejoin those boring men."

"No?"

"Stuffy men with dainty dinners? Not my scene either, Detective."

"Then why'd you come?"

"Oh, I was curious who Master X was planning to parade around this time. He always throws one of these for a new sub. We haven't had one of these dinners since he debuted Cece over a year ago."

The bartender dropped two more tumblers in front of them. "And? What'd you think of our newcomer?" asked Sam.

Amusement lit Mary's face and her eyes shimmered a glistening green. "I think her heart belongs to someone else."

"What makes you say that?"

Mary dipped her finger into the scotch, sucking the amber droplets from the tip. "They hardly touched each other all night. There was no passion, no tension between them. Nothing. However, when she looked at *you* . . ."

"We just have history. But trust me, she's moved on."

"Or so she wants you to believe."

"Me? I wasn't even supposed to be here tonight."

Mary pulled a tube of lipstick and a small mirror from her purse, touching up her lips. "True. Which only makes me wonder . . . who else are they trying to convince? And why?" With that, Mary motioned to the bartender. "Be sure to put these on my tab downstairs." With a tilt of her glass, she slipped back downstairs.

Sam chewed the inside of his cheek. Whatever Elliot and Jess were up to, he knew there was a good reason behind it. But if they weren't fooling Mary, chances were that others could see through them, too. "Excuse me," he said to the bartender. "I need a piece of paper and an envelope."

The bartender hesitated, then disappeared into the back with a nod. Moments later, he returned with a spare sheet of stationery, an envelope, and a pen. Sam grabbed them with a quick thank-you and scribbled a note.

> *Step things up. No one down there believes*
> *you two as a couple. —S*

Stuffing the note into the envelope, Sam scribbled *For Master X* across the seal and handed it to the server. "Could you please take this note to the man who organized the private dinner downstairs? He's dining with the woman in the purple dress."

"Yes, sir," the waiter said.

"And deliver it along with a gimlet?" Sam tossed a twenty onto the bar and finished his drink. He waited until he saw the server go downstairs with the drink and note in hand.

If Jess and Elliot were going to do this—whatever "this" was—they might as well do it right.

31

Dinner ended rather uneventfully not long after Jess and Elliot returned from the bathroom. But Sam never came back.

Elliot had the valet bring his car back around and once they were locked safely inside, Jess spun to face him. "Did you see how mad Epoly was? She was shooting you daggers from her eyes. She was picturing your face on a dartboard."

"Not my problem. It's not my job to babysit her subs. And if she treated them better, they would likely stay till dessert."

"You and I both know that Sam is anything but a sub."

He ignored that, turning the ignition on. From inside his coat pocket, he pulled out an item wrapped in a cloth napkin, holding it out for her.

"What's this?" Jess asked, taking it carefully from his palm.

"Open it," he said, his eyes glistening with humor.

Jess pulled the napkin back slowly. As realization hit her, she threw her head back against the car seat, laughing.

"A cookie."

"For a job well done," he said. "Now, we just need to get those bags unpacked."

* * *

When they reached the docks, Elliot pulled into a reserved parking spot and he led her to his personal yacht, docked and waiting for them. They climbed on the boat, loading the various suitcases stuffed with pills as well as Jess's personal bags on board.

"Before I take us back to my house," Elliot said, "let me show you around." The yacht had three levels and from the top deck, he led her down a set of stairs. The first door on the left and right were guest rooms. He opened the second door. "The master bedroom."

She glanced inside, noting the dark wood and subtle nautical decorations. "You travel by boat a lot?"

"Not as much as I'd like," he said, entering and pulling the suitcases behind him. He set them beside a large dresser. "So, for the masquerade tomorrow, I'll get the yacht across the border and into Canadian waters. By the time we're out of the country, it should be very late and most of the partygoers will likely be drunk by then. You and I should be able to slip away unnoticed and go down to the lowest deck and dump the suitcases overboard."

"What if someone sees us?"

"We'll be masked. Wear a simple black dress, something nondescript that's hard to pick out. And we won't open the suitcases at all. We'll just dump them overboard and get the yacht quickly back into the United States."

It was a good plan—or as good of a plan as they were going to get. "And the money?"

"I moved it into the safe in this room. If these guys threatening you are on board, we can give them their money at the party."

They walked back up to the helm that was just off the highest deck. "You think this is going to work?" Jess asked, nerves jumping around her belly.

"I think it's your best shot. Are you leaving town after the party tomorrow like I said?"

She hadn't planned on it. She knew she should and yet she couldn't bring herself to leave Sam and Matt and everyone else in the thick of things.

"Dammit, Jessica," Elliot cursed. "I'm not telling you to leave for good. Just get out of town for a long weekend. An act of good faith to show them you're wiping your hands of everything."

Again, she couldn't bring herself to answer him—to lie. Because she had no intention of leaving. She never did, if she was being honest with herself. "I'll lie low after. I promise."

"Okay," he said, backing the yacht away from the dock. "Look, I know this isn't ideal. Any of it, not even having to stay at my home tonight. But after a dinner party like the one at Hugo's? People would be expecting you to come home with me. And who knows how and if they are watching."

"I know," she said, watching as they drew farther away from Portland's glittering city lights.

Afterward, back at the house, Jess was set up in his guest room. She had hung up the few clothes she'd brought with her and now she sat on the most comfy bed in the universe, surrounded by her sister's paperwork.

Various invoices for pharmaceuticals, e-mails, receipts, labs, and studies of medicines surrounded her. The medical jargon was like a different language. She opened a particular file labeled with the name of the drug she had stacked in her closet—most of which was now piled on Elliot's boat.

Jess read on, doing her best to make sense of her sister's scribbled notes.

Biophuterol is a drug that brings more oxygen to organs, particularly the heart. The perfect drug for patients waiting on the transplant list. Extra oxygen to the organs improves blood flow, creating more time while they wait and preserving their organs, slowing down decay. Additional studies showed that when the drug was also given to the healthy families of patients who were donating organs (such as kidney, bone marrow, etc.), the drug aided the healthy organs being readied for transplant, making it so that the organs could be outside of the body for longer periods of time and thus making long distance transplants easier. Short-term use of the drug did not show long term effects, however it was found to be highly addictive. Side effects included dizziness, disorientation, increased heart rates and blood pressure.

She flipped to the next page, then cringed, nearly dropping the file on the bed. The next page was all images of human organs. Air pushed up from her stomach, bringing with it a dry heave. She photographed corpses for a living, but it still caught her off guard. She looked down at the photos again and this time her business side took over. Of course, when she photographed bodies, you typically didn't see all the organs and guts—*usually*. There was the occasional body mutilation case.

One picture showed a heart, twenty-four hours postmortem, a dull mauve color, bordering on gray. Another photo was a healthy heart directly postmortem, just before it was ready to transplant. It was plump and red. The third image was of a brighter, cherry red heart, the muscle tissue slightly more swollen than the picture of the nonmedicated heart. The color was incredible; almost unreal. The sort of red you saw in movies. The caption next to it showed that it was a heart that had been affected by Biophuterol.

The research went on and on for pages. Whatever this drug was, Cass was passionate about it. There were formal letters to her boss, pleading to begin trials in the US for Biophuterol. All of which were stamped *Denied*.

Jess moved the stack of papers to the side as Dr. Brown's

business card fluttered out of the shuffle, drifting down into her lap like a feather. She turned it over in her hands. On the back was scribbled *Call me* with his personal cell phone number. Not that that was anything new. Zooey had confirmed that even though she had been dating Dr. Brown, he was a ladies' man and had his eyes on Cass.

At the bottom of the file there was a stack of mail that had come to the house over the last week. Mail that Jess hadn't been able to bring herself to open yet. Even though it mostly looked like bank statements and bills, they were addressed to Cass. Addressed to a woman who was no longer breathing. Jess flipped through the sealed envelopes: a bank statement, a cable bill, a flier for home security. Jess pinched the flier between two fingers and ripped the thing in half, throwing it to the floor. *Too little, too late, Holden Watch Security System.* She was about to toss the next envelope to the side as well but she paused. It was a large envelope with a Mercy Hospital return address. It could just be more bills, something work-related. But instinct told Jess otherwise. She began tearing it open when a small knock sounded on her door.

She dropped the envelope from Mercy Hospital on top of the pile before saying "Come in."

Elliot poked his head in the room. "What are you doing?" He looked at the envelope beside her on the bed before entering the room. He wore navy-and-red plaid pajamas low on his lean hips, along with a thin, white T-shirt.

"Just catching up on some of Cass's mail. Bills and stuff."

"Well, I just wanted to make sure you were comfortable."

"Very."

"So . . . the yacht party tomorrow . . ."

". . . Yes?"

"I just thought that maybe we should have a chat about what's expected."

Jess looked down at the slinky tank top and shorts that she

always slept in and resisted the urge to cover her exposed skin. "Now?"

"Or later. I just fear we'll both get too busy. I don't want you to be caught off guard by how big this event is."

"Why? What's going to happen?"

He chuckled, crossing his arms, his hip against the door-frame. "You mean other than us both risking our lives to dump thousands of dollars' worth of drugs into the ocean? Other than us trying to return the drug money back to the original owners?"

"Yep, other than that." Jess stood, grabbing a robe from the hook of the adjoining bathroom door and flinging it around her shoulders in a show of modesty.

"Well, you've been to a smaller-scale version of this party before," he said. "You've seen what people do there. There are hookups, fucking, all over the place. This one will not be an exception."

Jess's throat went dry and her mind immediately went to this man's relationship with her sister. "And what's your point?"

"Well, I'm just warning you that we'll have to be . . . affectionate. If we're not, it will look suspicious."

"Affectionate. I can handle it. It'll be like an acting job. I'll consider myself back in high school, when I played Chorus Girl Number Four in *Oklahoma!*"

"*You* were in *Oklahoma!*?"

"Cass was trying to get me into more wholesome activities."

"She did always seem very concerned about you. Even when you were living far away."

Jess cleared her throat, staring at the fluffy, cream-colored carpet beneath her bare feet. She spread her toes, imagining it was sand and that she was on a peaceful beach somewhere.

Elliot turned a card over in his hands, running his fingers along the edge. "I received this toward the end of the dinner."

She reached for the note, recognizing Sam's handwriting immediately. The sight of it launched her back to being fourteen and the two of them sharing notes from their World History class. "They're not buying us? Who's not buying us?"

"My guess would be Epoly," Elliot answered. "That's who he would have talked with the most at dinner."

Jess handed the note back to Elliot. "So? We need to step up our game. Affection. Got it. We'll cuddle, hold hands, you can even squeeze my ass." Elliot took a step forward and flutters danced in her chest.

Why was he moving closer to her? She backed away as he kept advancing. His steps were quiet, with the grace of a wild-cat, and the look in his eyes was just as primal. "That's all well and good. But I have one concern left."

He was nearly on top of her now and Jess reached behind her, placing her hands on the wall. She didn't want to be backed into the corner like some scared little chipmunk. She could be a wildcat, too. She could be strong and raw and all those things that dominants possessed. His hand came down on her hip, slipping inside of the robe so that his warm, fleshy palm was flush against the strip of skin between her tank top and the band of her shorts. Her skin flared and she could feel herself flush from her stomach up to her breasts, her skin reddening at her cleavage. *Oh, God.* She hated that her body reacted like this even though her mind objected. It didn't feel bad, his hands be-ing on her. Just like the spanking earlier wasn't painful enough to warrant her tears. It was the embarrassment of it. The hu-miliation that had brought about that burning sensation to the back of her eyes. If things had worked out differently, if Cass hadn't died, this man before her could have been her brother-in-law. He could have been family.

His other hand cupped her jaw, fingers tracing the line of her chin to her ear and down her neck. Her breath staggered and she was momentarily at a loss for words until Sam's face sud-denly popped into her mind.

"You better remove those hands or be willing to lose them,"

she said. She didn't know much about self-defense and she was pretty damn sure that this man with all his money had some of the best black-belt training New England could offer. But that didn't mean that a kick to the balls wouldn't still hurt like hell.

He chuckled. "Don't worry, Jessica. I can't do anything with you. Not like what you're thinking." There was an underlying sadness to him that had been present since the first time Jess had laid eyes on this man, back in the elevator when she only knew him as his title, "Master."

Her eyes flicked down to his hand, still on her hip. "Then what are you doing?"

"We may be expected to kiss at this party. There are occasional games that require it."

She stepped back, forgetting that the wall was right behind her. The back of her head slammed into the plaster and she winced. "So . . . when that time comes, we'll kiss. *If* it's even needed."

"Have you seen a couple kiss for the first time? There are nerves. Jitters. People bumping their heads against walls," he chuckled. "First kisses are awkward and this group? They will know. They will know right away that we'd never kissed, let alone had relations before."

"Relations. Sounds like something my grandfather would say."

"I don't love being compared to a grandparent, but hey . . . whatever gets you in the mood."

Jess shoved his hand off her hip. "I do not need to be in any 'mood.' Consider me mood-less, buddy." But even through her objections, she could feel that he was right. If they had their first kiss in front of a crowd, she would be a basket case. She'd fuck the whole thing up.

Even as she pushed his hand away, it found its way back to her body, this time around her back, as he pulled her close to his body. "Elliot—"

But he didn't allow her to object further. He bent low, pressing his lips to hers, curving his fingers around the back of her neck and scooping into her hair. Her lips molded around his. Lips so different than Sam's. Not so needy, not as though he desired her, but like she was an item on a checklist to be crossed off. He was a good kisser. There was no doubt about that. But yet, she felt . . . nothing. Not a thing. No stirrings or dampness between her legs. There was no steely erection pressed against her hip. And with those flannel pajama pants he was wearing, she should have felt something if there was in fact something there to be felt.

She opened her eyes midkiss, his lips still working against hers, and she studied his face. He looked pained, the lines around his eyes pinched. As she pulled back, he opened his own eyes to find her looking at him.

"We're not gonna be playing Romeo and Juliet anytime soon, are we?" Jess laughed and despite the tears in his eyes, a smile cracked through like a bit of sunshine peeking through a storm cloud. A foreshadowing of better days to come.

"No, I don't think we are."

"But at least now it won't be awkward to fake it."

"That was my first kiss since . . . since . . ."

"I know," Jess interrupted.

"You do?"

"Well, I guessed. You should relax your face more when you kiss me. It looked like you were in pain—" Jess reached out, brushing her fingertips along his brow and he pulled back like he'd been burned.

"Don't touch my face," he snapped.

"What?"

"Just . . . don't. Especially not at the party. It will be a dead giveaway."

Jess rolled her eyes. "Fine. Whatever. When you kiss me again, keep your face relaxed. Talk about dead giveaways . . ."

"Okay . . . I get it."

"Or I'll bite your lip and really give you something to wince about."

"And the student becomes the master," he joked.

There was a terse pause and silence filled the room with something thick and heady. "Hey, Elliot . . . do you think . . . after all of this, we'll stay friends?"

Hell. If she thought the room was filled with something tense before, now she was utterly drowning in it.

"Friends?" he asked, his voice a short, hard staccato.

"Yeah. You know . . . friends. People who care about you, who you hang out with but don't fuck."

"I don't have friends," he answered simply.

"Well, that's sad. What about Lyle? Simon?"

"They work for me. That's not a friend."

"Don't you get lonely?"

"I never used to. Until your sister. And now—" His voice cracked and Jess jumped in to spare him.

"Well, I was thinking . . . I have no family left. And you and my sister were in love. It kind of, sort of makes you, I don't know . . . almost like a brother to me." Her face burned with an immediate blush as she realized how ridiculous she must have sounded.

"A brother," he said. She was about to tell him to forget it; he was taking way too long to think it over. "I'd like that," he said. "I mean . . . *after* all this. For the next few days, if I'm gonna be kissing you, I think it will forever damage me to think of you as a sister."

Jess chuckled. "Deal. Come Saturday, I'll think of you as my brother."

Her phone buzzed from the nightstand, Sam's name lighting it up. Jess grabbed it and spoke into the receiver.

"Hello?"

"Jess. We have another murder." Sam's gruff voice vibrated through the phone and she could hear—no, feel—his sadness and frustration. "Come down to the Eastern Promenade near the dog beach as soon as you can. Bring your camera. We don't have another photographer yet and we need you to take this one. Just for tonight."

"Of course. Not a problem."

"Jess," Sam said, and dropped his voice to a whisper. It sounded even more muffled than usual. "It's Dylan. Dylan's been murdered."

32

Jess rushed around the room, throwing Cass's paperwork along with what little of her own things she'd brought back into her overnight bag. Grabbing her sister's gown off the hanger, she balled it into a wad, stuffing it inside as well. That was why she didn't bother to own nice things herself—they typically ended up wrinkled and on the floor within a day.

Elliot reached inside the bag, taking the gown back out and hanging it up again. "Why don't you leave this here? I'll have Simon dry-clean it tomorrow."

She was too exhausted to argue.

After grabbing her work clothes, she stuffed her legs into her jeans, not even bothering to take off her pajama shorts. Same with her tank top; she slipped her button-down shirt over top and slid into her blazer. Thank God she'd thought to grab her camera before leaving her house that night.

"Where do we need to get you to?"

"Eastern Promenade. Just—oh, shit. Shit! The ferry? When was the last ferry?"

Elliot looked startled by her outburst. "About an hour ago.

It's not a problem. I'll take you on my boat. I assume someone can give you a ride home after?"

"It's so late . . . you don't mind?"

"I don't think we have much of a choice. Unless you prefer to take a midnight swim? I wouldn't recommend that, personally. I've only ever swum from Peaks Island to Portland twice and both times I had Lyle follow me in the boat in case I got caught in an undertow."

Jess just stared at him in disbelief momentarily before shaking the fog from her mind. *Is this guy for real?*

He smoothed her dress on its hanger, placing it carefully back in the closet. "Of course, I don't recommend that at all unless you've been training for a triathlon."

Jess laughed, but it came out choked-sounding. To avoid that hard stare of his, she grabbed the rest of her things, checking to make sure she had all the paperwork and her camera. Anything else she forgot, she could get later. "All right, Mr. Howell . . . lead the way to your yacht."

"Howell?"

Jess gave him a gentle push on his shoulders, urging him out the door. "Oh, come on. Did those rich parents of yours not allow you to watch Nick at Nite?"

"Actually, I don't come from money. As a kid, we were very poor. We couldn't afford cable. Hell, we couldn't even afford a refrigerator."

As they stepped outside the night's chill whipped across her face and neck and Jess shrugged her overnight bag higher onto her shoulder, her camera bag hitting her hip as they walked toward the dock. "Seriously? But . . . but you just seem so proper. Like you went to the best prep schools and—"

Elliot stepped aboard the boat, holding a hand out for her to guide her onboard. "Nope. Not even a little. I got a liberal arts degree at Southern Maine Community College and later took a two-week course to get my real estate license. I thought I'd be drowning in college loans forever."

"Your family, are they—"

"I was the oldest of four. My younger brother died when I was twenty. I'm paying for one of my sisters to study at Oxford now. And the other is significantly younger than me. She lives with my aunt."

Jess peered at him as the boat rocked, mimicking her own feelings about this guy. Just as she thought she had a firm grasp on who he was, just as her feet were steady, a new wake knocked her off balance. "And your mom?"

"She passed away as well." He was quiet a moment, turning the key. As the boat growled to life, its engine was louder than a nursing home on bingo night. Jess opened her mouth to speak and without even turning around, Elliot cut her off. "And before you ask . . . I never knew my father."

The boat vibrated beneath her and Elliot rushed to the ropes, untying them and tossing them onto the dock. Moving back to the helm, he turned the wheel, pulling the boat carefully away from the dock. "Have a seat. There's water in the fridge below if you need it and if you lift up that bench, there are blankets inside."

Jess stumbled back, sat down on a cushioned bench, and watched in awe as this strange and powerful man got her safely ashore.

Sam circled Dylan's body, taking a moment to stretch out the kinks in his neck. *Fuck. Poor kid.* His guts twisted and Sam had to blink through the spots circling in his vision. Sam bent to his knees, shining his flashlight over the powdery corpse. Dylan's lips were a purplish color, his eyes dilated and cloudy as they stared blankly ahead.

"I'm sorry, kid," Sam said.

"What do you think the cause of death is?" Matt asked, standing above him.

"I can tell you that it looks like an OD."

"Agreed," Christine, their medical examiner, chimed in from

beside him. "There's no external wounds. No sign of a struggle. Without getting him on the table, I'd have to concur that it was likely an accidental overdose."

Sam shined the flashlight on Dylan's nose and just below his eyes. "What about that redness at his nose? And the slight bruising beneath his eyes."

Christine looked closer, but shot Sam a look that said *you don't look like the medical examiner here.* "Could be anything. Sometimes redness around the nose and bruising of the eyes is simply a side effect of an overdose. Like I said, I'll know more when I get him on my table. Don't expect me to pull any rabbits out of hats here, Sam. It could be something, or it could be nothing. Fact of the matter is, we just don't know yet." She tucked silky black hair behind her ear and checked her watch with a sigh. "And I won't be able to move the body until your photographer gets here either. Where is she?"

Damn good question. Sam had called Jess over thirty minutes ago. "She's on her way. Did you get hair samples and fingernail swabs?"

"I've done literally everything I can without moving the body or disrupting it for imaging. Call me when the photographer's here." With that, she turned away in a huff.

Sam crouched down once more as emotion twisted inside of him. *Why the hell did this kid go back to drugs?* He seemed genuinely surprised and upset when Sam had told him about the recent fatalities related to O. For once, Sam had actually thought he may have changed a kid's life, convinced him to take the better path.

"You couldn't have done anything else, man. This isn't your fault," Matt said, practically reading his thoughts.

"Mattie, I don't think this was an overdose. It just doesn't make sense. Thirteen hours after he gives up information for our drug bust, he ends up dead? Why was he getting high alone on the beach? This kid was a social user. He did it to connect with friends and as a social outlet."

"Maybe the friends got freaked out and left him here."

"Why isn't he dressed warmer? He looks like he's in pajamas, for Christ's sake."

Matt scratched his goatee. "I don't know, Sam. Maybe it was a last-minute thing. Maybe he was high before he left the house and didn't get dressed properly."

Anger swelled in Sam. How was it that his own damn partner didn't see how this crime scene didn't match up? "Are you fucking kidding me right now? You don't find this situation strange? We saw him this morning. There was no bruising around his eyes and nose. That's a sign of an altercation right there."

"Okay, okay. Yes, it's suspicious. But Christine's right. We won't know anything until we open him up. And even then, you—*we*—need to tread lightly. Convince Straimer if it is a murder and go from there. No one here even knows you interrogated this kid. And they *can't* know, Sam."

Sam kneaded the back of his neck, working out the knots. "Jesus. When did you become my voice of reason?"

"Just call me Jiminy Fucking Cricket."

Larger waves started slapping against the shore and Sam looked up to find a boat approaching the docks. Several of the uniformed officers ran where the boat was headed in an effort to intercept anyone from entering a live crime scene. Squinting, Sam looked closer and saw Warner at the helm of the boat. With Jess standing just behind him, camera slung diagonally across her body. "Fucker," Sam cursed, but quickly tamped the flare of anger back down. This is what they needed. They needed their relationship to look more real. And what was more real than them showing up via boat together to a crime scene?

Jess's curly hair whipped around her face, wild and free like she herself once was. She hopped off the boat and turned to leave, but Elliot grabbed her hand, tugging her close to his body.

Sam couldn't watch. Even if it was fake—and he hoped it was—it was like a searing hot dagger being pushed through his flesh.

Time passed slowly despite the fact that he knew Jess was rushing to get over to the body. One button on her shirt was open, revealing a wrinkle of a tank top and a strip of tanned flesh at her abdomen. Sam wet his lips and as their eyes connected he could feel their chemistry in every inch of his body, clear down to his toes. It left a surge of prickling through to his core.

"You're late," he said as she approached.

"I'm sorry," she panted, out of breath from her jog down the dock to the crime scene. "I got here as fast as I could. The ferry doesn't run this late—"

"The body's over there. You know what to do." He wondered if his face looked as stern as his voice sounded, but then again, if she and Elliot had roles to play, then so did he. That of the jilted lover.

"Is it definitely Dylan?" she asked, pain glistening in the depths of her brown eyes.

"It's him, all right." Sam turned and walked away from her.

"You just need the usual shots, right? Nothing out of the ordinary—"

He spun around quickly, underestimating how close she was to him. He stumbled, his hands landing on her rib cage, thumbs brushing the underside of her taut breasts. He took a sharp breath before forcing his hands back to his sides.

Sam's cock grew hard within his pants, but he ignored the sensation. Ignored the ways this woman could turn him on and heat him up like a fucking campfire. Finally, he answered her question.

"You know what I need," he said, before he turned and walked away.

33

Jess finished her photographs relatively quickly, all things considered. Maybe she just wanted to get the hell out of there. She'd never had to photograph the body of someone she'd just seen alive less than twenty-four hours before. Even though she barely knew this kid, it still knocked the wind out of her to look so closely at his lifeless eyes. Eyes that had been bloodshot, but still lively hours earlier while he divulged all sorts of information to Sam. That couldn't have been coincidence.

She pulled the camera off her neck, pausing at Dylan's feet. From that angle, she could see up his nose and she crouched, pulling the camera to her face once more. She zoomed in as tight as she could on his nostrils. She couldn't be certain, but it looked an awful lot like drugs were packed into his nasal cavity—almost as though someone had shoved the drugs in forcefully. She snapped the last picture, making a mental note to point it out to Sam before she left.

Though her job was done, Sam's was only just beginning. As she walked to the edge of the promenade toward the impromptu snack and coffee station, she found Sam and Matt huddled away from the group, in a private meeting.

She gave them an extra minute together, pulling the envelope addressed to Cass from the hospital out of her duffel bag and tearing it open. A stack of stapled, photocopied papers fell into her hands with a note clipped to the front. It was mono-grammed stationery with the initials RGB letter-pressed to the front. Jess flipped the note open.

> *Cass,*
> *I found these last night while I was working late at the hospital. They're watching me, but I knew I had to get them to you. Be careful. Watch yourself. And we can go to the police together.*
> *Your friend,*
> *Rich*

What the hell? Jess flipped the envelope over, looking at the postmarked date—September fourteenth. The day before her sister's death.

"All done?" Sam's voice was raspy, and he sounded almost as fatigued as he looked. *Dammit,* she thought to herself, and shoved the letters back into the envelope, doing her best not to appear as unnerved as she felt. Her feet sunk into the sand, making it even more difficult to stand tall than it usually was around Sam.

"Yep," she said, and her own voice was also weary, reflective no doubt of her exhausted body. It was just after three in the morning and they'd all been up since nearly six. It didn't seem human that Sam could still function after hardly any sleep the night before. "Be sure to check his nasal cavity," she said. "I got a macro shot of it, but it looks like there may be some powder forced inside."

"I noticed the bruising at his eyes and redness around his

nose. Now that you're done, we can move the body and have a closer look," he answered sharply, not looking at her directly. "Good job. Go home, get some rest. If you could get us those images in the morning that would be great."

"I'll deliver them first thing." She paused, shifting uncomfortably. "Well . . . good night." Moving aside, she pulled out her phone, searching for a cab company.

Sam's baritone voice came from over her shoulder, far closer than she expected him to be. "What are you doing?"

"Calling a cab, what does it look like?"

"I don't think you need one."

"We've been through this. We can't be seen together and you won't be done here for at least an hour—"

"Not *me*," he grunted, then jerked his head up to the parking lot beside the beach. There was Elliot's limo with Lyle sitting on the hood, staring at his phone. He looked up in time to catch Jess and gave a little wave.

"Guess Elliot wanted to make sure I got home safely," Jess said.

Sam nodded. "I hate that I'm about to say this . . . but I like him for that. He seems . . . okay."

A warm sensation flooded her stomach and for the first time in a while, Jess felt like she had family watching out for her again. She was too independent for her own good sometimes. She knew that. And yet, now and then, it was nice that someone else was there to pick up the slack. She looked to Sam. It would be nice if she could let him be that person. Someone else to stay home and wait for the cable guy. Another human being to help out when a pipe burst or when a package needed to be signed for. That warm feeling exploded into a fireball as her eyes connected to his and little sensations popped off in her chest like mini-fireworks.

"You should get home," he said.

"I should."

Another pause. More eye contact.

"Jess—" His voice was firm, but it also came out in an amused sort of chuckle as she snapped herself out of the daze.

Gathering her duffel bag, purse and camera bag, she was about to say good-bye, but she blinked, Sam's face coming more into focus despite her exhaustion. A dark trickle ebbed its way out of one nostril. "Sam . . . your nose. It's bleeding."

She lifted a hand to his cheek, the rasp of his stubble scraping her palm.

He jerked out of her touch, pressing a finger to his nose and looking at the scarlet stain that streaked his hand. "Shit," he groaned. "You got a tissue?"

Jess nodded, diving a hand in her bag to pull out one of those little travel tissue packs. "Here. Are you okay?" she asked as he tipped his head back, pressing the tissue against the bloody side.

"Fine, fine. I . . ." He seemed to stop, thinking before continuing. "I'll be okay. Probably just pushed myself a little too hard today."

"Why don't you let Matt finish up here—"

"No. This is my case. Dylan was my responsibility."

Jess held in a sigh, simply nodding instead. There was no point in arguing when Sam got this way. He was stubborn. A trait she recognized and understood because she was the exact same way. Something they had connected over at a very young age when they both wanted to play with the same set of Legos in preschool. "Okay," she said. "Just take it easy, okay?" She gave his shoulder a little squeeze before walking up to Lyle's car.

It took another hour and a half after Sam put Jess into Lyle's car before he finished his own work at the crime scene. His limbs were weary, the night chill was transitioning into a morning dew, and in a few hours the sun would be cresting over the ocean. Slowly, he made his way up to the parking lot where his car awaited. Only a few more minutes and he could collapse into bed. His head was pounding. He finally understood where that phrase *splitting headache* came from. There was no escape from this headache. No amount of Tylenol could help. Nothing. The moment his car came into view, he noticed that something was wrong. A padded envelope was pinched between his windshield wipers and his hand instinctually went to the gun on his hip as he scanned the area for shadows or any bit of movement. Everything was still. Cautiously, he walked up, comforted by the fact that dozens of uniformed officers and Matt still roamed nearby. After diving a hand into his pocket, he slipped on a latex glove he was still carrying from the crime scene and carefully opened the envelope.

A torn piece of stationery fell out along with a memory card for a digital camera. The exact kind of camera that Jess used. Sam carefully unfolded the note, which read:

She's a heavy sleeper.

The sweat from a long day's work chilled against his flushed skin and he dove inside his car, grabbing his laptop from the backseat and shoving the memory card into its reader. Twenty images were on the card, all of Jess's new house. There were very standard interior shots like something you'd find in a real estate listing. And then the last two images, of Jess fast asleep in her bed. The covers were pulled up high around her chest, her head turned to the side, mouth parted.

This fucker had been *inside* her house while she had been sleeping.

The ride back home was pretty smooth and thankfully Lyle was quiet most of the way. Almost as if he could sense how exhausted Jess was. She really just needed some quiet time to think. And read. But she knew better now than to take that piece of paper out anywhere other than in the safety of her home. *Even still... could it really hurt? A quick peek?* The windows were tinted and Lyle had his eyes on the road.

She stole a quick glance at him in the driver's seat, eyes fixed straight ahead, focused. Quietly, she pulled the envelope out of her purse. Just the first page. She'd only glance quickly at the first page and then slip it back into her bag. The paper rustled in the nearly silent car, as loud as an alarm blaring in the middle of the night. She froze, waiting for Lyle to react. But he didn't. She turned the radio on from the backseat and glanced at the first page.

It was an attorney's notes. Personal notes for a potential medical malpractice suit that resulted in death. No... two deaths. And personal medical records. For her parents. Mr. Nicholas Walters and Mrs. Renee Walters.

Jess's head felt too light for her body and stars danced behind her eyes. The music that she had only just put on seemed to warp in her ears, producing a horrible, tinny sort of sound. Her breath shuddered with each inhalation. What the fuck was going on? What did any of this have to do with her parents?

She squeezed her eyes shut, willing her brain to work at full capacity. She couldn't fall apart. Not now. And she sure as hell shouldn't be reading this anywhere in public. She quickly folded the papers three times and then stuck them in the inside pocket of her jacket along with the note from Dr. Brown. The envelope it came in was too puffy to fit in her pocket, so she shoved it inside her duffel bag on top of the rest of the mail. Something—instinct or maybe paranoia—made her take a pause and she grabbed a stack of the junk mail and slipped it inside the envelope, tucking the flap closed before falling back into her seat. She held her breath, puffing her cheeks out before slowly releasing it through tight lips.

The more she learned about her sister, the more confused she got.

Lyle pulled into her driveway behind her car and stood to

open the door for her. He yawned as she stepped out, dipping his head and covering his wide-open mouth with the back of his hand. "Sorry about that," he said.

"It's okay," she said with a glance around at the neighboring houses. "I'm sorry Elliot dragged you out of bed so late for me."

"I don't mind. I wasn't even asleep yet."

"Well, thanks again." Lifting her bags and sliding her purse over one shoulder, she headed for her front door, pulling out her keys.

"I'll wait until you're inside," Lyle called after her with a wave. "Flip the outside switch a couple of times when you're locked in and safe."

Jess gave him a nod, unlocked her front door and walked into her foyer. Shutting the door behind her, she switched the main light on, turned to lock the door behind her, and flickered the lights for Lyle. She watched as his headlights backed out of her driveway and the car took off down the street.

Even though she was exhausted, out of habit Jess dragged her memory card out of the camera, plugging it into her laptop and uploading the photos. She was way too tired to edit, but she could at least have them culled and ready for the morning.

After thirty minutes of work, she dragged her weary body up the stairs. As she came closer to the master bedroom, she heard music softly playing.

It was a familiar song by the Eagles. *Did I leave the radio on when I was getting ready?* Slowly she stepped into her sister's dark bedroom. The curtains—curtains that she knew she had pulled tightly closed, were now wide open; a Bluetooth speaker was suction-cupped onto the center window, playing the tune.

She backed out of the room. She had to get out of there.

She turned to run down the stairs as cold metal jabbed into her back and a gloved hand came down hard on her mouth.

"Not a word," a man's voice said.

34

That voice... *I know it. I know that voice, but from where?*
She had to get him talking. Keep him talking and maybe it
would jog something in her memory.

Her toes pressed into the hardwood floors at the stop of the
stairs. She whimpered against the gloved hand smashed against
her lips. Sweat and moisture beaded between the thick material
and her skin. A tiny shiver hit her shoulders, but she willed it
away. Willed the fear and terror back somewhere deep inside of
her.

"Where is it?"

"Where is *what?*" she tried to say, but it came out muffled
from behind the pressure of his hand. The gun pushed harder
into the small of her back and she yelped, craning her neck to
free her mouth. "Whatever it is you want... take it," she panted.
"Take it. I don't care."

His chuckle sent a cold shiver racing down her body. "*Whatever* I want?" His hand brushed down her hip to her thigh and
as he slid it back up, his thumb brushed over her pelvic area.

She gulped down the bit of bile that threatened the back of

her throat and something hard that she didn't know existed in herself anymore took over. She felt cold. Numb. Like stone, this man would have to take a sledgehammer to her to break her down at this point.

"If *that's* what you were really here for, you would have taken it already." She hardly recognized her own hollow voice.

"You're not afraid." It wasn't a question. And as his torso pushed against her body, she felt . . . nothing from him. Absolutely nothing. No arousal at all.

She noted this, but at the same time, she wasn't a complete idiot. There was no need to poke the hungry lion when you were the tethered, sacrificial lamb. She tried to take a step back, but his body prevented her from moving anywhere and she hated being at the edge of her steep staircase. "I *am* afraid," she said. "Is it the money you want? Cass's money? That's what this is all about, right?" Jess moved her eyes as best she could without alerting him that she was looking around. There was a strip of skin between his sleeve and his glove . . . he was white. Not a lot of arm hair. Shifting to look down, she saw that he was wearing dress shoes . . . loafers, maybe leather. Not cheap-looking. Of course they weren't cheap-looking; he was a drug dealer. He had money to afford the good stuff.

"Money?" The grim sound came out as half chuckle, half grunt. "Sure. That would be nice, too." There was an unnatural deepness to his voice, like he was trying to disguise it. Like he knew she might recognize him.

She gulped. "I don't have it. Not here. But I'll have it tomorrow night at the masquerade on—" she stopped, catching herself just in time before she said Elliot. "—Master's yacht."

"Warner has five bedrooms on the second-level deck. Leave the money in the first one on the left."

She nodded, not trusting her voice just yet.

"Now," he continued, "Your sister's mail. Where is it?"

"Her mail?" she squeaked, inhaling on a jagged breath.

"M-most of it was already open. I barely looked through anything myself yet."

His hand came down hard on her hair, squeezing and yanking her neck back, the gun pushing further into her spine. She yelped and this time it was real fear that quivered in her voice.

"I don't need your fucking play-by-play. Just tell me where it is."

The act was gone. The veil had dropped. And the reality of her situation slammed into her like a sixteen-wheeler careening down a highway. Tears pricked behind her eyes and her throat felt too tight to answer him. "I-it's downstairs . . . by the front door."

The gun nudged her forward down the steps. "Show me. Keep your hands where I can see them."

She stepped cautiously, her bare feet cold against the chilly stairs. Her jacket from earlier was flung carelessly across the banister and she could see the corner of her parents' medical records peeking out from the pocket inside.

"Put your hands flat on the door. And don't do anything stupid. You can't run faster than a bullet."

She looked at the beveled glass, the window cut out in her door, squinting her eyes and trying to catch his reflection in it. All she could make out was the blurry outline of a dark figure behind her. His laugh was far deeper this time and he shoved her body harder into the door in front of her. The glass was cold against her forehead and his breath was hot and stank of gin as she felt his mouth trail against the back of her neck. This time, his erection was very present and pushed into her backside.

Oh, God. I'm going to die. Now. Tonight. She forced her eyes open to look out the window. *Shut your brain off. Don't feel anything,* said a little voice inside her that sounded too much like Cass for her to ignore.

One hot tear cut through her makeup, falling down her

cheek as the man behind her pushed his erection harder against her. Jess blinked as headlights came into focus. There was a car pulling into her driveway. Hope sparked in her chest. Someone was here. Someone was going to save her.

Either that, or he was going to kill them both.

A sliver of hope shined through like a quarter amidst a pile of dirt. The will to live sparked inside of her. "Her mail's in the duffel bag," she choked out. "Just take it." The sound of the car engine outside sputtered off and the lights went out.

The man pushed off of her and she heard a rush of movement from behind. She looked down in time to catch the man hunched over the duffel bag, unzipping it. A mask covered his face and a hat hid his hair—she should have known he would be prepared.

He gave a satisfied grunt and without looking back at her said, "Get the *fuck* out of Portland. We've given you every chance. You have until Monday." He didn't give her time to ask any questions before taking off out the back door. Jess unlocked the front door, threw it open, and fell into Dane's arms.

"Jess!" he exclaimed, her weight nearly knocking him back off the steps. "What's wrong? Are you okay?" Her body shook as his strong grip wrapped around her and wetness stained her cheeks, soaking into his soft cotton shirt. His chest was pure hard muscle, tensed against her.

She couldn't answer his question yet. She didn't even bother trying. Fisting the sleeves of his shirt, she just clasped him closely. She was alive. She wasn't hurt or taken advantage of. The thought alone caused her throat to close. And she owed that to Dane. She didn't care what his reason was for showing up at her house in the middle of the night. She just didn't care. He crooned some soothing sounds against her hair until her tears had diminished. Then he gently pulled her back, grasping her shoulders.

"Are you hurt?" He scanned her face, her body for any trace

of damage, his palm eventually landing on her jaw, cupping her face. "Jess, goddammit, you've got to talk to me." He peered into her house.

Jess ran her hands across his arms. He was real. He was here. And she was going to be fine. Somehow she managed to sputter out an explanation—she told him about the man in her house and how he threatened her, though how Dane made sense of it was well beyond her. Even still, he seemed to understand every word.

"He's gone?" he asked.

"I-I think so."

Dane looked around before stepping into the entryway and grabbing her purse, jacket, and camera bag from the floor. "Come on. Lock up."

"Where are we going?" Jess's hand trembled as she slid her key into the lock.

"Anywhere but here."

He helped her into the passenger side of his truck before getting behind the wheel and peeling out of her driveway.

Jess closed her eyes, her head feeling heavy on top of her shoulders, as though her neck had to strain simply to stay upright. Eventually, she let it fall against the seat, her eyes closing, thankful for the silent ride.

She must have fallen asleep, but when she opened her eyes, only a few minutes had passed.

"I'm going to take you to my house. Is that okay? I can call whomever you want me to once we're there. Sam or Elliot—whoever," said Dane from the driver's seat.

She desperately wanted to see Sam, more than anything. She wanted to curl up next to him in bed and let him stroke her hair until she fell asleep. But seeing him would mean explaining that someone broke into her home. And going to his home this late in the evening would just cause more danger. For all of them.

"Your house is fine. As long as you're there, too," she said wearily. "It's too late to call anyone."

"I promise I'll be there all night. I can even sleep in the room with you if that would make you feel better. On the floor, of course."

Somehow, she didn't even think that would be enough of a distance to appease Sam. The very fact that she was going to be spending the night in Dane's house was likely enough to piss him off. "Dane?" she asked, barely recognizing her own voice. She was exhausted. "What were you doing at my house so late?"

His jaw jumped, but he glanced quickly to Jess before bringing his eyes back to the road. "I was out with Lyle when he got the call to pick you up. I-I wanted to say good-bye."

All the weariness was gone in a flash and Jess sat straight up, turning her body to face him. "Good-bye?"

"Well, not for forever or anything. I just might have to go out of town for . . . for another small job. And I didn't know how long you'd be in town for, so in case, I thought I'd come tell you that I'll be gone for a bit."

"For how long?"

"A week . . . maybe two?"

Jess grew quiet. She was sad to see Dane go. She knew he was keeping something from her, but she didn't feel like she was in danger around him. "I'll probably be going back to New York soon, too." *You have until Monday.* She shuddered at the memory of the thick, gruff voice in her ear.

"Yeah? It's probably safer there. At least until this all blows over."

If it all blew over. "That's what I'm told."

Dane was quiet for another tense moment. "But is it what *you* want? You want to go back to New York eventually, don't you?"

A sob bubbled in her chest and Jess looked out the window

before it could explode into another tearful breakdown. "No. I want to find the people who did this to Cass and get justice for her death."

Dane took a right turn out of the downtown district and pulled into a quiet neighborhood in South Portland. "You think you're getting close?"

She placed a hand to the folded medical records in her jacket. "I know I am."

35

The next morning, the smell of fresh brewed coffee and the sizzling of bacon in a frying pan woke Jess from a deep slumber. Her body was stiff and aching, a painful reminder of the nightmare attack the night before. She whimpered as she rolled to her side to check the time. Six-thirty. That left her a couple of hours to get the photos filed for Sam.

She was suddenly very grateful that she had put her clothes on over her shorts and tank-top pajama set the night before. Otherwise, she would have been sleeping nude in Dane's guest bedroom. Even still, the tiny shorts left little to the imagination—it was a little more skin than she cared for Dane to see. She peered out the door, making sure he wasn't in the hallway, and just as she was about to run out, her toe hit a folded robe on the floor outside her door. She bent, lifted it, and read the attached note.

I have breakfast and coffee ready downstairs.
I'll keep it warm for you.
—Dane

After sliding her arms into the soft terry cloth, she finished up in the bathroom and slipped her pants on under the robe before she went downstairs for breakfast. Dane was sitting at his kitchen table, reading *The Sound and the Fury* and drinking a cup of coffee.

"Faulkner?" she said as she walked in.

"Surprised?"

Totally. But she wasn't about to admit that. "Just figured you as more of a Hemingway guy."

"Hemingway has his moments, even if he was a drunken asshole ninety-five percent of the time. I left you a mug next to the coffee machine. Sugar is out and half-and-half is in the fridge."

Jess helped herself to the coffee, noticing the heaping plate of bacon and scrambled eggs beside it. "Holy crap, that's a lot of pig on that plate."

"You don't have to eat all of it."

"Isn't some of it for you?"

She peered around the column separating his dining area from the kitchen and saw as he held up his own plate. She grabbed hers along with the coffee and sat across from him, eyeing the food like a virgin in a whorehouse. "Please don't tell me you eat like this every day? You'll never make it past forty."

She glanced up, catching his weary gaze before he quickly slipped his mask back on. There was a sort of ghostly pallor to his skin that she hadn't noticed the other day.

"I don't eat red meat," he answered quickly. He set his book down beside his plate. His breakfast was entirely different from hers. It looked like egg whites with some sort of herb, a slice of smoked salmon, and half a grapefruit.

"Why'd you go to the trouble of making it for me, then?"

He shrugged. "I had leftover bacon from when a friend was visiting. And I remember your sister once telling me that you two would always splurge on the really good cuts of bacon when you were in high school. Even when you couldn't afford it. She said that some women turned to chocolate or booze, but for you both, bacon was your comfort food."

"That's quite a memory you got there."

"When it comes to your sister, it's damn near photographic."

An alarm on his phone went off and he hit a button, pulling pills from out of his pocket and swallowing two. Realization pinged in Jess's brain and she fell back against her chair, nibbling on a piece of bacon. "Of course," she said aloud. "I'm such an idiot."

"What?"

"You have a heart condition, don't you?"

He froze, his mug of black coffee half-raised to his lips. Even his grip on the handle seemed to tighten "I do," he said after a long pause.

"And you're the reason Cass was trying so hard to get Biophuterol in a drug trial here in Portland."

His jaw tightened and he stood, taking his plate with him. "Your sister was philanthropic. She wanted to produce drugs to help people, not to make money."

Oh my God. It's all falling into place. "And when she couldn't legally get the drugs into your hands . . . she did it illegally. You're the reason Cass got involved in all this."

The dishes crashed into the sink. "Fuck. Yes, okay? Yes. It's my fault—"

"I didn't say it was your fault. I said you're the reason. There's a difference."

"Well it *is* my fault. If it hadn't been for me, she wouldn't have felt such an urge to help." His body sagged and Jess got up, moving over to stand with him. "She saved my life. Without those drugs, I wouldn't have lasted another week with my heart as weak as it was."

"But the drugs helped?"

"They changed my life. I'm still not perfect, but they allowed me to get to this point and now—" He stopped.

"Now?" Jess thought back to her reading the other night. "Are you growing immune to the effects of the drug?"

"Starting to," he said. "It's only meant to bridge the gap while you're waiting for a transplant."

"You've been waiting a while?"

"Over a year. I don't want to jinx it . . . not that I believe in those things . . . but I may be getting a new heart. Soon. I got the call yesterday."

"And that's why you came to say good-bye last night," she said, finally understanding. "Cass would be so happy," she said, "that it all wasn't for nothing." Stepping forward, Jess placed her arms around Dane, pulling him in tight for a hug. "Congratulations on the new heart, Tin Man."

He chuckled against her shoulder, squeezing her tightly back. "I'm glad you know. I kept telling her that I could find another way to get the drugs. That I could go to Canada and get them in myself . . ."

"But she worked in pharmaceuticals. It was probably easier for her to bring in cases of medicine from over the border, huh?"

"She fudged some paperwork. No one suspected a thing. Until your boyfriend found her picture at border patrol."

"You could have told me sooner about all this. You know I don't think you killed Cass. Even with the lies you told me . . . the look on your face when you talk about her? You loved her."

"I did." His voice cracked.

"But they're still going to need an alibi, Dane."

He shook his head, pulling out of the hug. "I can't give you one. And if they put me on the stand, I'll plead the Fifth—"

"That's the biggest misconception of trials," Jess interrupted. "Pleading the Fifth only works if you're guilty of something."

His chiseled, pale face turned to hard stone before her eyes. With a single nod, he repeated, "I know. As I said, I'll plead the Fifth."

36

As hard as she tried, Jess wasn't able to get anything more out of Dane. The ride back to her house was almost silent, not the comfortable silence she'd come to accept at times. This one was terse and made worse every time she attempted to talk.

Thankfully the drive was short and their good-bye even shorter. Two hours after getting home Jess was showered and had her flash drive loaded with the edited shots she'd taken the night before at the crime scene. When she walked into the precinct Sam rushed toward her, his eyes wide and wild, bloodshot like he hadn't slept a wink the night before.

"Jess." He grabbed at her shoulders and yanked her into his chest, crushing her in a hug. Years of backbreaking training to become detective had solidified Sam's body into practically a weapon and his strength, even in this show of affection, was quite literally taking her breath away.

Hundreds of thoughts blazed through her mind, the most potent one being the way Sam's arm was hooked around her waist. The way his body pressed against hers, melting her against his hardened frame.

"Where the hell have you been all night?" She cringed as what she thought was a sweet moment hemorrhaged into pure fury.

"How did you—"

"Come here," he snarled, taking her arm. Despite his anger, his touch was tender. He brought her into an empty office where he bent over the computer, tapping keys like a madman. "I called you all night long. I slept in my car outside your house waiting for you to return before I gave up and came here to wait."

"Why—why would you do that?" Had Dane called him about the attack and not told her?

"Because of this." He stood, pointing to his computer screen. "Are these your images?"

She looked at the thumbnails. They were the images she had taken of Cass's house the first day she arrived. She had thought she might be able to use them to sell the place. "Yeah. Why do you have my pictures?"

He held up the memory card reader, showing it to her. "So this is your memory card?"

Jess licked her lips nervously. "Yeah, I guess. I mean that's the brand I use. And if it has my pictures on it—Sam, what is going on?" She'd never seen him so angry. Yes, he'd been mad at her in the past, but this was something entirely different. This was more than a tantrum from a dominant personality not getting his way. It was a mixture of fury and terror; his eyes blazed with both and his angled features were tight.

"What about this image?" His voice lowered as he moved the cursor, enlarging a picture of Jess sleeping.

Like an avalanche beginning at the top of her head, every muscle in her body slowly lost control until she was trembling. Even her teeth were chattering. "Wh-where did you get that?" But even as she asked, she already knew the answer. Her sister's murderer had gotten into her house more than once. There was a pattern. All this time, she thought he was looking for the money or the drugs . . . but, no. It was more than that. It was the power play he got off on. He had enjoyed last night. It was fun to him—not only threatening her, but being turned on by her terror as he pressed his gun into her back. And he had been there looking for her parents' medical records. Not the money. Not the drugs. Records that she hadn't been able to bring herself to look at since before the attack last night.

"Jessica." Sam was breathing nearly as hard as she was. "I need you to tell me the truth. And whatever the answer is, it'll be okay."

"The truth? The truth about what?"

"Has anyone been spending the night at your house? Anyone other than me?"

An indignant laugh popped out of her mouth despite her fear. And slowly, her concern for her life morphed into outrage at Sam's question. "Do you actually believe that I've been with anyone else? How can you even think that?"

"I'm not accusing you here, Jess. I know I seem . . . well, I haven't given you any reason to trust me enough to tell the truth. But this is for your own good. If you've been with anyone—anyone who might have stayed the night—"

"No!" she shouted, then looking around, lowered her voice. "No. No one."

"Not even Elliot?" he asked, his voice tighter than before. "He's never spent the night? Never tied you up and driven you crazy?"

Mortified, her face flamed, initially with embarrassment that quickly morphed into need. The memory of her tied down with Sam going down on her caused her body to tighten in all the right areas.

"I haven't been with anyone else. Though the world is supposed to believe that I'm fucking Elliot, I can't. I won't. And not to mention he doesn't want to, either. That's not what we are to each other. I've only been with *you* since I arrived. And for some stupid fucking reason you're the only one I *want* to be with." Tears danced in her eyes and she ducked her face down in an effort to hide them. Pain splintered inside of her, leaving wreckage in its aftermath.

"Jess." Everything about Sam softened as her name slid off his tongue. "I'm sorry . . . as a detective, I use tactics to get the truth out of people. I—"

"Forget it," she said, turning for the doorway. "I understand. You're just doing your job."

As she reached the edge of the desk, his forceful body pinned her against the door. His breath was hot and rough against her ear and it sent waves of warmth spiraling down her body.

He linked his fingers in hers, tugging her arms above her head as his teeth grazed her ear with a wicked nibble.

Sliding his other hand down the length of her arm, he scooped it into her pants, popping open the button and unzipping it first. She panted, biting her lip to quell the moan building in her chest as his fingers dipped below the elastic of her thong. Nimble fingers slid over her sensitive flesh, stopping to cup her between her thighs. He paused before curving his finger and stroking her clit.

"Damn, you are so fucking wet."

Every all-too-sensitive inch of her body cried in pleasure as those fingers crept toward her swollen, aching core.

His mouth moved on top of hers and he drank her whimper, rolling his tongue into her mouth with a skilled lick. He pulled away from the kiss, and his teeth grasped her bottom lip, nibbling and sucking as he pulled away. "How hard would you come for me?" he asked, thrusting two fingers inside of her. "How many thrusts would it take?"

Oh, yes. Yes, please. She needed it. Her head fell back against the wall and as she opened her mouth to answer him, he took her in another kiss, speeding up his finger thrusts and adding pressure to her clit with his thumb.

He pulled his fingers slowly out of her and Jess heard her own shattered cry, squeezing her eyes shut.

His fingers were damp as he slid them back to her ass, letting the moisture and slow pressure ease one finger inside her tightest area. She moaned as the sensation, utterly different from any other, took hold of her body. It was an easy, lustful stretch and his finger worked her open, wider, with skill so adept and wicked that it could only be described as an art form.

He continued until he was fully inside, filling in an area where she hadn't even realized she needed him. His touch was searing and as he placed his thumb gently back onto her clit, she jumped. Everything was heightened; with one finger, he managed to fan a single flame into a blazing inferno.

"Sam, please," she pleaded.

"You like that?" he asked as that diabolical finger shifted back, nearly pulling entirely free before he slid it back inside of her again. A gradual, steady push, this time not stopping until he was buried deep.

She arched her back, searching, fighting for that right angle, the last thrust that would catapult her over the edge. It was so close—so very in reach. It was right there, and yet, she felt paralyzed. As though it was being dangled in front of her, just beyond where she could grab it.

He dropped his lips to her strained neck, running his tongue along the roped muscle there. "Is this what you want?" he asked, flicking his finger faster over her clit.

"Yes, please, yes—"

He pulled back from her neck. "Look at me, Jess."

She opened her eyes, the soft yellow light warm around his chiseled face. "Call me Jessica," she said. She had no idea why, but with Sam she wanted him to take control. To handle her body in ways she could never be capable of herself.

"You want me to call you by your full name?"

During sex, absolutely. It felt so good. "Yes, *sir.*" As the word left her mouth, the wet heat poured harder from her sex. The word came so naturally in the heat of the moment. And felt so right. Right for her—for *them*.

A flaming need overtook her as he pumped a finger into her vagina as well, the heel of his palm adding even more pressure to her clit. "Yes, yes . . . just like that," she said as an incoherent cry shattered the quiet office. Thrusting her hips into his hands, she writhed against him and clawed at his shoulders with clenched fingers. His mouth devoured her, his tongue raking over hers, but Jess met his kiss with an even greater claim of her own. He was anything but tender as his raw, animal nature took over in pleasing her. But that was okay—she didn't need tender. She didn't need him to make love to her. She needed release. Explosive, mind-blowing release.

Her brewing orgasm crackled against her spine as he massaged her with agile, swift strokes. Her vagina pulsed a warning— a demand for relief just before the orgasm slammed into her fast and hard, rocking through her body. Her arms jerked around Sam's neck as her sex and ass convulsed around his fingers, tightening and releasing, leaving her helplessly weightless in his arms. A groan climbed up her throat and blended with Sam's as it burst from her lips. The room warped around her and even as the spasms slowed, he continued to pump inside her, making sure he had milked every bit of pleasure he could from her body.

She slumped against the wall, her legs beginning to work again as his fingers eased carefully out of her body. When she opened her eyes, she was met with his sensuous smile. He released the hold on her hand and brought his fingers to stroke the svelte column of her neck. That orgasm should have satiated her need, but rather than satisfy her thirst for Sam, it seemed to only further trigger her hunger.

He twirled a section of her hair that had fallen from the confines of bobby pins, stroking it between his thumb and finger before he pushed it back and away from her face. They rested there, his forearms framing her body on the wall behind her.

After a few minutes, Sam straightened her blouse as she zipped up her pants. "Well," he said, "should we get your crime scene photos down to CSU and find these bastards?"

The reality of their situation came slamming back into her. The panic and terror she felt the night before as a man waited in her house. "Sam, the reason I wasn't home last night and why I didn't pick up my phone—someone attacked me. Inside my house. Whoever's doing this still has access."

Sam's face became red as he sucked in a sharp breath, pushing his lips together in a hard, thin line. "What happened? Why didn't you call me?"

"I think . . . I think the only reason I'm alive is because Dane was there and scared him off."

His face flamed a million shades of scarlet. "What the hell was he doing there? You know what? Never mind. That's the least of our concerns. First we have to figure out what they want inside that house . . ."

"I've been trying to figure that out, as well. At first, I thought it was Cass's money or . . . something. But last night—I found this." She pulled the medical records from her purse and smoothed the stack of papers on Sam's desk, explaining the note from Dr. Brown to Cass. "I think the man who attacked me was looking for this."

Sam squinted, flipping through the paperwork. "Did you read this?"

"I started to but I haven't had time to read all of it."

"What do your parents' deaths have to do with Cass's murder?"

"I've been trying to figure that out."

He scanned the pages, his eyes flitting from left to right while Jess read from beside him. "I have no fucking clue what this says. Damn medical jargon. I only understand one out of four words," he said.

Jess collapsed into a chair, dropping her face into her hands. "Damn. I was really hoping you'd have some answers."

Sam shook his head, folding the papers and handing them back to her. "No. But I know someone who might."

"Someone we can trust?"

He thought about that a moment. "Right now, I don't know who we can trust. But she may be our only hope. We should still lie low, especially regarding our relationship."

"I don't know that our relationship matters as much now in the grand scheme of things."

He took her hand and pulled her to her feet. "You may be right, but I'd rather not take any chances. Have I mentioned lately that I'm sorry?"

"For?"

"Everything. For not being there for you when we were teenagers. For helping my mother cover up the car accident. I'm sorry."

Sadness tingled in her chest and Elliot's words from earlier buzzed in her head. *Cass knew the most unforgivable secrets are the ones that take the most courage to be honest about.* "I know you are. It must have been really hard for you to tell me the truth after all this time. And it was a long time ago. We were both young and stupid."

"Yeah, but your stupidity didn't ruin lives."

She sighed. "If I forgive you, Sam, then you have to also forgive yourself."

The silence was tense, but not altogether uncomfortable. He squeezed her hand, pulling her out into the hallway. "Come on," he said. "Let's go find out what the hell these records say."

37

Sam led the way down the elevator and into the back of the hospital where the morgue was. After walking down the long corridor, he opened the door to where Christine was elbows deep in Dylan's autopsy. Her lab coat was stained crimson and she had several bright lights craned over the body. She blinked, looking up at them as they entered her exam room.

"McCloskey?" she said, startled, before looking to Jess. "Jess, hi. What can I do for you?"

"We had a question. Neither of us really understands medical writing and we thought you could maybe have a look at this and tell us what it says?" Sam nodded to Jess who stepped forward, handing the medical records to the ME.

She held up her gloved hands, signaling for Jess to hold on a moment. "Unless you want Dylan's DNA all over your papers, that is."

Jess scrunched her nose. "No, thanks."

Christine snapped the gloves off, tossing them into a special bin beside her table, and then held out her clean palm. "Okay, let's have a look." She took a few minutes to read, flipping carefully through the pages. "It looks like a lawyer was trying to get a malpractice suit off the ground, but he didn't have much of a case. And the medical records are old. Twelve years or so?"

Jess nodded. "Yeah."

"Who's the lawyer?" Sam asked craning his neck to see.

"Um . . ." Christine flipped to the first page. "Burt Horowitz. Of Horowitz & Schacter law firm." She pressed her glossy, red lips together, her black hair pulled into a sleek ponytail. "Where'd you get this? They don't typically release records like this to the family."

"Oh, um, I don't really know. It was in my sister's personal effects when I picked them up." Jess glanced nervously at Sam, who flashed her a quick, reassuring smile. "I was young when they died and no one would really tell me anything because I was a minor." She gave her best innocent performance. "I was just hoping to find a little closure."

Christine smiled warmly at Jess, her brown eyes so dark, they looked nearly black. "I lost my dad a few years ago," she said. "I know the feeling. Here," she said, gesturing to a seat on the other side of the room. "Why don't we sit down . . . away from the corpse." She had a dark sense of humor, but Jess kind of liked that about the medical examiner.

"That'd be nice," Jess said, making her way around Dylan's body on the table.

Sam's phone chirped and he grabbed it from his pocket. "You good here alone, Jess? Some lab results just came in."

She nodded. "We're fine."

For a moment, it looked as though Sam was about to kiss her, but quickly thought better of it as he backed out the door.

From her desk, Christine grabbed a staple remover and held it up. "Do you mind if I unstaple it? Just a lot easier to read that way." Jess nodded and Christine took the seat next to her. "This must be really hard on you. Dealing with your sister's affairs and then this popping up amidst everything else."

Jess paused, careful not to reveal too much. "Yeah. Truth be told, it was a nice distraction."

Christine nodded thoughtfully before placing the second page between them so they could each look. "Well, anyway, this is really just a basic medical record. It has the detailed breakdown of when your parents were brought in as well as the names of the original EMTs who were on the site of the crash. Here are the ER doctors who were on call that evening. They usually list any surgeons later—with the surgical notes." She flipped quickly toward the back and nodded. "Yep, here they are. Anyway, it looks like your father was dead on arrival, but your mom was alive, but barely." Christine paused, looking up just in time to see Jess wince at the information. "Oh, shit. I'm sorry . . . I get into my doctor zone and I just sort of shut myself off from what I'm explaining. Do you want me to stop?"

Jess shook her head. "No, I'm fine. She wasn't conscious, was she? My mother."

Christine hesitated before looking back down at the papers, flipping to the next page. "No, she wasn't conscious."

"Why did they lie? They told me that she was dead upon impact like my father."

Wrinkles formed at Christine's pinched brow. "You were young, right?" Jess nodded. "Are you *sure* that's what they told you? Don't get me wrong, it's just . . . sometimes with trauma, especially when we're young, we mishear the information."

"I think I would remember them telling me my parents were dead . . ."

Christine's eyebrows came together, the moment of empathy flashing quickly. "Yes, of course. She was brain-dead on the scene. That might be what you heard."

Jess closed her eyes tightly, conjuring up the memories of that horrible night. *Could that be?* Her sister had been home for spring break from college. The call came from the hospital well after the crash. Well after the first responders had gone home. They said that they did everything they could, but her parents had passed away. At least she thought that's what they said. Then again, they were actually speaking to Cass and Jess was just eavesdropping. It's completely possible she had misheard.

"Here, this language right here describes the series of tests they gave to your mother several times at the hospital. They test these things over and over again with different doctors because they want to be certain."

Jess scanned the notes as Christine flipped to the next page. "And here. Your mother was an organ donor. This is the paperwork and notes on her surgery as well as the information of who her organs went to." Her brows knitted deeper together. "That's weird. It's against, like, every HIPAA law in the books for you to know who her organs went to. Where'd you say you got this again?"

But Jess barely heard the question. They had had her mom in surgery. Her mom was alive—maybe not functional, but her heart was beating, her blood was rushing, her lungs working. "You mean—I-I could have said good-bye?" The words choked Jess, locking up high in her throat.

"I don't know. According to the notes, she started crashing almost immediately on being brought in and they began harvesting the organs very quickly. There may not have been any time. I don't know if this helps at all, but it looks like your mom's donation saved a lot of lives. Her heart, her kidneys, her liver, bone marrow . . ."

Jess took a deep breath, calming her rush of sorrow. Putting it back deep inside her gut in a box that was tightly shut and locked. "It does help. A little. And just knowing exactly what happened to them will be good for me, I think."

"Good." As Christine handed the stack of papers back over to Jess, she dropped them and they fluttered to the floor. "Oh, jeez." They both dropped to their knees as they gathered the papers together. "Sorry . . . I'm such a klutz."

"You're preaching to the choir there," Jess said. Though she attempted to smile, it was halfhearted, the sorrow still taking up so much space in her body. Once they'd finished gathering the fallen papers, they each stood and Jess turned, finding herself looking into Dylan's dead, cold eyes.

"Such a shame. Found anything notable yet in him?"

"Other than a cocktail of drugs in his tox screen? No."

Jess froze. "What drugs?" She knew she had seen something shoved into his nasal cavity, but Dylan had specifically said in his interview with Sam that he didn't do any drugs other than O. He didn't do anything that would permanently harm his brain. It was Sam who told him that Biophuterol was dangerous.

Christine went back to her clipboard. "The usual. Heroin, cocaine, meth, O. I don't know when these kids are gonna learn."

"Yeah, right." On the other side of the table, a cooler of ice sat half-hidden from view. The sort of container that people bring to football games or carry their lunches in, only slightly bigger. It was white with a red top and some sort of sticky residue on the side, as though there had been a sticker there and the adhesive never washed off. Jess recognized a couple of bright red organs sitting on top of the ice and her mind went directly back to the reading she did the night before about Biophuterol's effects. "I didn't realize you iced the organs during the exams."

Christine sighed, pulling her gloves back into place. Her patience with Jess being in her exam room had apparently worn off. "It's precautionary. Just in case someone decides they want to run a second tissue sample, I prefer to keep the organs as preserved as I can until we're ready to dispose of them."

Christine reached into Dylan's chest cavity, pulling out his heart. It was bloody and cherry red, just like in the picture Jess had seen the other night. Christine held the heart up like some kind of ancient relic. "I'm impressed," she said. "Even some of the detectives here get squeamish at seeing a human heart so up close."

Jess remained calm even though her belly roiled at the sight. "Guess I'm desensitized. Is that normal for a heart, post-mortem? To be so bright . . . so, I don't know . . . oxygenated?"

Christine nodded, putting the heart on a scale. "Sure. Pretty normal. This one's in pretty good shape for a drug user."

The effects of Biophuterol weren't exactly common knowledge yet. Jess wanted to blurt out that was because the sole purpose of Dylan's drug of choice was to keep organs preserved, but she kept quiet. Instead, she backed up to the door. "Well, I'll leave you to it. Thanks again for this."

But she still had so many questions. Why would someone go to such great lengths to get her parents' death records? And why was Dr. Brown so nervous that he had to secretly snail-mail it to Cass?

Nothing was adding up.

38

After Sam left Jess with Christine in the morgue, he rushed upstairs just in time to bump into his partner.

"Hey," Matt said. "You look weird. What's going on?"

"Nothing, I'm fine. Lab results are in." Sam thrust the information into Matt's hands and he skimmed it quickly.

"They found chloroform on his clothes?" asked Matt.

"Yeah and Jess was right. The drugs were impacted so deep in his nose, it looked like they were forced. This wasn't a simple overdose. He was given something to pass out and killed while he slept," said Sam.

"Well that explains the lack of defensive wounds. Still no cause of death from Christine?"

Sam shook his head. "She's down there working on it."

"It's still most likely an overdose."

"Yeah, a forced overdose." Sam said.

"Should we go interview his mom? She may know if he was going out to meet someone."

Sam's attention was only half on Matt and what he was saying as he searched for the Law Offices of Horowitz and Schacter on his phone. "Hm? Oh, yeah. Sure." *Bingo.* Their practice moved out of Portland to Brunswick eleven years ago. "Why don't you take Rodriguez and go interview the mom without me? I've got something to check up on."

"What's up? Everything okay?"

"Yeah. Yeah, everything's good," he said. But if Matt's frown was any indication, he didn't believe him. He wouldn't have believed himself if he were in Matt's shoes.

Sam dialed Jess, even though she was just downstairs. She answered on the first ring.

"I have to go check on some things for a couple of hours. Are you going to be okay here?" he asked.

"I'll be fine," she said. To her credit, she didn't sound afraid.

"You sure? I could bring you with me—"

"I'll be fine. I'm just going to finish up the files from the crime scene and take a nap."

He didn't love leaving her alone, but he was done trying to control his friends and loved ones. "Okay. Matt's around. If you need anything give him a call."

"I will. I promise."

The drive to Brunswick was tense. Sam pulled into the sleepy Maine town within forty minutes of leaving the precinct. A white wooden sign creaked in the wind, swinging from a pole outside of the small brick-and-mortar office building.

He pushed through the office door and was met by an older but friendly looking receptionist. She had cotton-colored curly hair and glasses that hung off her neck on one of those beaded attachment things that people buy at Walgreens.

"Good morning," she said with a smile, her speech slow, but friendly. "Do you have an appointment?"

Despite his nervous energy, Sam returned her smile. "I don't. But I need to see Burt Horowitz. It's very important."

"Oh, okay. Let me see if he has an opening." Pulling her glasses high onto the bridge of her nose, she leaned over the computer screen. After several minutes and the slowest typing known to man, she looked up to Sam. "He can see you now." *Well, I should hope so,* Sam thought. *The place is completely empty.*

She hobbled to her feet and led him through a door into a back area that broke off into four different offices. Sam never liked lawyers. In his line of work, they were the bane of his existence, even when they were on his side. But even more so when they weren't.

The door at the end of the small hallway was open. There was a copper engraved nameplate adhered to the wall outside of it that said *Burt Horowitz.*

"Burt," the elderly receptionist said, "this gentleman is here to see you."

"Thank you," Sam said to her with a nod.

Sam entered the office behind her as a man in his midsixties stood to greet him. He was tall and lean like a beanpole. The man must have been six foot four at least. His hair was mostly silver, with just a hint of dark brown at his temples as a reminder of the color he used to sport. His face creased with a friendly smile, lines that were evidence of decades of happiness and laughter. Sam caught his own reflection in a mirror hanging behind Burt's desk, noting that the only lines creasing his own face were at his brow and eyes. Unlike the lawyer before him, Sam had zero smile wrinkles. *Until Jess reenters the picture,* he thought to himself.

"Thank you, Sylvie," Burt said, quickly shutting the door behind her. He gave Sam a wide-eyed look before taking his seat back behind his desk. "She can't type worth crap, has no idea how to use the Internet, and I swear that she was there for the birth of Christ."

Sam cracked a smile. "But?"

"But nothing." Burt grinned, throwing his hands in the air. "She's the worst receptionist in the world! She's been here since we opened our offices. There's a loyalty there."

"That's big of you."

"So, what can I do for you, Mr.—"

"Actually, it's Detective McCloskey." Sam reached across the desk, exchanging a firm handshake with the lawyer. He could almost get behind this guy. A man who valued loyalty and watched out for one of his own? He liked that. "Call me Sam."

"Burt Horowitz. But you knew that, already. So, what brings you in, Sam?"

"I'm here about a case you worked a long time ago. More than a decade ago, actually. But, it didn't seem like anything was pursued outside of a quick glance into some medical records. I was curious what made you initially look into it and why you ultimately dropped it."

"I'm happy to help. I just need some ID, Detective."

Sam nodded, pulling out his badge and identification card.

Burt glanced at his badge, directing his attention back to the computer. "What was the case? If you have the names of the people attached, I can likely search for it." He typed something into his computer. "I mean, I can't guarantee that I'll remember, but years ago Sylvie transcribed all our case files into this database. Not that that means anything. That woman's even worse with filing than she is with typing."

"Nicholas and Renee Walters." As soon as Sam said the names, Burt's entire demeanor changed. His friendly, welcoming smile dipped into a frown and those bright brown eyes sparked with fear.

He pulled his hands away from the keyboard and stared directly at Sam. "You need to leave," he said, and pointed to the door. "Out. Now."

"You look scared, Mr. Horowitz." Sam asked.

"Please, just go."

"Did someone chase you off of the case?"

"You could say that. I was hired to look into their deaths as a potential malpractice suit. I barely got the papers filed and medical records released to me before the threats began."

"What threats?"

"Our cat was left mutilated on our doorstep. Terrifying notes were left for us—at my office, at my wife's office. Our kids would come home with the notes in their backpacks."

"Did you report it?"

"No, and I've always felt horrible about that. And about what I had to do."

"What? What did you have to do?" Sam asked, the edge of the desk biting into his arm. But the pain felt good. The pain kept him alert. Present.

"For the first and only time in my life, I had to lie to my client. I told him that I looked into it and that there was no foul play. Everything was on the up and up."

"But it wasn't?"

"No, God no. Nicholas's records were fine. They all matched up."

"But Renee's?"

Burt shook his head. "I really shouldn't say any more. I can't risk it. I moved our practice out here to get away from Portland. To start fresh. Uprooted my family, my partner. Thank God he was willing to make the move, too."

Burt stood, opening his office door and holding it for Sam. "I'm sorry. I can't tell you anything else."

Sam stood and pushed the chair in. "Thank you for your time, Burt. Just one more question—who hired you to investigate? Who was your client?"

Burt's grip on the door tightened. Giving a quick look around, he dropped his voice as though someone may be listening in on them. "A detective on your force. A Detective Straimer."

39

Several hours and a nap later, nerves jittered in her belly as Jess left her house, dressed and ready for Elliot's yacht party. Her parents' medical records were tucked inside her clutch—after what happened the night before, she wasn't about to let them out of her sight. Even if they were seemingly unimportant, someone out there was willing to kill for them. And she wanted to know why.

She only had one stop to make before heading over to Elliot's.

She walked into the hospital and went up to Zooey's room. The guard's chair was empty, a book resting where he or she should have been. Jess waited, looking around before knocking quietly in case Zooey was asleep.

From inside the room she heard voices—women's voices. She cracked the door, peeking through. "Hello?"

"Jess? Is that you?" Zooey's voice sounded close to normal and she looked a whole lot better than she had during Jess's last visit. One of her wrists was still bound to the bed, but her hair was brushed and it looked like she even had some lipstick on.

"You're looking better." Jess grinned and walked through

the door, handing her the bouquet of flowers she had bought in the hospital gift shop. A woman sat beside the bed. She had the same dark hair and dark eyes, the same pert nose and bow-shaped lips as Zooey. "How are you feeling?" Jess asked Zooey.

"Not a hundred percent yet, but better," Zooey said, and smiled shyly. The woman beside her cleared her throat, touching a string of pearls that rested on her delicate neck. "Oh, sorry. This is my mom, Evelyn. Mom, this is Jess—Cass's sister."

Zooey's mother gave a quick nod and her lips pulled in something that resembled a smile. "Nice to meet you."

"Same here," said Jess.

"Exquisite dress," Evelyn said, taking in Jess's gown, from the sweetheart neckline down to the flared hem. "Givenchy?"

Jess nodded. "Good eye."

Evelyn's smile split wider—a real smile this time.

"You look beautiful. Off to somewhere special? What am I saying—look at you. Of course you are."

"I have a party. But I hadn't heard from you in a couple days so I thought I'd come by and say hi."

"Mom, could you go get me some coffee?" asked Zooey.

"It's four-thirty, you don't need—" said Evelyn.

"Decaf is fine," Zooey interrupted.

With that, Evelyn nodded and stood, leaving the room. Jess waited an extra moment after the door shut behind her before sliding into her seat. "So how are you really feeling?"

Zooey's head fell back, and she rolled her eyes to the ceiling. "She's only been here a day and a half and it's already miserable."

At least you have someone, Jess thought, but stopped herself before she could become bitterer. "So, I wanted to give you an update, but you cannot tell anyone, okay? A few of us down at the station know you're innocent in this and we're working to clear your name. I'm not going to let you take the fall for this if I can help it—"

"They're claiming I premeditated Rich's murder. That I . . .

I . . . like drugged his drink or something insane. Yes, I followed him to the bar, but I was angry and I just pushed him. *Barely* pushed him and he went down and hit his head. I didn't go anywhere near his drink, I swear."

"I know. We know. And because he was drugged by someone, that's why he went down so easily and so hard when you pushed him. This wasn't your fault."

"And Cass?" Zooey's eyes welled up with tears, her voice rising into a different octave. "I could never. She was my friend."

"You don't have an alibi for the night she died?"

Zooey shook her head. "I was home. Alone."

Jess clasped Zooey's hand. "We're getting close. Just hang in there. And—" Jess looked behind her to make sure no one was near the door, and dropped her voice. "Try to stay here in the hospital as long as possible. As soon as you're well enough, they'll arraign you and transfer you to a jail."

Her face drained of color and her eyes settled on the wall across the room. "Oh, God. I might go to jail, Jess."

It was quiet for a moment while Jess worked up the nerve to ask her the uncomfortable question. "Zooey—you said that Rich and my sister were friends, right?"

She nodded, shaking herself out of a daze. "Yeah, but Rich obviously wanted more."

"Did you ever overhear their conversations?"

"Once or twice, maybe. Why?"

"I think Dr. Brown knew something . . . something about Cass's death or even my parents' deaths. And I think it's what got him killed as well."

"What makes you say that?"

"I found a note. From Rich to Cass that he had mailed to her the day before she died. He seemed scared. And it included . . . medical records."

"Medical records?"

"My parents' medical records to be exact." The silence was thick and seemed to suffocate her. Jess sighed, her shoulders slumping as much as they could with the boning in the gown. "I sound crazy, don't I? I'm sorry—"

"What did they say?"

"What did what say?"

Zooey rolled her eyes. "The medical records. What'd they say?"

"That's the thing. They said nothing important. Just that my dad was dead on arrival to the hospital and my mother had no brain activity. She started to crash and they operated, salvaging her organs for donors before she died. That's it. Oh . . . and apparently it included information on the recipients of her organs. I guess that's a huge violation."

"Um, yeah. HIPAA laws mandate that they can never release another person's medical records. Do you have the records with you?"

Ignoring the lump in her throat, she reached into her clutch, handing the papers to Zooey. "You know how to read medical stuff, right? Working in pharmaceuticals?"

Zooey took the stack of papers, eyes narrowing as they scanned left to right. "Yeah. I mean, I'm not a doctor or anything, but I know most of the abbreviations."

The seconds seemed to tick by slowly, each click of the second hand from the clock on the wall like counting down a time bomb about to go off. Zooey got to the last page and flipped it over, looking through the stack once more. "This is all there is?"

Jess nodded.

"Huh." Zooey clicked her tongue, nibbling on her lip. "Okay. So, what you said was mostly right. Except a couple pretty big details. Doctors do a series of tests when they suspect a patient to be brain-dead—your mother didn't respond to any of the tests . . . except one. Now, sometimes that can just be a discrepancy and mean nothing. Other times, it can mean she still had enough brain activity for it to be justified that she stay on life support."

"What? You mean she—she could have lived? But why . . . why would they do that? Why would they ignore a test like that!"

"I don't know. Laziness? Arrogance, maybe? Who explained this to you?"

"A doctor at the precinct."

"And she also said that your mom started crashing, right? That's why they began the operation?" Jess nodded and Zooey gave another thoughtful "hm," her lips pressed tightly together in thought. "There's nothing in the notes here indicating any sort of medical crash. Her heart was stable, oxygen levels remained okay. She was in a coma, but that wouldn't have justified rushing her into surgery without first notifying the family."

"What the hell is going on?"

"I don't know. But there's no paperwork with the organ recipients' information here."

"There's not?"

She shook her head. "Nothing. Maybe your doctor friend was mistaken? She got some of the other stuff wrong."

"Or . . . Or she lied."

40

Jess gripped her set of keys so tightly that the jagged edges cut into her palm, leaving indentations. And she didn't even care. She didn't give a damn about the pain. What she did care about was the fact that Christine either lied about her parents' paperwork, stole some of it, or both.

With her free hand, she pulled out her burner phone, calling Sam. "Sam, something weird is going on and I think it's all connected. Call me back." She hung up quickly, trying to keep her message vague. He claimed his cell wasn't bugged, but that didn't mean that someone wasn't listening in nearby.

The parking lot at the hospital was surprisingly empty for five o'clock on a Friday. She expected more of a hustle and bustle from staffers trying to escape for their weekends. But it was pretty much just her. As she slid her key in to unlock her car door, she glanced up to see a shadowed figure—a man's reflection in her driver's-side window. *Fuck.* Her pepper spray was attached to her keys, which were currently plugged into her car door.

She removed her keys slowly, preparing herself to strike if

needed. But as she turned to run, a velvety voice greeted her in a French-Canadian accent.

"Bonjour, Ms. Walters."

"Gilles." His name came out in a breathy, panicked way that she quickly tried to recover from. "You startled me." She hadn't seen the French-Canadian representative that her sister worked with since they ran into each other at Cass's office. And since he'd put in over a million dollar offer on her house.

"My apologies. It was not my intention."

"What are you doing here?"

"Visiting Zooey. A terrible tragedy. It's so hard to believe that someone I trusted . . . worked alongside of for years could be a murderer."

"Alleged murderer," Jess corrected.

"I'm surprised to hear you say that. She's a suspect in your sister's case, is she not?"

"Innocent till proven guilty and all that. Don't they teach American law in Canada?"

He chuckled. "My entire knowledge of the American judicial system comes from episodes of *Law & Order*."

"Sadly, it's probably the same for most US citizens as well. If you believe Zooey to be a murderer, why bother visiting?"

He adjusted the silk pocket square coming to a point out of his suit jacket pocket. "After working together for years, it felt like the right thing to do." He paused, sliding that hand back into his pocket. "I hope there are no hard feelings about me pulling my offer on the house."

"No, none at all. It was . . . awfully generous. Well beyond any asking price I would have started at."

He shrugged, but there was a tightness to his movements. "Don't underestimate that house. Especially with the discovery of the tunnel beneath it. What a fascinating piece of Portland history you have there. Do you know the story behind the tunnels?"

Jess shook her head.

"Well," he continued, "it was said that the very wealthy and some of the high-end hotels had tunnels built below their buildings that connected to various theaters and restaurants around the city. The reason being, that it was so cold in the winters, it was a way for the wealthy to get home from the opera and remain warm." He smiled at this piece of history—one that Jess had never heard before. "It came back into use during Prohibition, too, as you can imagine."

"Interesting."

"Interesting?" he asked incredulously. "No, my dear Jessica, it is *fascinating.*" Jess studied the man. A man her sister worked with at the pharmaceutical company. A man who worked as her Canadian rep and whom she would travel with frequently. What were the chances that this was exactly who she was looking for? The man in her house last night didn't have an accent . . . but who knew if Gilles's accent was even real? But even if he *was* the man she was looking for, all she had were worthless suspicions and zero evidence to support them.

"Funny, I just assumed the widespread news and discovery of the tunnel is why you pulled out of your offer." If he was in the drug ring, that would be one hundred percent true. No access to the wharf means no easy transport for the drugs, therefore no justification for overpaying for her little pink house.

"You know . . . most people would think having a tunnel in their basement would be a safety issue."

"Oh, no. Quite the contrary. I found the house rich with history and style. Your sister's renovation maintained its historical essence, but in such an elegantly modern way."

"So, if you don't mind my asking . . . why did you pull your offer?"

A flush stained the apples of his cheek and for the first time since Jess had met this man, he seemed embarrassed. Unsure of himself, whereas he usually walked around with his nose in the air. He was so high on his horse, Jess was surprised he could see anyone else from way up there.

"I come from an affluent family," Gilles admitted, dropping his voice. "I always have. But . . . my grandmother recently passed away. She left me most of her fortune. It's all perfectly well documented. But a couple days ago, my family filed a suit. They don't think it's fair that I got the entire inheritance. I visited her every week. I played bridge with her. I made sure she was well cared for in that home. The rest of those vultures only saw her twice a year on holidays. They couldn't even tell me when her birthday was if I asked them." His lips thinned and anger flashed in his eyes. "They put a lien on my accounts. I can't access anything until this is all sorted."

"I'm sorry," Jess said. Either this man was a good liar, or he really was telling the truth. "You really cared about her."

"I did," he said, and nodded. "In any case, it seems my financial situation has changed. At least until my lawyer sorts all this out."

"Well, if you want to resubmit a lower offer once you get your financials sorted, come back and we'll talk."

"Yes?"

"Sure. Well, I should get going." She gestured to her car. "And you should get up there to see Zooey."

He nodded and turned toward the hospital.

"Mr.—um, Gilles!" Jess called after him. He paused, turning back toward her. "One more question. Why did you put in such a high offer in the first place?"

"Because I had plenty of money. It wasn't an issue to go over the asking price. What's an extra three hundred thousand dollars when you have millions?"

* * *

Jess left Sam another voice mail, this time asking if he had the ability to look up financial records for a Canadian citizen. She spelled out Gilles's name for him. *Dammit.* Why the hell wasn't he calling her back?

She threw her car into reverse and drove back to the precinct, pleased to find a spot right across the street. Just as she was about to shut off her engine, Christine exited the precinct. And clutched in her pretty, manicured hand was the insulated cooler from her exam room. The one in which she had organs on ice. Jess cringed at the sight. *What the hell is she doing leaving with that? Even if it was cleaned out and sanitized, why would you want to bring that home with you?*

Christine slid it on the floor of the backseat of her car before getting in and driving off. Jess backed out of her space and slipped into the street, following a couple of cars behind.

Christine took several turns, but luckily it was rush hour and no matter what streets she went down, there was always a steady stream of vehicles on the road. Jess didn't think she was spotted. And her little Subaru didn't really stand out as anything flashy around town. In New England, nearly everyone drove an Outback.

Christine pulled into the Casco Bay Ferry parking lot. Jess made sure to drive past and then skidded into a parking lot across the street.

She threw her car into park and jumped out, rushing to keep Christine in her sight. Jess dodged a car, crossing the street and pressing herself against the wall of a neighboring pub, peered out from around the side. Christine grabbed the cooler from her backseat and then sat on a bench overlooking the water. She crossed her knees, pulled out a book and started reading.

What the hell was going on? Something was in that cooler; Jess could feel it.

Jess ran inside the pub, her heart skipping as she saw an

empty table right next to the window facing Christine's bench. She tucked herself into the seat, careful to slide the chair back so that she could pull herself out of view of the window in the event that Christine looked up in her direction.

The watching and waiting grew tedious. Her eyes felt heavy and Jess found herself wishing she'd brought a book to read as well. Something to read; anything to keep herself awake. After almost twenty minutes, Christine put her book down and grabbed her cell phone from her purse. There was a lot of nodding from Christine and Jess squinted her eyes, wishing she could read lips. Christine's dark eyes scanned the dock and just before her eyes landed on the pub, Jess arched her back, stretching out of view. Was anyone in here? Had someone spotted her? Not a single person was on their cell phone, taking a call, though a couple people were texting. The casual pub was mostly filled with a young happy hour crowd. Jeans, T-shirts, a few business suits, but unfortunately nothing nearly as fancy as the gown she was wearing. Jess stuck out more than a hitchhiker's thumb. She glanced out the window again, just in time to see Christine leaving the bench and getting into her car. The cooler sat at the foot of the bench. It was a drop-off.

Jess grabbed her clutch, running for the door as soon as Christine's car sped away. She stumbled on the uneven sidewalk, cursing the beautiful Jimmy Choos Dane had given her, and then fell to her knees in front of the cooler. A note was taped to the top inside a six-by-nine envelope. Jess grabbed it, looking around at her surroundings before yanking the papers out of the envelope.

> *This was the best I could do. I thought these were the most important parts to retrieve. I can try again tomorrow.*

After reading the note Jess unfolded the rest of the papers. *Her* papers. Or more accurately, a list of the people her mother's organs had gone to.

Jess scrambled for her burner phone, nearly dropping it while dialing Sam yet again. "Sam McCloskey. You need to call me back. Now. Immediately. I'm down at the Casco Bay Ferry. Come now." She hung up quickly, still clutching her phone as she scanned the names of the patients. Nothing was ringing any bells. Flipping through the pages, she read the log of doctors and nurses and interns who were a part of her mother's surgery. When she came upon a series of names she did recognize, her heart leapt into her throat and she could hear the whooshing of blood pulsing through her brain.

Dr. Adams had been her mother's surgeon that night. The surgeon who made the call to operate and harvest her organs. He had three interns on the case with him—two who scrubbed in alongside of him: Dr. Marcus Moore and Dr. Christine Lee. The third intern who did not scrub in was Dr. Richard Brown.

A wave of searing hot pins and needles pricked her body and stars flooded her vision. She scanned the donor recipient list once again.

And there it was. A name that she wouldn't have recognized without first looking at the names of the doctors: Nancy Adams. Adams—a shared last name. His wife or daughter?

"You motherfucker," she said. "You killed my mother to get her organs."

Jess shoved the paperwork into her clutch and, with shaking hands, opened the cooler. There, on ice, was Dylan's heart.

The smell of fresh blood slammed into her, rocking her senses and for a moment, Jess was certain she'd pass out. She shut the lid again, locking it. Her phone, still clutched in her sweaty palm, vibrated and she quickly answered it.

"Sam, where the hell have you been—"

But it wasn't Sam. There was heavy breathing on the line and then a song started playing. The lyrics and melody of "Witchy Woman" flooded her ears. As Jess pulled the phone back to look at the number, a needle pierced her neck. While everything around her faded, one thing was still clear—the sight of Elliot's yacht floating before her. Then the world went dark.

41

Sam raced back to the precinct from Burt Horowitz's office, busting through the front doors as he arrived. Donnelly jumped from behind the front desk as Sam slid his ID card and got on the elevator, going straight up to Straimer's office.

He didn't bother knocking as he slammed open the door. It flew back, hitting the wall behind it with a bang. A woman screamed and jumped, spilling a few drops of water down her blouse. "McCloskey! What the hell's your problem?" Straimer shouted.

Sam nodded at Rose, the captain's wife, as she clutched her scrubs. "Sorry, Rose," Sam said. "Straimer, I need to talk to you."

"Sam," she said, moving toward him. "Word around the hospital was that you hit your head pretty hard. How's it feeling?"

"Word around the hospital? What the hell happened to patient confidentiality?"

"That's for outsiders. Of course we know what goes on within the hospital. The scrub nurses get all the good gossip first." She winked and nudged him with her elbow. "I was just leaving, anyway. I need to get back. I have to work late tonight," she said, speaking to her husband. "I'll make that pot roast tomorrow, though, okay?"

Straimer nodded, but his lips pulled taut against his teeth in the way they always did when he was pissed. "Sounds perfect. I'll see you back home, babe." He kissed her gently on the lips.

"Relax, Sam," she said as she passed by him. "Your blood pressure is probably through the roof with how hard you're always working." She squeezed his arm and slipped out as Sam shut the door as calmly as he could manage.

"What in the hell is so damn important that you had to kick my wife out, Sam?"

Sam's voice was raspy and his stomach growled. It was almost dinnertime and he had already blown through lunch after going to visit Burt earlier. But despite the fact he hadn't eaten anything all day, he was only hungry for answers. "Twelve years ago, you hired a lawyer to investigate the Walterses' deaths. Why?"

"Sam, what are you talking abou—"

"Twelve years ago!" Sam repeated, this time raising his voice in frustration. "You hired a Burt Horowitz to investigate Nicholas and Renee's deaths. Why!? I need to know."

"Okay, okay, calm down, Sam." Straimer took a deep breath, falling into his seat. A weariness seemed to settle over him. "You knew we were all friends, right? Nick, Renee, and I?" Sam nodded, saying nothing, but taking the seat across from his captain. "Well, nothing about the case seemed to be making sense. A hit-and-run, no witnesses. It just didn't smell right. But I was ordered to leave it alone and that some of the higher-up detectives were handling it."

"But you couldn't?"

"I was young and sad. Mourning the death of my two best friends. If Matt was killed in a mysterious hit-and-run, could you? What if it was Jess in that car with him?"

"Yeah, but Jess is the love of my life. Renee was just your

frie—" And then it slammed into him so hard and fast, it was like a sledgehammer bashing the thought into his brain. "Oh my God. You loved her. You were in love with Jess's mother?"

Straimer avoided Sam's eyes. "But she chose Nick," he said. Sam inhaled deeply, still smelling traces of Rose's perfume in the air.

"Does Rose know?"

"No, of course not. But I've always felt guilty. Even though I moved on and I love Rose so much—"

"There's always a piece of your heart that will belong to Renee," Sam finished for him. He knew just how Straimer felt. If Jess moved on without him, he could never fully get over that loss. "So you hired a lawyer?"

Straimer nodded. "I thought that maybe there was something in the medical records to indicate some sort of clue. It just made no sense. I was on the scene of the wreck—Renee was in bad shape, but I heard they got her vitals stabilized in the ambulance on the way there. It was Nick who was in the worst shape. So when we got to the hospital, I stayed with him. Rose was working that night and she went with Renee. I knew I should have called the girls sooner. Gotten them to the hospital to say good-bye, but I couldn't do it. I couldn't call them with that news."

There was a long pause as Straimer stared at his desk. Sam waited silently. He knew better than to push for more information in a moment like this. After a couple of minutes, Straimer took a deep breath and continued. "It wasn't long after Nick died that Renee crashed and they rushed her into surgery. It just all happened so fast. And so I hired the lawyer out of my own pocket to see what he could find. But there was nothing *to* find. I was just trying to make sense out of senseless death."

Guilt clawed through Sam's stomach. "Captain . . . I have to confess something to you." His voice was hoarse and he had to stop and clear his throat. "When I was fifteen and you all interviewed me about where my mom was that night. . . I lied. I wasn't with her. And she hadn't been home all night. She and her boyfriend had a fight and she stormed off to go for a drive to clear her mind. She was drunk." He could feel his face heating with anger. Anger at her, at himself, at the loss that Jess and Cass suffered because of his own flesh and blood. "I tried to stop her and—and when she came home, hysterically crying, she begged me to lie for her. For them. Her boyfriend got rid of the car for her and I . . . I lied." He rested his hand on his badge, and the cool metal felt refreshing against his heated skin. "I should probably turn this in." He set the badge on Straimer's desk.

"Sam . . . I know. I've known for years. Since before you became a cop. It took me a while, but I found surveillance footage outside of a local shop that showed your mom behind the wheel that night."

Sam's stomach roiled and he thought he was going to be sick. "Why didn't you do anything? Why didn't you say anything?"

"Because by the time I discovered the truth, your mom had already died. Bringing the truth to light would have only ruined *your* life. And you weren't the guilty party."

"I was! I am. I lied to the police! I obstructed justice—I went against everything I've taken an oath for—"

"You were also fifteen. And scared. And your mom, who you loved despite her faults, begged for your help. A lot of kids would have done the same thing. Nick and Renee's deaths are not your fault, Sam."

A lump settled hard in Sam's throat and he ignored that stinging sensation behind his eyes. "You hired me anyway. You pushed me to become a detective."

"And every day you prove to me that I made the right choice."

For the first time in years, Sam felt like he had family in Portland again. "Captain, did Rose ever know about your feelings for Renee? They say women have a sense about these things."

"I suppose. We never really talked about it, but as we got older and she realized she couldn't have children, it became harder and harder for us to be around the Walters. Their family was everything we wanted and I think it just hurt her. So we pulled away from them."

"I just came from Burt Horowitz's office in Falmouth. He lied to you. He did find something in his research. Someone threatened him to get him to keep his mouth shut. And I think it has something to do with Cass's death, too."

Like an explosion, Straimer banged his fist against his desk, standing and pacing the room. Sam could feel his anger. Anger mixed with a satisfaction flowing from his captain. A validation of his suspicions from all those years ago.

"I knew it." Straimer's eyes flickered with rage. "I fucking knew it."

"What are we gonna do about it?" Sam asked, his voice surprisingly calm.

The captain stopped pacing. "We need a warrant. I need to get a warrant for those medical records."

"We don't need a warrant. Jess has the records."

"Did she get them legally?"

Sam pressed his lips together. This was a gray area. The phone on Straimer's desk rang and he picked it up, flopping back into his chair. Sam pulled his own phone out of his back pocket. "Shit. Captain, my phone's dead. Can I use yours?"

But Straimer was saying something into the phone and didn't hear him. After another second, he handed the phone over to Sam. "It's the hospital," he said. "They said they've been trying to get in touch with you for hours. Something about a CAT scan appointment you missed yesterday."

"Son of a bitch," Sam said, and took the phone. "This is Sam," he said into the receiver.

"Detective, it's Dr. Adams." The voice didn't seem nearly as friendly as it had earlier in the week when he had called to check in.

"Dr. Adams, yeah, hi . . ."

"We had an agreement for you to stay on active duty."

Sam rubbed his fingers against his forehead. "Yeah, yeah. I know. I'm sorry. The appointment completely slipped my mind."

"If you don't come in now, right this second, I'll be forced to call your captain back and tell him I'm removing you from active duty."

"No, no . . . don't do that," Sam answered quickly. "I'm on my way." He was already standing, gathering his things before he even hung up. He tossed the phone back to Straimer. "I forgot about my doctor's appointment. I'll try to find Jess when I'm done and then we'll come straight back here."

"Come to my home," Straimer called as Sam ran out. "I'll be at home. Get Jess and bring her straight there with those medical records. Even if they're not legal, at least we'll know what we're looking for. We'll be safe at my house."

42

The world was rocking as Jess blinked awake. Her head pounded and a low vibration of sound hummed through the room. Jess groaned and rolled to her side, feeling a soft mattress and silky high-thread-count sheets beneath her.

She jolted up, but the blood in her head rushed, slamming against the base of her skull. She groaned and pressed her palm against her moist forehead. Sweat glistened there despite the chill that ran through her body. *Where am I?*

Her vision was blurry, but she blinked hard, forcing herself to concentrate, and through her foggy sight, the room started to look familiar.

She swung her legs off the bed, noticing her discarded Jimmy Choos in the corner. Her memory of the afternoon slowly filtered back into her mind. The cooler. Dylan's heart. The medical records.

Oh, no. No, no, no, no . . . She stood quickly, too quickly, as her stomach flipped and the world rocked again, catapulting her back onto the bed.

Using the bedpost, she pulled herself to her feet, fighting her nausea, and stumbled toward the dresser where her clutch was. Inside were her keys, but her pepper spray had been removed from the key ring. Her credit cards and ID were in her wallet, but no medical records.

"No!" she cried, and threw the purse at the closed door. With what little strength she had, she ran to the door, twisting the knob and pulling. It was locked.

Another surge made the room tilt and she realized it wasn't just her disorientation causing the room rock, but rather the floor instead was tilting. She pressed her back against the door, taking in her surroundings. The walnut furniture. Rope accents. Nautical décor. She knew this room. It was Elliot's master bedroom . . . on his boat.

Jess clamped her eyes shut. No. She couldn't freak out. Not yet. She needed to keep a level head and get out of this alive. It couldn't be Elliot. It couldn't be the one person she had turned away from Sam to trust. Someone had drugged her . . . that much was obvious. But if it wasn't Elliot, then why the hell had they brought her to Elliot's boat?

She launched herself off the door, opening every drawer she could find and rummaging through various folded clothes. She needed a clue, a weapon . . . anything. In the bottom drawer, beneath dozens of folded socks, her hand slipped around something cold and metal. She gripped it, pulling it out. She had a brief reprieve from her fear at the sight of the Swiss Army knife. She looked down at her gown and hissed a frustrated sigh. She had no pockets, no bra, nothing. She lunged for her clutch on the floor, dropping the knife inside. It wasn't ideal, nor exactly easy to grab, but it was better than nothing.

She tucked the clutch under her arm and flung open the closet door. Stacked on the floor were the suitcases of drugs she and Elliot had brought from her house last night. She bent, scooting the suitcases over and feeling around the floor. All the way in the back of the closet was a safe. A very large safe.

Her hands trembled as she turned the closet light on. All of the drugs, all the pills they had transported from her house, were stacked on the shelves in the walk-in closet. But if they were there, then what was in the suitcases that she and Elliot were supposed to dump into international waters tonight?

She hovered over the suitcases, unzipping the top one carefully. Inside, instead of the drugs that they had loaded the suitcase up with, there were bags and bags of candy. She ripped open one of the bags, which was full of breath mints.

Oh, God. Her blood froze over in her veins, sending chilly vibrations down her body. Elliot was keeping the drugs for himself.

Jess zipped the suitcase shut and backed away from the closet. Her throat burned and felt swollen, but with a steely resolve, she ran for the door, knocking. "Hello? Elliot?!" she called. "Anyone? How—how did I get here? Elliot, come on, open up!" *Dammit.* She pressed her ear to the door. Maybe he wasn't even on the boat. It was faint, but on the other side of the door, she heard footsteps.

She knocked louder. "Master," she called with another knock. "Sir, may I please come out?"

A key rattled on the other side. "Jess?"

She pulled back from the door as it unlocked and swung open. "Lyle? What are you doing here?"

"I always come to the boat early to set up for his parties beforehand. What's going on, what are you doing in here? Were you locked in?"

Lying had never been her strong suit. But she had no choice . . . this one had to be good. "I don't know." She put a hand to her head. "I'm really dizzy and—and the last thing I remember was opening my sister's mail this morning. Everything else is kind of hazy."

"Come here." Lyle took her hand and guided her to the bed. Running into the en suite bathroom, he filled a glass with water and handed it to her. "Did he . . . did Elliot do something to you?"

Concern reflected in Lyle's shimmering eyes. It didn't take much for Jess to start crying; the tears were already there just waiting to fall. "I don't know. But . . . I think he might have."

"Oh, God. No . . . not again. I-I can't let this happen again. N-not to you."

"Let what happen again? Lyle, tell me, please . . . what do you know?"

He froze, rushing to the doorway and looking out into the hallway before shutting the door. "We have to get you out of here, Jess. He did it. He killed Cass. I was there that night and he just . . . he shot her." Tears spilled down Lyle's cheeks and he pulled at his hair, making the rusty red strands stand straight up to the ceiling.

"Why? Why did he kill her if he loved her?"

Lyle shook his head and wiped the back of his hand under his nose. "He doesn't love anyone. Money is his one true love. He discovered Cass was bringing in this new drug and he got pissed that there was someone trying to smuggle something on his turf. She didn't know it was him, but he sent her all these threatening notes. Bullied her into smuggling the new drug in for him after she wanted to quit. All she wanted was a few pills for a friend, but he had an expensive client willing to pay top dollar for continuous large shipments. And then he found a way to make her his sub—an even better way for him to keep tabs on her."

"But why? Why kill her then if they had a good thing going?"

"Because," he said, regret consuming his soft voice. "The police caught her. They recognized her picture or something at border patrol. She was working with them to gather evidence. And the call she made to you . . . it was the last straw for him. The last betrayal."

Jess gulped, her throat closing. Words were damn near impossible. "You know about that call?"

He nodded. " 'You're in the frame'? I don't know what it means, but it seemed like a sister thing. Look," he said, kneeling in front of her at the foot of the bed. "I didn't pull the trigger. But I'm just as responsible. I can't let it happen again with you. I owe it to your sister."

Doubt clouded her mind for all of a second. He seemed genuine, but Jess sure as hell wasn't trusting anyone easily these days. Then again, she wasn't really in a position to choose her allies. She needed to get out of there as soon as possible. "What do we do?"

He stood, holding out a hand. "We're going to get you off this boat," he said.

"How?"

"There's a basement hull. Down there, we can crawl out through a hatch and get into one of the dinghies."

"Okay," Jess said, squeezing his hand. Uncertainty still popped down her spine but at this point she really didn't have much choice. She gripped her clutch, hearing the Swiss Army knife rattle around inside as a comforting reminder that she wasn't entirely unarmed.

"Come on," he said. "We need to hurry." He tugged her toward the door just as Elliot opened it and walked in.

Elliot looked truly startled, utterly taken aback as though he hadn't expected anyone to be in his bedroom. "Jessica? Lyle? I thought you weren't coming until later?"

Lyle stepped between her and Elliot, using his body as a shield. "Tell her, Mr. Warner," he said, but even in his bravery, his voice trembled. "She already knows all about the drugs."

Elliot's face changed rapidly from confused to regretful. "You know?" he asked, looking beyond Lyle to Jess. She couldn't find the words, so she just nodded. "It's true. I started dealing drugs when I was young and just out of community college. It turns out that having a knack for business applies to all businesses—drug dealings included. It got me my start in real estate. I'm sorry I didn't tell you, Jessica. The less you knew, the safer you were."

"Like Cass was safe?" Jess's voice cracked. "You lied to me. You got me to trust you. You got Cass to trust you—and Dane."

"I felt awful that Cass got involved in everything. You have to believe me. Even I have people I answer to."

Jess moved so that she and Lyle were standing next to each other. She was feeling stronger and braver by the second. "You killed her. You pretended to love her and you shot her, leaving her for dead in the ocean."

Elliot jerked back as though she had just struck him. "You think I killed her? Jessica, you have to believe me. Ask your detective—I have an alibi that night. It's airtight. After I left her at the masquerade, I was on a video conference call with a dozen international clients."

"You . . . what?" Her brain grew fuzzy again, like a static television. "But Lyle said—" Jess turned to look at Elliot's trusted employee a second too late. If only she had looked a moment earlier, maybe she would have seen the gun sticking out from underneath his jacket. Or maybe she could have stopped his hand as he reached for it. But everything happened so quickly, and Lyle grabbed his gun, aimed for Elliot's gut, and pulled the trigger.

43

Sam got to the hospital quickly. He ran up the stairs to the fourth floor into the neuro department and rushed up to a startled receptionist. "I'm here, I'm here. I'm supposed to be seeing Dr. Adams. He called and told me to come in right away."

"Oh, yes. Mr. McCloskey?"

"That's me."

"He was pulled away for a family emergency. But he cleared you to go see Dr. Moore instead."

"Dr. Moore?"

"Mhmm," she said, disinterested, her eyes locked onto her computer screen. "You know where his office is? He'll meet you there and take you down to radiology."

Sam turned to the stairwell. He knew just where Moore's office was. He took the stairs several at a time, anxious to get face-to-face with the man who'd been toying with him for days. He wanted to look him in the eyes and hear his confession, the man he was convinced had killed Cass and Dr. Brown, someone who was supposed to be his best friend. The man who was responsible for torturing Jess. He wanted to throw Marcus

Moore against the wall, tighten the cuffs around his wrists, and drag him off to jail. He was so close . . . the doctor just needed to make one little slip-up and then Sam could officially arrest him.

Moore's office door was cracked slightly open. It didn't matter to Sam that he was in a hospital, surrounded by witnesses. Or that he didn't think the doctor would necessarily attack him there. Something about the situation felt completely off. He touched a hand to the gun on his hip, wrapping his fingers around the handle. With his other hand, he pushed the door and it slowly creaked open. "Dr. Moore?" he called again.

Soft music played from inside the room and though it took a couple of seconds to recognize the tune, when it hit him, it slammed into him like a wall of bricks. *"Witchy Woman."*

Sam's gaze darted around the empty office. There had to be something, *anything,* that could implicate the man in even one of his crimes. Then he could get a search warrant and nail the bastard. But the doctor was too damn smart for that. A song playing on repeat on his stereo was circumstantial at best.

Sam grabbed his cell phone, cursing as he remembered the battery was dead. Instead, he grabbed Moore's office phone, pausing just before he dialed Straimer. Instead, he hit *redial.* A series of beeps sounded in his ear and then a woman's voice answered.

"What are you still doing at the office?" she snarled. "Get down to Warner's boat now. People will be arriving any minute. I'm waiting for you in O'Malley's Pub next to the dock." Sam looked at the time—it was only six.

Without saying a word, Sam slipped the phone back into its cradle. Warner's masquerade. Sam cursed and paced the office, scanning the cluttered space for any other clues. There were more questions than there were answers. Why the hell would a doctor get involved in distributing drugs? Why would he risk it? Especially since the only drug he was distributing seemed to be a new prescription medication. It didn't make any sense. This had to be something bigger. Something more involved than the drug trade.

Sam dialed Straimer's home number on the office phone. "Captain—get to Elliot Warner's yacht at the pier next to O'Malley's Pub. There's a black-tie masquerade event happening there tonight and if we don't get to that yacht by seven, I have a feeling we're going to lose all the evidence in this case."

"Black tie? Sam—"

"Captain, just find yourself a tux and a mask and gather as many uniforms as you can who clean up nicely. Go to Mary's Chowder House and ask for Epoly. Tell her I sent you and you need to get into that party. She'll help."

"You need to give me more, Sam. I need more than this if I'm going to be pulling uniforms for backup—"

"My cell is dead, but I'll meet you on the yacht. It leaves dock in an hour." He hung up, racing out of the office.

"Oh my God."

Jess clutched her stomach and fell to her knees beside Elliot. Blood flowed from under his body, spreading into a pool. If she hadn't known better, hadn't seen Lyle shoot him with her own eyes, it would have looked like a spilled glass of red wine seeping out beneath him.

Elliot was trembling, his face gone white. His bloodstained hands clutched the hole in his stomach. "How could you do that?" Jess asked, looking up at Lyle. Gone was the innocent-looking man wanting to help her escape. Instead of the weepy brown eyes he had flashed her earlier, they were now dull and beady as his lips tightened into a scowl.

"So you believe him over me? You believe his lies?" Lyle shouted.

She did believe Elliot. He wasn't the one who pulled a gun. And he had looked genuinely surprised to see her in his master suite. She knew that admitting the truth was suicide, but she nodded all the same. "Yes. I believe him."

Rather than the sneer she expected to see, reverence gleamed in Lyle's eyes. "Well, then you're not as stupid as I thought you were. I could have given everything to your sister. Everything he offered her, I could have provided, too."

Blood trickled out of the corner of Elliot's mouth and his words were quiet. She could barely hear him speak. "H-he always wanted to take over the drug trade. I wanted out. I wanted to walk away."

"Shut up!" Lyle screamed, cocking the gun and raising it, this time aiming at Elliot's forehead.

"That would be a waste of a bullet," Elliot said, and gave a throaty chuckle despite wincing in pain.

"You wanted out so that you could begin a life with *her*. You wanted out so that you could take her away from me."

Despite her trembling limbs, Jess stood up and started backing toward the door. Lyle was a lunatic; totally delusional. "How could Cass have made such a terrible choice?" she managed to say with a steady voice.

"I—what?" Lyle's eyes were wild, bloodshot with fury.

"Elliot didn't love her. He used her like a little one-trick pony. If he loved her, he would have been able to keep her in line, isn't that right?" Jess took a cautious step forward. "Is that what you would have done?"

"He was too soft. That's why she strayed and went to that detective instead of remaining loyal to the business," said Lyle.

Jess took another step forward, carefully reaching out her hands and stroking his arms. "But you . . . you wouldn't have been afraid to tell her the truth. You weren't afraid to tell me." She sucked in a breath, pushing her breasts into his chest and curling her arms around his neck.

"All your sister needed was a firmer hand," Lyle said. His palm cracked hard against her ass, squeezing like it was a piece of fruit to be crushed. Jess cried out, falling against his body. His mouth crashed down onto hers and he bit her lip hard enough that blood spilled over her tongue. Tears burned in her eyes, but she pushed them away, right along with her pride. *Play along,* a little voice said. *Stay alive.*

"Now, *that's* how a man kisses," she said, brushing her finger along Lyle's lips.

"This outfit won't do for tonight. Not if you're going to be my date," he said.

Jess pulled back, letting her hand fall to her clavicle. "You're asking me to be your date?"

Small tremors slashed through her core as she watched and waited for his response. There was nothing else she could do.

"I wasn't asking. I'll be right back—I always keep some backup outfits in my quarters for my subs."

He left Jess and Elliot in the room, locking it from the outside. Once he was gone Jess didn't waste any time. She rushed to the chest of drawers, grabbing as many spare clothes as she could, and carefully lifted Elliot's shirt off his chest. She tied the materials in a makeshift tourniquet around his waist. "Breathe, Elliot," she said. "You're going to get out of here alive. The fact that you're still conscious is a good sign."

"I trusted him . . ." Elliot sputtered. "I trusted him with Cass. Trusted him to keep her safe."

"Don't think about that right now. When Lyle and I leave, put pressure to the wound. There's got to be a doctor somewhere on board."

"Downstairs," he rasped, the single word taking way too much of his effort for Jess's comfort. "There's an operating room down in the hull."

"What? *Why?*"

He grasped her hand in his bloody one. "Stay alive, Jess. I'm so sorry I dragged you and Cass into this."

Jess cupped his head, placing a wadded-up shirt under the

crook of his neck. "Don't do that. We don't have time for re-grets and this is not good-bye." With that, she wiped her bloody hands on another shirt as best she could, and then threw it in the closet.

"There's more to this than just drugs. There's a whole team of doctors—"

The lock turned and Elliot groaned, shutting his mouth as the door opened. Lyle stood in the doorway and held up a new outfit . . . if it could even be called that. He handed it to Jess. "Here you go."

Jess stared at the leather strips of the gown, horrified, doing her best to disguise her disgust. "Isn't this a black-tie affair?"

"BDSM black tie is a little more . . . open to interpretation," Lyle said. He nestled into a chair in the corner. "Get dressed, Jessica. I want to watch."

44

Sam made it down to the pier in less than thirty minutes. Granted, his cuff links weren't fastened and he'd barely had time to grab a scarf that was different from the color he usually wore at these functions. The color of your scarf denoted your role in the community as a dom or sub, so by changing it he hoped to confuse the regulars. No one could know it was him at first glance. Luckily, he'd had a larger mask in his closet, one that covered most of his face. And before throwing his tuxedo on, he covered his hair with baby powder to change the color. Glancing in the mirror, he could almost pass for someone different. He just needed a little luck.

There was only one problem. He didn't know what the ticket item was to get on the boat this time. It was usually something challenging to get ahold of. In the past it had been a dead fish or something equally bizarre.

Whatever was needed to board that boat as a party member, he was sure he didn't have it on him. He needed to get creative if he was going to make it on the boat. Jess and Elliot should already be on board, greeting the guests, playing out their little ruse. Whatever it was they had planned, they knew that Dr. Moore was going to be on that boat tonight. They knew and they had been planning this. Without him.

Hired bouncers walked the perimeter of the boat's deck. *Elliot sure knows how to throw a bash,* Sam thought as he strolled to the edge of the dock, pretending to check out the various angles of the yacht. He scratched his chin, feigning interest in the woodwork and dinghies hanging off the sides while the rest of the masked partygoers gathered at the gangplank. Several hostesses waited to check their ticket items, but he was still too far away to see what they were holding.

Sam eyed a small ladder that trailed up from a dinghy, hovering just above the water and leading to the middle deck. His eyes followed the line up to where a bouncer was forty feet or so above, pacing back and forth, but he didn't seem to be focused all that hard on Sam's side of the dock. The bouncer's sights were set on the front of the boat, where partygoers were gathering. There was a chance that Sam could jump onto the escape boat and climb up the ladder without anyone seeing him.

A small chance. A fucking miniscule chance. But he had to try something. He glanced to his left in time to lock eyes with Mary, who was turning the corner and heading for the party. She stilled midstride. Even from far away, he watched as her head tilted, looking from him to the boat. She gave a barely visible nod and then she strutted toward the entrance and flung her arms out dramatically. "Hello, my Mainer fetish group!" she called in a singsong voice. All heads swiveled in her direction, including the bouncer's above Sam. He moved to the side of the boat until he was entirely out of view, checking out the commotion below.

That nervous tension uncoiled in Sam's belly—even if just for a moment. He'd have to remind himself to get Mary a damn good Christmas gift. Backing up a few steps, he took a deep breath. It was now or never. She wasn't going to be able to distract everyone for long.

He ran and launched off the edge of the dock, leaping onto the safety boat hanging off the side of the yacht. The edge slammed into his stomach, damn near Heimliching his lunch right out of his belly. His toes dipped into the water, but he pulled himself over the side until he was flat on the floor of the little rowboat. It certainly wasn't his most graceful move ever, but it worked. He paused, waiting to see if any of the bouncers had heard his *Mission: Impossible* moment. From the other end of the dock, he could still hear Mary's high-pitched voice distracting the crowd.

Sam sat up, glancing up at the deck beyond the ladder. He couldn't see anyone, but at this angle that didn't mean the bouncer wasn't still there.

Sam channeled that grueling year of detective training and jumped onto the ladder, pulling his entire body weight like a chin-up.

He reached the top, curling his aching arms around the edge of the ship and kicking off of the top step of the ladder to throw his body weight over the edge.

He landed with a thud, his back slamming into the floor of the boat. He sucked in a needy breath—holy shit. He and Matt seriously needed to lay off the doughnuts.

"And that, ladies and gentleman, is my toast!" he heard Mary's voice echo from down below, followed by the sound of dozens of clinking glasses. How she managed to get flutes of champagne passed around for her toast was beyond him. He had long stopped trying to figure out the mysterious ways of Mary.

Sam heard a bass chuckle from somewhere to the right and he pulled it together, forcing his breath to slow down as he rolled to his feet. He walked calmly and as slowly as he could manage in the opposite direction. It was all about looking like you belonged.

"Hey!" the bouncer shouted after him, but Sam didn't turn around. He continued walking toward where he could hear the other partygoers mingling. "Hey, you! How did you get down here?"

Sam sped up his footsteps, taking the stairs up to the top deck three at a time, and then blended into the crowd, turning in time to see the bouncer hopping up the steps and scanning the crowd. *Come on, Jess,* Sam thought, also searching the crowd. *Where are you, baby?* There was an uneasy burrowing feeling in his gut. He hadn't heard from her all day, even thought it was his own fault for forgetting to charge his phone.

The crowd got bigger and bigger as more and more masked men and dolled-up women filtered onto the yacht. He could only hope that Straimer had made it on with Matt and Rodriguez and a few others. But with the sea of masked people floating around him Sam didn't recognize any of his team.

A man a little younger than Sam stood up at the highest point of the boat, bottle of champagne in hand, and began to speak. He looked familiar, but it was hard to tell who he was behind the black mask that covered half of his face.

"On behalf of our host this evening, our beloved Master X, I wanted to welcome you to our yearly gala—this year, a regatta! There is plenty of food and enough alcohol to drown your livers . . . and your sorrows. Am I right?" He held his hand out, gesturing for someone to join him in the spotlight. It was a woman. Not just any woman—Jess.

Sam didn't know what he was expecting Jess to be wearing that night, but nothing could have prepared him for the woman who stepped up beside that man. A man who wasn't Elliot. Sam didn't like it. He didn't like it one bit.

Sam's entire body clenched, muscles steeled and ready for battle. He had to keep cool, think with a level head. The leather dress Jess was wearing could have been painted on. Where it wasn't skintight, it had well-planned shreds, stretching across her body in strings. Her hips and thighs were covered by nothing but little scraps of leather that came together in a skirt.

Spaghetti straps filtered into two triangles that barely covered her nipples and the outsides of her breasts but then gaped open, revealing a swell of cleavage and skin all the way down to her belly button, baring her flat stomach. Heels that looked like they needed to be registered as weapons made her muscular legs look like they went on for miles.

A full head of russet brown hair peeked out from under the speaker's mask and it hit Sam like a spotlight. The driver. The mystery host taking Elliot's place was his driver.

An awareness took hold as Sam realized that all other dominants in the room were staring at Jess, their jaws practically hitting the deck. Their eyes bugged out of their heads and the jealousy of other women on the boat swarmed around like a hive of bees. But Sam knew Jess better than any of them. And that confident swagger that he knew and loved about her wasn't present. Something was wrong. Elliot's driver tugged her into his hip, embracing her with one arm and holding his champagne bottle with the other. He popped the cork. Champagne spilled out over the edge of the bottle like a volcano erupting with white, fizzy bubbles. The crowd cheered and music started to play from somewhere. The yacht began to pull away from the dock

Where the hell is Elliot if someone who worked for him is giving the welcome for the party? thought Sam. It didn't settle right.

Sam watched as Jess scanned the crowd. Was she looking for him? Pushing his way through the masked revelers, he tried to make himself stand out, stand taller so that she'd see him, but she looked right past him and into the crowd beyond. His sense of hope deflated. But just then Jess paused and her eyes scanned back the way they came, landing on him. She squinted from behind her mask. Sam gave her a little nod. After a quick glance to the man beside her, Jess angled her head lower. Signaling . . . *signaling what? Something under them maybe?*

Sam shook his head as discreetly as he could, conveying he didn't understand. Jess's shoulders slumped, defeated.

Jess brushed her fingers against the arm of the man beside her, which curved possessively around her waist. His fingers clamped onto her hip and Sam's hands flexed instinctually at his sides to keep himself from charging. Jess said something in the driver's ear. She gestured to the bar, motioning with her hands that she wanted something to drink. Sam's grin widened as he realized those hand gestures were meant for him, not the driver. The driver nodded and Jess brushed past him, on her way to the bar.

There was a jolt of excitement and he pushed aside the pride he felt for Jess at how well she was handling this. There wasn't time for that now. He shoved through the crowds, also making his way to the bar.

"Two Woodfords on the rocks," Jess said to the bartender, and then gave a quick glance around. Only a few feet away was yet another bouncer, almost as though Lyle had sent a prison guard with her to ensure she behaved.

"Are you okay?" Sam whispered in her ear.

"No." Her voice was a gut-wrenching rasp across his senses.

"What's going on?"

"One floor below deck. Second room on your left. Save Elliot. He said something about doctors being on the bottommost floor . . . about this being about so much more than drugs . . . whatever that means."

"Save Elliot—why? What happened?"

"Just *go.*" The words didn't even qualify as a whisper, but were just mouthed in his direction. She was in serious trouble.

"I could arrest him now, if you saw something and can testify—"

"These bouncers will catch you before you even try to make a move, Sam. And he will kill you. You have to wait for the right time."

The bartender brought Jess two whiskeys and her demeanor shifted immediately. She turned and took them back to the driver.

It had only been about ten minutes since the "host" had popped the champagne, but they were already in the middle of the water with no plans to hit land until well after midnight. It was an easy place to dispose of bodies. Of drugs. Of almost anything.

"She's right, you know," a woman's voice said from beside him. It was low and sounded tighter than his grip on the edge of the bar. "And I can help you." He turned toward the voice. Shock didn't begin to describe how Sam felt when he saw who was standing before him, ready to help.

45

Lyle took one glass of Woodford from Jess's hand, the ice creating a sweaty moisture clinging to the outside. He took a sip, then thrust it back into her hands as though she was his waitress. *No . . . worse than that,* thought Jess. A waitress drops off a drink and is done with it. He was treating her like a piece of human furniture.

"I saw you chatting with someone over there. Was it who I think it was?"

Fear rose like a storm cloud on an already dark day. Jess fought to keep hold of her wits. "I can't read your thoughts. I don't know *who* you think it was."

He jerked her arm, yanking her closer to him. "Don't be fucking cute with me. Your detective is on board, isn't he?"

"He is, but he's not here as a detective. He's here as my ex-boyfriend and a fellow dominant in the community. There's nothing for you to worry about. He'll get over me eventually." She batted her eyelashes at Lyle, nibbling the corner of her lip. "He can't take me to the places I need to go. He's not man enough."

He yanked the glass from her hand, drinking the contents in one gulp before tossing it onto a side table. Still grasping the upper part of her arm, he pulled her down the stairs, throwing her into one of the rooms. The door slammed shut behind him. "You know where we are?" She looked around, not recognizing the room from Elliot's tour the night before.

"It's the playroom," Lyle answered impatiently, pulling the revolver from his waistband. His index finger stroked the trigger, his pure joy from holding the gun evident by the gentle smile on his face. "You ever been shot before, Jessica?" he asked.

She dug her feet into the carpet as he gripped her arm, pulling her deeper into the room. "I'm going to take your silence as a no," he continued. "Well let me tell you, it hurts like a bitch. For years, I ran drugs for Elliot like a little fucking errand boy. I was being groomed to take over. I couldn't wait for him to retire and give the drug ring to me. It didn't seem like he was ever going to leave. And that's when they came to me with an even better offer. I'd still be a runner, but the pay was three times what Elliot offered. And though having organs in my car is a little messier than drugs, the money more than makes up for it. I didn't even give a shit at that point if Elliot stayed or left. Except one stipulation of my new job, the one catch, was that I had to keep on pretending that I was his errand boy. I had to keep tabs on him. And your sister. Make sure they were doing everything they needed to."

"Oh my God," Jess gasped as the pieces all fell into place. "Organs. You're illegally harvesting organs, aren't you? Is Elliot a part of this?"

"Your precious Elliot wanted nothing to do with this. They managed to blackmail him into using the boat for surgeries, but other than that, he's squeaky clean. If you don't mind being in love with a drug dealer, that is. He's a fucking moron. The money from the drugs is nothing compared to what we get for organs. Hundreds of thousands. And the more kids we get hooked on O, the more organs we have to sell."

"Christine harvests them during her autopsies." She meant it to be a question, but even as she asked it, she already knew the answer. Had seen it with her own eyes when Christine dropped off Dylan's heart.

"You're a smart girl, you know that?"

"But, my sister . . . she didn't . . . she didn't know about this, did she?"

"No," he grunted. "She was clueless. Until that moron doctor friend of hers stuck his nose where it didn't belong. He and your detective friend practically pulled the trigger themselves."

"But they didn't pull the trigger—*you* did." Jess winced as he jerked her closer into his body. "I thought you cared about Cass?"

"I did!" he shouted, his voice becoming shriller with every passing moment. "I fucking *loved* her. But she betrayed me. She betrayed all of us. Went behind our backs, working with that detective. Calling you, trying to leave a clue because she feared for her life. I wasn't planning on killing her that night exactly. But she was going to die. No amount of love I had for her could have stopped it."

"You said someone else was there when she died? . . . Who? If I'm going to die as well, I need to know."

"Marc was there. He and I were always in charge of getting the drugs from the parties."

The other night when Lyle dropped her off. She had opened the medical records in his backseat. She didn't think he was paying attention, but of course he was. She had stayed awake long enough for him to get down to the tunnel and sneak into the house and attack her.

"My phone—the phone I lost the night Cass called . . . the night she died. Did you orchestrate that, too?" she asked.

"We have people in New York . . . all over, really. It wasn't hard for us to get that phone out of your possession."

They'd been watching her long before she ever knew any of this existed. A raging fear coursed in her body, leaving her desperate and shaking. "I-I mean, I understand. You had to do what you had to do to survive. To . . . thrive." She smoothed her hand up his chest, curving her palm around the back of his neck.

His grin twisted painfully as his free hand latched onto her throat, squeezing. "You can drop the act now, Jessica," he growled, slamming her head against the wall behind her. Pinpricks of various colors blurred in her vision. Her purse slipped from her grasp and hit the floor as she attempted to open it, attempted to access the knife buried inside. "I knew you were lying in Elliot's bedroom . . . and yet, I thought this could be fun. Give you hope. Then again, I didn't expect your boyfriend to show up tonight."

Jess clawed at his hand around her neck, wheezing for a breath, any oxygen she could get into her lungs. There had to be an escape. It couldn't end like this. The pain as his grip tightened was nothing compared to the pure glee she saw in his eyes as he literally stole the last breaths from her body.

The pain melted into weariness; an exhaustion that was planted deep in her bones. He knew just when to ease up on his grip to keep her conscious. He wanted her to feel it. To be present until the utter last moment. If only she could get the gun from his hands. Turn it on him. But her brain wasn't sending the signals to her arms fast enough anymore.

A pounding settled in her brain and just as she thought the world was going to go dark again, Lyle released her throat. She gasped for air, coughing, her lungs burning as she was able to breathe again. There was a pounding in her head—*no, it isn't in my head*, thought Jess. It was knocking on the door.

"Boss, there's a situation out here," said a voice from the hallway.

Lyle growled, lunging for the doorknob. But Jess knew that voice. Would know it anywhere. She slid along the wall, grabbing her purse and getting out of the way. As Lyle unlocked and swung the door open, a fist slammed into his face. His neck rocked backward as Sam launched himself at Lyle, but even after taking the first blow, Lyle was ready for the fight. Sam had his gun in the air, but Lyle was faster. He yanked Jess by her hair, pulling her back against himself like a human shield. This time the barrel of Lyle's gun pushed into her skull. Drops of blood from Lyle's nose dripped down her arm.

"I will fucking make a Rorschach painting using her brains if you don't back off," Lyle snarled.

Sam kept his gun drawn, but maneuvered his body out of the way of the door. "Let her go. Release her and we can work something out."

Lyle snorted, the movement causing another spray of blood to fan out down Jess's arm. "You don't think I'm stupid enough to believe that?"

"What do you want, then?" Sam said.

"I want you to go out there and call off your men. Tell them to stand down. Whatever it is you say to get them to back the fuck off. Or I will put a bullet in her head."

"Okay. You got it." Sam's voice was cool. Too cool. And his relaxed state was chilling in its lack of emotion. "But you've got to let her go."

"You're kidding, right? She's the only reason I'm alive."

"Take me as your hostage instead."

Jess couldn't see Lyle behind her but he tightened his hold around her hair. "You must think I'm stupid. Switching out a woman like her for a man who could overpower me? Not a chance. She comes with me until I'm safely off this boat."

"And how exactly are you going to manage that? Walk through a party of hundreds of people with a gun and a hostage?" Jess could see the tightness of Sam's muscles despite the calmness of his voice. She could see it in the white-knuckled grip he had on his gun.

"I have a plan. Now . . . call off your men."

Sam's eyes flashed before he called into the hallway. "Stand down! He's coming out and he's got Jess."

Lyle kept his eyes on Sam as he exited the room and backed down the hallway. The empty hallway, Jess noticed. She was positioned flush against his body, still acting as his shield. They reached a staircase, but Sam followed, the barrel of the gun pointed in her direction. Though she knew he was careful, waiting for his shot, it was unnerving staring into that steel cylinder. One wrong move on either side of her and she was a dead woman. "Stop following me, Detective!" Lyle's voice sounded more panicked with each passing second.

"Or what?" Sam said.

"I'll shoot her!"

"You'll lose your only bargaining chip and you'll be dead less than a second after you pull the trigger. And you know it. You're smarter than that . . . Lyle, wasn't it?"

Lyle's steps slowed behind Jess and her scalp was being pulled so hard that the nerve endings were close to being numb. "Where's your team of people, Detective?" He cackled in her ear. "There's no one else here, is there?"

She could feel the anxiety in Sam, even from how far away he was down the hall, just as much as she could feel the readiness in his body, the way his muscles were braced to react at any moment. "I told them to stand down. They're obeying orders."

She could feel Lyle's heart slamming into her back and it mirrored her own racing pulse. He pulled her down a small set of stairs and then they stopped, as if they were pressed up against something. *A wall? A door?*

Sam rushed to the top of the stairs. "The thing is, Lyle, I don't think you're going to kill her. I think you care about her. And you already had to kill someone else you cared about, didn't you? You already had to kill Cass."

Lyle inhaled sharply, a small sniff at the base of Jess's hair before he spoke. "Death is the ultimate form of control." His voice was venomous.

Jess clenched her eyes shut, not wanting to look behind her, but also aching to know where she was being taken. Lyle kicked at the door, using his foot to knock. She heard a curse from inside.

"We cannot open this door!" a male voice called from inside.

"It's an emergency!" Lyle shouted.

"You'll have to kill me to take her through that door without me, Lyle. And the second you move the gun to point it at me instead of her, I'll have my clear shot to your forehead. And you know it. Better to give yourself up now," said Sam.

"You know what else I know?" Lyle said. "You're here *alone*. And inside this room are more of my people. Armed. Ready." Lyle kicked at the door again. "Let me in, goddammit. Now!"

Jess slowly moved her hand, unclasping her purse. With Lyle's body rocking and him kicking the door, he didn't feel her as she pulled out the Swiss Army knife, opening one of the blades.

Sam's eyes followed her movements. He shook his head in warning, but she had to defend herself. She couldn't stand there like a victim anymore. Curving her palm around the knife, she hid it in her hand, pressing it flush against her wrist and forearm, the point digging into her flesh.

There was more murmuring from the other side of the door and as it swung open, Lyle ducked inside. Sam launched off the top step, knocking the door wider just before it shut. There was a commotion of shouts and screams and Jess used the distraction to plunge her knife into Lyle's thigh. The other noise around her dulled as the room filled with his scream. His gun fell and skittered across the room, landing in a corner near a stainless-steel rolling cart. Jess shoved off of his falling body at the same time she made eye contact with Christine, dressed in scrubs. Christine wasn't a killer. She was a surgeon. A medical examiner who had participated in some very shady things. But she didn't strike Jess as being a murderer. And yet, it was as though a rubber band snapped between them and they both lunged for the gun.

Behind her Jess could hear grunting and punches being thrown and shouting, and she wondered if Sam had lost his gun in the struggle. She needed Lyle's gun. Without it she was helpless. *They* were helpless. She and Christine landed on the floor at the same time, hands grasping for the weapon. Jess pulled her knee up, delivering a sharp blow to Christine's nose. The woman cried out, hands going to her face as blood flowed through her fingers.

"You fucking bitch!" she screamed.

"You bet your fucking ass I am," Jess yelled, and kicked the woman again, her foot connecting to her chest. The hard blow sent Christine onto her back.

Jess stood, wrapping her hand around the warm metal handle of the revolver. She was dizzy. Her throat ached and each breath felt like fire entering her lungs. But she had the upper hand, at least. She swiveled, backed against the wall, and grabbed Sam's gun where it had rolled into the corner.

Both Dr. Moore and Sam were bloody from fighting. Dr. Moore had a scalpel clutched in his palm as a weapon. Jess clicked the safeties off and aimed one of her guns directly at Moore's head. "You," she said. "Drop the knife and get your back against the wall."

His snarl sounded like something a caged animal would make, but he did what she said, his hands going in the air.

"Walters!" a voice called from somewhere behind her.

"And you," she spun, facing Lyle, his hands clutched around his leg, the Swiss Army knife sticking out of his thigh. "You fucking killed my sister." She stepped closer, cocking the gun.

"Jess," Sam said. But his voice sounded far away. She heard

her name again. And then again, but she just kept advancing on Lyle.

"She thought you were friends—and you shot her in the chest."

Lyle's eyes were calm, his expression filled with a satisfaction that Jess wanted to wipe clean. "What do you care?" he asked. "Oh, she told me all about you. How you'd never call, never visit. She knew what she was getting into with this business. She couldn't possibly have believed she was getting out of it alive."

"Jessie." Sam's voice was like a warm wave lapping over her, calming her and she let it wash into her senses. "Jessie, give me the gun."

"Listen to him, Ms. Walters." It was the first time the second voice registered in her mind. She turned, releasing the guns into Sam's palm and she could feel the entire room give a collective sigh as she unarmed herself. Jess turned to see who had been talking to her, calming her.

"Lulu?"

The mousy submissive looked anything but in the moment. She had a gun raised and her lean strong biceps and triceps were tense. Her mouth was set into a firm, determined line.

"Actually," she said. "I prefer Agent Kinney." She held out a badge with her spare hand. "FBI. You're all under arrest," she said, turning her attention to the room of doctors and Lyle.

Jess spun to Sam.

"She's been investigating these parties and Mercy Hospital for over a year now," he explained.

"Everyone, hands in the air ... I want to see your palms." She had her gun aimed not at Dr. Moore, and not at Christine or even Lyle. Jess followed the line of where the barrel pointed: directly at Dr. Adams.

"Ms. Walters, Agent Kinney, Detective McCloskey," Dr. Adams said in a calm voice, looking up at them through surgical glasses clipped to his head. "I think I should point out that by putting my hands in the air, I would be effectively killing this man on the table. And considering we three doctors are his only hope for survival, you may want to think twice before shooting us."

Jess had been so amped up on adrenaline and fighting for her life, that she didn't realize what was going on in the room surrounding her. There on the surgical table, unconscious and with his chest cavity spread wide open, was Dane.

46

The boat had docked two hours ago and the doctors were still in surgery inside the boat. They said it was too risky to move Dane. Pulling a man with an open chest out into a unsterile environment would cause sepsis—and them barging in the middle of his surgery put him at enough risk as it was. Elliot had been rushed in an ambulance to the hospital, in critical condition. Everything in Jess's world was crashing down. She sat on a bench overlooking the boat and Matt sat beside her, putting his arms around her shoulders.

"Sam still in there?" she asked.

Matt nodded. "So is Agent Kinney. And Straimer. They're safe."

"And Dane?"

"He's in good hands. For being a group of criminals, they're also all brilliant doctors, I'm told."

"Is Dane going to jail?"

Matt took a second's pause before answering. "Buying organs is illegal."

"And Elliot? If he survives?"

"He went to the FBI a couple of months ago. He traded information for immunity—for both him and Cass. But she died before he was allowed to tell her everything."

There was movement on the boat as a stretcher was being moved carefully down the ramp. EMT workers rushed to meet it, gently taking over the gurney. Dane was alive, though awfully pale-looking, with tubes coming out of his nose and mouth. Agent Kinney led a handcuffed Dr. Moore and Christine while Straimer carted Lyle out, his hand gripped tensely around Lyle's arm. Sam was the last out, pushing Dr. Adams in front of him.

Jess jumped off the bench and before she could make it a couple of steps, Matt had her around the waist. No matter how hard she tried to wrench out of Matt's grasp, to break free and get to Sam, he refused to release her.

Tears streamed down her face. He was bleeding . . . Sam was bleeding through his tuxedo shirt. "I just need to see him," she cried, and pushed against Matt.

She closed her eyes, falling into Matt's hug. "I just need to see that he's okay," she cried.

"Jess." She swung around, hearing Sam's voice and her eyes widened as he was suddenly standing there in front of her. Rodriguez took Dr. Adams, walking him toward the police cruiser, and Sam pulled her into his arms. He was here. *Oh God, he's okay . . . bloody with the makings of a black eye and a split lip . . . but okay.*

She ran her fingers over his face and his shoulders, her trembling hand hovering over the bloodstain at his shirt.

He shook his head, grabbing her shaking hand and kissing her knuckles. "It's not deep. Moore got me with the scalpel, but I pulled back at just the right moment." He gently touched the bruises at her neck, his dark blue eyes swirling with shadows. "Are you okay?"

"I'm fine." She was dazed, shaking and in shock . . . but she'd be fine.

"Damn right you are," he said. "You should get checked out by the EMTs anyway."

She shook her head, gripping his forearm. "No, not without you—"

"We *both* should."

She couldn't exactly argue with that. He cupped her face and dipped his mouth gently to her lips, his forehead warm against her. "I love you, Jess," he declared. "I loved you back in pre-school when you would sneak into my lunchbox and then tell me it was Charlie Gardner stealing my pudding snacks. I loved you in fourth grade when you would let me cheat off your math homework. I loved you all through high school and even on my darkest days, you were still a beacon of light, shining from afar to bring me home. And I love you now. More than ever."

"Saying 'I love you, too' just doesn't seem enough . . ." She pushed onto her toes, kissing him again. "But I do love you, too."

She looked back as Rodriguez Mirandized Dr. Adams outside her cruiser. "I need to talk to him, Sam. I need closure."

He nodded, lacing his fingers into hers and leading the way toward the car. They walked up just as Rodriguez was pushing him into the backseat. "We need a minute," Sam said to the officer. She nodded and stepped back.

Jess opened the door to slide into the front seat and Sam moved to get in on the other side. "I need to do this alone," she said, stopping him.

To her surprise, he didn't argue. Didn't try to talk her into having him there with her. He simply stayed where he was.

She climbed into the front seat of the cruiser and stared at the doctor through the plexiglass partition. "Dr. Adams," she said.

"I want a lawyer," he said.

"I'm not in here officially. You have so many charges against you . . . the stuff with my parents is probably the least of it. I know you killed my mom."

He rolled his eyes. "Your mom was brain-*dead*—"

"Maybe," she cut him off. "Maybe not. And because of you, I'll never know. Because of you . . . I never got to say good-bye to her."

He lifted his gaze, the blue and red flashing lights passed over his creased face, lined with years of wrinkles. "She would have died anyway, Jessica."

"But she wouldn't have been alone! On some exam table! She could have been holding her daughters' hands." The sob burst from her chest and with that explosion, his face slackened into something that resembled remorse.

"And without your mother, my daughter wouldn't have lived another week. I'll never forget Renee Walters. I thank her every day."

"Don't do that. Don't turn yourself into a martyr. You're a murderer."

He nodded. "I am that. And yet . . . I'm also a savior to many. So many people would have died without the organs I've provided."

Jess wiped her eyes with both hands, letting the tears wash down to her chin. "Good luck convincing a jury of that," she said, before she got out of the car and slammed the door.

Sam was there waiting, a few feet away, his expression so grief-stricken, so filled with pain that it made her breath catch even more.

"Come on," he said, wrapping his arms around her waist. "Let's both go get a clean bill of health."

EPILOGUE

Three Days Later

Sam heard the shower shut off as he carried the last of his boxes inside the pink house. Pink. He chuckled. If anyone had told him as a kid that he'd someday be living in a pink house, he would have body checked them.

He entered, kicking the door shut behind him. Luckily, he didn't have all that much stuff to begin with and it made moving in pretty damn easy. Now if only he could convince Jess to let him repaint the outside.

He dropped the box in the foyer, yanking his shirt over his head. He winced, looking down at the fourteen stitches he'd needed under his rib cage, and climbed the staircase to where he now heard her rummaging around in the master bedroom. He may have undersold just how good Moore had gotten him with that scalpel. He grimaced as hunger for Jess spiked through his body. A few weeks ago, she had been nothing more than a memory. Someone he was certain would never want to see him again, let alone share a home and a bed with him. And in a matter of days, she'd planted her little roots, anchoring herself to his soul.

"I'm home," he called from the stairs so not to startle her. She scared very easily these days—for good reason. He moved into the doorway and came to a cold, hard stop. *Oh, sweet Jesus*—the sight of her sucked the breath clean out of his lungs. Her lavender robe clung to her body, draping her damp skin in soft-looking silk. Her hair fell in wet curls down her back and her firm, rounded ass called to him, tempting his hands and caused his stirring erection to harden further, thirsty for her body.

"How was the debriefing?" she asked.

"A long one," he said. "Looks like they're going to be able to cut Dane a deal in exchange for his testimony against the organ trafficking."

"Good."

"That's where he was, the night of Cass's death. Having a meeting with Adams about buying a new heart."

"And that's why he couldn't give you a real alibi," she finished for him.

"Kinney mentioned that there was a weird discrepancy in their bookkeeping, though. It looked like there was a fifth person being cut in on the cash, but none of the four are talking."

"Elliot doesn't know who it is?"

Sam shook his head. "Apparently not. Elliot didn't know about Christine or Dr. Adams, either. His only contact was with Dr. Moore and Lyle."

"That's weird." Jess chewed her bottom lip in thought as Sam walked over to her, pulling her lip from her teeth.

Her pouty lips thinned and her brown eyes flashed back at him. "Sam," she warned, putting a hand to his chest and pushing him back. "We have to go to the hospital, remember? We have, like, a million people to visit."

He chuckled, noting the deliberate dare that flashed in her expression. "Well, then," he challenged, popping open the button on his jeans and pushing them down over his hips. "I should change."

Her breasts were heaving faster, harder and he could see the outline of her nipples distinctly through her thin silk robe. He cupped the back of her neck, pulling her close against his body. "How is it that you can drive me so fucking crazy? You make me want to stroke you and worship you, while at the same time I want to paddle that tight ass when you don't listen to me." He grinned and trailed his fingers down the sensitive sides of her waist.

She lifted her chin in a show of defiance. "When have I not listened to you lately?"

He loved that tone now. He loved when she got heated and playfully defiant. It meant they were both in for some spanking later. "Well, for starters, I noticed those damn ceramic frogs are still out front."

"They're cute!"

"They're girly."

She jutted her bottom lip out and tossed her hair. The seductive movement sent every bit of his body into its most hardened state.

His fingers moved to the ribbon keeping her robe loosely closed. The only thing separating their bodies was a thin rectangle of silk and the cotton boxer briefs he wore. He tugged at the belt. Her cheeks flushed even pinker as he slipped the soft material off her shoulders, letting it fall to the ground.

"Well, now we're definitely going to be late," she said. Her gaze was hungry, sweeping his body and it was so intense that it practically branded him like her touch.

They each moved their lips to the other's at the same time and with that kiss, Sam felt more than a decade of loneliness, of aching, of emptiness slip away, the tension melting from his muscles as he pushed his tongue into her mouth.

The kiss started sweet but quickly morphed into something

more primal, more urgent and she was panting against his mouth, clawing at his shoulders. She fought to catch her breath as he slowly drew a line from her neck down over her breasts and over the landscape of her stomach.

He was careful to touch her gently with his calloused fingertips—she claimed she was no longer sore, but he knew she wouldn't admit it even if she was still in pain. He rotated his touch, circling her inner thighs. She panted, spreading her legs for him.

His hips jerked, longing for that firm grip of hers as her fingers dipped into the elastic waist of his boxer briefs, pulling them down over his straining shaft.

He groaned, dropping his head back as she pumped her hand against his cock harder. He blinked open, watching as she slid her other fingers down between her dripping thighs, teasing him, stroking her wet heat for both her pleasure and his.

She stroked the base of his cock, curling her fingers around his sack, heavy with need. His hand hovered beside her, brushing against her inner thighs, stroking and worshipping her smooth skin.

"How wet are you?" he asked

Her answer came in a rough breath. "So wet. Pulsing for you, Sam."

He dropped to his knees in front of her to get a better view and she eased herself back onto the bed, spreading her legs wide. She dipped a finger into the slick wet depths, pushing it all the way in to the knuckle before slowly pulling it back out. He watched, gripping his own dick and stroking himself slowly, longing to bury his tongue into her hot, wet pussy.

Her heels dug into the mattress, hips pulsing higher as she thrust her finger inside herself again. Their panting breaths filled the silence along with the sound of wet flesh meeting frenzied motions. "Fuck, yeah, that's beautiful."

"Sam." She moaned his name in the way he'd only imagined she did when he wasn't around. Her eyes blinked open, fighting to maintain eye contact. He took her finger pulling it free from her sex before drawing it into his mouth. He burned to feel her around his hard cock. To feel her pulse against his tongue and he crawled over top as she fell onto her back. He moved into position, sliding his erection between her thighs, pushing against her wet opening, so ready for him.

With a flick of his hips, he was inside her, slipping into her aching pussy. Searing heat burst into his mind and he gripped her knee, spreading her even wider. He thrust harder inside her with deep, hard movements. Her hands dug into his shoulder, nails biting his skin and even that felt fucking good. The pain mixed with sweet, impending pleasure. He could feel the hard clench of his balls, the tightening of his brewing release.

She arched into him, using her body weight to thrust him deeper inside her. Her neck elongated with an animal-like groan and he was utterly captivated by her expression, so full of desire and freedom. She damn near took his breath away.

Her muscles clenched around him and he grunted as her contractions squeezed him, milked him, her release taking hold of her shuddering body.

"Jessica," he demanded, "look at me."

Her eyes snapped open, obeying his order immediately. He increased his rhythm, pumping into her clenching cunt harder and faster as her moans became louder.

But even as she cried out, her eyes stayed directly on him, just as he had asked. Her obedience caused a violent pleasure that rocked through him and he flicked his hips, pushing his hand against her clit in subtle but effective circular motions. He wasn't going to last much longer. "Come for me, Jess."

She jerked against his body, letting go in a release that rocked hard through her body. He thrust himself one last time, spearing into her as his own release spurted inside of her. He collapsed on her body, careful not to let his weight fall entirely on her and her arms rested on his back, caressing his tense muscles in soft little strokes.

His heartbeat pounded against hers until eventually, the rhythms lined up, matching. He shivered as the last tremor bulldozed through his body.

Jess linked her hand in Sam's and he groaned as she dragged him to their last stop at the hospital.

"Please tell me this is it. She isn't really even a friend," he said.

"Zooey was Cass's friend. And I'm trying to lay down roots and get my own good group of girlfriends going. Or do you prefer me to spend all my free time with Dane and Elliot?"

He jolted upright from his slouch at that, holding up the bouquet of flowers he was carrying. "Fuck that. After you."

Jess entered Zooey's room and stopped, looking around. "She's . . . she's gone. I thought she wasn't being discharged for another day."

Sam walked to the edge of the bed where her chart was kept. He flipped open a page, shaking his head. "That's what they said up front."

"Do you think her mother forced her to get an early discharge? That woman is a beast to be reckoned with. I sure as hell wouldn't want to be the nurse to say no to her." Jess turned her attention back to Sam, who was standing stiff as a statue beside Zooey's hospital bed. Restraints hung unused over the side. Jess pulled out her phone and dialed Zooey's number. "Sam? What is it?" she asked as she waited.

He jerked his chin toward the bed. "There. On her pillow." There was a tension in his voice that she knew all too well. And she didn't like the sound of it one bit.

Jess could hear the phone ringing on the other end of the line, as she walked slowly to the other side of the bed. Zooey's voice mail clicked on, playing "Witchy Woman" in lieu of a voice-mail message. Jess gasped, dropping the phone onto the bed.

There, resting on Zooey's pillow was a propped-up tube of scarlet lipstick.

See how the story began in Katana Collins's

WICKED EXPOSURE

Nothing left to hide . . .

A forensic photographer with the NYPD, Jessica is devastated to receive word of her sister's death in a robbery gone awry. But when she arrives home in Portland and the local PD asks her to take pictures, she finds more than she bargained for. With each new photo she exposes more of her sister's secret erotic life. And when she shares her discoveries with Sam, the super-sexy local detective, she experiences passion she never knew possible. But Jessica soon learns she's merely a pawn in a deadly game of betrayal and revenge and begins to wonder if her next picture could be her last. . . .

Read on for a special excerpt.

A Kensington trade paperback and e-book on sale now!

familiar hollow feeling carved out into her chest as she looked around the three-story home. Lifting the coffee cup in her hands once more, she turned it over, examining it. The porcelain was smooth and the edging was gilded with a pewter design.

Never in her life had she felt so alone. Their parents died when Jess was a freshman in high school—a car crash. A fucking hit and run to be exact. One that left her parents caged under their crumpled car. A shiver tumbled down her spine. She was alone now. Totally and completely alone. She had no grandparents, no cousins, no aunts, no uncles. Her sister was the only family she'd had left. It was depressing how quickly Jess had been able to pack up her belongings and come to Maine. There was no one she needed to call; no one she needed to check in with.

For a while, that had seemed freeing, having zero ties to any place. Being able to pick up and travel whenever she wanted. But now? Now it just felt damn lonely.

Jess sighed and turned the water on, soaping up a sponge. "When I get home, I need to get a dog or something," she muttered to herself. "Something that will miss me when I'm gone."

"Dogs are a lot of work, you know," a voice behind her said.

Jess screamed, spinning to find a man standing there. The soapy mug slipped through her wet fingers, shattering across the linoleum floor with a deafening crash.

The man eyed the broken cup for all of a moment before bending to clean up the pieces of shattered ceramic.

"W-who are you? Why are you in Cass's house?" Jess trembled, pressing herself against the counter and feeling behind her for a weapon. Her fingers grazed a knife's handle and she wrapped her palm around it, sliding it behind her.

The man looked up at her from his crouched position. He

had light brown hair and striking blue eyes. The smallest hint of an amused grin flashed across his face as he stretched to a standing position, dropping the broken glass into the trash can. "I'm sorry." He brushed his palms on his jeans and extended a hand. "I'm Dane."

Jess eyed his outstretched hand, still clutching the knife behind her. "Hello, Dane" she said, and paused. "You didn't answer my question."

He gave a light chuckle and dropped his hand back to his sides. "Well, since your first question was 'who are you?' I actually did answer you. And you—wait a minute." His eyes narrowed and scanned her face before the smirk spread to a full on grin. "You're Jess, right? Cass's sister?"

Jess relaxed her shoulders, giving a little nod, but didn't let go of the knife yet.

"I've heard a lot about you. It's nice to finally meet you."

"And yet, I still know nothing about you and why you're here." Fear trembled at the base of her belly. The guy seemed okay; nice, even. But that didn't change the fact that he was a stranger lurking in her sister's home.

"Cass set up an appointment for me to have a look at some leaky pipes upstairs."

"She must've done it weeks ago." Jess narrowed her eyes, studying the man up and down.

"Yeah, it was a couple weeks ago. I was called out of town for a job in Boston and Cass didn't seem to mind the extra wait."

He walked over to the far right cabinet, grabbed a pint glass from the top shelf, and filled it with water. Her eyes wandered over his shoulder to the thin bookshelf on the other side of the room. A framed photograph of her sister and this man—Dane—rested on the top shelf. The two of them in front of Cass's bright pink house, each holding a hammer and grinning from ear to ear.

"You seem awfully comfortable in her home." It was an observation as well as a question. Jess loosened her grip on the knife and slid her hand away from it. She took a few kickboxing classes at her gym. In a worst-case scenario, she could deposit a quick kick to the groin and run like hell.

"Ayuh," he said, his Maine accent becoming more and more prominent as Jess spoke to him. "Cass and I have been friends since she bought this place. Needed quite a bit of work at first." He looked around as though remembering an old friend. "Wouldn't be able to tell it now, huh?"

"Yeah. Except for that awful color outside."

Dane laughed. "Now, that's true. Cass was never about to change that, though. It was one of the reasons she bought the damn place to begin with."

"So, you and Cass were . . . friends?"

Dane nodded. "Absolutely. I taught her how to boil a lobstah."

Jess snorted. Her sister damn well knew how to boil lobster. They were raised here in Portland. Which meant Cass used the excuse as a way of getting closer to this guy. The thought brought a warmth in Jess's chest. "Well, how hard can it be to throw a lobster in a pot?"

"You'd be surprised. It's more humane to kill them first, anyway." From his pocket, he pulled a little orange bottle and tossed a pill into his mouth, swallowing. He drank the rest of the water with a glug and wiped his mouth with the back of his hand.

Jess wasn't sure exactly why she was warming up to the guy, especially considering the hellish week she'd had—but she was nonetheless. And her instincts were usually spot-on.

"So, where's Cass, anyway?" he asked, glancing at his watch. "Still at work probably, huh?"

Sorrow frosted over in her gut. "Oh God," Jess whispered, covering her mouth. "You don't know."

Dane tilted his head. "Know what?" His chest hitched. "Is Cass okay?"

Jess inhaled slowly through her nose. She'd had to make a few of these calls already and they ripped her heart out every time.

"Dane, I'm so sorry . . . Cass died."